A Song For Joey

A novel by Elizabeth Audrey Mills

A Song For Joey
by Elizabeth Audrey Mills

Published by Elizabeth Audrey Mills on Createspace
A Song For Joey © 2012 Elizabeth Audrey Mills

Second edition - August 2012

All rights reserved. Without limiting the rights under copyright reserved above, no part of this publication may be reproduced, stored in or introduced into a retrieval system, or transmitted, in any form, or by any means (electronic, mechanical, photocopying, recording, or otherwise) without the prior written permission of both the copyright owner and the publisher of this book.

This is a work of fiction. Names, characters, places, brands, media, and incidents are either the product of the author's imagination or are used fictitiously.

Email: elizabeth@itsliz.net
Website: www.itsliz.net

Cover from a photograph by Dan Welch
(www.publicdomainpictures.net)

~1~
August 1945
Paolo

Libertà! Paolo smiled at the word, rolled it around in his mouth, savouring the taste, as he closed the little gate of the farmhouse and set off along the familiar lane. The war was over and he was a free man again.

Humming a tune he had heard on the radio, he strolled leisurely down the bumpy path beside the hedgerow, clutching a small bundle containing all his possessions.

After a while, he stopped and gazed affectionately at the endless, flat, open fields all around, musing wryly that this was not really so different from his life over the last two years - after all, he had been almost free anyway. No prison camp for him; he had worked as a farm labourer - with lodgings in the farmhouse and two bob a week in his pocket - in exchange for his promise to not escape. As if he would want to run away from this pleasant place and return to Italy under that madman, Mussolini.

He inhaled a deep breath of warm, scented, summer air, and a big smile erupted across his face. With arms extended on each side, he did a little dance, his face lifted up to gaze at the broad blue sky, feeling the heat of the summer sun like a lover's caress.

At the end of the lane, where it joined the winding country road, he sat on the grass verge and waited for the bus that would take him to Great Yarmouth. The piece of paper in his top pocket had the address of a guest-house where he would be able to stay until he could be repatriated.

His war had been short. Conscripted in 1942, trained for two weeks, then sent into battle in Tripoli, poorly trained and badly equipped (his rifle had dated from the First World War, and there was a gouge in the stock that looked very much as though a bullet had ricocheted off it). He promptly made sure that he was captured by the British, along with the rest of his unit. He was not a fool; he had no intention of fighting and dying for Il Duce Pazzo; and besides, he had his family to think about. He had simply waited for the Allies to arrive, then surrendered to them.

And here he was, two years later, free as a bird, with a pocketful of cash saved from his earnings. The British government had even given him a suit to wear - yes, it was brown and cheap, but it fitted, and was smarter than the Prisoner of War overalls he had been wearing for the last two years.

He laid back in the long grass, hands behind his head, watching the crows in the big elms beside the road, listening to the hum of bees in the wild flowers nearby and the song of a skylark over the field of waving barley behind him, savouring every moment.

This was a good life. One day he would return to his wife and children in Italy, but not just yet - first, a little holiday at the seaside. Mussolini may be dead now, but why rush back when a new life was just beginning for him?

-♪-

The bus dropped him at the busy market in the centre of Great Yarmouth, and for a while he amused himself with some relaxed browsing at the stalls, even bought himself a tie for tuppence.

Then, conscious of the instruction to make his way directly to the guest-house and report to Mrs Cartwright, he began to ask, politely, in his broken English, for directions to Trafalgar Road.

The first man he spoke to looked at him in disgust, before muttering something under his breath and stamping off. Puzzled, Paolo tried again, with a similar result. He began to realise that his accent was betraying his origins, and Italians, clearly, were not popular in England at the moment.

Fortunately, his salvation appeared before him in the form of a tall man in a blue uniform.

"Good afternoon, Sir," said the policeman, ponderously.

Paolo smiled nervously. "Good af'noon, Signore, Officer. I have not'ing wrong done, I t'ink?"

PC Archie Randal looked him up and down, while Paolo squirmed. "That's what I'm here to find out," he replied, non-committally.

Archie had served as a sergeant in the military police in France; it was a job he had loved. But, when he returned home after the war ended, he found himself discharged - they had too many men, and he was close to retirement age. Onto the scrap heap with you, Sergeant Randal! He had immediately applied for a job with the civil police, and was snapped up thanks to his army record.

"Do you have identity papers?" he enquired, his eyes seeming to probe Paolo's brain, seeking out everything he had ever done wrong. Civvy street hadn't changed Archie much, he still had the bearing of a non-commissioned officer - erect, with head high and shoulders back.

"Oh si, yes, certo." Paolo ferreted the little cardboard folder from his inside jacket pocket and passed it to the officer, along with his letter of release. Archie scrutinised the ID card.

"You are from Italy, I see," he said, looking up to examine Paolo, who nodded, nervously.

Archie then unfolded the off-white sheet with a Whitehall address. "Ah, you were a prisoner of war, and now you are released; is that correct?" He refolded it and slipped it into the little book, then held it out to Paolo.

"Yes, sir. I will returning Italy in some days." Paolo took the papers and pushed them back into his pocket, waiting anxiously for the officer's response, reminding himself that this was not the Polizia, with their pistola and their attitude, this was an English bobby.

"What are you doing here?" the policeman suddenly asked.

"Perdono?"

"Why have you come to Great Yarmouth."

"Ah, I have a residence ... " he fished in his top pocket for the address of the guest-house and passed it to the officer.

"Do you know where this house is?" asked Archie.

Paolo shook his head.

Archie nodded. "Then I will show you. Walk with me."

The two of them set off, the policeman's shoes making

a steady, rhythmic clicking sound on the pavement. Paolo noticed that, with each step, Archie's head turned left and right, like a clockwork robot, his eyes missing nothing, his mind constantly analysing, assessing, archiving.

They emerged onto Temple Road, and walked south, passing a large area where bomb-damaged houses were being demolished. Men swarmed and machines throbbed, raising clouds of dust; huge lorries roared in and roared out again, laden with the debris of wrecked lives. They reached Trafalgar Road, and PC Randal took Paolo to *The Nest*, Gladys Cartwright's Bed-and-Breakfast.

When they reached the brightly painted front door, Archie gave a firm rap on the brass knocker, and a plump woman of about fifty appeared.

"Hello Gladys," he said, cheerfully.

"Archie!" she responded, a broad smile on her smooth, plump face. "Who have you brought to me this time?"

-♪-

Gladys looked the stranger up and down, suspiciously. Her home was open to almost anyone, of course - guests from all over the world had stayed there over the years - but, according to Archie, this man had been a prisoner of war, and she was apprehensive. Still, she had his official letter in her hand, so presumably he was trustworthy. She led him up the stairs and showed him to one of her guest rooms.

It was a neat room - compact, but adequate. Centrally, a single bed set the theme and purpose of his stay. On one wall, a window admitted a bright shaft of midday sunlight, which sliced across a light oak dressing table, continued over a rag rug on the floor, to the opposite wall, where it cast a spotlight on a matching wardrobe.

"I charge three pounds twelve and six a week, with breakfast and dinner included," she said, brusquely, adding, "Payable in advance."

The man nodded. "I can pay you, signora, I have some money saved, and I will find work."

He put his small bundle of possessions on the bed while he took some cash from his pocket and carefully counted out some of the coins and notes he had hoarded. His savings, which earlier that day had seemed such a fortune, were suddenly revealed for their paucity. He had enough for another two weeks, then it would all be gone. He needed to get a job, soon.

Gladys accepted the handful of money, checked it, then handed him his key. "I'll give you a receipt when you come down for dinner. It's served at six o'clock sharp."

She left him to settle in, and he wandered over to the window, which was neatly festooned with pretty floral curtains. He considered her brusque manner; perhaps she, too, hated Italians. He hoped he could win her over with his usual charm and bright smile.

The view from the window was pleasant. On the opposite side of the road that passed below was a grassy strip with trees and flowers, and beyond that a row of small houses. To his left he could see the sea, and, to his right, a stark, red-bricked church. He looked at his watch, it was only two o'clock; time enough for a little exploring.

Abandoning his neat bundle - containing only some

underpants, a couple of shirts and his few personal items - and set off down the stairs and out of the front door.

Trafalgar Road consisted of a long row of bay-fronted houses. Several had name boards outside, declaring that they offered 'Bed and Breakfast'. Unknown to Paolo at that time, Great Yarmouth had been a popular holiday resort before the war. Now, many of the guest-houses looked shabby and neglected. Only *The Nest* was clean and neatly painted.

He ambled in the warm afternoon sun down to the wide, sandy beach, then stood quietly for a while looking out across the water. Europe was over there, reeling from the years of killing and destruction - Germany, Belgium, France and Italy, torn apart. What lunacy makes men wage war, he wondered, not for the first time. As usual, there was no answer, could be no answer.

A broad promenade stretched in both directions parallel to the sea, and he strolled slowly along the parade of cafés, hotels and amusement arcades, many of them closed and boarded up. He also saw some of the damage caused by German bombs and naval shells. Carcases of buildings teetered on the edges of craters, their insides exposed like dolls houses, their wallpaper peeling, the corners of upper rooms clinging stubbornly, their edges frayed like lace.

At five o'clock he made his way back to Trafalgar Road and climbed the stairs to his room. There he closed the door and opened his knotted bundle of clothes, carefully unwrapping the shirts inside, to reveal a little wooden picture frame.

It had travelled with him into war, and stayed with him

throughout his captivity.

He gazed affectionately at the family group in the photograph - his wife, Caterina, their boisterous son, Josepe and little baby Helena (she would be nearly four years old now). He tried to imagine them as they might be, but could not - he had missed so much of their lives.

Opening a drawer in the dressing table, he gently put the picture into it and covered it with his few clothes. Then he went down to dinner.

-♪-

When he reached the dining room, he found that there were already a few people seated. He chose the only empty table - unwilling, for now, to deal with any more hostility - and looked around.

There were four, square tables, with plain white cloths, laid with knives and forks at each station, and with a little vase of white and yellow flowers in the centre. Two of the tables had one occupant each - men in work clothes, remote, disinterested. The other held a large man in loud, laughing conversation with a young woman.

A door opened, admitting a mouthwatering smell of cooking, and a waitress entered, carrying three plates of food. She looked around the room, then walked past Paolo to deliver her cargo to the three other men. On her way back to the kitchen, she stared curiously at Paolo, before disappearing through the door, reappearing almost at once with two more meals.

Seeming almost to be tormenting Paolo, she walked past him again and served the young woman. Finally, she came back to him and placed his dinner carefully before him. She had to lean towards him to do so, and he was treated to a generous glimpse of cleavage and a waft of perfume, reminding him of pleasures lacking in his life for two years. But, he noticed, her expression was challenging, the twinkle in her pretty eyes was more curious than friendly. Hypnotised, he watched her rear as it undulated back to the kitchen.

Rita knew the effect she had on men, and she was not oblivious to the fact that he had noticed her cleavage - it had not been revealed by accident.

In the kitchen she asked her mother about the new guest.

"You watch out for him, my girl. He's foreign, was a prisoner of war. Don't you go flirting with him." Gladys knew she was wasting her breath. Rita was always getting into trouble with men.

Rita smiled to herself as she helped Gladys to prepare the jam roly-poly pudding and custard for afters. Foreign, was he? Good lovers, some of those European men. Shame he wasn't American, they always had cash to spend on a girl. She remembered that airman, Hiram; what a great time they had shared before he went back to his base.

After a little while, she peeped into the dining room, noticing that everyone except the young chorus girl had finished their first course. She bustled in and cleared all the plates, leaving the foreign man until last again.

When she finally reached him, she treated him to a little smile, not much more than an upturned corner of her mouth, but he responded happily with a big, toothy grin.

She felt that surge of excitement again; she had him, now she would play with him for a while.

When dinner was done, and everyone else had left, Paolo stayed behind, hoping for a chance to speak to the attractive waitress. But she didn't reappear, it was Gladys who came to clear away the dishes.

"There's no more," she barked.

He shrugged and left. But, instead of returning to his room, he decided to go for another walk. The evening was fine and warm; he loved these long English summer days, almost like home.

Rita, meanwhile, was quizzing her mother about the stranger.

"How should I know," grumbled the older woman. "He arrived with a letter from the government, saying he was an Italian POW, released pending his repatriation."

'Italian?' Rita was intrigued; she'd never had an Eye-tie.

'Wonder what he's like between the sheets,' she pondered.

'Well, there's only one way to find out,' she smiled to herself.

-♪-

"Mum, I'm pregnant."

Gladys froze, her mouth open, her cup halfway to her lips. They were sitting in the Front Parlour, as Gladys liked to call it, enjoying tea and scones before continuing with the cleaning and decorating. The winter months were always quiet in the guest-house: there were no shows on at the theatres, no holidaymakers, so it was the time for repairs and maintenance.

A heavy silence followed.

Rita seemed unembarrassed, belligerent. "Well, someone say something."

"What do you suggest?" Gladys snapped, "Well done?" She glared at Paolo, who looked as though he was trying to shrink into his chair and become invisible. "I take it this young man is responsible?"

"Of course it's him, who else could it be?" Rita countered, though some of her bravado was gone. She knew her mother was referring to her string of lovers.

Not long ago, she had been seeing that lad from the Pleasure Beach, and before him there was the American airman, and before that many others. Rita soon became bored with her boyfriends, once the excitement of a fondle under the pier had gone, and another man would soon catch her attention.

"How should I know? I can't keep up with you. All these chaps you bring home, and the ones you think I don't know about! You're getting a reputation, young lady. Now look what's happened, you've gone and got yourself knocked up!"

There was a long uncomfortable silence, during which Gladys put her cup down in its saucer and folded her arms across her bosom, glowering at Rita and Paolo in turn. Paolo seemed to be struck dumb, and though Rita kept looking at him for support, he kept silent, his chin buried in his neck, his eyes on the table.

"Well, what are you going to do about it?" Gladys demanded.

Another pause, while the two youngsters looked

anxiously at each other.

"Maybe I could . . . you know . . ." stammered Rita.

"What?"

"You know . . ."

Gladys knew perfectly well what Rita was hinting at, but she had no intention of making it easy for her. The silence dragged on.

Rita was now feeling sheepish, all her former bravado ebbing away. She couldn't have a baby, she just couldn't, it wasn't part of her plan. She began to feel resentful of Paolo - she hadn't fallen before, why had he gone and ruined everything by making her pregnant?

"Come on, out with it girl!" Gladys leaned back in her chair, defying Rita to say the words.

"Well, I've heard there are women who will get rid of it for me, for money." Even as she said the words, Rita cringed. She knew her mother was strongly opposed to abortion, even if they could find someone who could do it.

"Oh no, madam, that is not an option. You created a life inside you, and every life is precious. It's about time you accepted some responsibility."

Rita's embarrassment turned to anger, and she stood up and shouted at her mother: "You can't tell me what to do! I'm twenty years old, I can run my own life!"

Calmly, Gladys looked her daughter in the eye. "Yes, you can, and a fine mess you have made of it so far."

Rita stared back for a moment, then turned and stamped out of the room, her high heels clicking on the polished floor as she disappeared into the kitchen.

Gladys turned to Paolo. "You don't seem to have much

to say," she hissed.

He shuffled uncomfortably in his chair. "I am sorry, Signora Cartwright."

"Sorry won't butter any parsnips," she grumbled. "Are you prepared to marry Rita?"

"Parsnips? Marry?" He paused, noticing her expression. Gladys was a small woman, but somehow she seemed more intimidating than a lion at that moment. "Well, yes, I suppose so."

"Suppose so?" screeched Gladys, incredulously. "You make my daughter pregnant, then you 'suppose' you will marry her? You two seem to have everything in the wrong order. The idea is meant to be that first you marry, then you have children, or do they do it differently in Italy?"

"No, no, Signora, I did not mean that . . ." he struggled for the words. "Of course we will be married, as quickly as possible. It is just a surprise, I had not expected it."

"Well, here is a lesson in biology, Paolo: a man and a woman have sex and that is the way babies are made. Did you not know that?"

"Yes, of course," he agreed, miserably, humiliated.

"But you did not think to take precautions?" She almost whispered the words. But when she spoke quietly, reasonably, it was even more menacing. She didn't wait for an answer. "I have a dinner to cook, one of the many responsibilities I have, which, it seems, also now include thinking for my stupid daughter and her beau." She too departed to the kitchen, leaving Paolo feeling that he had just survived a mauling.

-♪-

The wedding was hardly a romantic occasion. It took place on a cold, wet and windy afternoon in February, 1946, at St Johns Church, only five minutes by car from the guest-house. Rita had wanted a Registry Office wedding, but Gladys would not hear of it.

"It's not a proper wedding if it's not in a church," she declared, and that was that.

Gladys studied her youngest pensively as she finished getting ready. What would Arthur have made of this, she wondered. Little Rita was his darling. Poor thing, she was only thirteen when he died, and was very upset. Gladys thought that, if he had been a bit more strict with her, Rita might have not been such a handful all her life. Now look at her, beautiful but wayward.

She looked lovely in her wedding dress, creamy-white, long, but loose, to hide her swelling belly. The family had pooled all their clothing coupons to get it.

The war may have been over for nearly a year, but food and clothing were still rationed. Every household had a book of tokens for everything from meat to paraffin, in quantities according to the size of family.

Rita's big brother, Ernie, chauffeur for the day, stuck his head around the door. "Time we were going, girls."

"Ready, then?" Gladys asked, her head filled with mixed emotions: pride at her lovely daughter, shame that she was marrying in haste.

"As I'll ever be," sighed Rita.

"It's the right thing to do, love, you know that. Your baby needs a proper family."

"I just don't want to throw my life away, mum. I'm only twenty, I should be having fun."

"Seems to me you already had a bit too much fun," Gladys frowned, looking down at Rita's tummy, significantly.

"It doesn't notice, does it?" Rita was immediately anxious again.

"No dear, it doesn't show, yet, but it soon will if we don't get a move on." She smiled, reassuringly.

Out front, Ernie was waiting in his Morris Oxford, which he had decorated with ribbons. He jumped out as they appeared, threw away his cigarette and held open the rear door for Rita and her mum. One or two neighbours had gathered at the sight of the beribboned car, and stood in little groups, watching curiously.

They drove slowly up Trafalgar road, turned left into Nelson Road, and then down York Road to the church. Saint John's was a compact cluster of buildings of traditional Norfolk flint, but in a strange Gothic style, crammed into the junction between Lancaster Road and York Road. On a nicer day it could have looked much more attractive, but to Rita, seeing it through the condensation inside the car's window, it looked cold and grey and heartless.

When the car pulled up, they were met by Rita's youngest brother, Thomas, holding a big umbrella to shelter the bride. Rita and Thomas were always the closest when children, and he had begged to be allowed to give her away. Rita took his proffered hand as she stepped gracefully from the car, then they waited under the umbrella for Gladys, before processing regally through the big, oak doors and into the vaulted church, echoing to click of Rita's heels and the muttering voices of the tiny congregation.

Paolo stood waiting before the chancel with his best man, a friend he had made at the bakers where he now worked. Rita took her place beside him, looking up at his face with a nervous smile. He had bought a good suit from his earnings, and she thought he looked very smart.

The vicar intoned the required admonitions, and the small congregation mumbled the unfamiliar words of familiar hymns. Before long, they were all sheltering in the arched doorway, taking photographs of each other, and when all was done to everyone's satisfaction, they processed back to the guest-house for the wedding feast. This was little enough; although the family had given Gladys as many food coupons as they could spare, and she had worked hard to make the most of them, it was scarcely a banquet.

When the food and drink were all gone, the guests departed, declaring the day a success. Gladys and the young couple sat down with a cup of tea, before the clearing up would have to begin.

-♪-

Rita struggled with pregnancy. She hated being fat - men had stopped noticing her and none of her clothes fitted any more. And, as she grew larger, so Paolo seemed to lose interest. He seemed to spend more and more of his time at work, and when he was at home he preferred to sit in the little front garden, smoking and watching the girls go by in their pretty dresses.

It was a beautiful summer; long hot days and sultry nights. But she found she was increasingly sleeping alone. Paolo went out drinking with his pals most nights, and didn't return until after midnight; she would sometimes find him next morning, sprawled out on the sofa in the front parlour. Then, one night, he didn't come home at all.

Rita, huge now, began to panic. She feared that something terrible had happened to him. Gladys phoned the police for her, but they had no knowledge of him being involved in anything. Eventually, the two of them walked round to the bakery.

Tom Wade, the baker, did not seem pleased to see them when Rita waddled in, followed by Gladys.

"Huh! Sending women to make his excuses now, is he?" he grunted, lifting trays of bread from the oven into a cooling rack. "This has been happening too much, lately, Gladys. How does he think I can cope on my own? He might at least have the decency to get you to phone in when he's too pissed to get out of bed."

Gladys frowned. "He's not here, then?" she asked, a chill gripping her heart.

"I wouldn't be doing this if he were, Gladys, I should be loading up the delivery vans with the drivers, they always get in a muddle if I leave them to do it on their own." He noticed Gladys's concerned expression and Rita's advanced pregnancy. "Is he not at home, either?"

Gladys and Rita shook their heads. "Who does he go drinking with?" Rita asked.

"Well he used to go with Charlie, one of the drivers, but

Charlie told me they haven't been out together for weeks."

Rita felt tears running down her cheeks. Suddenly, she had a feeling she knew what he had been up to.

Gladys took her arm and gently led her towards the door. "Thanks, Tom," she called over her shoulder, "I'll let you know when we find out more."

"Thanks, Gladys."

As they opened the door, he called out: " ... erm ... sorry Rita."

-♪-

When they arrived back at the B & B, Paolo was there, packing his clothes into a suitcase.

"What's going on?" Gladys demanded as Rita gave a little groan and collapsed into a chair.

"I am leaving. I have enough of this place and enough of you," he growled.

"What about Rita, what about your baby?"

He laughed, a kind of cough. "My baby? I am not so sure. I hear about your many men," this directed at Rita. "Maybe the baby not belong me, maybe you trap me for become a father."

Rita gave a howl, then found her voice. "No! The baby is yours, I promise you, Paolo. Please don't leave me to go through this alone."

Gladys grabbed his arm. "You are not leaving, young man, you must not desert your wife and child like this."

He shook himself free. "You cannot stop me. I am returning to my home in Italy. England is not a nice place."

"You are a coward!" Gladys shouted. "Afraid to accept responsibility. A real man would stay."

Paolo did not reply. Instead, with a glare at the two women, he snapped his case closed, the sound ringing like two gunshots in the small room, and marched wordlessly out of the door.

Rita was sobbing in her chair, her body convulsing.

Gladys was worried for her. Emotional scenes like this were not good at eight months pregnant. She reached down and took her daughter's hand. "Come in the kitchen with me and I'll make us a cup of tea."

Meekly, all her spirit gone, Rita stood and followed her mother. She sat on a chair at the kitchen table while Gladys filled the kettle and lit the gas ring under it with a match.

Rita expected her mother to rant and rave about how it was her (Rita's) own fault - her bad choice in men, her casual attitude to sex, all the years of anguish she had caused her mother - but, instead, Gladys was sympathetic. She talked quietly, as she spooned tea into the large, brown teapot, reassuring Rita that she was not alone, that she would always be there for her. Then, when Rita's tears had stopped and her drink was finished, Gladys sent her up to bed for a nap.

While Rita was resting, Gladys phoned Sergeant Morris at the Police Station and told him what had happened.

"There's nothing much we can do, Gladys, love," he said, sympathetically. "Did he take anything that didn't belong to him?"

"Not as far as I know, Jim."

"And there was no violence?"

Gladys snorted, "He knew better than to try anything like that!" she declared.

"Well then, Gladys, we can't touch him, even if we could find him. Sorry."

Gladys had developed a simple philosophy in life, which had seen her through two wars, eight pregnancies and widowhood at the age of only thirty-five. She once described it to her brother, Walter: "There's no point in using up energy worrying about what you can't have, concentrate on what is realistic."

She thanked Sergeant Morris and put the phone down, then sat thoughtfully for a few minutes. Paolo was gone, there was nothing they could do about that. What had to be faced now was Rita's pregnancy, and the raising of her child without a man in the house. "We can do it, between us," she said out loud, her mind clear. With a little smile on her face, she stood up, straightened the cushion on the velvet armchair, and went to the kitchen to begin preparing dinner. After all, they still had a living to earn and guests to feed.

-♪-

Later, though, in the night, her sleep was shattered when the stillness was broken by a scream. Gladys stumbled from her bed and ran to Rita's room, where she found her daughter sitting up in bed with an expression of horror on her face. What she saw made her shudder: Rita, her clothes and her bed were crimson with blood.

The poor girl lifted her bloody hands and stared at them, then up at her mother. "What's happening, Mum?" she pleaded.

"It's just your waters breaking, " Gladys lied. "You're losing a bit of blood at the same time. Don't worry, it looks worse than it is; it often happens."

She pulled a blanket from the wardrobe and covered her daughter's shivering body. Keep this over you, love, while I phone for an ambulance."

This was bad. In all her own pregnancies, and those of her daughters that she had attended as acting midwife, she had never encountered anything like it. She ran downstairs to the telephone on the hall stand and rang 999. When she had explained the situation, and been assured an ambulance would be on it's way, she ran back upstairs to her daughter.

"Right, my love," she said softly to Rita, who was sobbing and shaking, "the ambulance will be here in a jiffy."

She brought a bowl of water and a flannel from the bathroom, then took her daughter's hand and began to wash the blood off it, smiling reassuringly. "You'll be fine, lovie. Millions of women have given birth, it will all be ok."

In truth, however, she was worried. Rita's skin had turned white, with a waxy sheen, and her eyes had started to drift and close. She kept talking to her, asking questions, forcing her to stay awake.

She heard the bells of the ambulance in the distance, racing through the dark streets of Yarmouth. With agonising slowness, they came closer.

When they stopped outside, she ran down to open the front door, and the crew, in their smart black uniforms with red piping, entered and took over. They carried Rita, now unconscious, out to the ambulance on a stretcher, and Gladys climbed into the back with her daughter. With bells ringing, they set off for the cottage hospital as fast as the tight streets would allow. She held Rita's hand and talked to her, hoping she could hear.

After a while, Rita's eye's flickered open. "I'm scared, Mum."

"Don't worry, dear, you're in good hands, you'll soon be holding your baby."

"Mum, I know you're lying. I'm going to die, aren't I?"

What could she say? Rita was right, she had little hope that her daughter would survive this. "Honestly, darling I don't know. You have lost a lot of blood, and I don't know what's caused it."

The girl visibly gathered herself. "Mum, I want you to promise me you will raise my baby if I die."

Gladys could see that her little girl was slipping out of consciousness again. "Alright, dear, I promise. If it comes to that, I will take care of him for you. But don't think about that now, just save all your strength."

"There's something else, Mum." Her voice was now scarcely audible, and Gladys had to lean close to her daughter's face to hear what she said. "Please, mum, give my baby my married name, Paolo's name."

With tears running down her face, she whispered "Yes, darling, I promise. Your little baby will have the best I can give him, and he will be proud of his mother."

She saw Rita's eyes close again, and heard her breath escaping slowly from her mouth. She was dead.

The ambulance stopped and the rear doors opened. Gladys watched in a dream as the crew quickly carried

Rita into the hospital. She followed, dejectedly, then stood alone in the corridor as her daughter was rushed away through swing doors. After a few minutes, the doors opened again and a nurse came through. She ushered Gladys into a little room.

"Mrs Cartwright, I'm Sister Ruby," the nurse said. "I'm sorry to have to tell you that there is nothing they can do for your daughter, but they are trying to save the baby." She reached out her hand and touched Gladys's arm, gently. "Would you like a cup of tea?" Gladys nodded, and Ruby left her, returning shortly with a mug of tea.

She was still sipping it when Ruby came back, carrying a small bundle of rags in her arms. The bundle was making snuffling and coughing noises, and Gladys realised it was a baby, wrapped in a sheet.

Ruby smiled. "Gladys, would you like to hold your granddaughter?"

~2~
May 1946
Belinda

Nobody believes me when I say I can remember my own birth, but I can see every detail of it in my mind. As I write now, so images float in the air around me, like smoke from a cigarette; I have total recall, I can watch it as many times as I like.

But the memory is strange, because I don't see it through the eyes of the little baby me. Rather, it is as though I am an observer, floating above the scene, looking down on myself, like a camera filming from up near the ceiling.

I can see the room - white walls and tiled floor. I see green-robed figures, their eyes blinking between masks and caps, and metal tools glinting in the glaring lights. Laid out on the table below me is my mother's pale corpse, opened up - like the carcase of a Christmas chicken - as the little body in which I am to live is lifted from her womb by the surgeon, his tunic spattered with her blood.

And though I am watching, godlike, from on high, I recall the shock of the smack that made me cough out the amniotic fluids that choked my lungs, and shout my first protest ...

"When did you start singing?" - Penny Wardle, journalist of the New Musical Express, interviewing me in February 1964.

"The day I was born," I replied ...

For eight months and three days, I was part of her body - I shared her blood, took oxygen from her lungs. Every sound she heard, I heard; every feeling she experienced, I experienced. I lived through her. When she died, part of me was wrenched away, and part of her is forever in me.

We passed, my mother and I, at the place where this world touches the next. We were like two people meeting at the elevator doors, one of us waiting to emerge into the world, the other about to depart.

She seemed surprised to find me there. '*Oh, my beautiful baby!*' she cried. Her hand reached out and she brushed my cheek with her fingers. There were tears in her eyes. '*I will never see you grow up, will I? Won't be around to help you. But you'll have your Gran, she'll be better at it than I would have been, anyway.*'

I couldn't answer, of course.

Then she drifted past me into the lift - the doors closed and she was gone. It was time for me to join myself. As I floated down, I watched the surgeon pass my tiny body to a nurse, and as I snuggled into my cosy new home, she carried me into another room and held me out to another woman.

"Gladys," she said, "would you like to hold your granddaughter?"

-♪-

Let me tell you about Gran - my lovely Gran, short and plump, with her rosy cheeks and her grey hair tied back. She is the constant of all my best childhood memories -

strong and kind, her warm smile and soft touch helping me to grow.

She ran a guest-house, *The Nest*. It was hard work, but she was willing and uncomplaining. Early every morning she was in the kitchen, cooking breakfasts for the lodgers. Then, when they went out, she would clean their rooms, before returning to the kitchen to begin the dinners.

There were always a few people staying; three or four of them at a time, usually - less in winter, more in summer. Sometimes they were itinerant workers, or fishermen between trips, occasionally a smartly-dressed door-to-door salesman, but very often they were entertainers - singers, actors and dancers from shows in the various theatres around Great Yarmouth, who returned to stay with Gran every season. Some only stayed a short while, while others remained for the whole summer season.

The place always seemed full and lively. After work each evening, the performers would return to the B & B with bottles of beer or whiskey and get drunk together. Then they would sing bawdy songs, laughing and joking until, one by one, they passed out or staggered upstairs to bed.

I was usually sent to bed before the party really warmed up, but, while I was allowed to stay, I loved to listen to the music and the stories they told. I joined in when I could, if I knew the words of a song. If not, I would dance. And when I didn't understand the jokes, which was usual, I laughed anyway. Gran kept a sharp ear on the proceedings, and if anything became too risqué for her granddaughter, she soon told the men to behave.

When the evening ended, however, and the men were asleep, there was little rest for Gran. She would clean the place before retiring to bed herself, then be up again before dawn, repeating her daily routine.

But she was always cheerful, content with her life and a constant source of wisdom and encouragement for me. Whenever she could, she involved me in the things she did. She took me shopping, and discussed the needs of the guest-house. She introduced me to all the tradesmen who called to deliver her orders - the milkman, the greengrocer and the butcher. She showed me how to lay the fire in the front parlour, how to repair a torn cushion, and how to make a "proper cup of tea". When we had a quiet hour or two on a warm day, we walked to the park, or, if it was cold or wet, we set up a little folding table near the window and played Ludo or Snakes-And-Ladders, watching the trees swaying on the green opposite, or the raindrops sliding crazily down the glass.

-♪-

Gran taught me a little bit about babies, and mummies and daddies. Not the impersonal, biological facts, but the way families grow and fit together.

"Your mummy was my baby," she said, brushing my hair back from my eyes as we sat together in the window seat, watching the leaves being swept in eddies by the winter wind. "She died while you were being born."

"Why?" I asked, as children will.

I understood about death; Gran had explained about

that when I found a dead bird in the garden, but I couldn't think why anyone would want to die.

She smiled sadly. "We don't usually get to choose. I expect God wanted her to be one of His angels," she said quietly.

"She was very pretty," I said after a moment.

Gran looked at me with a puzzled expression. "Yes, she was - a beautiful girl. But how do you know?"

I shrugged. "I met her, when I was born," I said. "She was on her way to Heaven. She stopped and touched my face. She said she couldn't stay to look after me, but you would do it better, anyway."

I could see tears trickling down her cheek, so I sat on her lap and wrapped my arms around her neck. She held me tightly, and I could feel her body shaking.

"Come with me," she said suddenly, sniffing. We stood and she led me to the big mahogany dresser that occupied the whole of the opposite wall. Opening the glass doors, she reached up to the top shelf, way above my line of sight, and took down a photograph in a pretty porcelain frame. It showed a young man and woman standing in a garden, smiling. "Do you know who this is?" she asked, handing it to me.

I studied the picture carefully, then shook my head, unsure what to say. The young woman in the photo looked a bit like my mummy, but not exactly.

"That's me and your Granddad on our wedding day," she said, taking the picture and looking at it wistfully for a moment, before putting it back into the cabinet. "How about this one?" She produced another, larger one, this time in a silver frame.

It showed a group of people, posing formally around a settee, some seated, some standing behind. I recognised Gran at once, sitting in the middle, surrounded by younger people, men and women. One face stood out. "That's my mummy," I said, pointing, smiling with the recognition.

Gran seemed to freeze, staring first at my finger, then at my face. "Yes," she whispered, "it is your mummy, my baby girl Rita, with all her brothers and sisters."

Suddenly, a strange expression on her face, she reached up once more and, groping to the back of the cabinet, produced another photograph. It was just a plain picture, no frame, and showed two people, like the first she had shown me, though the clothes were very different.

"There's my mummy again," I said.

She nodded, watching my face carefully.

I looked at the man standing beside her. They were both smiling, holding each other close. I pointed to him. "Is he my daddy?"

"Yes, he is Paolo, your daddy.

"What happened to him? Did he die, too?"

She shook her head sadly. "No, petal, he had to leave, to go back to Italy."

"Why?"

"It was where he was born. He and your mummy had a big argument and he left."

"He shouldn't have left us," I said fiercely.

"No, petal," she replied quietly. "He shouldn't have gone."

-♪-

Here's another snapshot; from my private album, the one in my head. Me, aged four, playing out front, sitting on the stone steps, with the bright blue front door open behind me. As I show you this memory, I can hear the seagulls shrieking, feel the warm sun against my skin on that summer day, smell the flowers in the colourful hanging baskets that Gran always tended so carefully. I'm making a little home for my doll, Rosie, out of cardboard boxes and odd things I had collected. Gran was usually busy in the mornings, so I found things to keep me occupied, and Rosie was my play-friend.

I didn't have any other friends. Some kids would occasionally pass, but they never played with me. They called me 'Wop' and, even though I didn't know what it meant, it still upset me, because of the disgust in their voices and the sneers on their faces. I told them, angrily, to go away, but they didn't stop, they just laughed and chanted it over and over again, until I ran indoors to get away from them.

I asked Gran what it meant. She was shocked and angry at their behaviour.

"'Wop' is a horrible word! It is used by some ignorant people as an insult to people from Italy. You have heard of Italy, haven't you?"

"It's where my daddy went."

"Yes, that's right. Italy is a country a long way from here; a beautiful country, warm and green. That's where your father was born, and somehow those kids must have found out. For a while, England was at war with Italy, but your dad refused to fight against us, and became a prisoner of war here in Norfolk. When he was released after the war, he met your Mum and they fell in love."

"What can I do then, Gran, when they shout like that?"

"Well, I could tell those children off, and you know I would do that for you, but I suspect it would only make them worse. The best thing to do is just ignore them, so they don't get any fun from upsetting you. Can you do that?"

"I'll try, Gran."

Actually, I quite liked the idea of being Italian - it sounded romantic and mysterious. I went into Gran's bedroom and looked at myself in her long mirror. Did I look any different from the other kids? I couldn't tell. My hair was black, always cut by Gran into a simple pageboy style that I liked. Maybe it was a bit blacker than anyone else I had seen? And my face: were my brown eyes unusual? Or my cheekbones? Was my skin lighter or darker than anyone else? I didn't think so; but, from that day, I started to imagine I was an Italian princess, much more important than those kids.

I followed Gran's advice. As soon as the kids started taunting me, I glared at them haughtily and swept elegantly (I thought) indoors. It felt good, because the more they shouted, the more I knew I had beaten them.

-♪-

In the mind of a child, everything is normal. Looking back through the eyes of little Belinda, the world looks simpler then than it is now. But that is because there were few pressures on a five-year-old; life for adults was just as hard as at any other time.

For anyone who did not live through those early postwar years, it is hard to understand how very different life was then. Almost all the things we take for granted now were either not yet invented or too expensive for ordinary folks.

In nineteen fifty-one, for example, when I was five years old, television was yet to become accessible to the masses; we relied on radio for entertainment and the latest news. There were no automatic washing machines - we did our personal clothes in the big sink in the kitchen, and sent the bed linen to the laundry - but we did have a vacuum cleaner, a rather frightening beast that was as tall as me and made a dreadful noise when it was switched on.

Telephones were just beginning to become more common in ordinary homes, though businesses had quickly recognised how useful they were, and Gran had owned one before I was even born.

Floors were rarely carpeted - more likely they had a covering of linoleum (which we polished) with the odd rug dotted around. Central heating was for the wealthy, the rest of us had open coal fires in each room and draughts from every door and window. Washing dried on a line extended down the garden (if you had one), water was heated in a kettle on the gas cooker.

Little girls played with dolls or helped their Gran (or at least tried to); boys played marbles, or football, or scrapped. We wore sturdy clothes, designed to last, and if something became torn, we mended it. I had two dresses

- while I wore one, the second was in the wash.

Boys wore short trousers of grey flannel, and leather shoes with scuffed toes. We didn't feel deprived - you can't miss what you don't even know exists - and we didn't question the way of things. If you had something, you assumed everyone had the same. I thought everyone had a Gran to look after them, didn't know what it was like to have a mother and father.

Each year, on my birthday, Gran took me to my mum's grave, at the huge cemetery on the other side of town, and we laid flowers and talked to her. She never answered me - I don't know if Gran had any response. Gran also talked to God ... a lot. She used strange words like 'thou' and 'thine'; I figured God must be foreign.

On Sundays, we went to St John's Church, a short walk from *The Nest*. She left me with Mrs Murdoch, a skinny, nervous woman with mousey brown hair and frumpy clothes. Mrs Murdoch ran the Sunday School.

Actually, I liked Sunday School. While I sat with crayons, drawing pictures of baby Jesus and camels in the desert, I could hear the grown-ups singing and praying in the main hall. We children had our own songs and prayers, and I joined in enthusiastically. Whenever I think about it, I can smell that little back room and the children with whom I shared it. I felt safe there.

-♪-

At the age of five, I started to attend Infants School. With that word - school - come memories of pencils and paints, a little bottle of milk every morning, echoing voices in cold rooms, smells of unwashed bodies and urine, dinners of boiled potatoes and cabbage and tapioca pudding.

For the first time in my life, I was thrown into close contact with kids of my own age, and I was not equipped. The only children I had met before had shunned and taunted me, making me sullen and withdrawn. In the lessons, I avoided speaking to anyone, and at playtime, I found a spot where I could be alone. But it did not save me from the attentions of a gang from the 'big' school, led by a stocky, red haired boy named Thomas O'Reilly.

Every day, he and his chums shouted abuse at me over the wall from their part of the school. "Dirty Wop! Smelly Eyetie! Your mother was a whore!"

If I managed to evade them in school, they waited for me afterwards ... then it was worse. They jostled me and pushed me to the ground, they took my satchel and threw it into nearby gardens (where I then had to beg the people to return it to me), and sometimes they punched me or hit me with sticks.

Teachers became frustrated with me as I slipped further behind in the classroom, and couldn't tell them why. I began to pretend to be ill in the mornings, so Gran would keep me at home, but she soon became suspicious.

"What's up, pet?" she asked me one day when I complained of a headache. "I know there's nothing really wrong with you, so why don't you want to go to school?"

Silently, I hung my head, unable to answer, afraid that, if I started to tell her, I would cry.

"Belinda, darling, we don't have secrets, do we?"

I shook my head.

"Well then, you can tell me, that's what I'm here for."

I tried to think how to tell her.

"Gran, tell me about my Mum. Some kids say she was a whore! What is a 'whore' Gran?"

"Oh my lovely, is that what's happening at school?"

I nodded again.

"Right, let's get this straight, your Mum was not a whore, she was a respectable married woman. Those kids have no business saying bad things about you or your family, tell me their names and I will go round to see their parents and give them a piece of my mind!"

"Oh no, Gran, that will make them hate me even more! Please don't."

"Well they can't get away with it, Belinda dear. I simply will not stand for them making you afraid to go to school. I'll take you there now, and then I'll have a quiet word with their headmaster. All right?"

"Ok, Gran."

She walked to the school with me and delivered me into my class, explaining quietly to the teacher why I was late. Then she left me and went to find the headmaster of the Junior School.

-♪-

In our living room we had a 'radiogram', a beautiful piece of furniture the size of a sideboard. It was made of light brown, almost orange-coloured, wood, with a dense, swirling grain. Gran polished it lovingly, and it was often admired by guests.

But it was the inside that captivated me. Behind its

elegant, curved doors hid a radio and a gramophone - wonderful technology that opened up a whole world of excitement.

In cupboards at each end were stacked Gran's collection of records, and I played them whenever I could, dancing around the living room, singing along with Vera Lynn or Glen Miller and his orchestra.

Whenever the world outside started to hurt me, I would turn on the radiogram, listening to the humming and fizzing of the valves and smelling that unique blend of wood oil and and hot electronic components, then hearing voices and music as though by magic.

The radio stations tended to be mostly talk, with sometimes a comedy show, but occasionally they had music programmes. Then I might have a special treat, because every so often there would be a new recording to thrill me. I loved the steady beat and complex rhythms of the jazz records, and soon became able to pick out the distinctive sounds of different bands and the voices of the singers. Many of the records came from America, a mystical land, far away across the ocean, where music seemed to be a living thing, constantly growing and changing.

When I first heard the exciting sound of Les Paul exploring the amazing sounds he could achieve with an electric guitar, blended with the sweet tones of Mary Ford's voice, I was ecstatic. They created a complex sound by recording and re-recording themselves, playing one tape back while adding fresh harmonies, and recording all that onto another machine. It's process I later came to know as 'overdubbing'.

I wanted to be part of that beautiful, new music, and experimented day after day, singing first one, then another of the harmonies Mary created, then trying some of my own. Music became as much a part of me as my hands, as important as as my heartbeat, as natural as breathing.

Gran would watch and listen as I danced around, singing happily. Then she would applaud enthusiastically. "You have a rare gift, Belinda my love," she would say. "I don't know where it comes from - certainly not from me, I can't sing to save my life, and your mother never had much of a voice. Perhaps there is an Italian opera singer in your ancestry somewhere, who knows."

That, of course, set my mind off on fantastic journeys of imagination, in which I would see myself on a stage before an enormous orchestra, singing to adoring crowds of opera lovers.

-♪-

For several months after Gran spoke to the headmaster, the older kids seemed to leave me alone. My confidence began to grow, and my lessons improved.

Then, unexpectedly, the following summer, O'Reilly and his gang were waiting for me as I walked home. They pushed me into an alley, and two of them held me while O'Reilly began pulling at my clothes, tearing open the buttons of my blouse, sneering at me and laughing.

"Stop it!" I shouted. "Leave me alone."

"Oh, the wop wants us to stop," he taunted. "Shall we stop, boys?"

"Naahh!" they all chorused, and began to shove me forwards and back between them, chanting again: "Wop! Whore! Wop! Whore!"

My world became a blur, as I was spun around and pushed from one boy to the next.

I was terrified, fearing they were going to kill me, when, suddenly, all movement and noise stopped, and I stumbled and fell. Then I heard a familiar voice, and looked up to see Mr Watkins, their headmaster, standing at the mouth of the alley, glowering at the boys.

In a voice that conveyed both his anger and his authority, he boomed: "O'Reilly, Scott, Perkins, Andrews, get home right now, I will deal with you in school tomorrow."

Chastened and embarrassed, the bullies shuffled past him and out of the alley, Tommy O'Reilly earning a special glare from the irascible head, who grabbed his arm and leaned down to speak in his ear: "You've gone too far this time, boy. You are in serious trouble."

He pushed the bully towards the end of the alley, then turned to me. "Did they hurt you?" he asked.

I was sobbing. But, with the boys gone, I was able to answer: "Not much sir, but they tore my blouse."

"They will pay for that, I promise you. Can you cover yourself enough to get home?" I pulled my blouse together, and he walked me to the B & B, where he told Gran what he had seen.

"I will deal with them most severely," he assured us as he was about to leave.

"Sir?" I said.

He towered above me, but crouched down to answer.

"What is it Belinda?"

"Thank you, sir."

He smiled and touched my hair with his hand. "Those boys must learn to treat a lady with respect," he said, gently.

-♪-

Gran cleaned me up and gave me fresh clothes to wear. When she was sure I had recovered, she sat me down with a cup of tea and some bread and butter, while she got on with preparing dinner for the guests.

Ted Bailey, a comedian staying with us, found me sitting pensively, alone in the garden, a little later.

"What's up, Princess?" he enquired.

Many of the entertainers called me "Princess", it was a nice gesture that helped me to feel part of their exciting lives. Ted had been a regular at the guest-house every year since before I was born; he was a jolly man, kind and caring, and he was like an uncle to me. I told him about the kids tormenting me, though I didn't mention what O'Reilly and his gang had called my mum.

"Ah," he said with a wry smile. "I am only too familiar with taunts like that. In my case it's because of my size."

Ted was indeed a huge man, tall, broad and plump, with a wild head of mousy brown hair and twinkling blue eyes.

"My way of dealing with them was to clown around and tell jokes, to try to make them like me. Eventually, when I was old enough to look for a job, I figured that if people wanted to laugh at me, I would turn it to my advantage.

That's why I became a comic."

I smiled at him, grateful for the insight. "But I'm hopeless at jokes," I said, "I always forget something important, and I can never think what to say when they start jeering."

"Oh, we all have different gifts; mine is humour, yours is something different." He leaned back in his chair. "Do you know why they do it?" he asked.

"What do you mean?"

"Well, people, kids especially, usually attack someone else because they are different, like wild birds do if one has white feathers, or something else that marks them out. Anything unusual unnerves them, scares them, so they respond aggressively."

"But that's just it, I'm not different from them, I look the same and talk the same. Why are they picking on me?"

"Because, my little lovely, you are prettier than any of the other girls and cleverer than any of the boys. And you can sing and dance as good as anyone I ever saw."

I blushed. I did not think I was pretty, or smart. And as for singing and dancing - well, couldn't everyone do it?

"I tell you what: would you like to come to see the theatre where I'm working?" he asked.

Everything else was forgotten in an instant. "Oh yes please, that would be great. Thanks, Ted."

After consulting Gran, he took me to the Windmill, a spectacular building on the seafront, only five minutes walk from home. I had passed it many times, and marvelled at the huge, brightly painted sails that adorned its façade, but I had never seen inside.

At first, as we entered the auditorium through the doors

from the foyer, it was too dark to see, but as my eyes adapted to the gloom, I saw the rows of seats, stacked up in tiers, falling like a wave to the foot of the stage. There was a smell, one with which I have become very familiar over the years, a mixture of stale cigarette smoke, the sweet aroma of popcorn, the accumulation of body odours of the thousands of patrons whose bums had pressed into those seats, the hot dust rising from spotlights, and a kind of oily smell I could not identify, but later came to know well - the smell of greasepaint.

Several women were hard at work, brushing the seats and the floor, collecting rubbish and dusting the enormous blue-and-gold-painted crests that adorned the walls, and someone was perched at the top of the tallest stepladder I have ever seen, working on one of the great chandeliers hanging from the beautiful, ornate ceiling. I was spellbound; the whole scene was magical.

On the stage, I saw men erecting scenery, pulling on ropes and arranging wires that trailed across the floor. In the centre stood three young, blonde-haired women, singing into a microphone, to the accompaniment of a piano hidden in the orchestra pit. The song was 'The Tennessee Waltz', which I knew well from a recording by Patti Page, but they were singing it in beautiful three-part harmony.

"See those girls?" Ted asked me; I nodded. "Well they are going to be famous before long. I never heard such beautiful voices. They are real sisters, too, Joy, Teddie and Babs, The Beverley Sisters. You watch out for them."

As each person saw us on our wanderings, they called

out a greeting to Ted. He was a very popular man, and we stopped many times to chat. He introduced me to everyone as his Princess, and they all made me feel welcome. After a while, I knew that this was what I wanted to do with my life: become an entertainer.

-♪-

Almost every day after that, for the rest of his stay in Yarmouth, Ted took me to a theatre. By the end of that season, we had visited every one. At each, he introduced me to the staff, backstage crews, entertainers and managers. Everyone seemed to know and like the jolly and sincere comic; showgirls flocked to put their arms around his plump body, and men shook his chubby hand.

In The Empire, an austere-looking grey building, we found rehearsals under way on-stage for a new summer variety show. The director, a tall, thin man with a pelmet of shoulder-length, grey hair and a nose like an eagle's beak, broke off from instructing the young artistes to warmly greet Ted.

"Ted, darling, so wonderful to see you," he gushed in a beautiful Glasgow accent. "Who is this delightful creature you've brought to see me?"

"This," said Ted, without a hint of irony, "is my friend Princess Belinda. She is going to be famous one day. Belinda, this is Douglas Barrett. Doug and I have known each other since we were both starting out. Now he has his own touring company."

"Hello, sir," I said nervously.

"Hello Belinda my love," he replied with a big smile

and an outstretched hand, which I accepted, feeling rather overwhelmed by his exuberant personality.

"Who have you got in this show, Doug?" Ted asked, scanning the troupe on stage, who were gathering in little clusters, talking in whispers while the great man was otherwise occupied. "I don't see anyone I know."

"Nay, I doubt you will," the eagle replied. "These are all relative newcomers. But I've got some names joining us later in the week: Teddy Johnson will be here tomorrow, and Anne Shelton is joining us on Friday for a wee while."

I was amazed. Here were names I had heard on the radio, world-famous singers whose records I had played and whose songs I had learnt, being talked about on first-name terms. I felt a glow inside, a surge of happiness to be touching the edge of this fantasy world.

-♪-

Later that same week, Ted took me to The Regent (which was mainly used as a cinema, but held summer shows) and The Hippodrome, a stunning indoor circus, where they also put on huge variety spectaculars. I talked to some of the successful entertainers of the time who were headlining lavish productions, and to ambitious amateurs, willing to work for peanuts just to be on the stage. It was magical, the greatest adventure of my life, and I loved every second. I had expected show-business people to be snobbish, but everyone I met was incredibly open and welcoming, I felt as though they accepted me.

"They're not all so friendly," Ted said when I

commented on how nice they all were. "Some think they're a class apart, so stupid they don't even talk to each other. They start to believe the myth of their own publicity."

"Do you know all the stars?" I asked.

He laughed. "Not all of them, but I've worked with quite a few: Matt Monroe, Arthur Askey, Billy Cotton, Alma Cogan; she's lovely, Alma, completely un-star-like, soft-spoken, always happy, incredibly sexy." He trailed off, smiling, lost for a moment in memories.

I took his hand. "Thanks for what you are doing for me, Ted," I said.

"Princess, you're going to be a star too, one day, I know it. When you make it to the top, I hope you'll think fondly of old Ted."

He looked down at me and grinned, and I squeezed his arm.

~3~
January 1953
Oliver

My days all began on the beach. No matter what the weather, I would be there every morning, walking along the golden sand, close to the water's edge. I didn't care if the wind was whipping my hair into my face and the waves were bursting savagely into huge clouds of spray and foam, or if the sky was blue and the sea as still as a painting, it was just good to feel close to the power of it. What I liked was that the sea was the same for everyone, it didn't care if you were rich or poor, or even a Wop.

Early mornings were the best, before school; then I was alone with nature. The beach had been swept clean by the tide, all footprints and litter gone. Then the gulls would swoop and screech overhead, fighting over the crusts of bread I often took them, and swarms of tiny sanderlings would hurtle along the frothy tides reach in perfect formation, perilously close to the waves, then swirl and land like a picnic blanket thrown onto the wet sand, to prick and probe for hiding marine creatures. Walking alone, leaving fresh footprints in the virgin sand, skipping aside as a sudden wave rushed at my feet, I would believe that I owned the beach.

Later in the day, people would begin to arrive, but for a while it was mine alone. In the summer, holidaymakers would emerge from their hotels and caravans as the sun sprang from the horizon, swathes of them jostling in the shops and amusement palaces, determined to have fun.

This was post-war Britain and, though the fighting was over, the hardships mostly remained. So the adventure of a holiday by the sea was attracting hordes of visitors to places like Great Yarmouth. Once they started to arrive on the beach, staking out their little territories with windbreaks and deckchairs, I would return home for breakfast before going to school.

-♪-

One wild winter's day, another figure appeared on my beach. He was a bit older than me (I was six by then, and he would have been about eight), tall and skinny, with ginger hair. We eyed each other as we passed, but did not speak. On the second such occasion I glared at him through the rain that slanted, freezing, across the space between us, willing him to go somewhere else. But on the third day he was back again, and this time with a cheery wave and a cheeky grin; I glowered back but, undaunted, the next day he was there, and this time he stopped to speak.
"Hello."
I refused to answer, or even to meet his eye, but stared at the sand before my shuffling feet.
"Do you live near here?" he asked, undeterred, his voice carrying strongly against the wind, and bearing a distinctive accent.
"Yes," I muttered into my chest.
"I moved here last week. I live over there."
I saw his arm raise and point towards the north beach. Following it forced me to raise my head, and when I

turned back to him, he was smiling. I quickly looked down again.

"You don't say much, do you?" he said, and I could hear the amusement in his voice.

"Don't have to," I grunted.

"My name's Oliver, what's yours?"

"Belinda."

"Can we be friends?" His voice sounded serious for a moment, and sincere.

I was suspicious. No-one of my own age had ever wanted to be my friend before. Why would he?

"S'pose so."

Suddenly, his hand came into view, extended in a handshake. At first I jumped when it appeared, but, still half fearful of a trick, I took it.

Nothing bad happened, and I looked up again to see his broad smile. Despite my resentment at his invasion of my private beach, and my nervousness that he would turn out to be like the other boys around Trafalgar Road, I could not help liking him. He had a simple openness that was endearing.

"See you tomorrow then, Belinda?"

"Ok." I watched him walk away, heading for north beach. He turned once and waved, and I waved back, then returned to my sea and solitude, but with a new sensation deep inside and a smile on my face.

-♪-

We met every day after that, and I was surprised to find myself looking forward to each encounter. He told me that his family had come to Yarmouth from Sheffield, hoping to be allocated one of the new prefabs that had been erected in Gorleston, but had been turned away. Sheffield suffered terribly in frequent night bombing raids by the Luftwaffe, and when Oliver's father had returned home from his army service he found that they were homeless. They had been moving from place to place ever since, staying with family or friends, or living rough.

We squatted on the sand behind a breakwater, to shelter from the relentless wind, so we could hear each other speak.

"There's a village sprung up on North Beach, little shacks made of corrugated iron and bits of wood ... all homeless people. My folks have built one for the four of us," he told me.

"What will you do now?"

"Probably try again for a prefab, I suppose, wherever they are building them."

"What's a 'prefab'?"

"It's a kind of house. See, there's a shortage of homes, 'cos of the war; there's thousands of families like mine that have been bombed out, and they can't build new houses quick enough. Usually it takes months to build one with bricks and mortar, but someone came up with this idea of making all the walls and roof and floors out of concrete in a factory, then putting them together quickly, wherever you want them."

I asked him about the bombing of his home town. He told me that the German planes had targeted Sheffield because of its steel industry and the factories producing essential weapons and supplies for our troops, and they virtually destroyed the city. Huge areas were devastated, and thousands of families killed or made homeless. He was too young at the time to understand what was happening, but he told me how terrified he had been of all the noise.

"Every night, the sirens would go off, and we would all run down the garden to the Anderson Shelter." Seeing my incomprehension, he explained. "It was like a little cave, a hole dug in the ground, with a dome made of corrugated iron set into it, and then covered with the soil and grass from the hole." As he described it, he drew a picture in the sand with his finger. "It was supposed to be safer than staying indoors," he said. "I suppose it was, really, 'cos we was in it when our house was hit."

He stopped speaking, and I looked up from his drawing to see that he was gazing off into the distance with unseeing eyes. I edged closer and put my arm through his, and he turned to me and smiled.

After a minute, he resumed. "It wasn't just us; the whole street was flattened by a stick of bombs. We could hear the planes coming, same as every night; droning engines, getting louder. Usually, there'd be a whistling sound made by the first bombs as they fell, then the bangs would start all around us, and the ground would shake, and that would go on all night. But the night we lost our house it was different. Right from the start the bangs were louder, closer. Then, suddenly, the door to our shelter came flying open, and we were lifted up and slammed down by the shock wave of a bomb exploding very near. I remember my mouth was open, but couldn't hear myself scream; the blast had deafened me."

Again he fell silent. I didn't know what to do to help him. His lips were pressed so tightly together that they were white, and his hands gripped each other under his chin, as though protecting his heart.

"I ... I have never talked about this before," he said quietly.

"You don't have to, if it's hard."

He shrugged, and even managed a small smile. "It is hard, but actually it's good to let it out. I have kept it in all this time. No-one in the family wants to talk about it, see, never even mentions it. It's as though they think that, if they pretend it didn't happen, maybe it will un-happen." He gave a little wry snort, then settled back into thoughtful silence for a while.

With an effort, he resumed. "When we came out of the shelter, not one building in sight remained standing. I looked up and down our street - every house was gone, there were fires everywhere, smoke and dust rising in a pall; it was a scene from the worst nightmare imaginable."

I had seen the boys in Trafalgar Road playing killing games, running after each other with pretend guns, shouting "Bang, bang, you're dead!" But when Oliver talked, there was no excitement in his voice, no laughter, just the flat tones of dreadful memories shared and a calmness that failed to hide the terror he had seen and felt.

A bond had been forged between us; an understanding.

-♪-

Our meetings became the highlight of my days. He asked me about my family; I told him about Gran and my life with her. And, as we walked along the shore, deep in earnest conversation, it felt natural to talk about my Italian father, who I had never met, and my pretty mum, who died having me.

One wild and wet January day, he held my hand as we walked, and didn't let go until we said goodbye at the edge of North Beach. I didn't mind.

But nothing is forever. The next day, I waited for him at our place, but he didn't arrive. The wind, that had started to build up before dawn, buffeted me as I stood alone on the shore, and hurled the first stinging frozen raindrops into my face like shards of glass. I looked up and down the beach, seeking out his familiar walk, increasingly anxious with each minute that he was late.

Eventually, I stayed long beyond the time for school, standing futilely on the swirling sand in the howling wind and sea spray all morning, before I finally accepted that, for whatever reason, he wasn't coming. I went home and cried into my pillow for the whole afternoon.

That evening I couldn't eat my dinner, and when Gran asked why, I told her I didn't feel well. She gave me a hug and made me a drink of Ovaltine and hot milk. I was sure she must have seen my red eyes, but she sensed that I didn't want to talk and left me to tell her in my own time.

At bedtime, I lay awake for hours, listening to the wind shaking the house and the rain lashing the windows. My thoughts of Oliver were interrupted by great crashes of thunder, and at some stage I heard raised voices in the darkness outside.

Suddenly my bedroom door opened and Gran called out to me.

"Belinda, get dressed quickly!"

I could tell by her tone that something serious was happening, so I did as she said, then met her on the landing. She was holding a lighted candle that cast a dim glow, barely illuminating her and the two lodgers who were staying at that time. She pointed down the stairway. At first, I couldn't make anything out, then, to my amazement I saw that the bottom steps were under water.

"The storm and tide have flooded the town, we may have to get up on the roof," said one of the men, dramatically. He normally spoke little, a big, rough man, a labourer from up-country looking for work, but now seemed to be enjoying himself.

We followed Gran into the front bedroom, her room, and went to look out of the window. The town was in darkness - no street lamps were working - the only light came from flashes of lightening that briefly revealed, in stark black and white, a stunning parody of the landscape I used to know, transformed into a scene from a nightmare. The whole town seemed to be sinking into the sea.

As I looked eastwards, towards the beach, I could see huge waves breaking on the promenade. Beneath us, all the pavements and gardens were hidden under the flood waters that, whipped into waves by gale force winds, were slapping and bursting against the sides of the houses. Already, the downstairs windows were completely covered.

Here and there some brave people with small boats were risking their lives in the swirls and eddies, rescuing trapped households, while the rain lashed them, and the winds tossed their tiny craft like flotsam.

Gran opened the window and shouted down to one of them, a man punting what appeared to be one of the paddle boats from the park, using a long plank of wood to push it slowly along. There were two small children sitting in the boat, clinging to the sides as it lurched dangerously.

He looked up. "Sorry dear," he called back, "I can't carry any more. I'll try to come back for you as soon as I can."

"Take my granddaughter," Gran pleaded, "she's only six."

He took a moment to assess his status. There was room for me, but he was clearly hesitant. In the event, Gran didn't give him time to say 'no' again - she and one of the men lifted me up and heaved me over the window sill, my legs dangling over the abyss, supported only by their hands.

I screamed with fear, the heaving waters seeming to reach up to grab my feet.

"Belinda, we're going to lower you to the boat," she shouted hoarsely against the howling wind.

Seeing her determination, the man manoeuvred his rocking craft close to the house, and when he was directly below me, Gran and the lodger lowered me until my feet were just a few inches from the pitching floor of the boat, then let go. I landed awkwardly in the well between the seats, and cried out with pain as my ankle twisted. The man grabbed me by one arm, trying to steady the pitching boat. He pushed me down into a seat as water splashed over the sides, beginning to fill the tiny space around our feet.

"You kids will have to bale out!" the man shouted, struggling to start the boat moving in the right direction again.

I had only a fleeting moment to look up at the window, where Gran's worried face lingered briefly, then I began desperately scooping water over the side with my cupped hands, urging the other kids to do the same. They were younger than me, a boy and a girl, holding on to each other, afraid to move.

"Come on!" I yelled at them, "If you don't help we will all drown!"

The boy, he could have only been about four or five, began copying me, and after a moment, the girl did the same. I couldn't tell if we were making any difference, but we must have kept up with the water coming in, as the boat didn't sink. I concentrated on baling, trying to ignore the waves that slopped in over the rim of the tiny craft with every movement. Huge raindrops stung my eyes, and the boat tipped and spun terrifyingly.

After what seemed an eternity, we lurched to a stop, and when I looked around, I saw that we had run up onto dry land, somewhere near the market place.

"Quickly, kids, jump out," the man said, urgently.

I scrambled out as best I could, but collapsed as my ankle gave way when I tried to stand on it. For a few moments I lay in the road, water lapping over me, too exhausted to even try to get to my feet, then strong hands grabbed me and scooped me up. Through the rain and tears of pain I saw that I was in the arms of a soldier, his khaki uniform turned nearly black by the water that had soaked through it, his face, inches from mine, etched with tiredness, his teeth clamped together in a grimace of grim determination.

-♪-

He carried me to a hall, filled with a great mass of people, where volunteers were caring for refugees like me. A doctor bandaged my ankle, and one of the helpers brought me a mug of soup. Then, for several hours, I sat alone, watching the door, waiting for Gran to appear. Though safe and warm, I was scared, and needed the reassurance of her warm voice and loving smile. She surely could not have stayed in the house all night; but if not there, then where?

One thing I knew, I could not find her on my own, and I couldn't walk far - I needed help. I looked around the hall. There was an ebb and flow of dazed humanity. Some arriving, others gathering their possessions and leaving, everyone seemed to be talking or arguing, eating, drinking or sleeping. No-one seemed to be in charge, the only sign of organisation was in one corner where a kind of cafeteria had been set up, with members of the WRVS serving soup and bread. I hobbled across and approached one of the women, who was standing idly, smoking a cigarette..

"Excuse me," I said, timidly.

She looked down at me and frowned. "What are you doing away from your parents?" she demanded, brusquely.

"I'm ... " I began, but she cut me off.

"Go back to your mother and let me get on with my work." The old witch! She was doing nothing!

"My mother is dead!" I shouted, fighting off the tears that were welling up.

One of the other women standing nearby stopped what she was doing and crouched down to talk to me, glaring at the harridan.

"Tell me what has happened, dear," she said gently, with a reassuring smile.

"A boat rescued me in the night and brought me here. I can't get home, it's under water, and I can't find my Gran." I burst into tears as the words came out. I felt so lost and helpless and alone. "And I hurt my ankle."

"Oh poor thing," she said. She foraged in her pocket and passed me a hankie. "My name is Sue, what's yours?"

"Belinda Bellini, miss."

"Right, Belinda, here's what we are going to do. First you sit down here and rest your ankle, and I am going to get you some cocoa. Then we can work out how to find your Gran." She helped me to a chair and brought me a mug of hot, milky cocoa to drink. As I sipped it, she asked me about Gran and where I lived.

"I think we need to let the police know where you are," she suggested. "Your Gran will be sure to get in touch with them. What's her name?"

"Gladys Cartwright, she bought me up after my mum died. She runs a guest-house in Trafalgar Road. *The Nest*, it's called."

Sue left me to finish my drink while she went to telephone the police station. When she returned, she brought a sticky bun for me.

"Inspector Randal knows your Gran, so he's coming here himself to help you find her." She smiled, "You have friends in high places, Belinda."

-♪-

I had known Mr Randal since my childhood. He was an occasional visitor to *The Nest*, sometimes bringing guests, sometimes responding to phone calls from Gran about doubtful characters staying or enquiring. Gran called him Archie, and he always stayed for a cup of tea and a chat. He was what I think is everyone's image of a policeman - tall, clean-shaven and smartly dressed, and he carried himself with a confidence that said "I can handle anything".

He had been offered, and declined, a post as Desk Sergeant; I recall him telling Gran that he would go mad if forced to stay indoors. But eventually he had promotion thrust upon him, and found himself tethered to a desk. Even so, he used every excuse to get out and "do some real policing".

A patrol car pulled up outside the hall doors, and I saw Mr Randal climb out and enter the hall. Sue escorted him to where I was sitting. He smiled when he reached me, and sat on the bench beside me. "Hello Belinda, how is your ankle?"

I showed him my bandaged leg. "It's ok, thank you -

hurts a bit, but not as bad as it did."

"Good. I've brought you a walking stick, to help take your weight." He produced a battered old stick with a curved handle. "It has been in our 'Lost Property' cupboard for over a year - I had to clean the dust off it."

He grinned. "Now, I'm trying to find out where your Gran is. She's not in the guest-house, which is still flooded, but we don't know where she's gone."

He saw that I was crestfallen. "Don't worry, we will soon find her. In the meantime, you need somewhere to stay. We have a list of people who have volunteered to offer a temporary place for folks like you who can't get home. I'm going to take you to a couple who have said they would prefer young people; their kids have grown up and moved away, so they have a spare bedroom."

When this scene plays through in my memory, as it frequently does, the next line echoes round and round my head. As he helped me to my feet, he said: "Mr and Mrs Grainger."

-♪-

I wasn't sure about living with strangers, but I could see there was no other way; and it was only temporary, until Gran came home. Mr Randal took me in his police car to a smart semi-detached house on the outskirts of town, on the Caister road. There I met the Graingers, a middle-aged couple. Mrs Grainger ("Call me Phylis, dear.") was a small, frail-looking woman with her hair tied up in a bun. She wore a long, pleated, tartan skirt, a plain blouse and a thick woollen cardigan. She seemed nice enough when she greeted me with a hug and a lot of 'oohs' and 'aahs'.

"Ooh, look at the poor thing," she cooed, holding me at arms length to study me. "Don't worry lovie, we'll soon get you clean and warm and a hot dinner inside you, won't we Jack?"

"Yes, dear," her husband replied, absently. "Course we will."

He was a plump man, with thinning brown hair pasted back with a shiny, greasy dressing. In his yellow-stained fingers, he cupped a smoking cigarette. He wore an old, sleeveless pullover, dotted with holes, over a grey shirt, and grubby corduroy trousers. He stared at me in a strange way, as though assessing me, weighing me up."

Inspector Randal left, and Phylis led me upstairs to her cosy bathroom, chattering all the way, like a mother hen clucking at her chicks.

"Let's get you out of those damp clothes," she said, turning the taps of the big, white, enamelled bath. She crumbled a lavender bath cube into the steaming water that gushed forth. I sat on a chair while she unwound the bandage from my swollen foot, tutting and sucking in her breath.

When there was enough water in the bath, and after she turned off the taps, I waited for her to leave, so I could undress in private, but she hustled me along. "Come on dear, don't be shy, I've had daughters of my own." She began to help me off with my ruined clothes.

No-one but my Gran had ever seen me naked, and I was acutely embarrassed at being exposed in front of a stranger, but she seemed unconcerned.

"Hop in, dear," she chirped, testing the water temperature with her fingers.

I clambered into the foaming, tinted, sweet-smelling water. It felt good, and soon I relaxed. Gradually, warmth began to soak into my flesh, and I allowed her to sponge off the grime from my back and shoulders.

"That's more like it, now you look better," she enthused as she lifted me out. She dried me off, then wrapped a towel around me, and sat me on the chair again to carefully wind the bandage tightly back around my ankle.

"Now, come through to the bedroom and I'll sort out some clothes for you. I have lots, left by my daughters when they flew the nest."

She led me along the landing. Mr Grainger was loitering at the top of the stairs, and my embarrassment returned when I felt his intense gaze on me. There was something about him, a kind of arrogance, that reminded me, for some reason, of the boys who tormented me at school. I avoided meeting his eyes, chilled by the hardness of his expression.

Mrs Grainger, Phylis, took me into a pretty little bedroom, decorated in pink and lemon, with frilly curtains and dainty furniture. Rummaging through drawers and cupboards, she produced dresses and undies and shoes, which I eagerly tried on. When we were satisfied that I looked clean and tidy, she took me back downstairs to her kitchen.

Once again, at the foot of the stairs, I found myself running the gauntlet of her husband's stare. His searching eyes frightened me, and I clutched at his wife's skirt for protection.

She sat me at the table, then produced from the oven of the big range a plated dinner.

"Here we are, love. We ate ours earlier, but I saved some for you after Mr Randal phoned."

-♪-

That afternoon, Mr Randal returned. Phylis greeted him warmly at the door, but I noticed that her husband slunk away into the garden.

"I can't stay, Phylis. I just came with a little bit of good news for Belinda," Archie said. I saw him look over her shoulder at the receding back of Mr Grainger. "Can't Jack stay with us?" he asked.

"Oh, he likes to potter in his shed, doesn't much care for conversation."

Archie's eyebrows knitted, briefly, and he gave a little grunt, but said no more. I always had the impression with Mr Randal that he missed nothing.

Mrs Grainger took us into the front room, where Archie took a seat on an armchair and I perched on the pouffe.

"I'm glad to say we have found your Gran," he said, smiling. "She was rescued and taken to the big hospital in Norwich, suffering from exposure. I don't yet know how she came to be outside the guest-house, but we are trying to find the lodger who was staying with you, to see if he can help us." He saw how concerned I looked. "Don't worry, the matron at the hospital assured me that, although she has been through a rough time, she is not in any danger, and they hope to send her home soon." He stood up. "I'm really sorry, I have to rush off. I'm sure you understand, it's a busy time for us."

As he stepped into the hallway, I saw him look right, towards the kitchen and the back door. It was not an idle glance, I could see his shrewd mind was working. And, the moment the front door was closed behind him, Grainger re-appeared.

"Why did you go and open your big mouth, volunteering to have strangers in our house? Now the bloody coppers are coming and going. You know I like my privacy."

Phylis opened her mouth to reply, but he had turned and stormed off upstairs. She glared after him for a moment, then turned to me. "Come on, Pet," she said, pretending nothing had happened, "let's play a game of Snakes and Ladders, shall we?"

-♪-

That night I went to bed early, exhausted after all that had happened. I slept soundly, but woke with surprise before daybreak to the sound of someone opening my bedroom door.

I smelt the stale tobacco smoke on his clothes as he tiptoed across the lino to my bedside, heard his breathing. Then the bed creaked as he sat on the edge, his weight stretching the blankets tighter across me. He leaned over me and lifted the covers, peeling them back, exposing my body. I curled up, like a hedgehog, trying to protect myself, but felt his hand sliding down my bare arm, his foul breath heavy against my skin.

"What ... ?" I began to ask, but he clamped a huge hand

painfully over my mouth, stifling any further sound and making it hard for me to breathe.

Still with one hand smothering my face, he began to grope with the other at the hem of my nightdress. I felt the cold night air on my thighs, and began to struggle, desperately afraid and suffocating under his cruel grip.

Suddenly his breath was hot and strong on my face.

"Stop struggling, little girl, or it will be worse for you," he whispered, hoarsely, squeezing my cheeks harder to emphasis his words. I clawed at his hand, trying to pull it from my face, mumbling urgently.

"I'm not moving my hand until you promise not to make a sound. Do you agree?"

I nodded, desperately.

Cautiously, he released his grip, and I sucked in the welcome air, panting, my chest rasping with the effort.

"Now just be a good girl and no harm will come to you," he hissed.

I felt his hand on my leg, stroking my skin, sliding up my thigh. I tensed as it moved around to my tummy, then down between my legs.

I could stand it no more, and began to scream as loudly as I could. Awful pain slashed across my face as he angrily slapped me, then he was gone, running from my room.

Sobbing and shaking, I stumbled from my bed and groped around in the dark for my clothes. I was just putting on my shoes when Phylis ran into the room and switched on the light. Behind her stood her anxious-looking husband.

"Whatever is the matter, child?"

I could not speak. I ran past her to the door, but was confronted by Grainger, who stepped to block my way. Without thinking, I kicked him as hard as I could in the shin. With my small foot, it probably didn't hurt much, but it was enough to throw him of balance for a moment, and I dodged past him and stumbled down the stairs. At the front door, I panicked for a moment as I struggled with the lock, but then I was out into their front garden, through the gate and down the dark street as fast as my poor, damaged little legs could carry me. Running, half-limping, sobbing, I escaped from that monster as fast as I could.

-♪-

I hobbled along a wide, dark avenue, lined with trees. Large houses on either side of the road hid behind hedges in enclosed gardens, the sleeping citizens within unaware of the beast living nearby. I listened for sounds of pursuit, afraid to look over my shoulder as I hobbled on, but thankfully heard none. Eventually the pain in my ankle became unbearable and I had to stop, sucking in the cold night air and exhaling great clouds of steam, like the milkman's horse. Cautiously, I hopped into a gateway and looked back to see if Grainger was following me, but if he had started to chase me he must have given up, because there was no sign of him.

When my breathing had settled, I resumed my progress, but at a much slower pace. Now that my fear had subsided, the pain in my ankle was excruciating and I struggled to keep going. Also, having stopped running, I soon became aware of how cold it was. I had no coat, just the cotton dress given to me by Phylis, and I found myself shivering violently. Somehow I needed to get warm.

The street was still in darkness, punctuated with little pools of yellow light beneath the street lamps, though the sky was beginning to lighten over to my left, with the first rays of the sun. Looking around, I saw a light shining from the window of a small shop, and went to see if there was any shelter. It turned out to be a baker's shop, but it was closed - the light I had seen was coming through an open door inside, shining out from a brightly-lit room behind. However, drawn by an appetising smell of fresh bread that wafted from the rear of the building, I tiptoed around to the back of the shop, where I found an open door, which was emitting those gorgeous aromas and the sound of men's voices in light conversation. I stopped in the shadows beside the door, hidden from their view, feeling the escaping warm air gently caress my arms and legs.

Suddenly, unexpectedly, a man stepped through the door into the yard, where he stopped to light a cigarette. When he turned, he saw me hiding.

"Now then, what have we here?" said sternly. Come to steal some cakes, have you?"

He was a stocky man, but tall, with broad shoulders. He wore just a shirt, with the sleeves rolled up, over a pair of white linen trousers held up by braces.

"No, sir," I pleaded, "I was just cold and came to get warm."

"Better come inside with me, then." He turned to re-enter the shop, but I hesitated. "Come on, don't be scared, I won't eat you."

I followed him inside, where he called out to his colleague working there. "Jacob, look what I found outside."

The man addressed as Jacob turned and grinned at me. "What, you hungry, kid?"

"Not hungry, sir, just cold."

"I should think so, out in this weather dressed like that. Would you like a nice hot cup of cocoa?"

I nodded, vigorously, smiling nervously, relieved that they were not hostile.

"Go and sit over there, then, and I'll bring it for you," he said, waving an arm towards a couple of wooden chairs standing against the end wall.

-♪-

I did as instructed, and felt the heat of the ovens seep deep into my body, driving out the shivering cold. I watched him cross the room and pour some milk into a saucepan, which he put on a big cooker in the corner by the window. While he was busy, I looked around the bakery. The other man had returned to his cigarette outside, and I imagined that, to them, the cool night air must be a delight after being in the heat of their workshop. It was not a big room, just enough space for the two men to work side-by-side on a single, scrubbed wooden table on one long wall, while the whole of the opposite wall was occupied by a massive oven with three steel doors. One was open, revealing the glowing coals that were providing the heat that was thawing my bones.

He returned with my drink, and a little cake with a cherry on top. Then came the question I had been dreading.

"Why are you out alone at night in the middle of winter, little one?"

It was asked in a kindly way, and I wanted to be honest, but I didn't want to explain in detail about my situation, and I especially could not tell anyone what had just happened. My mind refused to revisit that place. So, instead, I just said "We were flooded out of our house."

"Well, you'll freeze to death in this weather with only that dress on. Where are your parents?"

"My mum died, and my dad had to go somewhere," I mumbled. Best not to give too much information.

"And why are you limping?"

"I sprained my ankle."

"So who is looking after you? And what's your name?"

"Belinda." Avoiding answering his first question.

"How do you do, Belinda," he said with mock formality, extending a plump, floury hand, which I shook, smiling shyly. He sat on the chair next to mine.

"I'm Jacob, and that there is "Donkey." He grinned at his colleague, just re-entering the bakery, after his cigarette. "His real name is Don, but we call him Donkey on account of his strength. He's the strongest man I know; can pick up two hundredweight-sacks of flour with one hand!"

Jacob looked to me like a jolly clown. His round, red face was warm, smiling and friendly, and his fat body, clad all in white, completed the impression of someone who was fun to know.

"Now then, Belinda. My conscience won't let me send you back out into the cold alone, dressed like that. So I'm going to leave Donkey to manage without me for half an hour," he looked across to his partner, who nodded, "and I will take you up to my flat above the shop, where my wife will fix you up with some warm clothes. Ok?"

At the mention of going to his flat, my mind filled with memories of being alone with Grainger. I began to panic, and my face must have told him something was wrong.

"Hmmm, there's something you haven't told me, isn't there?"

I nodded.

"Do you want to tell me?"

He was perceptive, and so kind, I hated myself for being afraid of him; he was nothing like Grainger. But the words would not form to tell him what had happened, my brain refused to allow the memories to the surface. After a while, I managed to say "There was a man. He touched me."

He looked shocked, and took a moment to consider his reply. When he spoke, it was with a hoarseness, a kind of suppressed anger that made his lips tighten and his words sound strained.

"I think I know what you are telling me, and I won't ask you to say any more, I can see it is very difficult for you to talk about it." He paused again, looking down at his knees for a few seconds, then he raised his eyes back to meet mine. "Wait here, I will ask my wife to come down to meet you."

He stood and walked stiffly towards the door leading through to the shop.

~4~
February 1953
Sanctuary

Jacob's wife was just like him - plump and pink and kind. Her name was Edith. She came bustling into the bakery behind him when he returned, with a concerned smile on her face. She chatted with me for a while, then asked me if I felt safe to go with her to the flat. I agreed, and she led the way to the stairs. I turned and waved to the two men as I left, and they each raised a hand in return.

"Jacob told me how you came to be here," she said, studying my face carefully. "You don't have to tell me anything if you don't want to, but I want to help you, and I can do that better if you tell me what you can. Is that ok?"

I nodded, looking down and shuffling my feet; Edith was nice, but I just wanted my Gran.

"Don't worry," she continued, "you're not in any trouble. Now, have you had any breakfast?"

"I had a cake and some cocoa with Jacob."

"Would you like a boiled egg and soldiers?"

I nodded again, happily; Gran often made me boiled egg for breakfast, it was my favourite.

Edith seemed to have a constant supply of words bursting to pour out. She wittered on the whole time she was cooking my egg, and continued while I ate it. I sat at the kitchen table, swinging my legs as I dipped the toasted fingers of bread into the lush orange yolk, while she told me all about life as a baker's wife.

When I had finished eating, I told her about my Gran and the guest house, and the flood. She took my clean plate and stood at the sink, washing it with a few other things.

"I heard on the wireless that hundreds of people had to be rescued," she said over her shoulder.

"Yes. Gran managed to get me out, but she was left behind; she's in hospital in Norwich, but I don't know how she got there."

"What I don't understand," Edith continued, "is: how did you end up over this side of the town?"

I was unprepared, and as I cast my mind back over the past 24 hours, memories of Grainger and his vile hands immediately returned, flooding my mind with sickening images, sounds, sensations and smells. It was as though it was happening all over again, and I cried out, involuntarily. In a second she was at my side, crouching down and touching my hand lightly with hers.

"You're safe now, Belinda, don't be scared. Jacob told me what happened. I promise I won't let anything hurt you while you're here."

I clutched at her arm and sobbed into her dress. The recollection had been just like reliving the whole torture, moment by moment, and still the memories rang in my head, leaving me shivering with emotion. She gently patted my back and stroked her fingers through my hair, making soothing noises until, slowly, the trembling eased and the racking sobs stopped.

She brushed the tears from my cheeks with a hankie that had appeared from nowhere. "Shall we try to find out where your Gran is?"

I swallowed, panting from the violence of my reaction, wiping my eyes with the back of my hand. "Yes, please."

Edith squeezed my arm reassuringly. "Good girl."

She took my hand and led me to where a big, black telephone sat on a small table in her hallway. With the help of the operator, she was soon talking to the desk sergeant at the police station, enquiring about Mrs Cartwright, of *The Nest,* in Trafalgar Road. She squatted beside me and held the phone so that I could hear the whole conversation. The officer checked his records and informed us that he had heard nothing, but would try to find out for us. Edith told him that she would make sure I was well cared for until we had news of Gran, and he promised to ring as soon as he had something to report.

After she replaced the heavy handset into it's cradle, she led me back to the kitchen and sat me again at the table. She poured me a glass of milk, and then sat opposite me, a serious expression on her face.

"Belinda, you have had some terrible experiences over the last few days. I want you to know that most people are not like that awful man. You are safe here. Jacob and I would be happy to look after you until your Gran returns, but you don't have to stay here if you don't want to."

"You're a lot like my Gran; I think I would like to stay with you, until she comes home, please," I said, seriously.

When I look back at those few days after the night of the flood, my mind oscillates between extremes of emotion, flicks from the awful moments of Grainger's abuse to the security and kindness of the time I spent with Edith and Jacob. In the scale of other, later events, it might seem that the abuse was insignificant, a small assault - but that's because it wasn't you who lived through it, whose innocence was violated, stolen, in a few seconds which meant nothing to that beast, but which cast a cloud over the rest of my life.

-♪-

My stay with the Macintoshes lasted much longer than expected. Gran's health was badly affected by the events that occurred after I was rescued, and it was months before I saw her again.

Inspector Randal came to see me with news about her and what had happened. He told me that the police had managed to track down one of the labourers who was lodging with us at the time, and he told Archie about that night.

We discovered that Gran had waited at her window for an hour after I was rescued, becoming increasingly worried about my welfare. According to the man, she suddenly shouted "I'm coming, Belinda!" and jumped into the freezing waters. It seemed to the man that she was trying to swim in the direction of the town, but she had not realised that, by then, the tide had turned, and a fast flow of water was rushing down Trafalgar Road towards the seafront. She was swept away, and that was the last he saw of her. He assumed she must have been carried out to sea.

The police found out the rest of the story from the Royal Navy. The crew of their rescue helicopter had found Gran at dawn, clinging to the telephone box that stood on the corner of Trafalgar Road and the seafront. They lifted her off and took her straight to Norwich Hospital.

Tough old bird that she was, she refused to give up on life, and was gradually nursed back to some kind of health. But it was an ordeal that had profound effects on her, physically and mentally. Her eldest son eventually took her to stay at his home in Yorkshire, where she remained for nearly six months.

Mr Randal also asked me what had happened at the Graingers'; he said that Edith had told him the little that she knew. At first, I didn't want to remember any of it, but he explained that it was important that other children were protected from men like Grainger, so I eventually managed to recount everything. I didn't hear any more about it, but Edith told me sometime later that the Graingers had moved away. I felt sorry for Phylis; she had seemed nice, and I thought she deserved better.

-♪-

When the news arrived, six months later, that Gran would be coming home, I suddenly had mixed feelings. I was overjoyed at the thought of seeing her again, of course, but had grown to love Edith and Jacob, who had cared for me as though I was their own daughter. I could also see that they were saddened at the thought of my departure.

The following morning, Edith helped me to pack my things, then she and Jacob drove me to Trafalgar Road to wait for Uncle Ernie to bring Gran from the railway station. We arrived early at *The Nest*, to find that all external traces of the flood were gone; it had been cleaned and repainted, and the little front garden had been replanted with summer flowers. We sat together on the low wall, and waited.

-♪-

But one thing I have learned is that once things change, they can never return to how they were. Gran was not the same person I had known before the flood. When the taxi pulled up and she stepped onto the pavement, blinking in the sunlight, squinting at the guest-house as though it was the first time she had seen it, I could tell that she was different.

I ran to greet her, arms outstretched. "Hello Gran," I called happily as I ran, but she did not respond, just looked at me, blankly.

"Gran, it's me."

Realisation dawning that she had forgotten me, I felt my voice catch. She continued to stare at my face, uncomprehending. I blundered on, my earlier joy gone, a kind of panic rising in my chest, my words falling out, making me sound like a Red Indian in a bad movie: "Me, Belinda."

"Belinda?" She spoke slowly, pronouncing the word as though she had never said it before.

"Yes, you remember, Belinda, your granddaughter."

She just shook her head, confused, and my uncle cut in. "Don't bother her now, she's been through a rough time thanks to you," he hissed. "Carry her bags in." He turned away from me and led Gran through the gate and up to the front door; I noticed that he had the keys in his jacket pocket, and that he cast a critical eye over the new paint as he unlocked the door.

Stunned, not knowing why he was so aggressive, I picked up the two bags, but Jacob took them from me, with a little turn of his head that said: "Don't let him get to you." We followed Gran and Ernie up the familiar red steps, through the hallway and on into the lounge.

"Where do you want these cases?" Jacob asked. "I can take them upstairs if you like."

"Who are you?" Ernie demanded, glaring at Edith and Jacob.

"Edith and Jacob Macintosh," replied Jacob, evenly, putting one case on the floor and extending his right hand to offer a handshake. "We have been looking after your niece since that awful night."

"Well," spat Ernie, ignoring the offered hand, "it's a shame she wasn't put into an orphanage. Been a burden on my mother ever since my feckless sister dropped her. Leave the bags there, the girl can make herself useful for once and take them up to mother's room."

"I really don't think she's strong enough for that, she's only seven years ... " began Jacob.

"I didn't ask for your opinion," Ernie interrupted, "and I don't appreciate your interference. If you are not keeping the little brat, I would like you to leave." He glowered at the pair of them.

Jacob looked down to me. "What do you want to do, pet?" he asked, softly. "You can come to live with us if you would like to." I saw Edith nodding behind him. "You know we would love to have you."

There is one moment in everyone's life, I'm sure, that decides their entire future; a crossroads. No matter how carefully we reason, we cannot know where each branch will take us. All roads lead over a hill to a future that is hidden until we are committed; then it is too late, we cannot change our minds, cannot turn back and try one of the alternatives. Once the first step is taken, it is irrevocable. This was the day I shall always remember, that definitive moment when I made the worst decision of my life.

I hugged each of them. "Thank you so much for everything. I love you both very much, but Gran needs me, I cannot leave her." And, with that, I destroyed a future that would have been happy and contented, and embarked on a life punctuated with harshness and pain. I waved goodbye to them at the door, watching until their Ford Popular turned the corner of Regent Road and they were lost forever.

-♪-

Uncle Ernie stayed for two days, during which he was as unpleasant towards me as he could be. Just before he left to catch a train back to Yorkshire, he grabbed my arm in a fierce grip, crouching down so that his eyes were level with mine.

"You had better take good care of my mother, or it will be the worse for you," he hissed. "I wouldn't leave her with you except I have to get back to my business, and she wanted to be in her own home. She sacrificed herself for you, you little bastard; she wouldn't be in this state if it wasn't for you."

"What have I done?" I stammered, frightened of him and close to tears. We were standing on the landing at the top of the narrow stairs, just outside Gran's bedroom door, and I felt very unsafe in his grasp, tottering a few inches from the steep drop.

"Done?" he barked. "She nearly died because of you. She shouldn't even be bringing up some damn foreigner's spawn. It's a pity my sister didn't get rid of you when she had the chance!" I felt his hot breath and spit on my face.

"Not my fault," I mumbled, looking at the floor, afraid of what he would do to me. But, to him, the conversation was over. "There's my taxi," he barked, releasing my arm and standing up. He picked up his case and walked out without a backward glance.

-♪-

Angrily wiping my tears and his spittle from my face with my sleeve, I turned and went back into Gran's room. Outside, a car door slammed.

"I heard voices," she said feebly from her bed. "Who was it?"

"It was your son, Ernie, Gran," I replied, absently brushing her hair away from her eyes with my fingers.

"Ernie? Why didn't he come in to see me?" she croaked.

"He had to get to the station to catch his train. Don't you remember, he's been here for a few days?"

Her eyes darted around the room as she tried to take this in, to remember. Then they settled on me, and took on a shrewd expression. "Who are you?" she demanded, shrilly, her little hands gripping the bedspread.

Tears sprang to my eyes as I tried to think how to reply. Every day ... several times every day ... she had asked the same question. It seemed she had forgotten all the times we had spent together, a whole piece of her life was lost without a trace, seven years of memories erased.

I forced a smile. This wasn't about me; she needed reassurance and help. "I'm Belinda, Gran. You remember me, Rita's little girl."

"Rita?" she cackled. "Where is she? Why isn't she home yet? I need her to help with the cooking."

"I'll help for now," I said. "Would you like a cup of tea?"

"Yes ... yes, I'd like that. And a ginger biscuit. What was your name again?"

"Belinda."

She tested the sound of my name. "Belinda. No, don't know it. But if you're here to help, you'd better get started downstairs, otherwise the guests will be arriving and we won't be ready."

I touched her arm as I left to make her a pot of tea. There were no guests due, we had no bookings, but it was not the time to put her straight.

-♪-

Gran gradually gained some strength through the warm summer, and was eventually able to leave her bed. She wanted to be busy, but soon became tired, so I fixed up a day bed on the settee in the front room for her, where she could watch television or sit up and look out of the bay window to see the world outside.

But soon autumn arrived, then Christmas. It was a quiet, sombre affair, though I put up some decorations, and she seemed to respond when I walked her to church on Christmas Day. We didn't mark the turning of the new year; Gran didn't know which day it was, and I saw nothing worth celebrating.

In the first few months of 1954, we worked together to get the B & B ready for summer, and it was a little like those earlier times. Although she didn't remember anything about me, she became used to my presence, and addressed me as Belinda. My eighth birthday passed without recognition, though I wrote a card for myself - it seemed important to me that the day was marked.

As one or two guests began arriving, we cooked and cleaned together, went shopping together, and sometimes even sat and talked about the day. But she was forgetful, and I had to watch carefully so that she didn't leave the cooker on or a tap running, and to make sure meals were prepared on time. I would come home from school half afraid of what I might find, though thankfully we avoided any catastrophes.

The summer was busy for me. Although nothing like the days of my childhood, when every room of *The Nest* was full, it was still hard work for an eight year old. But even those few guests fell away as another winter advanced, and we found ourselves with little to do. Gran became morose, and started spending most of the day in bed. I enlisted the help of a neighbour to carry the television upstairs into her room, and the man from Hardings Electrical came and re-routed the aerial for us. She watched everything, from 'Television Newsreel' and

'The Grove Family' to the potter at work in 'The Interlude'.

All through that winter, and every winter after that, she was a victim of fevers, and dreadful coughs that left her breathless. She became forgetful and bad-tempered, neglected her personal hygiene and aged dramatically. She seemed to have lost interest in the guest-house, became resentful of its demands on her, and it fell to me to run it as best I could.

I tried. I kept it clean, and even redecorated some of it. I worked hard every day after school, helping her, trying to do the things she used to do, remembering the ways she had taught me, but I was only eight years old, and there was so much I didn't know. I coped, just, but gradually the place became shabbier, the guests fewer.

In 1958, Gran was confined to bed by the doctor, and I became her nursemaid in addition to all my other tasks. I felt permanently tired. I was waking at five o'clock every morning to care for Gran, cook for what few guests may be staying, and do my homework. Then I spent the day at school, rushing home at dinner time to give Gran some lunch, then back to the classroom, where I often fell asleep during lessons. The teachers knew what was happening at home, and were surprisingly tolerant, but my education was slipping away from me.

-♪-

The one thing that kept me sane and helped me through each exhausting day, my constant companion, was the radio. In those days, the only official broadcaster was the

BBC, but sometimes in the evenings it was possible to pick up Radio Luxembourg, which floated erratically across from Europe. They played much more music - all the new records from America and the UK - but transmissions were prone to fading away into a hiss of static or a babble of incomprehensible voices from some unknown broadcaster with a more powerful transmitter. Still, it kept me in touch with the latest sounds.

It is hard to convey how important music became. It was not entertainment, and much more than pleasure. It connected with my soul, became part of me, echoing in my head, long after the radio was switched off and I dragged myself upstairs to bed. My mind was like one of those radio stations, with every song I had ever heard stored faithfully away, ready for instant replay.

There were ballads, sung by Connie Francis and Perry Como, and Rock n Roll was becoming hugely popular, with amazing records from the likes of Little Richard, Brenda Lee, Chuck Berry and, of course, Elvis Presley. British artists, like Tommy Steel, Joe Brown, Marty Wilde and Lonnie Donegan, were preparing the way for an enormous record industry, of which I was later to become a part. I learnt all the words, and danced around the house to the exciting beat. The whole essence of the new music seemed to be that life could be fun. Well, mine wasn't exactly fun, but music lifted my spirits and gave me a little push every day to get through the drudgery.

And though life was hard, I was still happy. In a perverse way, I enjoyed looking after Gran; it was as though I had been given a way to repay her for all she had given me through my childhood. And, even when she became bad-tempered, or forgot who I was, I still loved her.

-♪-

Gran died on the twenty fourth of April, nineteen sixty; I was thirteen years old and completely alone. I sat at her bedside, holding her cold, limp hand. Her breakfast tray lay on the floor where I had dropped it when I entered the room and realised she had gone, the contents strewn - her tea spilt, her toast scattered.

"I'm sorry, Gran, I failed you," I sobbed.

She had always been there for me when I was a small child, but when it was my turn to care for her, I couldn't save her. I straightened the sheet that covered her, brushed her hair from her face with with my fingers, then sat and talked to her, reliving the years we had spent together.

After a while, I gathered myself and stood up. I had responsibilities - someone must be notified. I rang Inspector Randal, and he came at once. He contacted Gran's doctor, to write a Death Certificate, and contacted uncle Ernest - yes, that Ernest, Gran's eldest son, who hated me - the feeling was mutual.

Ernie turned up two days later. At first I was pleased to see him, as he began to make the arrangements for the funeral, but his attitude to me had not changed, and he treated me like a slave. For the week leading up to the funeral, I had to cook for him and wash the dishes, wash and iron his clothes and run errands for him, and all this while still grieving for Gran; at least there were no guests to cater for. I did not go back to school.

On the day of the funeral, as I was getting ready to go with him to the church, he came into my room.

"Don't bother to get dressed up," he growled. "You're not going. I want you to pack your things and get out of this house. You had better not be here when I come back, or you will feel the back of my hand."

I was dumbfounded, and he had turned and marched out before I gathered myself enough to fully grasp the import of his words. I heard the front door slam, and sat on the edge of my bed, my head reeling from the shock of what was happening. With tears in my eyes, I looked around my little room. "What am I going to do?" I said aloud.

The house was empty and silent, not the lively home of my childhood. Memories paraded before me: guests singing in the lounge, Gran cooking, tea in the garden on a summer's afternoon. For a moment I was there again - I felt the warmth of the sun on my skin, heard the bees as they worked the honeysuckle and lavender bushes, saw Gran as she had been before her illness: plump, pink, busy, smiling.

Somehow, with the memories filling my senses, I was not surprised to hear her voice calling my name.

Belinda!

Gran, I thought, *I miss you so much.*

In the empty, silent house, she answered me: *I will always be with you, my love.*

Help me, Gran, I don't know what to do.

You must do as Ernest says. I am angry at what he is

doing, but I cannot change his mind. Belinda, go into my bedroom.

I did as she told me. I stood in the doorway of the room that held such a mixture of memories of my dear Gran. Once, it had been warm, with the smell of her perfume. This was where, as a toddler, I had tiptoed in the night for comfort from her loving arms when bad dreams frightened me, and where we had stood side-by-side at the window on the night of the flood. Now it echoed cold and empty, stark with images of the last few years when she had laid in that bed, slowly dying.

Stop those thoughts, she said, sharply. *That was not me, I had already left my body. Now, you have to act and I want to help you. Go to my wardrobe and get the little case out.*

I did as she said, and found a small, light suitcase at the bottom of her wardrobe. I stood with it in my hand and looked around the room.

Good. Now go to my jewellery box, on my dressing table.

I knew that box. When she was dressing for a special occasion, she used to unlock it and draw out her beautiful emerald necklace and earrings, her wedding ring and a simple, yet elegant, silver brooch in the shape of a bird, set with glittering stones. But when I looked in the drawer for the key, it was gone, and when I tried the lid of the box, it opened easily.

The little tyke! she exclaimed in my head. *He's taken all my best pieces!*

All that remained were a few trinkets - some small gold earrings, a plain silver necklace, a few old coins.

Take the box, Belinda, put it in the case, then get your clothes together before he returns.

Back in my room (my room no longer) I gathered together what few clothes I owned, and stuffed them into the suitcase; they didn't even fill it. On an impulse, I returned to Gran's room and threw in the silver photo frame with a faded picture of her and my granddad, all I would ever have of her. Time was passing and I was afraid that Ernie would return and find me still there, so I clicked the case closed and, with a final look around the little house that had been my home for thirteen years, I stepped out of the front door into an uncertain future.

~5~
May 1960
Spring

I stood alone at the end of Trafalgar Road with my little suitcase at my feet, watching the family return from the funeral. I couldn't believe I had nowhere to live; it seemed impossible. I half expected someone, an uncle or aunt, to come and take me back, but no-one did. I doubt that they knew I existed; they had never visited Gran in all my childhood.

It was the last day of April, 1960. In just under two weeks I would be fourteen years old. But there would be no party, no hugs from Gran, no smiles from my show-business friends, no presents. I was completely dispossessed.

In the daylight, I could see that the suitcase Gran had told me to take was old and battered. It was made of some kind of cardboard, painted brown to make it look like leather, but the coating was flaking off where it had received knocks over the years. Still, it didn't weigh much - hardly any more when full than when it was empty - my life in one suitcase, eighteen inches by twelve by eight. I owned nothing of any value, but I was glad I to have Gran's jewellery - perhaps it would give me a bit of security.

Gran? I tried, but there was no answer.

It began to get darker, and colder.

Finally accepting that there was no returning to *The Nest*, I thought of the only other people who had been good to me, Edith and Jacob. They had visited several times in the first years after Gran's return, but she never welcomed them, or even recognise them, and was very rude to them on one occasion; they never returned.

I had a clear memory of the bakery where they lived, and I knew it was on or near the Caister Road, so I picked up my battered old case and started to head north, through the centre of town.

After what seemed an eternity, I saw the railway station off to my left, and Caister Road ahead. But it all looked so different; new buildings had sprung up everywhere, like weeds in a flower bed, changing the appearance of the whole area. The road had been widened, and new roads cut away into new estates to my right and left. I reached the place where I was sure the baker's shop had once been, and stared unbelieving at the building that stood there, a modern car showroom. How could it be gone, the place that held so many happy memories? Where was the couple who had taken me in and cared for me?

As I opened up my memories of that road, images of the last time I had walked it alone rushed at me from all sides. Grainger: again I smelt his foul breath, felt his hands violating me, and again my body shook with the embarrassment, the shock, the anger.

By then it was completely dark. All around I saw lights gleaming from house windows - happy families settling down for the night, warm fires and hot dinners, televisions and conversations. There would be no more pleasant evenings for me with Gran and the show people. The laughter and music of those easy times echoed in my head, taunting me, forcing tears from my eyes. Cars drove past with a whooshing noise, their headlights briefly slicing through the darkness - busy fathers driving home from work, or setting off to the pub. I walked blindly on, hoping I was mistaken and the bakery would suddenly appear. The road continued, but there became fewer and fewer houses, until I found myself looking out over open countryside.

Shivering, I retraced my steps, the suitcase becoming surprisingly heavier in my hands with each step. Again, I scanned every building as I passed, hoping I was wrong, longing to recognise something in one of them that clicked with my memory of the little baker's shop, but there was nothing.

Eventually I reached the crossroads again and stopped. Tired and dejected, I put down the case and looked around, unable to decide what to do.

A short way off to my right was the railway station. I shuffled towards it, attracted by the lights and the possibility of somewhere to sit down. But when I reached the big, Victorian building, my confidence evaporated - it was deserted, black iron gates barred the entrance. This was the end for me; I had nowhere to go, no-one who cared if I lived or died.

I sat down on the stone steps and sobbed.

-♪-

"Crying won't help." A belligerent voice poked its way into my misery, making me jump. Wiping the tears from my eyes with my sleeve, I looked around, but could see no-one in the darkness. The voice had sounded young, but with a croakiness to it that made it hard to be sure.

I heard a cough, then the voice again from the shadows: "What's your name?"

It had an accent, like some of the people from London who had stayed at the .... I suppressed the thought of my lost home, afraid I would start crying again.

"Belinda," I said. "Who are you? Where are you?"

"My name's Joe. Don't worry, I won't hurt you. Over here, look to your left. Yes, you're looking straight at me. Walk towards the sound of my voice."

I did as he said and, as my eyes adjusted to the darkness, I saw a doorway, blacker against the grey of the walls. Piled up at the base of the door was a mound of flattened cardboard boxes and rags. The mound spoke: "What's up? Are you in trouble?"

"I've been thrown out, I have nowhere to live." Why was I telling this talking rubbish heap my problems?

"What's in the suitcase?"

Sudden anger surged through me, a defensive reaction: "Mind your own business! Nosy sod!"

"That's better! I like it. Let it out, Belinda, it's your weapon against the world."

The heap stirred, and something like the shape of a head appeared at one end, boxes cascading down like an avalanche. "Want a drink?" An arm materialised from the side, with a grubby hand holding a flat bottle.

I accepted it, unscrewed the top and took a sip. For a moment my brain failed to register the strange taste, and I had swallowed it before the warm fumes from it had reached my nose and the liquid had burned my throat. I coughed, feeling it searing my inside.

"What is it?" I spluttered, my eyes watering.

"Whisky. I nicked it from an offie when no-one was looking. It's good stuff, keeps the cold out."

As the shock of the first taste of the drink passed, I could feel its warming effect in my tummy. Encouraged, but with some trepidation, I took another swig; this time I was prepared, and managed not to cough as it hit my throat.

"'ere, steady on, leave some for me," he said, but I sensed it was meant as a joke.

I wiped the rim with the edge of my hand, then, screwing the lid on, handed the bottle back. "Thanks, Joe."

"No sweat. Look, if you don't have anywhere to sleep, you need to keep warm, like me. There's room in this doorway for both of us. Do you want to get under my boxes?"

Nervously, I put my suitcase against the door, at the opposite end to his head, then sat beside it and slid my legs into the heap. It was surprisingly cosy. I shuffled my bum down, feeling the warmth of his body, and tried to arrange some of the boxes around me, but they kept falling off.

"Bloody hell! You're letting all the heat out. You never did this before, did you?" he asked.

For some reason, that struck me as funny, and I began to giggle. "Ho yes," I said, putting on the kind of silly, pantomime-aristocratic voice I had heard my entertainer friends use, "I always spend me 'olidays in railway station doorways. It's the latest thing, doncha know."

I heard him unscrew the lid of the bottle again. "Here,

have another swig."

"Don't mind if I do," I said, taking a good gulp of the heady drink, then passing the bottle back.

"Tomorrow, if you like, I'll show you around. If you're going to survive on the streets, there are fings you need to know."

"Ok, thangs Jooey - I mean Jowey. Wha's happ'ned to my voish?" My lips felt numb, and I pressed them together with my fingers.

"It's just the whisky, taking away the cold," said his voice, suddenly distant. My vision became blurred, the shadows around me started spinning slowly, and without warning I suddenly felt sick. I just had time to turn my head away before the contents of my stomach erupted from my mouth.

"Yuk!" I said, wiping my mouth with my sleeve, "that tastes awful!"

"It don't smell too good, neither!" came the sharp reply.

I didn't care, the world was fading slowly, the cold and the sadness, swirling like water disappearing down a drain, before I passed out.

-♪-

I was awakened by a man's voice, god-like, from above, and a stirring of the body next to me.

"Come on kids, clear off before the bobbies find you," said the voice, not unkindly.

A misty, grey dawn had crept in, and I looked up to see a tall man wearing a smart, blue uniform and peaked cap.

"Ok Mr Parker, thanks," said Joey, rising from the

cardboard boxes like the Creature from the Black Lagoon. I had a headache, a piercing pain in my temples, and an unpleasant taste in my mouth, but I followed his example and stood up, holding the ball of agony that sat on my neck where my head should have been.

"And, Joseph, clear up that sick, please."

"Sure fing, mister Parker," Joey responded cheerfully, while simultaneously giving me an accusing look.

We collected up his boxes and carried them around a corner of the station. There we found a gap between two buildings and stuffed the boxes into it. Then Joey showed me where the toilets were, and he emerged with a bucket, presumably from the cleaner's stores, filled with water. Together, we washed away my sick and swept it into the bushes with a stiff broom.

As we worked, I studied my new friend. It was easy to think of him as a friend, even though we had only just met and I knew nothing about him; I felt ... well, comfortable with him. He was about eleven or twelve years old, shorter than me, with a dirty, pear-shaped face, sticky-out ears and a tangled bush of dirty blonde hair that erupted from his head like candy floss. He wore baggy, grey trousers and a distressed, green, school blazer, with the initials "A.P.S." on the breast pocket.

"Mr Parker is the stationmaster," he explained. He's a good sort."

Joey then took the tools back into the Gents' toilets, while I visited the Ladies for a wee and a wash.

" Hungry?" he asked as we emerged.

"Yeah, starving."

"Right, lets go see what we can find to eat then."

I picked up my case and he grabbed my hand and led me away from the station, along the road that, the night before, I had trudged alone and friendless.

"You will be amazed at the amount of good food there is to be 'ad for free," he said as we sauntered along. "The supermarket throws tons of grub away every day, stuff left from the day before that they're not allowed to sell."

-♪-

We arrived at the huge store that had sprung up on the outskirts of Great Yarmouth a year earlier, like Atlantis rising from the depths. I had never been in it; all the shopping for the guest-house had been ordered by phone from our traditional suppliers - the local bakers, butchers and greengrocers - and delivered to our door. Nor did I get to see the inside this time, for Joey led me around to the back of the building, where there was a row of large dustbins. After checking that no-one was watching us, he lifted the lid on the first and peered inside.

"See, Bell, at night they fill all the shelves with new stuff, and dump all the old out here," his voice came, muffled, from inside, "and a lot of it is good, eat-able food. Like this." He emerged, brandishing a French stick, which he passed to me.

We moved along the row, plucking goodies from the bins, constantly alert for anyone spotting us. I was amazed at what we found - sausages, eggs, fruit, bottles of milk, it was all perfectly good food, and I found it hard to understand the philosophy of the store that made them waste it. After a while, we were joined by another boy, who Joey introduced to me as Charley. He was a quiet lad, who scarcely spoke a word - unlike Joey, who chatted away constantly, in his intriguing London accent, about what to look for and who to avoid. Soon, our pockets were full, and we left Charley still rummaging.

"Charley's had a rough time," Joey explained as we headed of around the building. "His dad was in the army, got killed in France, and his mother drank herself to death on gin. He's been alone nearly all his life"

I stopped walking and looked back. Charley can only have been about ten years old, but carried himself like an old man. He wore a long overcoat, several sizes too big for his little body, and shoes that also looked huge below his short legs, like the over-size boots that clowns wear. His shaggy brown hair hung down over his face as he delved into the bins.

As I watched him working, I saw a movement at the far side of the yard, and Joey shouted from behind me, startling me: "Leg it!" A man had rounded the corner of the building and had seen us. Without even looking, Charley dropped to his feet from the side of a bin, and ran, amazingly quickly, towards us. Simultaneously, the man gave a yell and also began running. We turned and fled, heading for the rows of houses a short distance off.

"We 'ave to split up, Bell," Joey puffed. "Hide in a garden or somefing over there." He waved a hand towards the backs of some houses, then loped off in a different direction. He seemed to be surprisingly slow, and the man seemed to be getting dangerously close to catching him, but I could not help, and had to find somewhere to conceal myself. I ran as fast as I could into an alleyway, clutching my suitcase to my chest, trying to avoid dropping the goodies I had salvaged.

I found a narrow, overgrown path between the backs of some houses, and turned into it. After scrambling through a mass of bushes and weeds, I hid, panting, behind a heap of rubbish piled against a fence. Eventually risking a peek from the cover of a mattress, I looked back along the path. A man ran past the end, without even glancing in my direction.

I sat on my suitcase and laughed quietly. It was a small victory, and I didn't even know what it was that I had escaped from, but it felt good.

-♪-

Joey was waiting for me at the end of the road when I emerged. "You gave them the slip, well done," he chirped.

"I was worried about you," I said, "you didn't seem to be going very fast."

"Oh, I can do a turn of speed when I need to."

"You mean you were going slower on purpose?"

"Yeah, well ... you're still new to all this, I wanted to lead him away from you." He grinned, cheekily. "Don't worry about me, they never catch me. I know this town better than any of them."

We walked across the busy market place and down to the beach that I had once thought of as my own. A picture of Oliver flashed into my mind, so vivid that it seemed to me it must be visible to everyone around. Oliver smiling, talking, walking. I wondered where he was, what had happened to him, why he had vanished.

"You ok, Bell?" Joey was studying my face.

I realised I had stopped walking and was staring along the beach. I looked down, sheepishly. The memories of Oliver had transported me into the past and reminded me how important he had been in my life for a short while.

"I'm fine, thanks. I used to come down here every day. There was someone I cared about."

"A boy?"

I nodded, sadly. "It wasn't love, or anything like that; just friends. I wish I could go back to those days, they were good."

Joey stopped walking, put his hands on my shoulders and fixed me with an analytical gaze. He had to reach up, as he was six inches shorter than me, but his expression was that of a man twice his age. "Life comes in two bits, Bell," he said gravely. "Yesterday ... and all the rest."

He grinned. "Someone told me that, and it's stayed with me. He was a drop-out, a drunk who lived on the streets here in Yarmouth for a year or two, then vanished. I think he used to be a professor or somefing. Randolph, he said his name was, but I fink he made that up. Anyways, he was a very clever man.

What he actually said was: *'shit 'appens'*. I asked him what that meant, and he said *'what's past is past; it's what's made you who you are, but it doesn't decide what you will be'*. I didn't really understand it at first, but I think I do now. It's all about what you make of the stuff that happens to you, see. You can never go back. Life may deal you a handful of shit, you can't change that, but you can change how you let the shit affect you, and how you turn it into what you want to become."

We sat on a bench and started to eat our food; bread, cheese and cake, and shared a bottle of milk. Somehow, it seemed to taste better, knowing that it was not only free, but also would have been wasted if we had not rescued it.

"I understand what you're saying, Joey, but my memories are so strong it's like re-living things again and again and again. So the torment goes on every day - the people I've lost, the mistakes I've made, the things people have done to me, they keep buzzing around my head, reminding me. I keep thinking that, if I could go back and change one thing, it would all turn out differently. It's hard to move on."

Ignoring the whining tone that had crept into my voice, Joey cut through to the heart of the matter. "I fink you did love him. What was his name?"

I looked at him, amazed. "You are way older than your years, my dear friend." I squeezed his hand. "Oliver, his name was Oliver."

"Well, Oliver gave you some good thoughts, didn't he? Those are what you 'ave to cling to, Bell. Where is he now?"

"I don't know; that's part of the problem. He just vanished, the day before the floods. I figured his parents must have moved on; they were looking for somewhere to live."

He shrugged. "That's it, then. So he's still around, somewhere. Probly finking about you just like you're finking about 'im."

"Yeah, I suppose you're right."

"Bell, if the bad stuff is weighing you down, you've got to fink of the good fings, and friends are the most important fings of all."

I looped my arm in his and leaned close to kiss him on the cheek.

"I'm glad you're my friend," I whispered.

"'ere! Don't get all sloppy," he mumbled, wiping the sullied cheek with his sleeve, but he was smiling.

~6~
July 1960
Summer

Over the following weeks and months of summer, Joey and I were almost inseparable. We scampered for shelter together when an unexpected shower caught us unawares, huddled together for warmth when the north wind turned chilly, shared our food, and swam naked together in the sea on sultry summer nights. We talked as I had never been able to talk before, and I learned to admire and respect that little man more than I have never felt about any adult.

Joey's father was a disturbed, violent man, who regularly beat his wife and child after bouts of heavy drinking. Without a hint of emotion, Joey described a pattern of dreadful abuse; of nights when he hid in a cupboard to escape his father's rampages, hearing the horrifying sounds of his mother being beaten senseless. Eventually, she could take no more - she stabbed her husband forty-eight times with a carving knife. The young Joey, only six years old at the time, emerged from his hiding place when silence fell, and found her sitting in a pool of blood on the kitchen floor beside his father's body, singing softly to herself. A court found her not guilty of murder, but had her confined in a mental institution. Joey was placed in an orphanage. He hated it so much he escaped after only a month, and had lived on the streets ever since.

He passed on all his survival experience to me, showing me how to find food, how to stay dry, and who to watch out for. He also introduced me to some of the other dropouts in the town. Until then, I had not realised how many people were sleeping on the streets of Great Yarmouth. People like "Blinker", a man of uncertain years, but definitely over sixty, who drank wine from the bottle to try to drown out the sounds of gunfire in his head. Or Gertie, an apparently sweet old lady who could, in a second, change into a cobra, spitting venom at anyone within sight. They all knew Joey, and despite the fact that he was younger than any of them, they treated him as an equal, showing respect that at first seemed odd, but that I soon came to understand.

It all seemed so easy, almost Idyllic. The days were spent at leisure on the beach or in a park. If it rained, we dived into one of the amusement arcades, roaming up and down the aisles, dipping our fingers into the payout troughs on the front of the machines. Quite often we found a penny or two, and fed it straight into the machine in the hope of winning the jackpot. Once, we did, winning the top prize of one pound - we dined well that day, in a restaurant - fish and chips with peas and a cup of tea; a lovely dinner that was like a banquet to us. We were so bloated afterwards that we slept on the beach for an hour in the gorgeous sunshine. I felt at one with the world, part of the great wash of humanity going about their lives. But it was an illusion; this was summer, and life would become much tougher when the cold weather arrived.

-♪-

I expect you've noticed, haven't you, that my education has not been mentioned for a while? Well, the simple fact is that I never returned to school after I was thrown out of *The Nest* (how appropriate that sounds now - thrown out of the nest by a cuckoo - I must write that down). Somehow, the life I was living on the streets seemed to be in a different world, a kind of extra dimension, tagged onto the place I knew before, and my mind found it hard to contemplate returning to what, by then, was an alien environment - so I didn't. I presume that the authorities noticed my absence and checked the last address they had for me, Gran's guest house. I also presume that my dear uncle told them some lie to explain why I wasn't living there.

Actually, what with the bullying, Gran's illness and then my displacement, all my childhood education was skimpy. Of course, living rough I learnt a lot of things that are not on the curriculum - how to keep warm, where to get free food, how hide from the rozzers, who to trust (no-one) - but as for maths and English, history and geography, I knew very little. And what use would it have been to me? A knowledge of quadratic equations would be great if you happened to be a physicist, but useless when figuring out the best place to sleep, and erudition is fine for politicians, but doesn't cut any ice when trying to explain to the local bobby where the bottle of milk in your coat pocket came from.

So how is it that I am now able to write in good style, explain myself using reasonably good grammar and complex sentences? Money, that's how. When you are as rich as I have now become you can buy anything - fine food, a big house, a good education, even popularity, if you're clever enough and pay the right journalists.

As my wealth grew, so I began to indulge myself. Not in booze and drugs, or orgies of sex, as so many did - I had seen what they could do to a person, and had no intention of ever letting that happen to me again. No, I wanted - needed - to give myself some dignity. I wasn't seeking to replace the things that gave me confidence, such as the self-reliance I had learned from living rough, but to subdue the ghosts that constantly reminded me of what I had lost. Education, the formal kind that is considered to be the foundation of a civilised society, became an obsession, and occupied much of my middle life.

Now I can converse with the best of them in English, French and, of course, Italian. I can speak in public with assurance, comfortably debate science and history at dinner parties, or argue politics on television. These days I am well respected; I write articles, dine with the elite, sit on committees and support charities, although I fear that the revelations in this book will prove to be a shock to many of the good people I now mix with, and may dislodge me from my current comfortable perch. So be it. I seem to be unable to cope with being safe for too long - I need danger to keep me alive, challenges to prevent me from withering like a neglected potted plant.

But I am getting ahead of myself.

-♪-

A favourite haunt for me in that summer of 1960 was the music shop, Robinson's - just off the market - where they sold the latest records. It was the only place I went without Joey, who said he found music boring. We used to separate at the door, he to wander around the market, looking for a pocket to pick, or a trinket to slip under his jacket, I to saunter into Robinsons, pretending I was interested in buying a record, and taking it to the booth to play it. In those days, recordings had not long shifted from the big old 78s that were played on mechanical gramophones - producing strange tinny sounds from a twisted, conical trumpet - to 45s, neat vinyl discs that faithfully reproduced the original music electronically through loudspeakers or headphones.

Of course, I had no money - well, not enough for such luxuries - but it didn't matter, I only had to hear a song once to have it locked in my memory, then I would spend the rest of the day happily singing it. The staff knew I could not afford to buy anything, but they didn't seem to mind; I never caused any trouble, and always returned the records undamaged in their little paper sleeves, so they were happy enough for me to listen to the music. The manager, on the other hand, was less accommodating. The first time I met him he refused to allow me to try a record, and told me to leave, calling me a 'vagabond' and threatening to throw me out. I smiled sweetly at him and did as he said, then simply waited for him to leave the shop before going inside again.

The sixties was a time of almost magical

transformation in England, as the hardships of the early post-war years were gradually being replaced with better standards of living. There was a new optimism, a confidence that the world could be changed, and the drive for this was coming from young people. We had seen the mess made of things by the previous generations, now it was time for us to build something different. The term 'teenager' was still quite new, but it was teenagers that held the future, and we knew it. We showed our rejection of the past in the clothes we wore and the music we played.

Unlike me, many people of my age had money in their pockets and spent it on whatever they liked. For some, that meant alcohol and excess - there was an undercurrent of sex and violence that I found disturbing, but for many of us it was an opportunity for creativity. Music and fashions were moving in new directions, and the biggest force in this quest for novelty was in the popular music world. Influenced by the trends arriving from America, new bands were springing up in England, copying what they heard, then adding to it, blending sounds, experimenting with their own styles.

Even though I had no money, I felt part of this culture switch, because I could sing. The music shop had started to sell guitars, drums and amplification for those new musicians keen to display their talents on stage, and there were often small groups of them, trying out the equipment. Many were laughably bad - though most of them were blissfully unaware of it - but occasionally I would meet someone with a real gift. It was wonderful to hear the guitar played well, or singers who could sing.

-♪-

A musician who came regularly to Robinson's was Bruce Green, a talented guitarist who fronted a group called The Beacons. I loved to watch and listen as he showed off his skills. One day, he was playing a song I had just learnt, and I was standing to one side, singing along. He stopped playing and called me over.

"You sound ok," he said, tilting his head to study me.

"Start again, from the top, and let's really hear what you can do."

I grinned, always happy to sing. He played the introduction, and I came in at the right moment, singing out loud and clear.

Partway through, though, the manager came over and grabbed my arm. "I told you to stay away, kid," he hissed. "Now get out!"

Bruce stood up. "If you don't want her, then you can manage without my business, too," he said, calmly, putting down the guitar and looking sternly and confidently into the man's eyes.

I was amazed to see the manager's expression change. He released my arm and was suddenly apologetic. "Sorry, Mr Green sir, I didn't realise she's a friend of yours."

"That's ok, Hubert, you just leave her with me; I promise you won't have any trouble."

The manager hurried away, embarrassed, and I turned to Bruce. "Hubert?" I giggled.

He smiled. "Don't laugh, it's not his fault. Blame the parents."

"He seemed to respect you."

"Yeah, well, I spend a lot of money here. All the band's gear came from Robinson's, some of it imported directly from The States. I reckon I earned him more commission in the first three months of this year than he had in the whole of last year." He studied me carefully. "You ever sung with a band?"

I laughed. "Nah! I just love music, sing whenever I can."

"Do you fancy coming to The Beacon's next rehearsal? I think the guys would enjoy having you along."

I was stunned, and delighted. "Sure, I'd love that."

"Ok, Wednesday at seven o'clock at Saint Luke's hall. You know it?"

-♪-

I was nervous when I turned up for my first band practice; it's one thing to sing along with a record, another to work with musicians. I was sure they would be very technical, and talk about what key a song was in, or semitones or metres, words I had heard but knew little about.

When I walked in the hall, they were bustling about setting up amplifiers and the drum kit. Guitar cases were open, leads trailed like snakes across the floor. Two of the band, a man and a woman, were singing at a microphone; he was good, but she was awful - I suppressed a smile as she missed almost every note she aimed at.

Bruce saw me and called the others over. "This is little Belinda, folks; she's the singer I told you about. Belinda, meet The Beacons."

He waved a hand first towards the nearest person to him, a tall and well-muscled man of about eighteen. "This is Bob, our drummer. Next to him is Paul, who blows a mean saxophone. Filo, here, plays rhythm guitar and sings, and that's Alan, our bass player, with Ruby, his girlfriend."

I smiled at each one as he introduced them, and they responded with a wave or a word, all except Ruby, who just glared at me.

After a little more setting up, we were ready for the first song.

"What key do you sing in?" Filo asked, as I had feared.

I shrugged. "Whatever key you play in," I said. It was obvious to me, I adapted my voice to suit the song.

He looked at Bruce and grinned.

"What?" I said, puzzled.

"Nothing, love," smiled Filo. "It's just that most singers we've tried out can only sing in one key, so we have to transpose everything, and that can be bloody difficult sometimes. It's a treat to meet someone who fits in."

I took my place at the microphone. This was the first time I had ever used one, and I was unsure what to expect from it, but I had seen many artists using them, so I stood as I had seen them.

Bob counted us in, and the band launched into the introduction. They sounded great - it was just like listening to the record in Robinson's, and when it was time to sing, I did what came naturally. It felt fantastic.

The music I was hearing was made right there in that hall, with those guys playing and me singing; it was just like the record, but we were doing it.

They worked through a couple of dozen songs from their repertoire. When I wasn't taking the lead role, for songs that needed a male singer, Charlie took over and I sang harmonies and "whoot ... whoot" and "doo-wah-didit" in the background. I even found myself doing those little dance steps and hand-waving that the American girl groups did, and I was aware that had a huge smile on my face all the while. I couldn't remember a time when I had felt such a part of something so creative.

When our time for using the hall was up, I helped them dismantle and carry the gear out to Bruce's van, then we all went round the corner to a pub, the Plough, to talk about how the evening had gone. Apart from Alan, the band was enthusiastic about my contribution.

I wondered at first why Alan was so negative, looking for faults in my singing, but I saw that Ruby was prompting him, and realised that she was put out because no-one had been as encouraging about her efforts.

We talked about the songs we had done, others in their set that they felt would suit me, and even some new ones that they had considered before, but rejected because no-one could sing them.

It was a dream night for me, and as I made my way back to the station to rejoin Joey, I was floating on a silver cloud, singing again the songs of the evening.

-♪-

We rehearsed three times that week, working intensely through their whole set. The boys were anxious about an impending booking, for which they had been feeling unprepared, but by the end of the week, we were confident and in high spirits. It was to be quite a gig: a wedding reception, taking place at a country house in Bradwell, a village just outside Great Yarmouth. The bride and groom were friends of Bruce's family, and we would be performing for something like six hours to about two hundred guests. It was a huge challenge for a relatively new group and an inexperienced singer.

Bruce drove us there in the morning. We carefully set up all the gear on the little stage at one end of a marquee erected in the grounds of the mansion, tested and tuned it all and ran a sound check. As we were finishing, the caterers arrived and began arranging tables and chairs. We laid covers over our equipment and returned to Yarmouth to wait nervously for our start time - three o'clock in the afternoon. We sat around a table in the Plough, in a strange silence, each deep in their own thoughts, sometimes venturing out for a brief exchange, then retreating again into safe self-absorption.

At half past two, we returned to Bradwell to remove the covers and switch on the amplifiers, to allow the valves time to warm up, then we sat at one side of the stage until the feasting was over, watching the floor-show. Waiters glided around the tables, serving, collecting debris and generally pandering to the clearly well-to-do diners. Eventually, a horde of helpers swarmed into the marquee and descended upon the large tables, carrying them outside, leaving a large dance floor before the stage. The stuffed guests, displaced from the comforting support of the dining chairs, split into two groups: the men gravitating towards the bar, while the women decanted themselves onto smaller tables arranged around the walls.

There is a pattern to such events, I have learned. Someone, in this case the father of the bride, mounts the stage and uses the band's microphone to splutter and whistle a greeting to the guests; some banal jokes and exchanges then take place, then the band plays the first number. As this was a wedding, the boys played an instrumental piece for the happy couple to begin the dancing, after which we launched into our set. The afternoon drifted pleasantly enough into evening, with only one drunken brawl erupting near the bar, and in a flash, it seemed to me, we were finishing our last song.

-♪-

"Thank you, thank you," said Bruce, smiling and waving to the applauding crowd, letting them show their appreciation for as long as they wanted. Then, as the din subsided, he continued: "That was our last song. We are The Beacons, and we hope you've had a good time. Goodnight."

With a final wave, he turned away from the microphone, to the expected chorus of "More! More!" from the dance floor. One voice rose above the others: "Sing *Home Again*," he shouted. Several people picked up on the idea and they began to chant it. Why they wanted that song, I will never know - it was an old, wartime song, and not one we had rehearsed. I saw that Bruce was uncertain; he looked at me, anxiously, enquiringly, and I nodded. I knew the song well; it had been popular in the last months of the war, and was sung by Alice Moon in the old film *Lost Angel*. The rest of the guys were shaking their heads, so they sat together on the raised platform upon which Bob's drum kit was perched, while Bruce picked up his acoustic guitar and pulled up a stool. I stood alone at the mike.

Bruce was one of the best guitarists I have ever known. He played a tinkling, melodic introduction on his guitar, leading to a pause for me to come in. On the spur of the moment, picking up on Bruce's intro, I decided to start the song in a low-key, conversational style, with rests between each line. Bruce filled the spaces with some beautiful riffs, that made the number like a duet, two friends in easy chat. As the song developed, we raised the tempo a little to a steady, swaying beat, which Bob reinforced with some nice brush strokes on the drums, and I heard the rest of the guys following, quietly.

We reached the last line, and Bruce gently stroked the final chord, letting it ring and fade as I sang " ... for you, my love, to come home ... again ... to ... me," each word rising in pitch above the one before, until I ended with a note that I could not believe was coming from my mouth; it rang, like a wine glass stroked till it resonates and fills a room. When the last echo faded away, the marquee was completely silent, and I shyly turned from the mike, head down, sure that I had ruined the song by aiming for such an impossibly heavenly note. Suddenly there was an explosion of sound, and I looked up in shock. All the guys, Bruce, even Alan, and, as the room came into view, everyone in the audience, were on their feet applauding.

Joey was right, people liked my singing. Maybe I just might have what it took to be a star.

-♪-

From the day of the wedding reception onwards, I performed with them at all their gigs. These consisted mostly of pubs, youth clubs and a few piano bars in Yarmouth and outlying districts; we had two or more shows every week all through the summer. With my contribution, we performed practically every tune in the hit parade. We could play almost any style, thanks to the skill of the boys. We sounded good, and quickly became a favourite in the area - new bookings were arriving nearly every day.

Despite his rejection of me, I respected Alan for his skill on the double bass and his showmanship - he would spin it like a top between notes, or lay the great barrel of the cello-shaped instrument on its side on the stage and climb over it while still plucking it.

Joey came to watch sometimes, when the gigs were in Yarmouth and he could get in for free. Afterwards, we would walk along the beach, savouring the cool night breeze and the reassuring, steady sound of the waves breaking on the sand.

"You got sumfing special in your voice, Bell," he said seriously on one of those occasions.

"Thanks, darlin'." I had picked this up from him; he used it as an irreverent way of removing barriers of class, age or gender. In his vocabulary, every man was 'mate', every girl 'darlin'', and every woman 'missus', and I soon found myself copying him.

"No, listen, it's not a compliment, Bell, I'm trying to tell you sumfing important. I never heard no-one sing like you, except maybe Doris Day. It ain't just musical - your voice 'as a sort of ... oh, I don't know, I ain't got the fancy words to say what I mean. What I know is this: I look at the people when you sing, and they stop talking, or eating, or whatever they are doing, and they listen. They can't help it. It's like ... well, it's like your voice goes inside them and touches their soul." He stopped, embarrassed.

I sat down on the sand, and he flopped beside me. The moon was low over the sea, its reflection a broken brush stroke from horizon to shore. Together we watched the luminous waves throw themselves onto the beach, their line of foam rushing towards us, slowing and stopping, then drawing back with a hiss of sand.

"I never thought of it like that," I said eventually. "It's the other way round for me, the song asks me to sing it. As though it's imprisoned, and needs me to set it free."

Again, the comfortable silence wrapped around us. We were like twins in a womb; two lives sharing one experience - separate, yet inseparable - our thoughts floating between us in the warm, amniotic love that held us together.

After a while he rolled onto his side to look at me. "Promise me sumfing, Bell."

"What's that?" I asked, dreamily.

"That you won't let your gift go to waste." He looked at me gravely. "I can see it in your future: you could be a successful singer, if you go where your voice leads you."

I laughed. "You got gypsy blood in you, Joey? Maybe you could become a fortune teller."

"I don't mean see the future like in a crystal ball, silly!"

He leaned forward and pushed my shoulder, not hard, but enough to throw me off balance, and I had to throw out an arm to stop myself falling over. "Listen to me, and stop trying to be funny." He was smiling, but his voice had an authority to it, a tone I hadn't heard before, as though he was trying to drive his words through the clamour of thoughts and sensations that he knew filled my head.

"Too many people let their gifts go to waste and never make anyfing of them," he continued, forcefully. "We all have gifts - some are obvious, like yours, most are harder to see, but we all have them, and it is a crime if we don't use them. Yours is special see, because you can reach millions of people."

"Millions?" I scoffed.

"Yeah, millions. You could be a big star, Bell."

I traced patterns in the sand between us with my finger, as my mind took in what he had said.

"And another fing," he said, suddenly, breaking into my thoughts.

"What?"

"Keep your name, don't let them change it. Belinda Bellini is a good name, be proud of it. Promise?"

"Yeah, I promise."

~7~
September 1960
Autumn

As an outcome of all the gigs I was getting with the band, I suddenly had a little money of my own. Not big sums at first, but more than I had ever earned before; and, as the work flowed increasingly into our diary, so my income grew. I started putting it in my Post Office savings account. Eventually I had enough coming in each week to pay the rent on a small flat. Excitedly, I told Joey, and asked him to move in with me; it seemed logical and obvious to me that we should share everything.

He seemed unsettled by the idea. "Look, mate," he said, looking awkwardly down at his feet, "I don't want to spoil your plans. You go ahead, but I'm better out here."

"But ..." I stammered, puzzled at his reluctance, "you won't have to worry about keeping warm and dry, or where to sleep, and we will be able to have hot dinners."

"I know that. But when the Old Bill come looking for me, they'll know where I am, won't they? My way suits me best: I can have anything I want without being tied down. If I want to get up and move on one day, well, I just pick up me bed and walk. Know what I mean?"

I could tell he was uncomfortable, because his accent had become more noticeable and he was using little phrases that he rarely said normally. But to me, this was a chance to get some kind of comfort and safety back into my life.

"If I get the flat, we will still be friends, won't we? I

couldn't bear it if we drift away from each other; you are like a brother."

"Course we'll stay friends, yer silly tart," he laughed, ending with a little cough that he had acquired.

"And will you come to stay, sometimes?"

"Yeah, that will be great." He gave one of his cheeky grins. "You any good as a cook?"

"Good? The nerve of him! I'm the best. My Gran taught me everything she knew."

"Sunday roast? I haven't had a roast dinner since me mum died."

"Sunday roast better than anything you ever tasted, I promise," I smiled, happy to prove myself to him.

"It's a deal, then, Sunday dinner at yours. Me mouf's waterin' already."

-♪-

Although I was spending much of my time rehearsing and performing with the band, and my nights were spent alone in the comfort of a soft bed, Joey and I saw each other as much as possible. Every morning, I walked over to the supermarket to meet him, and we would forage together among the bins, before wandering down to the beach, or a park, to eat our spoils for the day. As always, our time together was companionable, comfortable, and I found myself thinking about the word 'love' - was this it?

Naturally, I asked him.

He was silent for ages, and I thought I had embarrassed him. When he spoke, he gazed out towards the horizon, where merchant ships shimmered like a camel train in the dunes of the Sahara desert.

He coughed. "I can't speak for you, but for me, yeah, it's love. Seems to me there's different kinds of love. Like, you love to sing, you loved your Gran, I loved my mum - I think I even loved my dad in a way. I fink you can love someone wivout all that romantic stuff. That's how I feel about you. I look forward to seeing you, I feel happiest when you're around, but I don't want to jump on your body." He turned to me and grinned.

"Well you know how to bring a girl down," I laughed. "There was me thinking I was as sexy as Elizabeth Taylor." But I hugged him. "That's exactly how I feel. It's as though we are two halves of the same person, separated at birth and now reunited."

-♪-

On Sunday, I was more nervous than I had ever been before. Even pre-performance butterflies were nothing compared with the near panic I felt at cooking my first dinner for Joey. It's not as though I wasn't a thoroughly experienced cook - I had spent the last seven years cooking breakfasts and dinners for the (admittedly few) guests at the B & B - but I wanted it to be perfect.

I was up at dawn on that morning, checking that I had everything ready. I had splashed out on a leg of lamb, and over the course of the morning, I roasted the joint - with some potatoes and parsnips - boiled more potatoes for mashing and steamed a handful of runner beans. I laid the table and relaid it three times.

Half an hour before he was due to arrive, I made the

gravy and whisked up the Yorkshire pudding mix. I swear, I checked the clock every two minutes, praying he would not be late and the dinner spoilt.

I need not have worried; at twelve o'clock prompt, he arrived, carrying a big bunch of flowers, which he presented to me with a flamboyant Shakespearian flourish of hands. I accepted the the bouquet, giggling.

"I want you to know," he said proudly, "that those flowers are not pinched from a graveyard, or anyfing like that. I got them by honest trade. I exchanged them with the lady at the flower shop for a bottle of whisky."

"And where, may I ask, did you get the whisky?" I grinned, knowing the answer.

He gave a little cough. "Well, I nicked it of course. There was a delivery waiting outside a pub, beer and wines and spirits; nobody seemed to be bothered to take them in, so I helped myself to the whisky."

I frowned at him.

"And some brandy," he continued, quietly, after a pause. "And a couple of bottles of beer."

Seeing my shocked expression, he carried on, almost whispering: "And a packet of tobacco. Well, two, actually; I couldn't make up my mind whether to have the Old Holbourn or the Golden Virginia, so I had both."

"And, pray, what time was this?"

Again he coughed, nervously, as though he expected me to scold him for being a naughty boy. "Er, not sure really," he muttered. "Might have been about five o'clock this morning."

I laughed out loud and hugged him. "Thank you, my dear friend, you always give me a smile, and having you here for dinner is gift enough for me, but the flowers are lovely, and I am very proud of you.

He beamed, simultaneously proud and relieved.

-♪-

The summer reached its zenith; the days were balmy, easy, dreamy. His face appeared before me. "Don't look so glum, Bell, show me those 'amsteds."

We were sitting on a bench beside the boating pool, watching the little paddle boats going round and round. It was mid-afternoon, the sun was a flaming torch, and we had found a little bit of shade under a canvas canopy. I had been deep in thought, and heard his voice float in on the breeze.

"'amsteds?"

"Yeah, it's rhyming slang, comes from 'amsted 'eef. Means teef, see?"

"What's an 'amsted 'eef?"

"No, silly, it's not a what, it's a place, in London. Ain't you 'erd of 'amsted 'eef?"

"It's a funny name for a place. What does it mean?"

He studied my face. "Are you pullin' my leg? You know really, don't you?"

"No, honest, darlin', I'm confused."

"An 'eef is like a big field, wild, like a prairie, wiv bushes and stuff."

"Oh, you mean a heath."

"Now I know you're 'avin me on! Yeah, that's what I said, a neef. So yer 'amsteds is yer teef - rhyming slang, see."

I laughed. "Is that how they talk in London?"

"Sometimes, yeah. There's lots of 'em. 'Apples and pears' is 'stairs'; see, it rhymes. 'Plates of meat' is 'feet'. 'Frog and toad' is 'road'. It's all done so the Bill doesn't know what we're talkin' about."

"What's the rhyming slang for ... I looked around ... 'duck'?"

"There's not a rhyme for <u>every</u> word, silly." He laughed. "Cor blimey, you're 'ard work sometimes."

I giggled. "I love you, Joey."

-♪-

So the summer drifted by comfortably, lulling me into a sense of well-being. I should have known that it would not last, of course; life is not meant to be simple. It follows a pattern: a spell of happiness, to make you think that the worst is over and things will be good from now on, then it is snatched away.

The change arrived insidiously. The little cough that had crept into Joey's vocabulary became more pervasive and worrying. At first, he laughed it off, blaming it on the dog-ends he sometimes smoked, but by September I could tell that it was bothering him, too. His breath was wheezy and laboured, his speech was frequently punctuated with long hacking spells, and sometimes he fell into awful spasms that took all his breath away and made his eyes flood with tears.

Worse was to come, when I noticed that he was wiping blood from his mouth afterwards.

-♪-

Anxious to nurse him, I persuaded him to stay with me "for a little while." I hoped that the improvement in his environment would cure him, but his condition continued to deteriorate, no matter what I did. On a cold morning in November, he had a bad bout and passed out on the floor. Desperately, I ran to find a phone box and dialed 999 for an ambulance. It soon arrived in a cacophony of bells, and the crew lifted his tiny body onto a stretcher.

I begged them to let me accompany him. At first they refused, but Joey had taught me that, to survive - to get what you want - you sometimes have to decide when to be truthful and when to lie. So I told them he was my brother, and they relented.

I waited in the hospital for an hour while they examined him, then someone, a nurse, came to fetch me. "I'm sister Andrews, " she said. "Joey is on the ward now. You can see him, if you would like to, but he is weak and mustn't be agitated, ok?"

"I promise."

"Right then, this way." She led the way and I followed, onto a ward and to his bedside, feeling eyes following me from every bed. There was a card on the wall over his head saying 'Joseph Bellini.'

He looked awful. His skin was pale and appeared almost translucent, as though it was made of candle wax, and his eyes were deeply sunk, with dark circles around them. His hair lay damp and straggly on the pillow. He was conscious, and tried one of his cheeky grins, but it was lopsided and forced.

"What you doing, getting me in this place? Blooming doctors pulling me about, anyone would think I was ill." He stopped, panting, drawing shallow, noisy breaths. Then his eyes slowly closed, like a blind being pulled down, and he fell asleep.

I turned enquiringly to sister Andrews, who said, quietly, "He has tuberculosis."

I had heard of TB, that it was killing thousands of people, and I asked, desperately, "What will happen to him?"

"You're his sister, Belinda, is that right?" She asked.

I nodded. "I'm all he has now." That much was true.

"Where are your parents?"

I remembered Joey telling me how Charley had lost his parents; for some reason, I didn't want to tell them about Joey's father. "Our daddy never returned from the war, and mother killed herself two years ago."

Frowning, she took my hand. "Will you come with me, please?" She led me to a small office at the end of the ward, with 'Sister Drake' on a little sign.

Once inside, she closed the door. "Belinda, I'm afraid the disease is at an advanced stage. We are giving him all the latest treatments, but he is very ill."

"Will he ... die?" I found I could hardly force the last word out.

She gazed at me in silence for a moment, as though unsure how much to tell me. She was a tall woman, stoutly built, with blonde hair, wearing a neatly-pressed, blue and white uniform, topped with a cap like a paper crown.

"Most people who reach this stage don't survive," she

said, gravely. "Are you both living rough?"

I shook my head. "I've got a flat, but Joey preferred to stay on the streets".

"That hasn't helped him. If he pulls through, we could get him into an orphanage, if you like, Belinda. It's not good to be living like he has been."

"He would never agree to go into a home." The words shot out, without hesitation. And there was another thought in my mind. I had heard about the things that went on in some of those homes: children starved, beaten and locked in cupboards, or even disappearing forever, and vivid memories of Grainger were all I needed to warn me that other terrible things could happen.

"If he gets better, I will take care of him," I whispered.

"I understand, Belinda, but he would very likely need constant caring. I wish you would let me help you." I could see from her face that she was sincere, genuinely concerned for me.

"Thank you, I know you are being kind, but we have learnt to take care of ourselves." Whatever happened from now on, I would trust only myself. The world is a cruel place, the way to survive is to be strong, make your chances, take what you want.

She shook her head slightly, but said no more.

~8~
November 1960
Winter

Joey never regained consciousness.

I sat by his bed for two days, dozing on a chair; eating food brought to me by the hospital staff, oblivious to the passage of time or my own welfare. For me, at that time, nothing existed in the world but the tiny body beside me; the only thing on my mind was that my best friend was dying, and I couldn't prevent it.

I brushed the lank, black hair from his forehead and dabbed at the beads of perspiration with a cool towel; I held his hand and talked to him constantly while I was awake; the nurses told me that I continued talking to him when I was asleep, urging him to keep fighting the disease that had no right invading his body. I was with him when he died, heard his last, painful breath escaping, felt his hand go limp in mime. I sat, silently weeping, until a nurse came and took me to the cafeteria. All I could think of was that there was no-one to arrange a proper funeral for him.

"What happens next?" I asked the young nurse.

"The hospital notifies the Registrar of Births and Deaths," she said, gently, "and the local council, who will arrange a simple burial."

"What about a church service, and a gravestone?" Suddenly it was important that he was buried properly.

"I don't know much, I'm afraid. I think there's a simple blessing by the vicar, but as for a stone, sorry, you would have to ask at the town hall."

My eyes thanked her, my mouth had ceased to function. After a little while, she had to get back to the ward, so I sat alone for a while, maybe a long while, I didn't know. He had been a vital part of my life for eight months, and now that he was gone I didn't know what to do. I remembered his voice, with its musical, sometimes comical, London accent, chirping on, telling me about his life, advising me in mine, encouraging me. I heard, again, as he told me what I was to do with my life: "*Belinda Bellini, you should be a pop star, making records*," he had said.

It was up to me, wasn't it? The only person who could make things right for Joey, and for myself, was me. I made up my mind, as I sat in the empty cafeteria, that I owed it to him to do my best for both of us. I stood up, left my cup of cold cocoa on the table and strode out of the hospital with a new purpose.

-♪-

As I walked out of the hospital into the grey, November afternoon, I paused to look around, to breathe in some fresh air, and to think. My world had changed in less than a year, and I had changed with it. A new, harder, Belinda had emerged, street-wise and self-sufficient, driven by a new determination. "*I can make it as a singer*," I chanted silently to myself.

Thoughts about music reminded me that the band had been booked for a big performance in Norwich the previous night, at which Bruce had heard there might be a record producer from London, looking for new talent. I found a telephone box and tried to ring Bruce, to apologise for not being there, but he was out. I shrugged my shoulders, no doubt I would see him later.

I headed for the town hall, to find out about burials. There I encountered a sullen, officious clerk who, peering over tiny spectacles like a character from the pen of Charles Dickens, grudgingly told me that I would have to talk to the vicar of a church if I wanted to know what to do. I thanked him brusquely and walked out, heading southwards beside the river, swirling grey at full tide, then across town to the only church I knew: St John's, where Gran had taken me to Sunday School.

The vicar was out visiting parishioners, but his wife was there. Over a cup of tea, I explained the situation to her, and she listened intently.

"Well," she said when I had finished, "first let me tell you the details, then we can work out what to do. Is that ok?"

I nodded, and she smiled.

"Right. All burials take place in the municipal cemetery attached to St Nicholas Church in the town centre. If there is no-one to pay for a plot, a place in a common grave will be allocated by the church, and we will hold a simple Christian service here, and at the graveside."

She saw that my face had fallen at the mention of a 'common' grave. It sounded like 'pauper's grave', a sign of destitution, a stigma.

"A Common Grave is not as bad as it sounds," she continued. "Joey will have a proper burial in his own plot, in a specially set-aside part of the graveyard. But there will be no gravestone, and the grave is only kept for one year, then it is re-used."

I sat quietly, considering what she had said, ideas forming in my head. "If I had some money," I began, hesitantly, "could I pay for a proper plot with a gravestone?"

She smiled. "Yes, of course, but do you have enough? What you would be buying is the right to bury Joey, and for a stone to be erected. It can be expensive: about seventy pounds for the grave, plus the cost of interment. Then there's the headstone; that can run to thirty or forty pounds, maybe more, by the time you pay a stonemason to carve an inscription. Can you afford that?"

So much! I shook my head, feeling a wave of helplessness break over me.

"It's not all bad news," she continued, seeing my disappointment, and reaching out a hand to touch my arm reassuringly. "I think Joey was only twelve years old, wasn't he?" I nodded. "Well, that means there's no internment fee. And we can help you a bit with the plot. Instead of buying it outright, you can pay a yearly amount of ten pounds to hold it until you can afford the bigger amount. Would that help?"

Could I find fifty pounds or more? My mind raced. I desperately wanted to give Joey a dignified burial and a proper grave, but it seemed out of reach.

I had some money: the rent for my flat for the next week was due, and I had saved my earnings from singing to cover it, so that was three pounds ten shillings. I also had the money I had been putting away in my Post Office savings account, about nine pounds. That gave me twelve pounds ten, and I would be homeless again. Maybe I could hold off the landlord for a week or so while I made some more, and perhaps Bruce would give me an advance. But where could I get another forty pounds?

There was one last hope, my Aladdin's cave, Gran's jewellery hidden in my case. I would sell the jewels and raise enough to take care of everything.

"I think I can do it," I said firmly, rising from my chair to leave. "How long do I have?"

She shrugged. "A week or so,normally, but we can delay it a little, if necessary. I will inform the hospital and the registrar that we are working with you on it."

"Right, thank you," I said, determinedly, "I will be back with the money as soon as I can."

-♪-

"How much?" I couldn't believe what I was hearing.

The little man in the jewellers shop shrugged. "Sorry love, most of them are worthless, they're just bits of tat. They look ok, but there's not an ounce of precious metal in them, and the stones are all glass. The only piece that's worth anything at all is the wedding ring, and that's only nine carat gold. If I melt it down, I'll be lucky to get two quid for it, maybe four quid if I can sell it as it is."

"No, I don't believe it. You're ripping me off. I'm not letting you have them for that."

I snatched them up and stormed out. But the story was the same at the next jewellers, and the next. "Honest miss, I'm doing you a favour at that price," became a phrase I heard several times. In the end I had to accept what was offered, a total of just thirty shillings.

Joey's gravestone had become an impossible dream.

Mrs Potter, the vicar's wife, was sympathetic when I returned to see her. "Come in love, my husband's home, you can have a chat with him."

We three sat together in their gloomy living room, with its dark furniture and heavy drapes. I sipped tea with them, hypnotised by the sonorous ticking of a gigantic grandfather clock, while we discussed my options, which were, obviously, seriously limited.

The vicar was a kind man, about fifty years old, already fast balding, with that leaden face so common among the clergy when they have to help parishioners through difficult times. "My advice, Belinda," he intoned, rather like his clock, "is to save your money until you can afford what you want. I don't like the idea of you getting into difficulties just to pay for a grave."

I shook my head. "No," I said levelly, "Joey is not going into a common grave. Even though I can't afford a stone for him, yet, I have enough to pay for a plot for a year, and I will get him a memorial with his name and everything, somehow." I blinked back the tears that were pushing at the corners of my eyes; tears for Joey and tears of frustration.

"We understand dear," said Mrs Potter, kneeling beside me and putting her arm round my shoulders. I couldn't help myself, suddenly I was sobbing into her bosom, my anger and self-pity, held back for so long, pouring out at last. She held me close, stroking my hair and murmuring gentle, meaningless sounds.

Eventually, I lifted my head. "I miss my Gran so much,

she would have sorted everything out for me."

"Perhaps she would. But it seems to me," she smiled, "that you are doing very well by yourself. You have been through a tough time, and pulled through. I admire you, Belinda."

I was amazed. Why should a woman - mature, comfortable, successful in her way - admire me? I was still a kid, no matter how hard I pretended otherwise; my life was a mess, I was worth twenty two pounds fifteen shillings. But when I looked into her eyes, I could see she was sincere. "Why?" I croaked.

"Because you are resilient. What happened just now was the first time you have let your emotions out, wasn't it? When life knocks you sideways, you fight back. I think you will go a long way, Belinda Bellini."

Her words were so like Joey's that they took my breath away. "Joey said that, too," I whispered.

"Then he was a very astute young man, and lucky to have you as his friend." She smiled again. "I will reserve a plot for him. The funeral will be next Monday, at ten o'clock, will you come?"

"Oh yes, please."

"Ok, it's all settled, then. Now I'm sorry, but we have to be getting ready to go out."

I left with four pounds five shillings in my pocket, but a new plan for the future.

-♪-

"Nice of you to turn up for rehearsal, Belinda. Shame you couldn't make it last night. After all, it was the most important gig we've ever done."

Bruce's face was twisted into an angry sneer, eyes screwed into little black slits, mouth pulled apart in a grim parody of a smile. The rest of the band lounged or sat behind him, equally hostile.

"I'm sorry," I mumbled, cut by their resentment. "My best friend was dying, I had to be with him."

He raised his arms, outstretched at each side, to shoulder height. "And what about us?" he whined, looking back to the others. "We don't count, I take it? You knew this was possibly our make-or-break moment, and you couldn't leave your chum for a couple of hours to support us. Well thanks very much. Maybe next time we'll have a standby, just in case you can't make it again, or maybe there won't be a next time.

"No, actually, there won't be a next time for you. No thanks to you, we landed a deal, so it seems we can manage perfectly well without you, after all. Goodbye Belinda, close the door behind you." I saw the others smirking, and Alan sidled up beside Bruce to enjoy the moment.

"Just like that? No thanks for all the work I put in that got you that gig," I shouted, angry with them, angry with myself for the tears that were stinging my eyes.

"Belinda, we were carrying you. We gave you a start, took a chance on taking in an unknown kid. We trained you, built you up." Now his eyes were bulging, and he spat out the words like bullets from a gun. "Now you think we owe you something? Wrong, kid, wrong in a big way!"

"One time!" I screeched. "That's all. Just once I had to

miss a gig, and that was to be with someone special when they died. But that doesn't count with you, does it? Don't you care about anyone except yourself?"

"Success is everything," he retorted. "If we are to make it big, we have to be totally dedicated, ruthless, single-minded. There's no room for sentimentality or weakness in show business.

"Yeah," Alan chipped in from behind with a sneer.

"Shut up, Alan!" I snapped. "I'm talking to the engineer, not his oily rag."

I had heard Joey say something like that once. It seemed to be the perfect response, and I felt great satisfaction in its effect; it was wonderful to see Alan's face turn purple with rage, and he stepped forward with his fists clenched.

Bruce stopped him with an outstretched arm, without taking his eyes off me. "Leave now, Belinda, before you cause any more trouble," he hissed.

"Oh, nothing could make me stay," I shouted. "If you think that's what it takes, if that's what ambition does to you, I don't want to be part of your dream. Friends are special, and if my friends need me I will always be there for them!"

I turned and stamped to the door, turning partway to throw a parting line: "Don't fool yourselves. If you are successful, you will never enjoy it, because you will be too busy screwing people, or waiting for them to screw you!"

Blood was throbbing in my head as I pushed through the door into the evening sunshine. Once out of their sight, the tears poured down my face as I walked away.

Now I really was in trouble - no money, no income, no friends, and by the end of next week I would be homeless again - I needed an angel to save me, but my little angel was dead.

-♪-

The day of the funeral dawned as bright and clear as a spring morning. After the service at St Johns, and the burial in the cemetery near the ruins of St Nicholas Church - flattened by German bombs in the war - I stood at the graveside, with the sun gleaming happily through the branches of the trees dotted around the graveyard, highlighting the beautiful copper and gold leaves that were gently fluttering down, as though it was not the saddest day the world had ever known. I had expected it to be a sombre day, mournful and melancholy, but clearly I was not in charge of weather arrangements.

There had been four of us at the graveside: little Charley, who I had met on my first day with Joey, the vicar, his wife and me. On the days leading to the funeral, I had called around to see all the drop-outs in the town, telling them what had happened to our friend, and asking them to come to the funeral. Several had said they would be at the church, but in the end it was just Charley and me.

Mr Potter reached the end of his liturgy, and we stood in silence, each with our own thoughts. I watched a newsreel of my memories of Joey - Joey laughing, Joey splashing naked in the sea at midnight, Joey Serious, Joey coughing up blood.

With my last two pounds I had bought a simple wooden cross for the grave, with Joey's name and the date of his death etched on it.

"I promise, my dear friend, that I will not rest until I can give you a proper gravestone and a real funeral," I said quietly.

I wanted it to be raining, to match my tears, not warm and sunny. Instead, I felt the warmth of the sun reaching inside me, filling me, touching my heart. I felt a hand taking mine.

With a thrill I heard Joey's voice: "*Crying won't help, Bell. Remember what I told you - Life comes in two bits: yesterday ... and all the rest. Life may deal you a handful of shit - you can't change that - but you can change how you let the shit affect you.*"

He was right. I had to overcome my sadness, be grateful for the good things, and make my own way. Thanks to him, I could now take care of myself. It was time to move on. The future was mine.

-♪-

The next day, I started hawking myself around the theatres in Great Yarmouth - asking for work as a dancer or in the chorus - without any success. It was not a good time of year. The summer season was over, and entertainers were being laid off, not taken on. Some of the managers wrote down my name and asked for my address - I knew they wouldn't be in touch.

Then my luck changed. As I was leaving The Globe, my chin on my chest, a man detached himself from a wall and stepped into my path.

"I heard you asking about work," he said. "What can you do?" He was tall, about six feet, I guessed, and in his twenties, slim, good looking, casually dressed in jeans and a leather motor-cycle jacket. He was smoking a cigarette, relaxed, almost arrogant.

"Sing, dance, anything," I said, shrugging, trying to sound cocky. I studied him carefully, unsure of his motives. He seemed nice enough, though, with a pleasant smile. "You got a theatre or something?"

"Nah! But I know them all. I'm, like, an agent; I can get you work, if you're any good. What's your name?"

"Belinda Bellini." Joey had always said it was a good name, with a professional sound to it. He said I would be a star one day; I hoped I could justify his faith in me. "What's yours?" (Look confident, nonchalant, Belinda, as though you've seen it all, done it all.)

"Gary Burroughs." He looked me up and down, and seemed to be satisfied with what he saw. "Have you done any stage work?"

"Loads," I lied. Well, I had done some with the Beacons.

"Ok, good, cool. Will you do an audition, if I fix one up?"

Too right I would! But I mustn't appear too eager, too needy. "Yeah, if you want. What can you get me?"

He laughed."Let's see if you can do the business, first. How can I contact you? Are you on the phone?"

"I don't stay in one place long enough to get a phone. I'm dossing with some friends, till I get proper digs." I was amazed how easily the lies were coming. "Where's your office?"

"Don't worry about that right now," he replied. "Meet me outside the Regent, tomorrow at twelve o'clock, I'll see what I can fix up. Ok?"

"Sure, I'll be there." I sauntered off, still trying to act cool, but my heart was singing. I had my first break.

-♪-

The next day, I bathed and changed into my only nice clothes, bought while I was earning money with the band. They were just an ordinary dress and shoes, not really stage wear, but they were all I had. They were still unworn, with the creases still in, and I hoped they would fall out. I also used a little of my precious make-up and perfume.

I studied myself in the mirror, seriously assessing my appearance for the first time since I was six years old. For the first ten years of my life, I had been content to be a child, playing at life; but that had been when I felt secure and loved. It seemed like a lifetime ago, so much had happened in the last few years. Now I was truly alone, surviving by my own resources. It was time to grow up.

And the girl in the mirror was not that child; here were the makings of a woman. My figure had started to fill out: I had good legs and a nice bust, emphasised by the narrow waist that six months of living rough had given me; and my hair - like coal, black and gleaming - had grown to a good length and settled seductively on my shoulders. I smiled at myself, and liked what I saw. I was ready to take on the world. Joey had taught me that I could do it, encouraged me and shown me the way; now I had to make it work, and I was determined to succeed.

-♪-

Gary was late. The clock above the entrance to the Regent had reached twenty past twelve, and I was about to leave, when he arrived.

"Ah good, you're here." He didn't apologise, seemed unaware that he had kept me waiting. That made me angry.

"You're late!" I hissed petulantly.

"Yeah, sorry. You ready to perform, then?" He seemed unconcerned. Arrogant pig!

Nevertheless, I followed him inside, where he greeted the manager as though they were old friends, then led me backstage. I remembered it all from my visits with Ted Bailey, my comedian friend from those innocent days, and the memories helped to boost my confidence.

"What are you going to sing?" Gary asked.

"Sweet Nothin's," I replied. It was a song recorded by Brenda Lee, a young American singer whom I greatly admired. She had succeeded in a rock music industry dominated by men, Little Richard, Buddy Holly, Gerry Lee Lewis and, of course, Elvis Presley. She could make her voice wonderfully raucous when she wanted to, though she was capable of delivering a gentle Country song too.

He raised an eyebrow, either surprised at my choice or impressed at my nerve, I couldn't tell. Maybe he didn't know the record, or maybe he hated it. He left me on stage, descended the steps and sat in a seat in the front row.

I stood alone on a stage for the first time, with no

microphone and no backing group, and the strangest thing happened: all my nerves disappeared. I knew I should be there, it was my destiny, I could feel Joey with me, urging me on.

I launched into the song, belting out the words in the way that Brenda Lee did in the record. It was as though the world no longer existed. I was so immersed in the music that I didn't realise I had reached the last word until I heard my voice echoing around the walls and roof, and heard a pattering of applause that sprang up from the back of the theatre, where a small bunch of people had gathered.

Burroughs seemed unimpressed. He stayed in his seat, his arms folded across his chest, a cigarette smouldering between his fingers. "Do another one," he said, dispassionately.

I glared at him; what was wrong with the man? Ok, if that's what he wanted ...

By way of contrast, I decided to sing a ballad, "You Always Hurt The One You Love," that I had heard performed by Connie Francis, but which I would give my own interpretation. I was nervous about throwing away the excitement of my first song, but I wanted to show him there was more to me than shouting.

Once again, as soon as I began to sing, I was transported into another universe; the theatre faded from my consciousness and I lived only for that song. When I finished it, I was startled by loud applause and cheering. I opened my eyes to the sight of almost a hundred people sitting and standing around the auditorium.

I felt a big smile take over my face. I gave a little

curtsey, then looked back at Gary; surely he must have liked it, everyone else had.

But he still sat there, expressionless. "Yeah, that'll do for now. Meet me back here tomorrow and I'll let you know if I can make anything of you."

-♪-

Another small crowd applauded enthusiastically. Their appreciation was welcome, but I had hoped for better things by then. Gary had lent me the money to buy an acoustic guitar, and I had learnt to play it - well, to strum a few chords to accompany myself, with the help of Bert Weedon's 'Play in a Day' book - and now I was singing to pay him back.

I smiled and thanked the regulars, of course, then left the tiny stage and took my place behind the bar for my only real job, serving drinks. Two months on, and I was still in Great Yarmouth; Gary had so far not managed to get me into any of the theatres, so I was reduced to making a small living singing in pubs, mostly his pub.

He owned the Bricklayers Arms, a small pub in Nelson Road, out of the town centre, but only a short walk from the seafront, and I had moved in with him. We lived in the flat above it. It seemed a fair deal for me; I contributed to our living expenses by working behind the bar, with a little to spare for myself - I saved what I could in my Post Office account.

Since I started performing there, trade had improved noticeably, with a large number of people attending just to hear me sing. Instead of being pleased, however, Gary seemed to resent my success, and took to spending all his time on the customer's side of the bar, making me work harder. Every night, the routine was the same: while I served drinks to the punters, Gary socialised with them, matching their consumption of beer and spirits.

Then, when the clock reached ten twenty-five, I would call 'time', allowing the serious drinkers to rush to the bar to buy their last pints. Licensing laws at that time forbade the sale of alcohol after ten thirty, but most nights the drinking went on in the Bricklayers until after midnight; Gary simply gave the drinks away, while striving doggedly to attain a state of insufferable, staggering drunkenness himself.

I became accustomed to leaving him to his puerile pleasures and going upstairs to bed alone. We had started to sleep together as soon as I moved in; it just seemed to be the natural thing to do. I didn't tell him I was under age - why complicate things? I enjoyed the closeness, it felt almost like love, though a quiet voice told me I was fooling myself.

"Goodnight everyone," I called as I left.

Gary's voice, raised above the mutter of farewells from the customers, shouted his usual slurred, empty promise: "I'll be up soon to satisfy your needs, baby!" He turned to his cronies, always the same heavy drinkers; "She's insatiable you know, can't get enough of me."

I sighed. "In your dreams, buster," I muttered as I closed the door and climbed the narrow, bare stairs.

At first there had been sex, initially careful and slow, but soon reduced to a quick release for him, leaving me unsatisfied and angry. After a short while, even that ceased, as he came to bed later and later, stinking of beer and breathing cigarette smoke into my face. Occasionally, he tried a drunken fumble, but never managed to raise an erection; I learnt to let him try, knowing he would inevitably fall asleep without achieving anything.

The flat was sparse, we never made enough money to furnish it properly, and Gary drank most of the profits. I made myself a pot of tea and carried it into the living room, a nice large, light room that looked out onto the corner of Nelson Road and Wellington Road. Sinking into the worn settee, I poured my first cup, then rolled a joint and leaned back into the lumpy upholstery. Gary had introduced me to cannabis - everybody was smoking it, he told me. I took to it quickly, it helped to relax me and make life seem a little bit less dreary.

I wondered again why I was still there. It was not the life I wanted; my career was stalled, Gary had not lived up to his extravagant promises to catapult me into stardom, and now seemed content to let me work as a barmaid while he drank himself into oblivion.

-♪-

"When are you going to get me some real stage work?" I demanded, petulantly. The summer season was about to start in the theatres, but I was still in the wilderness as far as the entertainment industry was concerned.

Gary was nursing a hangover. It had been two o'clock when he staggered up the stairs and flopped into bed, smelling like one of our dustbins. I had turned my back as he dragged the covers off me; thankfully, he was too drunk to try to grope me.

My day's work started at six o'clock, when I had to be up to receive a beer delivery. Thankfully, the drivers were sympathetic to my situation, and carried the kegs into the cellar for me, otherwise I would have been helpless; it was struggle enough for me to roll one into position and connect to the lines, I could never have lifted it.

When Gary had finally blessed me with his presence, it was ten o'clock and I had cleaned up the mess left by his cronies, washed all the glasses and polished the bar and all the chrome. We had reached a stage where he left everything to me.

He pulled himself a pint of bitter and sagged into a chair. "Don't nag me, baby, I'm not well," he whined, pathetically.

"You're not ill," I spat, hating myself for the shrill tone my voice had taken. "You've got alcohol poisoning!"

"Get me an Alka Seltsa, babe. My head's splitting."

"God, you're pathetic!" I snapped. "If you don't get me work soon, I'm moving out. You can try to run this place without me."

His face clouded over; his lips pulled back in a snarl. "Don't push your luck, kid," he snapped. "If you leave me I'll make sure you never get a job in Yarmouth."

I threw down the tea towel I had been using to dry the glasses, and stormed out into Nelson Street and down to the beach. There, I walked slowly along the waterline, as I had as a child, skipping aside as waves rushed at my feet, as though trying to grab me. I remembered the long chats with Oliver, and the companionable silences.

Slowly my mood improved. My thoughts drifted to Joey. Dear little Joey; what a tough life he had suffered, and how resilient he had to be, but always he was stoical and cheerful, until it was snatched from him. 'I must learn to be like him,' I thought.

-♪-

That night, after I called 'time, gentlemen please', with scarcely a hint of sarcasm in the word 'gentlemen', Gary called me over to the table where he was sitting with some of his friends. "Here, try one of these," he said, holding out a little piece of pink paper, about the size of a stamp, which he had removed from a small tin box that sat on the table with its lid still open.

"What is it?" I asked.

"Don't worry about what it is, just try it, it's good stuff, you'll enjoy it." He thrust the little square at me.

I hesitated, looking at Gary, the piece of paper, the tin, then at his mates, who chorused "Go on!"

"What am I supposed to do with it?"

"It's just blotting paper," he grinned. "Put it in your mouth."

I knew I should have walked away, I knew he was not to be trusted, but somehow, in that moment, a combination of bravado, his power over me, and my curiosity, took over my hand. I saw it reach out and take the innocent-looking scrap, then watched dispassionately as it came up to my mouth, which opened without any instruction from me. After depositing the paper on my tongue, my rebellious hand then picked up Gary's beer glass and raised it to my lips. I heard Joey shouting to me "*NO! Stop, Bell, stop! Don't do it,*" but it was too late, I had taken the first step on the lonely road to hell.

~9~
January 1961
Exploited

Now, before I continue, I have a confession to make: there is something I haven't told you.

Despite my total recall, there is one place, a hole in my memory which, thankfully, I cannot access. I do not wish to see into it, because it holds the darkest part of my life. Sometimes, I have momentary glimpses of the start of it - and the end - they are bad enough. I am thankful that my mind is preventing me from peering over the edge into the abyss of full recollection.

Gary fed me every drug he could get, and once he had me hooked, I was desperate for more. I will never know which substances he pumped into me, all I can say is that I became dependent on him maintaining my supply. He gave me pills and powders, I smoked, sniffed, swallowed and, yes, eventually, injected everything he gave me. But the drugs were just a tool; he used them to pacify and control me, keep me malleable and, ultimately, to sell me.

He started to hold parties in our flat, attended by sleazy characters I hadn't met before. They would arrive after dark, through the back door, and stay all night getting high, drinking, smoking, shooting and snorting to loud music.

And there were other girls - young, like me, with eyes that gazed unseeing into space.

Before my brain locks up, refuses to allow me any

further access, I can see disjointed movie clips of those nights, like flickering images projected onto a thick cloud of smoke.

There is no sense of time, one moment flows into another, which, for all I know, could have happened on a different night, or even in a different month. There might be six or ten or twelve people, laying around on cushions or lounging in chairs, taking turns to make lines of white powder, which they sucked up through their noses with straws made from banknotes. By then, I was doing the same, and usually my memory gives out shortly before recalling the kick that followed.

But sometimes I have little flashes; they are not pleasant. I look down and see my naked body, I look up and see men standing around watching as, one by one, they violate me, degrade me, pierce, slap, punch me. I feel nothing, the drugs insulate me from all sensations. I see them handing Gary money. I see him laughing and slapping them on the back.

As far as I can work it out, those little vignettes represent a period of about six months that is otherwise completely lost to me. I could not have saved myself. I was hooked on ... god knows what. Gary supplied me, then sold me to his friends.

When I probe my mind, all I can see is a shadow show, shapes swimming past, voices, echoing.

But one day, as I drifted out of my cloud, my body screaming for a shot, I found Gary laying unconscious on the floor of our flat, out of his head on something. No matter how I tried to wake him, I could not. It did not occur to me to worry about his welfare, I didn't care if he lived or died, I just wanted my shot.

Desperately, I staggered down the stairs and into the street, hoping to find someone to give me what I needed. As the mist shreds and drifts, I can see the disgust on the faces of strangers as I begged them to give me drugs, offered them money, or sex.

Then I found a familiar face. Thank god!

I didn't know his name, didn't care, he was someone I knew who might give me some heroin, anything to relieve the terrible pain that racked me.

"Please, give me some smack, anything, I'm dying!" I croaked. "I'll sleep with you, do anything you like."

He stared at me, puzzled, amazed. "Belinda? Is it you?"

Yeah, yeah, B'linda, whatever. Have you got any stuff, or not?"

He grabbed my shoulders with both hands, rocked me gently but firmly, forcing me to look in his eyes. "Belinda, it's me, Oliver, I came to find you. God, you look awful. What's happened to you?"

Oliver? I knew an Oliver once ... he left.

-♪-

My fuddled brain tried to make sense of the thoughts that suddenly flooded through it. There <u>was</u> something familiar about him. The hair, the eyes? He was older, but yes, it was him!

"Oliver!" I threw my arms around his neck and held onto him, felt his hands on my back as he hugged me close and I sobbed into his collar. "Where have you been? You went away without telling me. I missed you so much. So many things have happened."

"I'm sorry," he whispered, huskily. "I'll tell you all about it, but first I have to know what has happened to get you into this state. What's all this about drugs? I thought you were too smart to start down such a dangerous path."

The mention of drugs switched my mind back to my present predicament. "Yeah, drugs. Have you got any, can you get me some?"

He studied my face intently, so deeply that I squirmed with embarrassment. "Yes, I've got some, you will have to come with me to get them."

"Sure, lead on, kindly light."

He took me to a run-down house along a narrow path, and led me up a flight of dingy stairs to an attic room. As soon as we were inside, he turned a key in the lock, then put the key in his pocket.

"What you doin'? Why you locked the door?" I slurred, my whole face screwed up with the effort of concentrating.

"Sit down," he said, indicating a battered table and chairs. "I'll get you something." He lit a ring on the greasy gas cooker in one corner of the room and began rummaging in a cupboard, emerging with two mugs and a jar of instant coffee.

"What's this? You playing some kind of game. Where are my drugs?" I started to stand up, but he was behind me in one movement and pressed down on my shoulders. I was so weak I could not resist.

"Here," he said, plonking a mug of coffee on the table. "Drink this."

"I don't want that!" I spat. "Let me go! I need drugs."

Again I tried to get up, and when he restrained me, I lashed out, feebly. He grabbed me in a bear hug, pinning my arms at my side.

"Belinda, I want to help you. His face was close to mine, his breath warm on my sweaty cheek.

The closeness of him affected me deeply. In the short while we had known each other, all those years ago, there had never been any physical contact, and yet, there was an attraction that was completely different from how I felt about Joey. I felt my heart pounding against my ribs, like it wanted to break free and join with Oliver's.

Through the haze of my drugged state, I knew I loved Oliver. I relaxed and rested my head on his chest, wrapping my arms around his waist. I felt him kiss my dirty, sweaty head.

-♪-

Oliver kept me locked in his room; I was a willing captive.

He bathed me, fed me, talked to me, held me when the demons returned to stab me with their fiery forks, and when my body shivered uncontrollably from the withdrawal of the poisons on which it had grown to depend. For two weeks, he hardly left me. When he had to go out to shop for food, he locked the door, and was gone for just a few minutes. Slowly, I recovered, finding something like the real Belinda Bellini, leaving behind the broken facsimile created by Burroughs.

He washed my clothes. While they dried I wore a pair of his jeans and one of his shirts. He said they looked better on me.

We talked about my life and his, and about our feelings for each other. I learned that, on the day before the flood, he, his family, and everyone else in the shanty town on the beach, had been moved out by the police for their own safety, following serious weather warnings. They lost almost all their meagre possessions to the wild storm that night, but there was a good outcome: because so many families were thrown upon the welfare services of the local council, homes were found for all of them in Local Authority housing complexes being built in towns and villages all around Norfolk.

I told him about my evacuation from the flood, and about Gran's exposure and decline. He was shocked when I recounted being ejected from the guest-house by uncle Ernie, and solicitous over the loss of Joey.

Once we had opened the doors to discussing our relationship, Oliver told me that he had loved me from the first time we spoke.

"But you were only ten," I said.

"I can't explain it, it was just something I knew beyond any doubt, and it stayed with me all the time we were parted. As soon as I was able to leave home, I came here to Yarmouth to find you. It took a month, but it worked." He smiled, and kissed me. I realised that I had loved him too, that Joey's words were true - it is possible to love many people, each in a way that is unique to that person. I would always love Joey with warmth, as a brother; I loved Oliver with a heart-pumping flood of passion.

"What can we do next?" I asked. "I am still under-age, we can't be married for another three years."

"I don't mind that, I can wait, but there's another

complication: I've received my call-up papers, I have to report for National Service in a couple of weeks."

"Oh no!" I cried, we have only just found each other. Can't you get them to change their minds?"

He laughed. "I wish I could, my love, but little lives such as ours count for nothing in the big scheme that is National Security."

I sat in silent thought for a few minutes, unable to reconcile the chain of events that seemed to be dragging me from one crisis to the next. After a while, I asked softly: "Will you take me outside, please?"

"Are you sure you're up to it?"

"I think so. It's just that I've been in this room too long; I need to feel the pavement under my feet and the wind on my face, to see people and hear the gulls."

-♪-

We emerged from his bedsit, and I blinked in the late summer sunshine, feeling the warm breeze on my cheek and fluttering my hair. Hand in hand, we walked through the maze of narrow back streets towards the sea. I could hear the gulls screeching, smell the salty air. It was good to be back with reality.

Suddenly, I heard a rustle of clothing and a heavy footstep close behind, and strong hands grabbed me. Before I could cry out, another hand was clamped over my mouth. I could see Oliver struggling with two men, they were punching and kicking him, then I was dragged into an alley and lost sight of them.

I could hear the panting of my captors as they ran, half

carrying me so that my feet scraped along the pavement. A turn, and darkness, as I was hauled into a building, then light again as someone switched on a naked bulb. I was in a room with no windows, possibly a cellar; the walls were plain brick; it smelt musty. There was little furniture, a couple of wooden chairs and a table were all I could see. One of my captors moved around to face me.

"Thought you could get away from me, did you, Belinda?"

"Gary? What's going on?"

"Oh, I have too much invested in you to let you go. You were my little goldmine, I can't afford to have you wandering off, telling people my business."

The man holding me dumped me roughly into one of the chairs, and Burroughs sat astride the other, staring at my face. "Did you think you and your little boyfriend could hide from me forever?"

"To be honest," I said, with more bravado than I felt, "I didn't give you a thought."

He laughed, a harsh explosion, like a cough, then his hand lashed out and slapped me across the face, first with his palm, then, on the back-swing, with his knuckles. It was a shock - not just the pain, which was instantaneous, but because it was unexpected. I had grown to realise in the time I had known him that he was capable of anything, including violence, but until then it had never been directed at me. I cried out, and he grinned, an ugly smirk that held more than a hint of menace.

"Now let's hear no more cheek from you. You are here, and now here is where you will stay until I'm ready to let you out. Besides, I have something special planned for you tomorrow." He leered as he stood and walked towards the door.

As he opened it, and allowed his henchman out, he turned back to me. "Don't bother trying to shout for help, no-one will hear you, and Hoss, here," he indicated the brute who had held me, and who glowered at me through bushy eyebrows, "will be keeping guard outside the door. If he hears you making a noise, he will come in and silence you. Do you understand what I'm saying?"

I didn't answer. "I'll take that as a 'yes'. Oh, and don't expect your boyfriend to rescue you; my lads have taught him a lesson. If he lives, he will have more respect for my property in future."

The door closed, I heard a key turn and the light was switched off, plunging the room into darkness.

-♪-

Time passed. I had no way of knowing even if it was day or night, but gradually my eyes adapted to the darkness, and I could see the layout of the room in shades of grey and black. A thin slice of light shone under the door from the room beyond. I walked over and gave an experimental twist to the knob, and pulled, to be sure it was really locked. It was a heavy, solid wooden door with an old mechanism, which rattled as I tried it. Immediately, there was the sound of a fist hitting the door on the opposite side, and a voice shouting something incoherent. I jumped back.

I returned to my chair and sat down again, frustrated, angry and very scared. I thought about Oliver, and hoped that Burroughs was lying about him being beaten up, though it had certainly looked that way in the last seconds I had seen him. I also thought about our short time together again and our feelings for each other. It seemed that we were doomed to be dragged apart every time we met.

I think I dozed off a few times, I'm not sure, but I was pacing around the walls like a caged animal when the light was switched on again; it startled me and I cried out, holding my hands up to cover my eyes, which were watering from the sudden, unexpected brightness. The door was unlocked and the creature called Hoss came in bearing a tray. He gestured for me to sit in the chair and, when I had obeyed, he put the contents down on the bare concrete floor, his eyes constantly on me, and departed wordlessly with the tray. The lock clicked and scraped and the light went out again.

What he left behind was illuminated by the narrow searchlight that shone beneath the door: a paper plate with some bread and cheese on it, and a plastic mug of cold tea. Little though it was, I was glad to see it. I guessed that about eight hours had passed since Oliver and I had left his bedsit. By my estimate, that would make it about six in the evening, and I had eaten nothing since waking that morning.

The feeding process was repeated again, about another eight hours later, at what I guessed to be about two am. This time it was the cold remains of a Chinese takeaway and a plastic cup of flat beer. It tasted good. Afterwards, I resumed my pacing, round and round the room, re-running in my mind the events that got me into this mess, thinking of all the things I could have done instead, trying to work out a plan of escape. Failing.

After a while, I returned to my chair and napped for a little while. Then, my brain still seething with memories and thoughts, I paced the walls again for a while, then sat down and dozed, then walked some more. It seemed to me that something like ten hours passed, when I thought I heard a distant voice. I closed my eyes, waiting for the light to come on and another meal to be delivered, but nothing happened. I opened them again, and looked around the room, scolding myself for imagining things.

Beginning to feel really hungry, I stood by the door, listening for any activity. Trying not to make a sound, not even breathing, I strained my ears for the slightest murmur, but heard nothing. I let out my breath in a fierce puff, then sat down again and waited.

I may have nodded off again, I can't be sure, but it suddenly seemed to me that the air in the room seemed to move, a gentle, warm breeze against my skin, and I heard that faint voice again, saying my name.

"Who's there?" I demanded.

"*It's me, Bell*," came the voice.

"Joey? But you're dead."

"*I know, funny, innit? I've come to help - go and check the door.*"

I did as he said, but heard no sound from outside. Nervously I hammered on the wood with my fist. "Hey! Anyone going to feed this little goldmine, or are you going to let me waste away?" There was no response.

I pushed and pulled at the handle again, to see if the door would move. It was still just as solid as the previous time, but the lock and handle were very old, and seemed quite slack.

"*They've gone out, Bell. This is your chance to escape.*"

"Oh sure. You didn't happen to see where they put the key, did you?"

"*Very witty. You'll have to break the lock.*"

I cast around in the semi-darkness for a way to get the door open, but there were no tools in the room, nothing but the table and two chairs - old, heavy wooden chairs with curved, slatted backs. Heavy enough to break a lock? I picked up one and, holding it by two of its legs, raised it above my head and smashed it down on the floor, seeing the back splinter satisfyingly and fly off, leaving just the heavy seat attached to the legs.

At the door, I lifted it aloft again and swung it in an arc to crash down on the doorknob. Again and again I bashed at it, sweating and swearing with the effort, each time weakening it a little more. One leg snapped off the chair, so I changed my grip and kept hammering.

When a second leg came away, I put the battered remains down and tried the door again - it was definitely loose. I threw my shoulder against it. People did that in the films and the door always splintered and flew open, but not my door, all I managed to do was hurt my arm. "Silly cow!" I thought. "It opens inwards." I pulled at the handle, now hanging loosely, and felt the door move a little. "There must be something I can use as a lever," I thought, scanning the empty room.

"*Look up,*" Joey whispered in my ear.

I looked up. Screwed to the back of the door was a metal coat hook. I swung at it with one of the broken chair legs, and it flew off. Grinning happily, I picked it up and inserted it into the gap that had opened between the door and frame, pulling with all my strength. Suddenly the door flew open; I stumbled backwards and fell on the floor.

-♪-

There was no time to lose; they could appear any minute, and it would be bad for me if they found me now. Jumping back to my feet, I ran through the opening into the next room. In the dim light from an open hatch at the far end, I could see that it was packed with boxes, crates and barrels, and I recognised it at once. "It's the cellar of the Bricklayers," I said out loud, triumphantly. I was on familiar ground.

Running past the mass of kegs and pipes and up the stone steps, I reached ground level in seconds and paused to listen for any activity. The place was silent. I turned towards the front door to make good my escape, but stopped, a thought pricking the back of my mind; there was something I wanted to do first. I headed in the opposite direction, up the stairs towards the flat.

As I hoped, it was deserted. Anxiously, I headed towards the bedroom and lifted the mattress on the filthy double bed upon which Burroughs had relieved his sexual desires so many times on my unfeeling, unresponsive body. Shaking off the unpleasant memory, I groped underneath. It was still there, a fat pillowcase, which I knew held Gary's illegal stash.

I hauled it out onto the floor, then grabbed my battered

suitcase from the top of the wardrobe and tipped the mass of notes into it, spilling some over the sides, there was so much, pushing it down tight until the little case was bulging. As I snapped it shut I looked around the room with a surge of exhilaration at my newly acquired power, to see if there was anything else I could do. My eyes took in the peeling paper, the damp patches, the stained rugs - what a dump! How had I sunk so low? Suddenly a sense of rage rose inside me against the man who had so debased me. I wanted revenge.

I went back to the wardrobe and lifted the loose panel that I knew lay in the bottom of it, under a pile of smelly shoes. There, in the hollow of the base, was a plastic bag containing his stock of drugs - folded paper packets of cocaine, pouches of cannabis, syringes and phials of substances I didn't even know the names of. All the filth in which he had become a dealer.

Seeing that stuff for the first time since my last shot, my stomach lurched, and I suddenly realised how vulnerable I still was. Oliver had given me a precious finger-hold on sanity, but when I saw those drugs, my addiction kicked in again and I felt a craving rise up instantly in my chest. My hands shaking, I carried the bag into the bathroom and, with an effort of will, emptied its contents into the toilet, feeling a surge of pleasure. "Take that, you bastard," I muttered as I flushed it away.

Back in the bedroom, I took my favourite red coat from the wardrobe, picked up my suitcase and, pausing only to stuff a handful of loose notes into my pockets, ran down the stairs and opened the front door.

There I paused my flight for a quick peek up and down

the road, to make sure no-one was approaching. The heavy shadows on the houses opposite showed me that the sun was still low behind me, in the east - it was not as late as I had thought. With a shock I realised that Burroughs and his thug could simply have been asleep when I smashed my way out of the cellar, and would have been rather upset at my actions; they would have killed me, of that I was sure. Well, they weren't asleep, they weren't even in the building. I couldn't guess where they were, nor did I care, as long as they weren't where I was.

"*Joey?*" I asked, tentatively. There was no reply. Wherever he was, he had decided I was doing ok on my own.

The street was deserted. With no further hesitation, I ran down Nelson Road towards the town centre, the railway station, and a new life.

~10~
October 1961
The Lion In Winter

Great Yarmouth railway station echoed with memories as I arrived and walked towards the ticket office. This time, the gates were open and the entrance thronged with busy humanity, but my mind was filled with images of a dark night and a little man who became my brother. I paused in the doorway where, a year earlier, I had met a heap of boxes and been sick after drinking my first whisky. Pensively, I looked left at the doorway where I had slept for six months and found my other half.

Glancing over my shoulder, still apprehensive that Burroughs would appear in hot pursuit, I hurried to the ticket desk, pulling a pound note from my coat pocket to pay my fare to Norwich. Minutes later, two shillings poorer and clutching my ticket, I stood on the platform, waiting for the train to arrive. I still couldn't believe that I had made it, and half expected Gary and his thugs to leap from hiding and carry me back into captivity, or death. Suddenly fearful, I pressed myself into the wall, trying to become invisible.

But only the train arrived, air-brakes hissing, diesel engine throbbing, the warm, chemical smell of burnt fuel and hot oil surrounding it like a cloak as it waited to retrace its magical silver trail to the city. Soon I was seated in emerald green plush, in my best red coat and Oliver's jeans, staring nervously at the station entrance, watching every face that appeared.

After what seemed hours, I felt a throbbing through my feet as the great engine revved up, then the carriage gave a slight jerk as we began moving. The station buildings slipped by, and the great lake that was Breydon Water drifted into view, declaring the outskirts of Great Yarmouth and the start of open countryside; the marshes and windmills of Norfolk painting a scene of ancient rural tranquillity, in stark contrast to the nightmare I was escaping. I laughed gaily - I was free, I had more cash than I had ever owned in my entire life, and I was embarking on a new life, a fresh start.

-♪-

After a little while, the swaying of the carriage induced a more introspective mood, and I thought again about Oliver. What had happened to him? I tried to reach out my mind to him - calling his name silently - but nothing came back, not even an echo of my own thought. Through the window, the streams and marshes and flat fields of Norfolk slipped past like a parade, accompanied by the rhythmic, clockwork sound of the wheels on the tracks, adding more miles between us. I tried Joey, maybe he could find out for me, but he wasn't there either.

In half an hour, Norwich station arrived like a surprise guest at a party, and everyone spilled from the doors of the train onto the platform. I was carried out on the surge, then stood entranced, turning left and right to take it all in, jostled by angry travellers who grumbled as they pushed past this stupid girl who was daydreaming in their way. There were six platforms - six! Most were bustling with activity - men cleaning and oiling the enormous green, red and black engines, families and business people walking or running to get into or out of the carriages, carrying suitcases or briefcases, talking, laughing, frowning. It was a carnival of colour and noise that filled me with excitement.

-♪-

To a simple provincial girl, who had only ever known a small coastal town, Norwich assaulted the senses with noise, activity and sheer size. I emerged from the railway station, blinking in the bright, late-afternoon sunlight, carrying no possessions except my brown suitcase stuffed with money. Only my money! I smiled at the thought. I was rich enough to do almost anything I liked, buy anything I needed.

The station nestled in a junction of two busy roads, controlled by traffic lights, beside a river. Beyond the rooftops, a square castle stood at the top of a hill. A hill! There were no hills in Great Yarmouth, where the land seemed to emerge from the sea just enough to keep its feet dry, then was too tired to rise any further. Once again, people barged into me, as I stopped, blocking the station doorway, taking in the unfamiliar scenery, uncertain which direction to take.

The train ride had given me time to think and plan. First I needed something to eat - my last meal had consisted of bread and cold tea, and that had been about fifteen hours ago. Following the finger of the river as it pointed away to my right, I saw an elegant spire rise high above the trees and chimneys. And there, in my line of sight, was the illuminated sign of a café; my tummy rumbled, and in my pocket, my spending cash called out to me.

-♪-

After a wonderful dinner of roast beef with vegetables and thick gravy, followed by golden syrup sponge and custard, I felt ready to face my next challenge, finding somewhere to live. Back at the crossroads, I picked a direction at random and strode out with confidence, over the bridge that crossed the river by the traffic lights, and up the long hill towards the castle tower.

As I walked, looking into shop windows with curiosity, and constantly watchful for any notices declaring "Room to let", my practised eye also sought out doorways and alleys where a homeless person might sleep. It was a habit that remains with me to this day; my subconscious cannot accept that I am secure now, will never need to seek shelter. When you know where to look, and how to look, the homeless are everywhere. I saw many, but, aware of my vulnerability, did not approach anyone, did not need to, did not want to. For here, in this bustling, imposing city, I would begin my new life - never would I return to the streets.

-♪-

The gentle rise of the road levelled off, and I realised that I had been walking with my eyes downcast for some distance. I paused to look around me, and now found that

I was standing at a broad, busy road junction, at the foot of a large mound. Squatting on the top of the mound, the massive stone cube of Norwich castle lowered over its protectorate.

Beside me was a handsome grey stone building, with pretentious columns rising in pairs on either side of a rank of five stone steps. A balustrade sat across the top of the columns and, above that, the wall rose to an enormous triangle-shaped carving, like the peak of a roof, with a great stone garland hanging in a loop attached to each end of its base. The words 'Post Office' were carved in the stone below it.

Here was a way to remove one worry: I still had my Post Office Savings book - I would deposit my cash where it could wait safely until I needed it, earning some interest in the meantime. The decision made, I mounted the steps leading to the front doors, which were open, and emerged into a hall that could have been a palace ballroom. The wide polished floor and high, domed ceiling, created an echo, so that voices and footsteps resounded into every corner. All around the walls, arched windows, set in alcoves, cast shafts of sunlight sparkling with dust particles.

I felt very small as I took my case to a cashier and presented it with my account book.

She opened the case and stared in amazement at the mess of notes inside. "Do you expect me to count these?" she asked in a thin voice, glowering at me over her spectacles, her mouth pinched tightly into a pale slit beneath her razor-sharp nose.

"Yes please," I said, levelly. I could see her mind

working furiously - Who was this child? How did she get so much cash?

She snorted and angrily banged a "Position Closed" sign in front of me, then took the case to a desk at the rear of the room. I watched as she emptied all the notes out, her lips pursed, and began to rummage through them, sorting them into piles by denomination - brown ten shilling notes, green pound notes, and blue fivers. Several times she glared suspiciously in my direction as she worked.

Eventually the notes were all sorted, and she quickly counted them, listing the total values of each pile on a piece of paper. Instead of returning to me when she finished, however, she crossed to a large, red-faced man who sat at another desk, beneath one of the great arched windows that ran all around the huge hall.

She showed him the paper, her mouth moving. They both looked over at me. I smiled and waved, trying to appear nonchalant, whereas really my insides were tied in knots.

He stood, ponderously, towering above the little woman, and together they approached me. He was dressed formally in a black suit and waistcoat. His shoes gleamed like polished coal. Miss Pinchmouth removed the "Position Closed" sign and they both studied me minutely. I felt like an ape at the zoo.

"Is this money yours?" the man asked asked in a nasal drone, his fat jowls bouncing like balloons over his several chins. Pompous arse!

"Yes, thank you." I was becoming wary, and ventured no more information. I was terrified that I would give away something that would get me into trouble, yet, at the same time, I was becoming angry at their supercilious attitude.

"May I ask how it came into your possession?"

Who the hell did he think he was? '*Joey, tell me what to say,*' I said silently.

It was as though he was standing beside me, giving me confidence, whispering in my ear, prompting me.

"*Tell 'em your a bank robber.*"

"From robbing banks," I retorted, crisply. "I'm the notorious gangster Bonnie Parker, my partner Clyde is waiting outside in the getaway car."

I had found a comic book about them in a rubbish bin in Great Yarmouth market square earlier in the year, and had read the story to Joey, who had never learnt to read.

"The trouble is, see, I still can't get the hang of this bank robbing thing, and I keep paying it in instead of taking it out." I smiled again, sweetly.

His face twisted and he made a sound like 'harumph'. "There is no call to be rude and flippant, young lady. We are naturally puzzled that anyone would arrive here with a suitcase full of money, especially someone so young."

'*Say nothing,*' whispered Joey. I folded my arms across my chest and looked squarely at the man (who I guessed must be a manager) not saying another word.

"Well," he demanded, "what have you to say?"

'F*ight back, they can't hurt you. It's your money, not theirs.*'

"I tell you what," I said, raising my voice, "give me back my money and I'll take it to a bank. I'm sure they will be glad to have it."

They didn't move, but people had started to look across at us, and they were clearly disconcerted.

"Come on," I said, even louder, hearing my voice echo around the hall. "Are you going to give me back my money, or do I have to call for a policeman?"

All around the hall, heads turned curiously at this, and Mr Manager and Miss Pinchmouth squirmed with embarrassment.

"Hurry up," I said, looking up at the huge clock that hung over the counter, "the banks will be closing soon."

After a quick conference, the manager told his clerk to accept the money, then he departed without a further look in my direction, his shiny shoes clicking on the shiny floor, until he disappeared through a door at the far corner of the office.

Miss Pinchmouth, also refusing to look at me, copied the total figure from her sheet of paper into my passbook, and onto her transaction form, sealing the matter with two vigorous thuds from her official metal stamp. Her face was a frozen mask as she handed the book back, with eyes that almost emitted laser, beams like Superman, frying me on the spot.

I knew I had won, and it felt good. I took the little book, smiled, thanked her, turned and walked back to the doors, my heart thumping loudly in my chest, the sound of my own shoes making a clock-like rhythm on the parquet floor.

'*Thanks, Joey,*' I whispered.

'*It was a pleasure, Bell,*' came the reply.

-♪-

Back outside, I set off along a road that looped clockwise around the base of the castle mound. I could feel its weight, its mass looming above me. I stopped beside a gate, beyond which I could see a path winding up the steep slope. Viewed from this position, the grey stone edifice of the castle, with its battlements and slits, looked all the more imposing. I could imagine an attacking army standing where I had paused, looking up at the tower and wondering if they really wanted to storm up that hill, knowing they would be pelted with all manner of sharp projectiles by the defenders, who themselves were hiding safe behind their walls.

As the castle fell behind me, the road meandered away from the city centre and into a more residential area, with houses, shops and cafés lining the pavement. This part of town had a different feel about it - the noise was not the drone of traffic but the buzz of voices talking and shouting, babies crying, somebody singing a tune I didn't recognise. Then, at last, as the sun sank ever lower, I saw what I had been looking for - and had begun to doubt that I would find - a handwritten notice in the door of a public house that declared: "Bedsit to let".

As I pushed open the door and entered the poorly-lit bar, I saw heads turn and disinterestedly observe me through a cloud of cigarette smoke. My shoes stuck to the dirty floor as I walked nervously between the tables, my eyes took in the grubby walls and the yellow, smoke-stained ceiling - it was a dump.

If there had been a choice of places for me to stay, then I would have turned and walked out, and possibly altered the whole direction of my life.

I remembered another moment of decision, ten years earlier, when I had elected to stay with Gran instead of moving in with the Macintoshes; my choice then had not been in my own best interest but, despite the hardships that followed, I remain certain today that it was the right thing to do. In 1961, however, there was really no choice: if I didn't get a room in that pub, then it was a night on the streets that awaited me.

I strode to the bar, trying to assume an air of nonchalant confidence that belied my shaking legs. A young woman insolently ignored me for as long as she deemed expedient, then dragged herself away from a magazine she was reading, and approached me. "Yeah? What you want?" she muttered without removing the cigarette from her mouth.

"I've come about the bedsit that's advertised." I aimed my thumb over my shoulder, towards the entrance, indicating the sign taped there.

Wordlessly, she turned and shuffled to an open door behind the bar. "Steve, someone here wants the upstairs room," she shouted. Then, without even a look in my direction, she returned to her magazine. My experienced eyes scanned the counter top, it was covered with cigarette ash and glass stains, and there were glasses piled in a sink waiting to be washed. This Steve had a staffing problem.

-♪-

While I waited, I looked around the small public bar. The walls were painted a dark brown or maroon, but were hardly visible, festooned as they were with photos, letters and postcards. The few patrons had returned to their beers and their newspapers. There was no conversation.

A man emerged from a door at the end of the bar. He was dressed casually, but the clothes were clean and of good quality: a striped shirt, the sleeves rolled up, was tucked into neatly-ironed brown trousers. He looked to be in his forties, with a tanned and lined face. His hair was already thinning, but was cut in a way that suited him.

He studied my face before speaking. "Marlene says you're interested in the bedsit." His voice was deep and rich, with an accent I couldn't place.

"Yes, I just arrived in Norwich."

"It's four quid a week, can you afford that?"

"Oh yes. Can I look at it?"

"Sure." He lifted a flap in the bar to let me through then, with a glance at Marlene, who was too interested in her book to notice, led me through into a hallway, with one other door off and a flight of stairs. "It's on the top floor," he said over his shoulder as we climbed the first flight.

"That's fine," I replied, taking in the threadbare carpets and grubby, peeling walls.

We reached the top, where there was a small landing with one door at each end. He selected the left door, produced a key, and unlocked it.

I don't know what I was expecting to see, but as we

stepped through into a large room with sloping ceiling, I gasped.

Dust swirled in shafts of hazy, late afternoon sunlight that sliced the dingy room from two grimy windows, like spotlights, illuminating a bare bed, an assortment of rickety furniture and, in one corner, a gas cooker. It was dirty, dusty, smelt of stale tobacco and something worse. I loved it at first sight.

"I'll take it," I whispered.

"Ok. I want a week's rent, plus a week as security. Rent is due every Friday; if you are a day late, I throw your stuff out on the street. Got that?"

"Yes," I said timidly. He was such an imposing character that I felt ... not scared, but dominated - no, overawed - by him.

He saw that I was taken aback. "What's your name, kid?"

I pulled myself up to my full five feet three inches and looked up at him defiantly.

"I'm not a kid, mister. I may be young, but I'm no child. My name is Belinda Bellini."

"Sorry, Belinda." He seemed to mean it. "How old are you?"

"Seventeen," I lied.

He eyed me, doubtfully. "Fair enough. I didn't mean to be rough on you. It's just that some folks try to take liberties with me, and I won't stand for it." He stuck out a hairy hand. "Steve Flock, pleased to meet you."

I took the offered hand, feeling my own tiny fingers gently being squeezed in his firm grip. When he released my hand, I shook it ruefully, then fished in my pocket and counted out eight pounds.

"You got any bedlinen in that?" he asked as he took the money, nodding towards my battered suitcase which I had set down at the door.

I didn't tell him it was empty. "No, I only arrived in the city today."

What a strange new word it was, casually passing my lips: *city*. I knew that London and Paris were cities, but I had never set foot in one before. Again I felt that thrill, a combination of excitement and fear at the adventure upon which I was embarked.

"I am looking for work as a singer," I added. Then, as an afterthought, "Or a barmaid."

Unexpectedly, his face cracked into a broad smile. "A singer? My wife will be glad to meet you, she's a great singer." As he spoke, I saw something dawn on him. "Bellini? Are you Italian?"

"My father was Italian, he was a prisoner of war," I said pensively. "But he went back to Italy when the war was over. His name was Paolo Bellini."

"But, that means you are like family, Belinda. That makes all the difference. Come and meet Dolly, and we will sort out some sheets and blankets for you."

-♪-

Dolly Flock squealed with delight when Steve introduced us. "What a beautiful Italian girl," she effused. "Look at your hair! My goodness, Steve, she is such a treasure. Come in the kitchen, Belinda, and tell me about yourself. Are you hungry. You must be. I'll make you a sandwich.

There's some cold beef. No, it's no trouble. Can't have my pretty new friend going hungry." The barrage was relentless, accompanied by bustling activity around the kitchen.

Smiling, Steve headed back into the bar, while Dolly had me sit at the kitchen table while she made my tea, still chattering incessantly. She was slim, with thick, black hair, tied up in a bun. Within half an hour, I knew the story of her life. I discovered that she was well known around Norwich, and further afield, for her singing, and that they called her Dolly because most English people couldn't pronounce her real name, which was Addolorata ... "Add-ol-o-ra-ta," she carefully enunciated for me. She and Steve had been married for six years, but had no children. For a moment, she looked sad, but immediately changed the subject.

"So," she said, "tell me how this young lady came to arrive alone in Norwich."

"Dolly, it's complicated; forgive me if I don't tell you everything. There are parts of my life that are painful to recall."

She put a cup of tea and a plate of sandwiches in front of me, then sat opposite with hers.

"Belinda, dear, you tell me just as much or as little as you feel comfortable with. You'll find that we have quite a lot of guests passing through, and many of them have doubtful pasts. We don't ask questions. Everyone has their special reason for being where they are in their life."

"The thing is," I continued carefully, unsure quite how to explain it. "I ran away from someone who was brutal to me, and now I'm homeless. I have money; I ..." I hesitated. Did I need to tell her? Actually, it was a relief to let it out, to share it with someone, and I felt safe with Dolly. "Well," I resumed, "he exploited me for over a year, so the last thing I did when I left was to steal his money."

She laughed loudly. "Good for you, girl. Well, look, you don't need to worry, you are among friends now. You probably don't know it, but there are many Italian families settled here in Norwich, and we will take good care of you. Now, is it right you can sing?"

"Oh yes, I love to sing."

"Wonderful, it's ages since I shared a song with another woman. Come on down to the bar, and I'll get Steve to accompany us on the piano. He's not the best, but he can keep time."

-♪-

Not since the innocent days of my childhood with Gran had I felt so secure. Steve and Dolly took me into their hearts and introduced me to the huge community of Italian expats in Norwich, and they welcomed me like a long-lost daughter. I cleaned up my room and feminised it with nice curtains and new bed linen. Cleaning the cooker was a mammoth task, occupying a whole day, but when it was done, it looked like new. Well, nearly.

When my memories escaped from their box and invaded my consciousness, dragging me back down into the past, the view from my windows lifted my heart again. From my position, high up under the roof, I could see right across the river to the railway station, and beyond that to the high ground on the far side of the river basin. Nearby I saw the roof and floodlights of Carrow Road, the home of Norwich's football team.

The months passed, winter closed its icy cloak over my world. Christmas arrived and, once enjoyed, departed. The love of my new family wrapped around me like a warm blanket, encouraging and protecting me, so that I began to believe in myself again. Nobody ever again called me that horrible name, the one from my childhood.

Steve took me on to replace the lazy Marlene as barmaid, and I worked every day from opening time until the evening staff took over. After paying my rent, and buying food - both of which I insisted on doing, even though Dolly tried to insist that I should not - I still had a good amount left from my wages each week to add to my Post Office savings.

I carefully put ten pounds into an envelope and posted it to The Reverend Potter, to pay for another year for Joey's grave. Somehow, it was important to me that I used my own, honest wages, and not any of the dirty money I had taken from Burroughs.

Then, in the evenings, I sang - sometimes with Dolly, sometimes alone, and sometimes with other singers and musicians who were part of Dolly's entourage. Singers like George Keeble, who often sang with Dolly, Maggie Lopez, legendary blues artist, and other regulars like Joe Banks, awesome boogie-woogie pianist.

We performed jazz and blues numbers for an appreciative audience, and I found I was building a following of my own. I was also learning about the technicalities of musical notation, rhythms, styles and the jargon that musicians used. It was here that my unpolished talent became a glittering diamond.

As more people heard me singing at Dolly's, I also started to receive bookings from other venues - jazz clubs, folk clubs, theatres and dance halls all over Norwich. My reputation was growing, and when Norwich City Football Club won the League Cup, I was chosen to sing with the Barry Spence orchestra at the celebratory dinner.

-♪-

Barry picked me for the gig himself. Dolly had told him about me, and he had been to *The Lion In Winter* to see me perform several times.

I rehearsed with the band intensively for a week. It was not that I didn't know the songs - most of them were already locked in my memory - but that I had to learn their arrangements, when to step forward to the centre microphone, when to join the other girls for harmonies, and when to raise my hands to encourage the audience to join in by clapping to the rhythm. There were a few I had not heard before, but with my gift of remembering new things at the first hearing, and my newly-acquired musical knowledge, they presented no problems. I was confident that I would not let the band down.

On the day of the show, I found myself with butterflies for the first time. This was the biggest performance of my life, performing to nearly twenty thousand football supporters at their Carrow Road stadium, and with a full orchestra behind me. A gigantic platform had been erected at the edge of the pitch, open on all sides, but covered against any possible rain, with a roof that looked like an enormous parasol. Thankfully, the weather, though chilly, stayed dry, and the sky remained clear.

Early that afternoon, the musicians carried their equipment through the players' entrance out onto the pitch, and set them up on the stage. Then we all departed for the pub to wait for the performance.

At dusk, we filed out onto the stage, and I stared with awe at the swaying sea of heads all around. There was a continual hubbub from the excited fans, standing on the pitch or sitting in the terraces, all proudly wearing their Norwich City shirts or scarves in the team colours of yellow and green.

At the appointed time for the show to begin, the floodlights around the ground were switched on, bathing the crowd in an eerie yellow glow. George Swindin, the manager of the football team, and Ron Ashman, their captain, climbed the steps onto the stage, holding the trophy high in the air, to the delight of the crowd, who roared and whistled and clapped enthusiastically - the noise was like the thunder of the enormous Royal Air Force Vulcan jet bomber that had once flown over Great Yarmouth.

After the hubbub had subsided a little, the manager stepped up to the microphone. Even with the power of the public address system, it was hard to hear what he said.

"..... without you. Sorry we couldn't get to the first division this year, but we will do it next year." Again, uproar exploded from the massed fans, and it was several minutes before they had settled enough for him to continue. "Ladies and gentlemen, we hope you had a great party this afternoon. The enjoyment continues now with our evening show, featuring the top-class local Barry Spence Orchestra, with the beautiful voice of Belinda Bellini."

He rejoined the captain and once more they held aloft the gleaming cup, to more ear-splitting adoration, before trotting off stage.

And I was on, waving to the crowd, then singing first the Canaries' anthem, "On The Ball, City." I could not hear my own voice, and neither could anyone else, because the fans sang along at full volume. It was an amazing experience that helped to relax me for the remainder of the show. After that, we worked through our planned set, ending two hours later with a deafening repeat of the club's anthem.

-♪-

When the show was over, Barry escorted me back to *The Lion In Winter*, my diminutive five feet two inches making me look like an elf beside his towering six feet four. I had grown to like Barry immensely. I wasn't attracted to him, although if he had been younger I might have been, but I respected him for his caring nature, which balanced perfectly his total professionalism. No matter how much the members of his band bitched about each other and squabbled, as they did frequently, no-one ever said a bad word about their leader - they all loved him.

Barry was quiet for a while, and I began to worry that something was bothering him. I studied his face; from my position, ten inches below his chin, it was like looking up at Gulliver. His craggy face was set in a frown, with furrows between his eyebrows and his top lip drawn into his mouth. He noticed that I was observing him.

"Belinda, that was a good performance today, as good as anyone I have worked with, and that includes many top recording stars. I would like very much if you would consider joining us full time." I went to speak, but he continued quickly: "You would have a proper contract, and a salary, a good salary."

I thought about it very carefully. It was a wonderful offer - regular income and the prestige of working with one of the country's top bands, but ...

"Barry, I doubt I will ever get a better offer, thanks for asking me. But the fact is, and I can't really explain this, I need to make it on my own."

"I understand, Belinda, and I respect you for it." He put an arm round my shoulders. "For what it's worth, I believe in you, I'm sure you will be a big success."

"It's scary, though," I said, resting my head on his arm. "Here I am turning down a good, secure job for the sake of what ... pride?"

"It's not pride, and it's more than ambition. I can see in you something that has driven me since I was in short trousers - a deep love of music and a need to share that love. Am I right?"

"That's part of it, but there's more. Whenever I have relied on other people, they have either left me or misused me. I don't trust anyone any more, not even someone as good as you, Barry. So, to protect myself, I need to be in control."

"Well, I'll always be here if you need me, and I really mean that. Ok, one more question, will you join us for the tour?"

"I will have to ask Steve and Dolly, but if they don't mind giving me the time off, yes, I would love to."

-♪-

Three weeks later, with the blessing of my new family, I set off in a coach filled with sixteen men and only two women, on a three month tour of the United Kingdom. We played thirty-two venues, sometimes arriving within an hour or two of curtain-up. It was gruelling, exhausting and exhilarating, the best experience a young singer could have. I learned to deal with the bitching and whining, to cover up when someone boobed, to change into my stage gear while holding up a sheet to protect my modesty, and to carry on singing when a fight broke out in the audience (oh yes, it happened).

At the end of the tour, I slept for a week, but I will never forget that experience - though I did not realise it at the time, it was a lesson that prepared me for the future.

~11~
June 1962
Romance

As spring lifted its daffodil yellow face to the sun, and sparrows began checking out nesting sites, romance unexpectedly arrived in my life.

It happened during the evening of my eighteenth birthday - ok, my sixteenth, but, as far as the world was concerned, I was eighteen. I needed to be eighteen, the age of consent, voting age, drinking age. I hated deceiving my new friends, my family, but I had to become an adult.

That day was celebrated with joy by my new family, and culminated in a musical jam session I shall remember forever. Every evening at *The Lion In Winter* was filled with music, but on May eleventh, nineteen sixty-two, we raised the roof.

The place was packed with all the regulars, and the visitors who passed through - the awesome Mel Jones, the enigmatic Phil Switch, the delightful Magdalena Esposito, too many even to count as they arrived, drank, sang and left again.

As the evening progressed in wild party mood, and I alternated between singing on the little stage and helping Steve at the busy bar, I noticed a young man staring at me. He was about seventeen, I guessed, with short, dark hair and a face like a baby. I stuck my tongue out at him, and he responded in kind, making me laugh, and he smiled. After a while, I saw him leave.

Half an hour later, however, he returned, pushed through the crowd to the bar and nervously handed me a bunch of flowers, to raucous cheers from the patrons. Embarrassed, I shyly accepted them.

"What are these for?" I shouted above the noise.

He squirmed nervously, struggling to find the tongue that had earlier poked easily from his lips, and eventually stammering: "Because I like you very much, and ... er... I want to ask you to go out with me."

"What, now?" I couldn't resist teasing him.

"Pardon?" he shouted.

"You want to take me out now?"

He coloured up. "Oh no, no, no. One day when you are free. Perhaps we could go to the pictures ... er, if you like ... or, er ..." He trailed off, his face a picture of uncertainty. Suddenly, he remembered something. "Oh, my name is ... erm ... Luke."

"Are you sure?" I teased.

"Oh yes, definitely, Luke, yes. Luke Fisher"

Poor boy, I was being cruel. I gave him a smile. "Thanks, Luke, I would love to have a date with you. Come round in the morning, when it's quieter, and we can fix up something. Now let me put these lovely flowers in water, then I have a hundred customers to serve."

-♪-

The next day, when Luke came to see me, I told him I didn't want to go to the cinema for our first date. "Let's go to Chappelfield Gardens, instead," I suggested.

He looked disappointed. "But I wanted to treat you to an evening out."

"We can't get to know each other properly with a film blasting away. And I don't want you spending money on me - for one thing, it doesn't impress me." I didn't tell him the other reason, the one that really bothered me, the thought of being bought. "We can get fish and chips, then sit in the park and eat them."

So that afternoon, we met in the public gardens at Chappelfield. It was a smouldering summer's day, the air was still and heavy, people were waving newspapers in front of their faces - not for the English the practicality of a fan. We sat on a shaded bench beside the bandstand, empty and silent that day, like a wedding cake without those little figures of the bride and groom on top.

Luke was ill at ease, unsure whether to behave as a gentleman or as a wild suitor, and lacking experience in either role. Taller than me by a clear head, thin as a broom handle, with neatly cut red-brown hair, he looked to me like an undertaker in his black suit and polished shoes.

Nervously, he lit a cigarette and offered me one. I shook my head.

"No thanks, but it's ok if you do."

He lit it, then sat staring at the red glow.

"Have you had many girlfriends?" I asked, to break the uncomfortable silence.

"Oh yes, loads," he answered, too quickly.

I waited for more, but realised there was none.

"I brought a picnic," I said brightly, indicating the basket that Dolly had helped me to fill. "Would you like to eat now? We could sit under a tree in the shade."

He nodded, and helped me to lay out the blanket on the grass. I started to remove the various treats from within, rather like a magician producing objects from a top hat. My silly sense of humour made me giggle when I imagined myself, as the finale, lifting a table and chairs out of the little basket. He asked what had made me laugh, and I explained my random thought, but he seemed unable to appreciate the humour of it.

The meal proceeded painfully, awkward silences punctuated with brief exchanges:

"Would you like a sausage roll?"

"Yes please."

"Thank you."

"Will you pass the sauce, please."

"Certainly."

"Thank you."

The sandwiches vanished, the lemonade slowly descended in the bottle

After a while I found a slightly more successful line of conversation:

"Tell me about your family."

"Oh yes. Well, it's just my mum, my sister and me. My dad was killed in an accident at work. He was a farm labourer and died when he was crushed in a machine. After that, we were thrown out of the tied house, and Mum brought us into Norwich to get a council flat."

"Do you have a job?"

"I'm an apprentice at the Caley chocolate factory."

"That sounds interesting." (*Talk, for goodness sake!*)

"No, it's boring. All I do is make tea for the engineers. I

go to college three days a week, except I don't go, I bunk off." He paused, and I sensed he was waiting for me to make some comment. I refrained.

After more uncomfortable silence, I asked if he wanted any more to eat or drink.

"No thank you," he replied, formally.

Tired of trying to start some kind of meaningful conversation, I said, rather more acidly than I intended: "Help me to pack this stuff back in the basket, then."

That done, he walked me back to the pub. I hoped he would hold my hand, but he shuffled silently beside me, hands in his pockets. When we arrived, I thanked him for the date, and began to push open the door.

"Erm ...," he began, then rushed on, as though afraid he would lose his nerve, "would you like to come and meet my mum and sister? Mum told me to ask you to dinner."

"Thank you," I replied with an amused smile. "That would be nice. When?"

"Sunday."

"Ok, Sunday is my day off, and I don't have any gigs this weekend. What time shall I come round?"

"Mum said twelve o'clock for dinner at one. She said to tell you it's roast beef."

"Thank your mum for me, and say I'll be happy to come."

He smiled, then seemed lost for words again. Unexpectedly, he suddenly leaned toward me. I saw his face looming, and realised he intended to kiss me. I let him, but turned my head so his lips met my cheek.

As he turned to leave I said: "Where am I going for this dinner?"

Once again he was thrown into confusion. "Oh yes, of course. It's Kensington Place, the flats in City Road, number 67, on the top floor."

-♪-

Sunday dinner with Luke's family was a much livelier affair than our date had been.

His mother, Maggie, was chatty and friendly, welcoming me and talking freely. A big table was laid in their living room, covered with a bright cloth and set for five. The fifth place was for Maggie's boyfriend, Graham, a tall, stocky man in his fifties. Luke's sister, Daisy, was also easy to get along with, and dinner proved to be a noisy occasion, with everyone talking at once and food being constantly passed around, or stolen from someone's plate. By the end of it, I felt relaxed and happy.

I helped Maggie and Daisy to clear the table and carry the washing up into the kitchen, while the men went to the pub. When all was done, Daisy asked if I would like to listen to her new Beach Boys LP. I told her I loved music, and we went into her bedroom.

It was a colourful room, with posters of Duane Eddy, Billy Fury and James Dean pinned to the walls. Much giggling ensued as we sang along to the tracks, each with a hairbrush as a microphone. After a few songs, we flopped down on the bed to catch our breath, while we listened to an older album by Buddy Holly and The Crickets.

"So, you and Luke - have you had it yet?" she suddenly asked.

"Had what?"

"Sex, silly!"

"No, of course not," I said, trying to sound shocked.

"Why not, can't he get it up?"

I chuckled. "I've no idea and don't intend to find out."

She stared at me, intently, for a moment.

"You a prude, then?" I was learning that Daisy was outspoken and blunt.

It was my turn to study her. A beautiful mass of hair, red-brown like her brother's but with blonde highlights, tumbled in waves over her shoulders, framing a pretty face with too much make-up. I guessed she must be about eighteen, maybe seventeen, with large, bright eyes that gleamed with a joy of life.

I didn't want to appear naive, but neither did I wish to discuss my experiences while with Burroughs, which would make me seem like a whore. "Nah! But I don't do it with just anyone, I have to fancy them first."

"Don't you fancy Luke?" Still that challenging, probing look.

"No, he's too young." I grinned, remembering that he was actually my age, he just seemed younger.

"What about girls? You ever played with girls?"

That was a shock, and not something I had ever thought about. What's more, she had a searching look to her eyes as she waited for me to answer. To cover my embarrassment, I shook my head and looked away.

"I have," she announced. "It's better than with blokes. Girls know what's good, none of that fumbling and useless groping." She paused, studying me carefully.

"You ever kissed a girl?"

Again I shook my head.

Suddenly, she leaned toward me and kissed me lingeringly on the lips. After a momentary shock, I found myself enjoying it, and I responded, moving my face against hers as our mouths wrapped together.

-♪-

When we finally parted, she stared at my face, which I could feel was flushed. Her own had an amused expression. I couldn't believe how the experience had affected me, and returned her gaze, trying to understand what had just happened.

"Nice?" she asked.

In reply, I draped my arms around her neck and kissed her again. While we were locked together, she gently but firmly pulled me down, so we were lying side by side.

"That's better. You're nice to kiss, you taste like vodka."

I giggled, feeling relaxed, despite also being strongly aroused. A decision made, she sat up and peeled off her tee-shirt, shaking her hair loose, then reached behind her back with both hands and unhooked her bra, proudly releasing her breasts for me to see. I felt my eyes open wide with surprise. Perfectly formed, with brown areola and plump, erect nipples, they were swinging a little as she moved, rising and falling with her breath. I gazed at them hypnotised, then reached up and touched one, curiously, stroking it, my fingers gliding over her nipple. She closed her eyes, an expression of pure pleasure filling her face.

She ran her hand up under my jumper, where she

discovered that I don't wear a bra - I don't need one, nature had not been as generous to me in the boob department as Daisy. She gave a little cry of delight when her hand cupped one of my little gems.

"Belinda, your tits are wonderful! I wish I had smaller ones, these are a damn nuisance most of the time." She grabbed her own, gyrating them as though to ensure I knew what she was talking about. "I can't run without them flying all over the place, and blokes never look at my face when they talk to me, they just stare at my boobs."

Suddenly, she reached over and pulled my jumper up over my head. I raised my arms to help her, feeling slightly shy. But as soon as it was off, and she gazed admiringly at my skinny chest, I began to feel a surge of wantonness flood through my veins. I grabbed her again, pulling her body close to mine so that our breasts were crushed together. My nipples were tingling with excitement, and I could feel myself becoming aroused.

From that moment, passion engulfed both of us, and we writhed together, our hands caressing each other all over. I felt her pulling at the top of my jeans, and I reached down to help, popping the stud and running the zipper quickly down. Then I raised my hips to help her as she pulled them down to my ankles, from where I kicked them into the air. Her own jeans joined them, then our knickers, and we rolled on the bed, naked, kissing and exploring each other.

I felt her hand between my legs, and I opened them to admit her, then gasped with the surge of excitement that made my body shiver.

She taught, and I learnt. I had never been raised to such heights of passion, even when I had played with myself, and certainly never with any man. I returned every touch, every kiss, until eventually we both cried out together as our orgasms pulsed through our bodies and shook them in wild abandon.

-♪-

By the time Graham and Luke returned from the pub, Daisy and I had dressed and rejoined her mother. The three of us sat around the kitchen table, chatting easily, several empty mugs before us measuring the passage of time in cups of tea consumed. We heard the front door shut and the two men drifted into the kitchen unsteadily. Graham plonked himself into the empty chair next to Maggie and leaned forward to kiss her on the cheek. The expression on her face told everything.

Luke staggered over to me and put his hands on my shoulders from behind. "Hello babe, he slurred from somewhere over my right shoulder, with more bravado than he had ever shown when sober.

Then his face suddenly appeared close beside mine and he planted a wet kiss on my cheek. Astonishingly, he then moved his hands from my shoulders to my breasts, and squeezed them. I was on my feet in an instant, turning as I rose, and slapped him hard across his face.

"Don't you ever do that to me again," I shouted, my nose inches from his. I was breathing heavily, anger replacing the feeling of pleasant euphoria that had previously engulfed me.

He stepped back, stunned by the violence of my reaction, unable to speak, his hand rubbing the cheek where a bright red patch was rising. Out of the corner of my eye I could see the other three with various expressions of surprise and amusement. Recovering, Luke took a step toward me, a scowl on his face, his hand rising to retaliate. Not allowing him time to complete the move, I moved closer to him, so that again our faces were only inches apart.

"You're drunk, Luke. You stink of beer. But drunk or sober, no-one is allowed to touch me like that unless I first invite them, have you got that?" I heard my voice falter as I realised the irony in what I had just said, following my earlier romp with his sister. He was blinking furiously, whether it was because I was spitting in his eyes in my fury, or to hold back tears of pain, I could not tell, but he made no further move.

"I said 'HAVE YOU GOT THAT?'," I shouted. He nodded, keeping his head down, and I turned to the two women, ignoring the smirking Graham, who I blamed as much as Luke for getting him that drunk. Tears of anger and embarrassment were by then coursing down my face. "Thank you for the lovely dinner, Maggie, I have to go now."

Daisy was on her feet then, launching her own tirade at her hapless brother: "Cretin!" she shouted. "You've just ruined a lovely day." Then, with hardly a pause, she turned on Graham. "This is all your fault. You know he's not used to drink."

Graham's expression of amusement vanished instantly

from his face, replaced by a scowl. "Shut up, brat, or I'll teach you some manners," he growled, his gravelly voice carrying clearly the threat of his words.

It was Maggie's turn to lift her ample frame from her chair. "That's enough," she said to Graham. "I will not have you threatening my children. I want you to leave my house now, this moment."

"Nothing would make me stay," spat the man, grabbing his jacket from the back of the chair and marching, lurching, to the door.

"And you," she continued, turning to Luke, as we heard the front door slam, "get to your room and stay there."

"Sorry, mam," her son mumbled, dejectedly.

"Don't apologise to me, young man, it's Belinda you should be saying 'sorry' to." She hefted her hands onto her hips and glared at him, meaningfully.

"Sorry, Belinda," he said quietly to me, his chin on his chest.

I had sat down again, my legs were shaking and tears were running down my face. I couldn't speak. I reached out a hand and touched his arm to acknowledge his apology. He patted my hand, then left the room.

Maggie and Daisy both stood up and came to hug me.

"You don't have to go," Maggie said softly. "I'll make us all another cup of tea."

I nodded. "Thanks Maggie. Sorry I reacted like that and caused so much trouble. What about you and Graham?"

"Oh, don't worry about him. We were finished anyway, he was just using me and I was too lazy to dump him. You did me a favour, although I wouldn't mind betting he will be round here tomorrow with a bunch of flowers and wheedle his way back into my life. He knows when he's well off."

We sat, subdued and quiet, drinking our tea, and when it was done, I set off for home. Daisy took me to their front door.

"Come again, Belinda," she whispered. "There's lots more we can do together." She leaned forward and brushed her lips against my cheek, then held my face in her hands and kissed me passionately, her tongue pressing into my mouth. It was over in a second, but left me breathless.

"I'll be back, Daisy," I said hoarsely.

~12~
June 1963
Building a name

"How old are you, Belinda, really?" Dolly propped another plate on the draining board. I picked up a mug and began to dry it.

I didn't answer at once, concentrating on wiping the mug carefully before putting it away in the wall cupboard. She looked over her shoulder at me, and raised her eyebrows, smiling. I knew Dolly would never say or do anything to hurt me, she was special, and I wanted to be honest, but ....

"Eighteen," I lied.

"So, which year were you born?"

I did a quick calculation. "Nineteen forty-four," I said.

"Too slow, my love," she laughed. "I could see you working it out. Let me guess ... nineteen forty-six?"

Sheepishly, I nodded.

"So you're sixteen? When was your birthday?"

"May eleventh. I'm sorry for lying to you, Dolly. It's just that ... I figured, if I keep up the story, everyone will accept it."

"Don't you have your birth certificate?"

I hadn't thought about it. Casting my mind back, I realised I had never seen it. I shook my head.

"I wish you had told me your birthday, I would have loved to give you a party."

I put my arms around her waist from behind and hugged her. "You are just like a mum to me. I love you very much."

She turned in my arms and crossed her own behind my neck, so as to hold me without using her wet hands. "I hope you know how much I love you, too. You are like the daughter I never had."

We stood together like that for a minute, then she kissed my forehead before returning to the dishes.

-♪-

When November approached, I again sent ten pounds to The Reverend Potter. As I stood at the postbox, with my hand in the slot, my fingers still holding the letter, I thought again of that day, when I had looked down at the tiny plot with its wooden cross, and promised Joey a headstone and a proper funeral.

'Are you there, Joey?' I asked, tentatively. He didn't speak, but I knew he heard me.

Was I any closer to keeping my word? Sometimes I thought so, but my plan was big, and there was a long way to go before I could make it a reality.

-♪-

Dolly wanted me to meet some friends who owned a pub near Pottergate, a lovely, old part of Norwich, so we caught a bus from the top of Finklegate, heading for the town centre. I was glad, because it also gave me a good opportunity to visit the music shops in Saint Benedict's Street, which I always enjoy.

We scrambled onto the top deck - well, I scrambled,

Dolly followed at her own pace - and we occupied the front seats.

"His name is Emesto Conti," she resumed when we were seated. "His family has been in Norwich for generations. Avril, his wife, is English, but she can swear in Italian like a native." She stopped as the conductor came to take our fares, then continued: "They have music in the pub every night: popular music, jazz, rock and roll, folk music. They want you to do some sessions."

The bus stopped at the top of Saint Stephen's Street, by the Catholic Cathedral, and most of the passengers on the top deck filed down the stairs. I opened a window to let some of the cigarette smoke out, but froze when I saw a familiar and unwelcome face in the crowd below. Quickly, I sat down again, and slid lower in my seat, peering over the edge of the window.

"What are you doing?" Dolly asked, her voice tinged with amusement. I realised that my action must have looked strange.

"Down there," I replied, pointing. "See that man in the duffel coat, waiting to cross the road?"

She leaned across in front of me to look.

"Yes, what about him?"

I was still staring at him, and when he looked in my direction, I knew I was right. Although I was sure he couldn't possibly see me, sitting on the top deck of the bus, it felt as though he was staring straight at me. It sent a shiver down my spine.

"It's Gary Burroughs," I declared, simply. I heard her inhale sharply.

At that moment, a gap in the traffic allowed him to start

crossing, and I noticed two things simultaneously. The first was that he walked with a limp; gone was the arrogant swagger that typified the man who had abused me so terribly. The second was that he was accompanied by someone I recognised, but couldn't place at first. The face was familiar, but not associated with Burroughs.

"Graham!" I exclaimed, quietly, when I made the connection. Maggie Fisher's boyfriend. But what was he doing, walking with Burroughs?

-♪-

Under Dolly's guidance, I found constant work in and around Norwich. It was exciting for me, to be recognised wherever I went and to receive warm welcomes at all the venues at which I appeared. As a result, I had become reasonably well off, and could afford not only good clothes for day wear, but also dramatic outfits for performing. With Barry's help, I made backing tapes for all my songs, and now employed a 'roadie' to drive me to gigs and set up the complex equipment that now formed part of my act.

But *The Lion In Winter* was still my home, and my little room at the top still my refuge. Each morning when I woke I would stand at my window, dreamily looking across the river to the tree-covered hills beyond; it was the perfect way to start each day. Every time I looked, the view was different. Sometimes a mist would lay on the river, so that only the tops of a few masts, their wet flags hanging limply, were visible above the grey blanket. Other mornings might be crisp with frost or smothered with snow. In the spring of 1963, the valley was thick with every shade of green and peppered with flecks of colour in the gardens and parks.

The weather was balmy that year, and life was good. It had been good for so long that I had almost convinced myself that, this time, it would stay good, that the gods had relented and were allowing me to be happy. Almost.

Even so, when I heard a knock on my door that July morning, and Dolly's voice called my name, I felt my heart jump and my breath catch in my chest. At the back of my mind, I had a constant fear that someone would work out that I was too young to work in the bar, and remained unregistered with the Inland Revenue, so was earning money illegally.

I opened my door. With a tense expression on her face, Dolly asked me to go with her to her flat. Wordlessly we descended the stairs, and when we reached her kitchen, my concern seemed to be well-founded, for there sat two smartly dressed people at her table.

One was a man, about thirty-five or so, plump, but not fat, with neat, receding blonde hair. His companion was a slightly younger woman, also blonde. They stood as I walked in.

"Belinda," Dolly said quietly, "this is Dan Fleet, of Oberon, in London, and his assistant, Jenny Macarthur."

I nodded, nervously, and accepted the offered handshakes. Who was Oberon?

"Hello, Belinda," Dan said in a smooth voice with a faint Scottish accent, as we sat down on the four sides of the wooden table, "Jenny and I have been watching you working."

So I was right. They were from the police, I was a criminal.

"Have you heard of Oberon?" he continued, failing to note the look of panic on my face. He looked more like a banker than a policeman, with his little round spectacles and expensive suit. When I nervously shook my head, he smiled. "Don't look so glum, we have come to make you a proposition that we hope you will like. Oberon is one of the largest entertainment agencies in London. We have many of the top singers and groups on our books, and we want to add you to our stable."

The reversal of events to my expectations was more than my mind could accept, and I sat silently shaking my head in disbelief. Dan misinterpreted the action, thinking I was turning down the offer. He spoke quickly. "I promise you, Belinda, we are a legitimate agency, and you will have a proper contract. Jenny and I have been impressed by your performances and we believe we can help you to build a successful career."

"Belinda," Jenny chipped in as I sat in stunned silence, "you have a rare and special talent. I haven't heard anyone as good as you since I joined the agency last year." She stopped, aware that she was gushing. "Sorry, I bet that sounds false. Honestly, it's not. When Dan sent me out to check out DollyRalph's claims about you, I expected to be as disappointed as I have been on every other trip. But I was so amazed by your voice that I called Dan and asked him to come and hear you."

Dan was nodding. "I trust Jenny's judgement completely, and she is right. You could go right to the top, Belinda, if you want to."

-♪-

I could feel tears pricking the backs of my eyes; this was totally unexpected, too good to be true. I looked at Dolly; she grinned and nodded.

Finally I found my voice. "You phoned them for me?"

"Barry and I agreed. You have what it takes to be a star, if you want it, my darling. Dan and I are old friends, I can promise you he is genuine, and what's more he is a nice guy, he won't try to screw you, in any sense of the word." She grinned, impishly.

I turned back to Dan and Jenny. "Then the answer is 'Yes, please make me a star'."

"Oh, I can't do that, Belinda," Dan said, seriously. "Only you can make it happen. But if you have the talent, and I believe you have it in spades, and if you are prepared to work really hard, then we can help you succeed."

Jenny was beaming. "I'm really glad we found you, and I'm looking forward to working with you."

"So, what happens next?" I asked.

"We will take you to London with us and fix you up with somewhere to stay. Do you have a manager?"

I shook my head. "Should I have one?"

"Well, it will make life much easier for you, especially at the start. But it's good that you don't have anyone right now, because inexperienced managers are one of the curses in our line of work. If you like, I can introduce you to a good man who will steer you safely through."

"What will all this cost me? I know you folks aren't doing this for me out of the goodness of your hearts."

He grinned. "Good girl. Always ask that question. This is a tough business, and it's filled with sharks. Never sign anything without someone you trust watching. And never pay anyone up front, ever. The agency charges you fifteen percent of whatever you earn in a year, and we get you on your feet before we take anything. That means that, in your first year, we pay out for recording studios, advertising agencies, all your tour arrangements, even the clothes you buy, and we don't get a penny until you start to earn. We could pay out half a million pounds in a year and not get anything back. That's why we need to make sure we only pick winners."

"And I'm a winner?"

"Oh yes, my dear, you most certainly are. You could be the best bet we ever made."

-♪-

So, after tearful farewells, I left Dolly and Steve and all my friends and travelled to London with Dan and Jenny in their chauffeur-driven Rolls Royce. I could not bear to think of leaving my little room, so I drew out some cash from the Post Office and paid Steve a whole year's rent to keep it for me.

On the long drive south, Dan and Jenny went through their plan for the first part of my career - songwriters, studios, record companies, publicity, and a tour supporting one of their established stars. By the time we reached the city that they referred to as 'The Smoke', I felt almost like a star already.

If I had thought Norwich huge, there were not words of

a scale to describe London. When Jenny said "This is London, Belinda", I looked out at seemingly endless rows of similar shops and houses on identical roads on both sides of us, dotted with parks and pubs, monuments, railway stations, tube stations and, every few yards, sets of traffic lights.

"How do you find your way around?" I asked. "It all looks the same."

They laughed. "Oh, you get used to it," Jenny smiled. "When we get near the river, it becomes much more interesting."

And so it did. About half an hour after entering the outskirts, we passed the Thames on our left, wide and grey and busy in its own way, with ships and boats of all sizes and a bridge every half mile. I saw places that had only been pictures in books before that day: our driver, Paul, took us past Saint Paul's Cathedral, Tower Bridge, the Tower of London, the Houses of Parliament, and Trafalgar Square, just so I could see them.

Eventually, we pulled up outside an elegant building with the words '*Imperial Hotel*' suspended in large golden letters above the entrance. Paul took my suitcase from the boot and carried it into the building, while I followed with my two new friends.

~13~
August 1963
Down To Business

The next morning, I enjoyed my first ever hotel breakfast, in the dining room of the *Imperial*. When I arrived, I found it large and busy, and I stood bemused in the doorway, uncertain of protocol. A young waiter rescued me.

"You are miss Bellini?" he asked softly. Surprised, I nodded.

"Miss MacArthur of your agency told me to look for you and make sure you have everything you need. My name is Connor." This introduction was delivered in a pleasant Irish lilt, and he had an open smile.

"Thank you, Connor. I'm pleased to see you. I don't know my way around and I'm afraid of making myself look silly."

"Ah, don't you worry about a little ting, I'll take good care of you." Somehow I felt he would.

He guided me through the breakfast routines, and soon I felt relaxed as I tucked into my scrambled eggs.

I was just enjoying a cup of coffee when Connor returned, followed by a plump, balding man in a pinstripe suite and shoes that gleamed in the light from the chandeliers.

"Miss Bellini, this is Mr Parkin, he is also from the agency."

"Good morning Belinda," the man said in a mellow, almost theatrical baritone. "Call me John, please. Dan has asked me to offer my services as your manager."

"Hello John." I waved to the empty seat opposite me. "Would you like a coffee, or anything to eat?"

He nodded to Connor as he took the proffered chair. "A coffee will be fine, thank you."

Connor gave a little bow and departed, returning in a flash with a fresh pot of coffee and another cup and saucer..

"So, John Parkin," I began, trying to sound assured, "I have an agent, why do I need a manager as well?"

He smiled. "Forthright, I like that. I think we will get along really well." He paused, resting his elbows on the table and steepling his hands, with his index fingers raised to his lips. "Well, your agent takes care of the work side of things, arranging tours, recording studios and so on. Incidentally, you will find Oberon is one of the best, and Jenny really knows her stuff. What a manager does is to look after you personally, taking care of your accounts, advising you on contracts, making sure you get paid, paying your bills, keeping the press off your back. Ah, you are smiling. You haven't had the pleasure of meeting reporters yet?"

I shook my head. "I'm just a girl from the country, John, they won't be interested in me."

"Maybe not yet. But it won't be long before you become newsworthy - then they will descend like a plague of locusts."

I studied him over my second cup of coffee. He was handsome enough, but a comfortable life had rounded all his edges and made him look like a turkey ready for the oven. Still, he had steely blue eyes under soft brown brows, and he seemed relaxed and confident. I liked him.

"And what does a manger cost me? I'm already down fifteen percent of my earnings to Oberon, soon I'll be working for nothing."

Again that wry smile. "You could think of it the other way round. A good agent and manager can bring in ten times what you pay them, Belinda, and I am a good manager. Most of my clients pay me ten percent; some like me so much they pay more." He grinned broadly. "But that's voluntary."

I returned his smile. "Well, Mr Parkin, you sold it to me. I don't know a manager from a milkman, but if Dan recommends you, I'm happy to accept his judgement. I guess I just got myself a manager."

-♪-

My next visitor was Jenny. She bustled in shortly after John had left, to talk about material for recording and performing.

"I want to try to get you as many new songs as I can, Belinda. Standards and covers are all very well, but they don't really make you stand out against other singers - you need a few songs to call your own. I have a couple of songwriters on the books who have produced successful material for our other artists. Will you come with me to meet them?"

"Sure. But I get to decide which songs I use, right?"

"Oh yes, always, but I think you will like the work these guys produce. They wrote '*No-one But You*' for Davey Black and '*Another Day*' for The Ambers."

I was familiar with both the tracks, and the artists who had recorded them. I was not impressed. I thought they were banal, commercial songs, knocked out to a formula by cynical writers, and the success of the records was purely down to the talent of the singers. However, I agreed to accompany Jenny to the offices of Stenner and Chambers (who sounded to me more like a firm of solicitors than creative artists) and we hopped into the Limo.

Abe Stenner and Marlon Chambers tried hard to look like trendy musicians, wearing the colourful, tight-fitting fashions of the time, but just managed to look ridiculous and false. Their music was the same, and after an hour, I was bored and had not heard a single song I liked. We left, with Jenny looking at me strangely.

As we stood on the pavement outside, waiting for Paul to return with the car, she asked: "What's wrong, Belinda?"

I was tense. I felt awkward about the way the meeting had gone, and knew I was being picky. But I was angry, too. It was my career, for goodness sake! I was not prepared to risk it by tying in with a couple of idiots like them. Unsure of my ground, I turned the question around. "What did you think of those songs we heard today, Jenny?"

"Well, they were ok, I suppose. Did you really not like any of them?"

"You see? You're being nice, and even then the best you could find to say was 'ok, I suppose.' They were all dreadful, Jenny! There are groups of lads in Norwich writing and performing songs that are a hundred times better than what we just heard."

She shrugged. "Ok, there are other writers we can try, are you up for it?"

"Sure, let's go. Don't get me wrong, Jenny, I'm not being difficult, but I have no time for fakes, and those guys back there have nothing original to offer."

-♪-

From the glamorous, expensive offices of Abe Stenner and Marlon Chambers, we moved to the grubby back rooms of *Groovy Tunes*. Three men - "Hi, I'm Jason," "Hi, I'm sexy," "Hi, I'm pissed - hahaha!" - were trying to outdo each other in looking laid back and Bohemian.

"These guys wrote 'Outa Town' for Jessica Lattice," Jenny had informed me as we pushed open the heavy Victorian doors. *Oh, great,* I thought.

The one called Jason, who seemed to be the only one interested in our presence (the other two had returned to their game of Monopoly), threaded a spool of tape onto a huge Grundig reel-to-reel recorder, while gesturing for us to sit down in two mismatched chairs.

"This one's called 'Make You Mine'", he announced as he pressed [Play] on the machine.

We listened.

When it was finished, Jason clicked [Stop], and Jenny looked expectantly at me. I looked at my feet. There was a long silence.

Eventually I said to Jason: "Jenny tells me you wrote 'Outa Town' for Jessica Lattice. Did you play this one to her?"

"Oh yes." He nodded vigorously.

"What did she think of it?"

He shrugged. "She didn't like it much."

Something about his manner made me persist. "What did she say, precisely?"

"Well, she said 'It's not very good'."

"Were those her exact words?"

"Er, not exactly, no." He was looking very uncomfortable.

"What <u>did</u> she say, exactly?"

After a long pause, he finally said, quietly: "She said it was a total load of fucking shit, actually."

I stood up and glared at him, leaning toward him with my hands on his desk, a tight, satisfied smile on my lips. "So your top recording star, the one who had your only big hit, told you it was a total load of fucking shit, but you thought you could offload it on this green kid from the sticks. Yeah?"

His mouth opened and closed a couple of times, but no sound came out. His hands flapped like a performing seal.

"After all," I continued, "if I flop, it's not your fault, is it? - 'Well, she didn't have the experience, or the fan base. It wasn't the song, it was the singer' - That's what you would say, isn't it? But if my talent turns it into a hit, like Jessica did with 'Outa Town' (which was also a total load of fucking shit, by the way) then you get to bask in my glory. Yes? No way, buster!"

I turned to leave, Jenny rose to follow, and we left without another word.

Paul was waiting outside in the limo. My heart was

thumping, my breathing fast and deep. After a short, silent journey back to my hotel, Jenny and I had a drink in the bar.

"Not a day that could be called a success," she finally said over her Pernod.

I became defensive. "I can't believe those people make a living from that tripe," I declared, then bit back on any further outbursts.

"I didn't mean to sound critical. I'm on your side, honestly." She leaned forward. "And, while I'm being honest, I agree with you - all the songs we heard today were just ordinary, corny stuff. There wasn't a hit among them."

"Thanks, I was worried you wanted to push me into choosing something. I wish I could write my own, but I know I don't have the talent; I can write some good lyrics, when the mood is right, but I can't create a melody. The thing is, unlike those charlatans we saw today, I admit it."

"But we have to keep looking, Belinda. You need material, and soon. But you can relax for a few days. I'm travelling up-country tomorrow, following up on some new leads. No doubt it will be a waste of time, but it has to be done. While I'm gone, explore London, take in a show, visit a gallery or museum. Just have fun and relax. When I get back I will introduce you to our resident record producer and show you the recording studios, and we can resume our search for the right song. If you need transport at any time, ring the office and they will send Paul for you. Will you be ok?"

"I'll be fine. Thanks for all you are doing, Jenny. Sorry I'm being a pest."

"You're not, honestly. You are right to want things to be perfect, I want the same for you. We will sort it all out, it's early days yet."

-♪-

Jenny left, and I made my way dejectedly to the dining room for dinner. Somehow, nothing on the menu appealed to me, and I settled for a salad. Having eaten half, and pushed the remainder around my plate, I gave up and took the lift to the fourth floor and my room, with a notion to go to bed early.

But the day had one more surprise.

I was running through the day in my mind, for the hundredth time, when my phone rang, making me jump.

It was Dolly. Hearing her voice, with its lilting Italian accent, raised my spirits at once, but she sounded serious.

"Belinda, cara, I phoned Jenny to get your number."

"What's up, Dolly? Are you ok?" I feared that something had happened to her or Steve.

"I'm fine, but I had to ring you at once with some bad news." She paused. I didn't know what to think, but I was somehow not completely surprised when she said: "That man Burroughs was here today, asking after you. I pretended I didn't know who he was. He came in almost as soon as we opened this evening, bought a beer and sat at the bar drinking it. Then he started asking questions: Did I have a barmaid called Belinda? Where was she? I wouldn't answer him, asked him if he was the police. He laughed and said: 'Sort of'."

I remembered the day I first met him. When I asked if

he owned a theatre, he said he was "like an agent." What a lying, devious low-life.

"Well, cara, I told him I don't have a barmaid called Belinda, which is true, now, isn't it? He wouldn't give up, and asked if I knew anyone by that name, and I said 'Only my sister-in-law in Roma; she a-married to my little brother Enzo.' He wasn't amused."

She stopped talking, but I waited for her to continue; I sensed there was more.

"Belinda, he is a bad man. He radiates evil. I am afraid for you." He voice trailed off.

"He can't find me, Dolly my love. I am safe here."

I really believed it.

-♪-

On my first day alone in London I decided to explore the area around the hotel. I discovered that, wherever you go in London, restaurants abound - Italian, French and English - and pubs of all nationalities, too. A few doors down from the *Imperial* was an Irish pub, *The Emerald Isle*, and that evening I gravitated to the sound of fiddles being scraped and bawdy voices singing. Before long I was joining in and making new friends. They were wonderful, friendly and sociable people.

Connor, the waiter from the *Imperial*, was there, and came to sit with me. I didn't mind, I enjoyed his company. He was easy to be with, open and friendly, without making me feel pursued. He was also nice looking, with red-brown hair, freckles and warm hazel eyes. And he was great fun, not afraid to jump on the dance floor, unlike most of the men.

We spent a large part of the evening together, dancing, drinking and chatting. He offered to show me around the area the next day, and I was happy to accept. By the time he walked me back to the hotel from the pub, I was feeling happy, squiffy and very attracted to the young Irishman. I was disappointed that he didn't kiss me at the door, but it was our first night out together, so maybe he would be more adventurous the next time.

Back in my suite, I stripped off and showered to remove the sweat of the evening's exertions, then, as it was such a warm night, lay naked on top of the bed covers.

Sleep was slow to arrive. My mind was buzzing with all that had happened that evening - the music, dancing, the lovely people - and Connor. As I recalled the fun we had had together, I thought how nice it would be if he were to touch my body. There, for instance, between my breasts.

I stroked gently in little circles with my fingers, tracing down to my belly, then back up to cup one breast, rubbing the nipple with my thumb. It felt so good. I pressed harder against my breast, pushing it up and across my chest, then the other breast. I closed my eyes and pretended it was Connor's hands I could feel, raising first one nipple, then the other.

Groaning softly, I slid one hand down over my belly to my pelvis, arching my back with pleasure when it reached the centre of sensuality that is hidden there.

"Oh Connor," I whispered.

Round and round, back and forth I stroked. A little visit

inside, two fingers pressing into the little place that makes me shiver with delight, then out again, slippery and sensuous, becoming more insistent with every movement. My body was trembling as I writhed alone on my bed, softly calling his name.

-♪-

Over the following few days, when he had time between his shifts at the hotel, Connor walked with me to a museum or art gallery or just down to the river. He talked about his home in Kilorglin, County Kerry, his parents and their little hotel, his sisters (five) and elder brother, the beautiful countryside of Ireland and the hardship of life in a mainly agricultural area. When he asked about my life, I told him about Gran and my time on the streets with Joey. I left out the episode with Gary Burroughs, but talked proudly of my friends in Norwich, especially the wonderful Dolly.

Still I lusted after him, but still he made no advances on me. He seemed to be quite shy, and although he seemed to be happy to hold my hand as we walked around, he never made a pass. I decided to break the ice, tactfully of course.

We were sitting in the sunshine on the steps beneath Nelson's Column, eating a burger from one of the street sellers. "Do you think I'm attractive?" I blurted.

He looked at me, surprised. "Yes, very."

A pause.

"Well, would you like to kiss me?" So much for subtlety.

He stared at his shoes, stretched out before him on the steps. As the silence grew, I became worried that I had offended his pride. When he finally spoke, it was so softly that I had to strain to hear: "I thought you knew, Belinda darlin', I'm gay."

I froze for a moment, stunned. "Oh Connor, I'm so sorry. No, I hadn't realised. No. Oh damn! I am such an idiot."

Inside, I was crushed. An idiot indeed. There must have been plenty of clues - he thought I knew, after all, so it must have been obvious to everyone else except this stupid girl.

"You'll probably be embarrassed to be seen with me now, I expect." His voice was hoarse, as though he had been there before, knew what to expect.

Dragged out of my own self-pity, I struggled for words. "What? Why? Oh Connor, no, certainly not. I love being with you. I haven't enjoyed anyone's company as much since Joey died ... " I felt my voice catch and fail, as memories of my times with Joey suddenly flooded my mind, like liquid from a shattered bottle.

Connor heard the change in my voice, and he gently took my hand. "Missing him?" He asked. How like him to be more concerned for me than I had been for his feelings.

I nodded. "He's always with me, but I hadn't realised how much your friendship has become like it was with him."

He looked surprised. "You don't think _he_ was gay, do you?"

That hadn't occurred to me, and I took some time to

consider it.

"I don't think so. We talked about love once, and he said he didn't want to jump on my body." I smiled as I recalled that moment. "But I think that had more to do with the nature of our relationship. We were ... " I struggled to find words to describe the way Joey and I felt about each other.

"Like brother and sister?" Connor suggested.

"A bit, but the bond was even tighter than that. I read about twins, once. Because they develop together in the womb, they are sometimes like two parts of one person, and they can often communicate even when they are apart. That's kind of how it was between Joey and me. Although we weren't really related, it felt as though we should have been."

He squeezed my hand. "I wish I'd met him."

"I'm sure you would have liked each other."

After a moment, he added: "You won't tell anyone about me, will you?"

"I wouldn't dream of it. There's no reason why I should." I wanted to reassure him, show him that I was open-minded and accepting. I remembered my afternoon of passion with Daisy - should I tell him about it? No, it would sound patronising.

An awkward silence settled briefly, as my thoughts ricocheted inside my head, then he suddenly leaned over and kissed me on the lips. It wasn't passionate - nothing like Daisy's kisses, for example - it was a token of friendship and understanding, and made me feel very special.

-♪-

"Are you with anyone? I mean, do you have a ... a..."

"Boyfriend?" He grinned. "You can say it." He leaned over and poked me with a finger.

"Sorry I didn't know what to say; I never knew anyone ... like you ... before."

"You probably do, but didn't realise it. It's not something we tell folks as a rule, for fear of being beaten up."

I was shocked. This was something I was completely ignorant about. "Does that really happen?"

"Oh yes, me darlin', all the time. I've not suffered violence yet, though I live in fear of it every day, but get a lot of verbal abuse."

"I don't understand why people have a problem with it."

"Well, me neither, but while the Church is against us we don't stand a chance."

I looked at him. As far as I could tell, he wasn't any different from any other man. Oh, he was definitely in the 'handsome' category, tall and muscular, every girl's dream, in fact, but I couldn't see any clues that set him apart. He looked around us before leaning closer to me to speak.

"To answer your question, yes, I do have a regular feller, Sigi - Seigfried. He's from Germany, dances with the Royal Ballet. Oh, he's not a star, but he's trying hard. We don't see each other much - he's always rehearsing or performing or touring. He is so beautiful, and graceful."

"Tell me about him."

"Ah, well now." He leaned back on the steps, arms and

legs stretched out in a star shape, like that drawing by Michaelangelo (but clothed, of course - though the thought immediately sent my imagination ricocheting off into an amazing, and completely inappropriate, vision of Connor laid out naked on the steps).

Unaware of my thoughts, and missing the grin I was trying to hide, he gazed up into the blue sky, and continued, with a smile of nostalgia. "He came to the hotel with a whole gang of dancers from The Ballet; they had a table booked. It was like a flock of flamingoes landing, so it was; all noise and colour. I knew he had seen me; I could feel his eyes on me as I worked, following me from table to table - every time I looked his way he was staring at me. And when I was serving at their table, he kept speaking to me, calling me over. I was getting all flustered, and they laughed at me, but I didn't care, I laughed with them. The next day, he met me after breakfast and we went walking. That night we slept together."

His eyes had a dreamy look when he turned his head to meet my eyes. "I love him like I never loved anyone, Belinda darlin'. He's The One for me."

I hugged him. "I'm really happy for you, Connor, my lovely brother."

-♪-

"Today is my last day of freedom," I announced to Connor. "Jenny phoned to say she will be back from her travels this afternoon."

He and I were walking along the embankment. The

summer of 1963 had seemed to go on forever, but now the temperature was dropping and winter was well established. I was feeling relaxed, happy and excited, all at the same time. London, always a vibrant place, was alive with the new mood of the sixties. Fashions had become brighter and more daring, businesses were thriving, and radios everywhere brightly proclaimed the new music - which was often crass, sometimes challenging, but always loud, and I rode on the sound like a pillion passenger on a motor-cycle.

"She'll be crackin' the whip then?"

Not for the first time I studied my handsome companion. Away from his work, Connor followed the latest styles - his hair was long, his suit trousers tight, his shoes pointed; he looked great. Once again I wished he was not gay - he could have talked me into bed without any trouble. I giggled at the thought, and he looked at me, puzzled.

Hastily, to cover my embarrassment, I said "Yes, Jenny wants to book a studio for rehearsals. And we need new songs. She says it's no good rehashing old ones, audiences these days want novelty, and she's right, of course. At a push, we can cover new records from America, but then you have two versions of the same song competing for chart position - the best you can hope for is to get a bit more than half the sales, it's never good."

"I can see what you mean. I always thought you must have hundreds to choose from."

"In a way we do, but if I record a song, it has to be right for me. For instance, most are written for male singers, with words or sentiments that wouldn't fit with a female performer. And anyway, there are not many 'good' songs coming along, I've discovered recently that most of the stuff churned out by the so-called 'professional' writers is rubbish. Some artists settle for what they can get, but it can be a bad decision that could ruin their career."

We stopped and sat on one of the stone seats set into the embankment, our breath forming icy clouds that were whisked away by the busy breeze. Behind us was the Thames, twinkling in the late morning sunlight, before us the busy street, with streams of red buses and black taxis, cars and motorcycles. A short way off, a busker, wearing a worn, military greatcoat with patched sleeves and tattered edges, had laid out a cushion to sit on and was unpacking his guitar.

"You could end up like him," Connor said, indicating the busker with a nod of his head.

I turned and looked. The man was in his thirties, and though shabbily dressed, somehow still managed to convey a sense of dignity in his bearing that suggested he had once known better times.

I nodded, sadly. "Exactly."

-♪-

In the silence that followed, the busker began his first song. His voice was clear, with a huskiness that hinted at a hard life, and the words he sang were new to me, like poetry set to music. I watched the people walking past. Most ignored the man, some sneered with disgust at the state of his clothes or the fact that he was, effectively, begging. But many others paused, drawn by the sound of his music, and dropped coins into his cap, set on the pavement at his feet. He thanked each one with a smile.

When the song was finished, Connor rose from the bench to move on.

"Not yet, Connor love, can we stay for a while?" I said. The man's singing had moved me, and I wanted to hear more.

"Sure, I was enjoying the music meself," he smiled, sitting down again.

After two more songs, I stood, followed by Connor. But instead of moving on, I took the few steps that carried me to where the busker sat. It is hard to describe how I was feeling at that moment. The word I want to use is 'trance', but that sounds too dramatic. So does 'hypnotised', yet both words are true. There was no choice in my actions, I had to talk to him.

He looked up at me, and smiled. "Hello," he said in that same husky voice, now with a hint of an accent.

I smiled back, unsure what to do next. "Do you mind if I sit with you for a moment please?" I asked, nervously.

"Course you can, pet, I don't often have a pretty girl wanting to sit beside me these days." He laughed. "Most of them run a mile when they get downwind."

I sat on the pavement at his side and, looking confused, Connor sat next to me.

"I know a lot of songs, but I never before heard any of those you sang this morning," I began.

"Ah well," he said, smiling again, "you wouldn't. Them's my own creation. I make them up."

No wonder I didn't recognise them. "They are very moving, yet beautiful." It was all I could say.

"Well, thank you, pet. Aye, they're bonny enough." He grinned. "Nearly as bonny as you, my dear. What's your name?" His gaze was direct and confident, despite his circumstances. It was like being scanned by an x-ray machine, my innermost feelings exposed.

"Belinda," I stammered.

He extended a hand. It was surprisingly clean. "Bill Argent, fallen star. Pleased to meet you, Belinda."

I accepted the offered hand, and held it for a moment. "This is my friend Connor."

He shook Connor's hand, then tuned back to me. "Well, Belinda my dear, you wanted to talk to me. Are you from one of them churches, come to save me from my sins?"

The question was so unexpected that I laughed out loud. "Oh no, certainly not. Mind you, my Gran would have loved to hear you say that, Bill. She was always making me go to Sunday School in the hope I would get religion. It never worked, though."

Unsure of myself, I hesitated. I knew what I wanted, but didn't know if it was possible. Eventually I opened my handbag and took a pound note from my purse. As I gave it to him I asked: "Are you here every day?"

He accepted the note gratefully. "Thank you my dear, that is very generous. Yes, I'm here at the same time every day, unless it's raining or snowing. Will you be coming back?"

"Oh yes, you can be sure you will see me again." I leaned over and kissed him on the cheek, then stood up. Connor shook his hand again and we left. As we walked away, Bill began another beautiful song and Connor gave me a puzzled look.

-♪-

It was late afternoon, and I was back in my hotel room, relaxing with a magazine, when Jenny called around. After welcoming hugs, we sat down with a bottle of wine and I asked her about about her trip. She described the painful details of another fruitless journey across the country to hear music being murdered by talentless hopefuls.

"But enough about me, how have you been settling in?"

"Oh fine, thanks. John Parkin and I have met a few times. He is sorting out my tax affairs at the moment, which is tricky, considering I don't exist as far as the tax office is concerned. I also made a new friend."

"Tell me more," she smiled. "Is romance in the air?"

"In my dreams, yeah," I replied, wryly. "I fancy him like mad, but he's gay. Still, we are good friends, and that's nice too."

"It is, for sure," she said. "Now, I have work for you. Tomorrow I am taking you to a studio to look at the rehearsal facilities. I want you to make yourself comfortable with the team there and way things are done. In the meantime, I need you to give me a list of a dozen or so songs you want to work on, with a view to an album. For the time being these can be any standards or cover songs you like, but if you have any of your own songs, I'd like to hear those too."

She paused, waiting for my response.

"Ok," I said, marshalling my thoughts. "I can easily let you have a list of my favourite existing songs, but ... "

It was my turn to pause, not sure how to introduce my

idea. Would she laugh, or think I was mad? "Jenny, I haven't written anything much myself, but I want to run something past you. I have found a good songwriter, but he's not with any of the established outfits. Would you be prepared to listen to him?"

"Where did you find him?"

I hesitated, unsure how it would go down. "Busking on the embankment," I blurted.

She grinned. "Honestly? You're not kidding me, are you?"

"No, straight up. I heard him today. His songs are all original, and they are unbelievably good. Can you come to the embankment with me tomorrow morning at ten to listen?"

She laughed. "This is a first for me, Belinda honey. Sure, why not. Meet you in reception at nine thirty."

So it is that a momentous decision was made that launched, not one but two careers.

~14~
November 1963
Paddington Nights

We found a perfect spot near to where Bill would soon be setting up. It was a pavement café, serving breakfasts and coffee to the crowds on their way to work. We bought ourselves coffees and took seats where we could observe Bill and hear him, but where I was hidden from his view.

It wasn't long before he had taken his pitch and unpacked his guitar. I watched jenny carefully as he began to sing. If anyone had been observing me when I first heard him, I suspect they would have seen the same reaction as I saw. Her eyes opened a little wider, a small smile pulled at the corners of her mouth. After a few bars, she turned to me and raised her eyebrows, then returned her gaze to the man who occupied our thoughts.

She listened to two full songs, then, while he was still singing the third, she indicated with her hand for me to stay, while she rose and walked the few steps to where Bill was performing. He gave a little nod to acknowledge her presence when she stopped in front of him.

When the song was done, they talked, and I saw her take one of her business cards from her handbag and write something on the back before passing it to him. They shook hands and she returned to me.

"I've told him to bring some songs suitable for a female singer to the studios this afternoon. If he comes, and if the songs are any good, he could earn himself a lot of money. I like what I've heard today, Belinda, I'm glad to brought me here."

I was pleased, both for Bill and to have my judgement accepted and validated.

"Now, my friend," she continued, "we have work to do."

We left the café and she hailed a black cab. "Lancaster Road, West Eleven," she said to the driver as we climbed in.

-♪-

The cab dropped us outside an elegant, white-painted, three-storey house in Notting Hill. The sky was darkening, and I heard a distant rumble of thunder from the west. I imagined Bill, sitting on the embankment with his guitar, looking over his shoulder to judge how long he had before the rain arrived. In my opinion, it would not be long.

Jenny and I climbed the flight of stone steps that rose to a polished mahogany front door, inset with panels of stained glass. On the wall to the left of the door a neat, brass sign indicated that this was the address of "Hugo White, Record Producer." Beneath it was another, saying, simply "The White Studios."

Next to the signs was an antique bell-pull, which Jenny yanked, producing a melodic tinkling somewhere indoors. A box, tucked into a corner, squawked something incomprehensible, and Jenny spoke her name into it. There was a click, and the door opened.

I followed her into an entrance hall that looked to me like a palace ballroom. The floor was tiled in a beautiful mosaic picture of a peacock, with tail spread in magnificent colours. Fine, mahogany furniture was spaced along the walls; velvet curtains hung languidly, drawn into slim waists by golden ropes; and a flight of thickly-carpeted stairs carried the eye up to a balustraded gallery.

It was along this gallery that a man appeared, casually dressed in a smart cream-coloured jacket and maroon trousers. His face was tanned, setting off his bushy, blonde hair and, when he smiled, highlighting his impossibly white teeth.

"Jenny, darling," he beamed. His voice was cultured, but with a hint of an Essex accent that he was unable to eradicate. He reached the foot of the stairs and engulfed Jenny in an enthusiastic hug.

"Belinda," explained Jenny, disentangling herself from his embrace, "this is Hugh White, our record producer. Hughie, this is Belinda."

He turned to me, still with that luminescent smile. "Hi Belinda, love. I have heard so much about you. It's a pleasure to meet you." He held out a slightly plump hand, but his handshake was firm and confident.

"Come through, come through," he gushed, waving an arm towards one of the doors off to our right. We followed him into what proved to be a luxurious office. All the pre-requisites had been installed to make an impression - rich carpet, leather-topped mahogany desk, a massive green leather settee and several expensive-looking chairs.

In addition, the walls were covered with guitars of all kinds, peppered here and there with framed gold records.

A polished brass chandelier, with fake candles pointing upwards and glass bangles hanging down, dominated the centre of the ceiling.

"Now, Belinda," Hugh began in a business-like tone as we all sat down around the desk, "I can provide everything, from the best engineer in the country to the best support musicians. And once we have you on tape, I will sell you to one of the record companies. But first, Belinda, love, we have to do something about your name. You need something punchier, easier for the punters to remember .... maybe 'Linda Lean' or something like that." He locked eyes with me. This was a man accustomed to getting his own way.

I turned to Jenny. Her face was carefully expressionless as she returned my glance and shrugged.

Joey's voice rang in my head: *"Keep your name, don't let them change it. Belinda Bellini is a good name, be proud of it."*

"Hugh," I began carefully, deliberately using his first name - I would not be intimidated - "my name is Belinda Bellini. That is what I will be called." It was a simple statement, no emphasis, no histrionics. I held his eyes, by which he was trying to master me. He would not, and the battle of stares would have gone on forever, if I had not broken the atmosphere with a smile.

-♪-

My only previous experience of recording was when Barry and a few of his musicians had crowded into someone's garage in Norwich, with a tape recorder, to make some backing tracks for me. White Studios were as much like that as a jet aeroplane is like a roller skate.

As we emerged at the foot of the stairs from Hugh's office, Jenny and I were met by the engineer, Eric Last, who took me on a guided tour. It was fascinating.

He started in the control room, showing me the console used to record such stars as Rebecca Strait, The Farm and Pete Lattimer. Beyond the control room, he led me around booths and cubicles, each with microphones (which he proudly told me were the latest Neuman models from America) and headphones. This, he told me, was how they separated the sounds of singers and musicians, which were then recorded individually on Eric's eight track desk.

Jenny stood in the background, grinning at my enthusiasm as Eric explained some of the techniques he used to get distinctive sounds for his various clients. After a while, though, we returned to the control room to plan the day.

"I am trying to get you onto the UK leg of Tony Fortinelli's European tour," she explained. "but we need a record out as soon as possible, so the punters have some idea of who you are. If we can get some plays on Radio One it will raise your profile. That's why I want Bill to come up with some good songs for you."

"What about musicians?" I asked.

"I've got some guys coming in this afternoon. They are session musicians, real professionals, experienced with studio and stage work. I want four or five of them to tour as your backing band. They have all performed together before, today will be a chance to see how they get along with you."

I felt my heart quicken. Professionals? What would they make of a inexperienced little girl from the wilds of Norfolk, who had never even been in a recording studio before?

Jenny noticed the expression on my face. "Worried?"

I tried to smile, but could tell it didn't work. "Yeah, what if they hate me?"

"Then we sack them. It's that easy, Belinda love. We are paying them well for their skills, they will do what I say or they will walk." She looked fierce, and I could believe what she said. Then her face broke into a smile: "But they will love you, I promise. I've worked with all of them before, they are honest guys, you'll see."

-♪-

Bill arrived carrying his guitar case in one hand and a professional-looking briefcase in the other. He looked surprised to see me, but smiled in greeting.

"Bill is now on our books as a songwriter," Jenny told me.

Clearly nervous, Bill opened his case and passed a bundle of handwritten sheets to Jenny. "I've brought about a dozen songs for you to pick over. They may not all be from a girl's point of view, but I think any of them would sound good with a woman's voice."

Without even looking at them, Jenny handed them straight to me. "I've learnt that I can trust Belinda's judgement in musical matters," she grinned.

I glanced at the sheets. They consisted of lines of lyrics with chord names above them. I needed to hear them before I could sing any. "Can I have some time to go through these with Bill?" I asked.

"No problem. I want a chat with Eric, anyway - and the boys, when they arrive. Will an hour do?"

"I expect so. Is there somewhere quiet we can go?"

Eric nodded. "Yeah, there's an office upstairs. I'll show you."

-♪-

Once alone in the office, Bill confronted me. "So you're behind this, are you?" he asked in his gruff voice, but he was grinning.

"I couldn't say anything until I knew what Jenny's reaction would be."

"I thought it was odd that two women showed interest on successive days. Thanks for putting in the word for me, pet."

"Your music did it, Bill. Someone was bound to grab you someday, I'm just glad we found you first. Now, what have you got for me?"

We sat side by side at the big desk, and I laid out the sheets. He picked through them and chose one. "I could imagine you doing this one," he said, handing it to me, nervous again.

"Sing it for me, please."

He unpacked his guitar, checked the tuning, then, with a opening chord, began to sing the one called 'Paddington Nights'. I followed the words on the sheet as he sang, and recognised it as one he had sung on the embankment. On the second verse, I joined in, and on the third he stopped singing and let me finish it.

My face must have been something to see, I knew I was grinning like an idiot. "I love it, Bill. One thing that drew me to you is that you write songs about your life, and I can relate to some of the things you've been through. I've decided I want to make people aware of the hidden people, the ones with no voice of their own, because they have fallen through the gaps in our society. But the message must be subtle, it must be the music that people hear first. I love 'Paddington Dreams' because it is about hope from despair. It is definitely one to try with the band."

He stared at his feet. "I can only write what is in my heart, pet. And I'm sorry it's not a proper music sheet, I never learnt to write those quavers and things."

"I can't read them, so don't worry about it. What's the next one?"

By the time Jenny came up to collect us, we had played through six songs, all of them suitable, and had selected two to run through with the band..

"You guys getting along ok?" she asked as she entered.

"Aye, bonny," said my new songwriter.

-♪-

The musicians were setting up as Bill, Jenny and I came down the stairs. Jenny called them over and introduced us, then Eric took me to a booth, for a sound check, before retiring to his control room. I could see him through the big window, from where he looked down upon the studio.

"Ok. Belinda," his voice suddenly arrived in my

headphones, making me jump, "give me some lah lah lahs."

I duly made some noises into the microphone. "Thanks, Belinda. Andy, now you." And so on, through the band until he had a level for everyone - Andy 'Judge' Morisson on guitar, Nick Frame who played bass guitar, 'Legs' Aspinal, trumpet, Marco Lane on saxophone and Benny 'The Boots' O'Brien, the drummer. Bill was included - he sat on a stool, with a mike for his guitar.

Jenny, meanwhile, had been photocopying Bill's song sheets, and she circulated, distributing copies among the band. "Who plays what, here?" asked Marco, eyeing the sparse notes on the sheets suspiciously.

"That's up to you guys," Jenny replied, in her authoritative voice, "you've worked together often enough. Improvise. Ready, Belinda?"

"Yes," I said, nervously. "I'm going to sing 'Paddington Nights' through with Bill, first, so you can get a feel for it."

As we played the song, I could hear Bill through the headphones, strumming and harmonising, and, gradually, I heard the other guys experimenting with backing ideas. By the end of the run-through, we had quite a good sound, and after six more times, Eric announced it was good enough for a take. An hour later he was satisfied with it, and we moved onto the second song.

It was a gruelling, repetitive, frustrating afternoon's work, and I loved it.

Performing on stage is only one aspect of music; essential, of course, but impossible until you have everything else perfected. Creating, refining, and developing a song is where it all starts, and it was a joy to be part of that process. By the end of the day we had bonded as a team, and I knew we were a good one.

As we were clearing up, Jenny called us all together.

"I've got us a slot on the UK venues of Tony Fortinelli's tour, starting in three week's time."

The guys groaned.

"Ok," she smiled, "I know what you think of him, but it's a good gig and will pay well. Are you up for it?"

There was a chorus of answers from the band, which included a fair bit of swearing, but seemed to amount to a general acceptance.

"How do you want to be billed?" Jenny asked. "Only I have to get your name on the posters and promotional stuff."

After a brief consultation, Andy, who seemed by consensus to be their spokesman, said; "We'll stick with 'Daylight Robbery', Jen."

"Good, 'Belinda Bellini and Daylight Robbery' it is. I'll write to you with the details and an appointment to sign contracts. In the meantime, back here tomorrow morning at eight sharp for more rehearsals. Belinda, we need six good songs for your set on tour, and two of them to submit to the record companies as a single before the weekend. See you bright and early, guys."

-♪-

There was a colourful poster on the side of a bus waiting at the traffic lights in Regent Street. I had stopped walking and was staring at it, without realising why, for several seconds before it dawned on me that it was announcing a performance of The Nutcracker, by the Royal Ballet at Covent Garden. Connor had carried on walking, oblivious for a moment, but became aware that I was no longer beside him, and came back to stand beside me. "Ah," he said, wistfully.

"Shall we go?" I asked.

"What! Do you know how much those tickets cost? More than a week's wages for serving at tables, that's for sure."

"No problem, I can afford it; it will be my treat. Wouldn't you like to see Sigi in action? C'mon," I urged, hugging his arm, "call it an early birthday present."

He thought about it for ages, looking first at me, then his feet, then off into the distance, then back at me, a slide-show of emotions flitting across his face. Eventually, the bus moved off, and the Connor show stopped at 'Happy Smile.'

"Ok. Yes. Oh yes please, Belinda my love, there's nothing I would like more."

And so we did. I telephoned the booking office and ordered the tickets as soon as we returned to the hotel - and he was right, they did cost as much as he could earn in a week. Because of his working hours, I booked a Sunday performance. I got seats in a box, the best in the house.

-♪-

We arrived at the Royal Opera House early, to savour the occasion.

It's a magnificent building. Joining a steady flow of arrivals, we climbed marble steps beneath towering white columns, so tall they seemed to meet at the top. In the opulent foyer, we collected our tickets, then stood gazing around at the crimson and gold decorations and the elegant clothes of the wealthy patrons.

We took our places about twenty minutes before the performance, and soaked up the atmosphere - the orchestra tuning, a buzz of voices as people arrived and found their places; a sense of expectancy filled the air. I had never experienced this before; I was always locked in my dressing room feeling my own nervousness. Today I could relax and be entertained.

Eventually, the house lights dimmed, the orchestra struck the first notes of the overture, and we were transported into another world. It was all I could have hoped for - colourful, graceful, uplifting. Connor pointed out his beloved Sigi, splendid in a red military uniform, tall, handsome and muscular, and a fine dancer; I could see why he had fallen for him.

-♪-

After the show, we decided to put off going out into the grey reality of autumnal London. Instead, we went up to the theatre bar, where we sat drinking coffee, watching people coming and going, listening in to their chatter about the show. Eventually, Connor looked at his watch. "Thanks for a wonderful evening, Belinda, darlin'," he said. "It's been great, but I have to get back to work now. It's my turn to lay up for breakfast."

He leaned over and kissed me on the cheek.

At that moment, Sigi came around the corner, walking with another dancer, laughing. I recognised them both at once. Connor had seen them too, and started to rise to his feet, a big smile on his face, but he stopped. We had both caught the look that passed between the two men when they saw him. He seemed to sag, to sink back into his chair like a balloon as the air leaks out. Sigi and the other man could not pretend they hadn't seen us, so they came over to our table. Sigi was bristling. He had been caught out, and he was responding by turning it against Connor.

"I told you never to come to my work," he snapped as soon as he reached the table, before anyone else could speak. His eyes flicked from Connor to me. "Gone over to the other side, have you?" he sneered. "Gone 'straight'?"

Connor seemed unable to answer. His face had coloured up, his mouth twisted. I went to stand, but he put a hand gently on my arm and shook his head.

He turned to the two men. "How long?" he asked hoarsely.

"What does it matter?" spat Sigi. He spoke with a strong German accent, but his English was perfect. "It was you who wanted to make a 'relationship'." He made the word sound like something unpleasant. "For me it was just a bit of fun. Sex, nothing else."

"You knew I loved you." Connor's voice had taken on a hollow, empty sound. I studied his face; it was like a white mask, drained of blood, expressionless.

"What do I care?" the dancer laughed, then turned away and walked out of my friend's life.

I took Connor's hand, and we walked silently out of the theatre and back to the hotel.

When we parted at the door, I said: "I'm so sorry, my dear friend."

He managed a wan smile and a little shrug of the shoulders. "My own fault. I fall in love too easily. Should have learnt my lesson by now. Goodnight, darlin'."

"Goodnight, dear Connor." I stretched up and kissed him on the cheek. "I hope one day you find someone who deserves you."

He turned and headed for his digs, and I closed my door with a sigh.

-♪-

The following day was Monday, and we both had the the day off. We started walking towards Trafalgar Square, with a vague notion of wandering around the National Gallery, or maybe Theatre-land. I was trying to think of a way to lift his spirits a bit.

The weather was edgy - sunny, but cold, with an unpredictable wind that took the heat from the air and ran off with it, and clouds that swirled as though the gods were about to burst through. There was a feeling that it could rain at any moment.

"Connor?" I said.

He cocked his head and turned to face me. He knew that when I said his name like that, with a question mark after it, I was going to ask a favour. Despite his low state of mind, he could still manage a little smile for his sister.

"What is it, Belinda, my little angel?"

"Where do you get your clothes?"

"Oh, Carnaby Street, sometimes, Oxford Street. Why?"

"You always look so good, so ... cool and trendy. Will you take me shopping?"

"Sure, I'd love to. Will we walk?"

I frowned. "How far is it?"

"Oh, about half an hour." He glanced at my face and grinned. "Ok, taxi it is, then."

We hailed a black cab that dropped us in Regent Street, just as the clouds gave up their contents. Rain pounded down on our heads so hard it was like being beaten with a rolled-up newspaper; within seconds our clothes were soaked through to our skin. We ran to the nearest clothes shop and bought some dry clothes and a raincoat each. Then we spent four wonderful hours diving into and out of the most amazing shops I have ever seen, on a buying spree that only stopped because we couldn't carry any more. We were festooned with carrier bags from San Trop, Nabertackle, Jake's, Sunrise and The End.

After another cab ride, back to the hotel, we dashed to my room and spent the afternoon trying everything on. It didn't matter who's clothes they were, we both wore them. I couldn't believe the outrageous outfits he and I had chosen - short skirts, fantastic flares, knee-length boots and clashing colours - it was as though all the rules about style had been thrown away and anything was possible. And it was.

Finally, exhausted, yet on a high better than any drug could deliver, we showered together, then climbed naked into my bed and slept, wrapped together like children.

I woke a few hours later, enjoying the warmth and

softness of his body against mine, the gentle rhythm of his breathing. It wasn't the wild passion I had first hoped for, but it was good, a safe bond of friendship. *'Joey,'* I thought, *'You don't mind, do you?'*

There was no answer, but I felt a kind of mental hug that said it was ok, or did I imagine it?

-♪-

With the Tony Fortinelli tour fast approaching, I found myself busier than ever.

For our rehearsals, the band and I had moved from the recording studios to the Star Theatre, a once-grand home of music hall. The last show there had been in the fifties, and it was sadly neglected by the time we arrived. We were using the stage to work out the routines for our set - where each of us would stand, any interactions between us, where the microphones needed to be, and so on. The years of experience that the guys brought with them was a huge help. Performance is only half about the music, the rest is the show you put on for the audience, and we wanted to give them a show they would remember.

We had decided between us that I would walk or run all over the stage while singing, and for this we had to buy the smallest hand-held microphones available at the time. I would also play up to all the guys during the performance - put my hand inside the front of Andy's shirt while he played a guitar solo, rub my leg against Nick's, blow in Marco's ear, and so on. The idea was to create a kind of sexual tension on stage, an innuendo that 'something' was going on between us. It was very tiring, but we felt it was effective.

-♪-

About mid-morning, Jenny arrived with a tall, smart man in tow. She waved her arms above her head to attract our attention: "Hold up, guys. Conference," she shouted above the clicks, hums and feedback of electronic amplification. With a pop, I switched off my mike, and joined the lads sitting on the edge of the stage, looking down upon Jenny and the stranger.

"This is Roger Trelawney," she said. "He's a professional photographer; I asked him to come and meet you. If you like each other, he will follow you around for a while, taking pictures for publicity, album covers, posters and so on."

Roger waved a greeting as she spoke. "I'd like to start right now," he declared in a smooth, deep voice, "unless you have any reason not to."

Jenny looked at me. "It's your call, Belinda."

"Yeah, go for it," I said.

"Great. Well, if you will all just carry on as if I'm not here, and I'll wander around, get the feel of things, maybe fire off a few shots."

He started rummaging in the big bag he had on the floor beside him, and produced two cameras and several other pieces of equipment. Jenny gave me a 'thumbs up' and departed, and the guys returned to their instruments. As we played through our set again, I watched Roger as he watched us. At first he did no more than observe, then he started to hold up a camera and fiddle with lenses. Not taking pictures at first, as far as I could tell, just playing with angles and lighting.

After a while, I forgot he was there, until an occasional flash reminded me, as he began to pop away at us.

The next day he had some ideas to try, and asked us to pose for some group shots. He wanted close-ups of my face from all angles, and he had brought some special lights and reflectors to get the effects he wanted. He also took a lot of casual pictures of us lounging around and talking.

-♪-

At mid-day, we took a break and all piled out of the theatre for some lunch, splashing through the slush from a recent snow shower, and bursting into the small café we had found a few doors down, like a steaming invading army.

We seemed to have so much to talk about, and usually all at once - when I think about it, the other patrons must have hated us for the din we made. With six chairs pushed around one table, we ate our soup, bacon butties, cakes and, in Nick's case, roast beef dinner, with hardly a pause in the chatter.

Joe's was a popular café, and the dinging of the little bell on the door was part of the ambient noise as people arrived and left. We were so engrossed in our exchanges that we ignored all the comings and goings. One person, however, wanted to to be noticed, and came straight to our table. It was John Parkin, my manager.

"So this is where you're hiding," he shouted above the general hubub.

"Hi John!" I cried, jumping up. "Bring a chair. Guys, make room for another body."

"No," he said quickly, holding up a hand. "I can't stay, and nor can you. I need you to come with me."

"Why, what's up?"

"Miss Bellini," he said, failing to suppress a smile of pride, "you have a recording contract."

With a scraping of chairs, the boys were suddenly all on their feet and gathered around him. "That's fantastic! Who with?"

"Barleycorn Records. It's an amazing coup. They have some of the biggest stars; we have never managed to place any unknown acts with them before, but they loved your demo. 'Paddington Nights' will be the 'A' side, with 'Gotta Larf' as the 'B'. Hugh White called me to get you and Bill to meet him down there now to sign a contract. I need you to break away from rehearsals for an hour to come with me to clinch the deal. Now. Ok?"

As if I was going to say 'no'. I looked around at the guys, who were beaming and giving me assorted thumbs up signals. "You bet," I grinned, giving him a big hug.

-♪-

Even though I had handed over all my affairs to John to deal with on my behalf, there was one thing I was determined to keep for myself. At the end of October, I put ten pounds into an envelope and posted it to The Reverend Potter, to pay for Joey's grave.

-♪-

Aware of the impending tour, Barleycorn pulled out all the stops, and had 'Paddington Nights' coming off the presses before the end of the week. Hugh, John and Jenny then set about nailing everyone who might play it on air - the disc jockeys on Radio Luxembourg and the few producers on British radio and television who had any interest in pop music.

For my own part, I was involved in what seemed like endless preparations for the tour - signing contracts, more studio work with Daylight Robbery, more stage rehearsals, photo sessions, and receiving lessons in stage make-up.

On the last day before we set off to Blackpool for our first night of the tour, Jenny phoned me. I was relaxing in my hotel room; standing at the window, looking out at the hailstorm that was pounding London.

"Watch BBC television tonight at six o'clock," she instructed. I could hear the excitement in her voice.

"What will I see?" I asked.

"A special edition of Juke Box Jury," came the crackly reply.

"Are they playing my record?" I exclaimed, trying not to let my hopes get too high.

"Oh yes. But not only that. This week they have a special panel ... The Beatles are making a guest appearance. You are going to be judged by the most influential people in pop music today."

I felt my stomach lurch. There was no doubt in my mind that, whether they loved me or hated me, they could decide my future.

Jenny hung up, and the rest of the afternoon passed in slow motion. I tried sleeping, but my mind was flowing with wild thoughts. I eventually went down to the restaurant, where Connor was on duty, and told him the news. He went wild with enthusiasm and gave me a hug that lifted me off my feet and swung me around. When he put me down, we were both laughing.

He looked at his watch. "Only an hour to go, I must away to spread the word. Meet me in the lounge at six and we'll watch it together."

"Oh Mr O'Connell, you can be so assertive sometimes."

At five to six, when I wandered into the lounge, it was packed. A cheer greeted me from the assembled staff and guests who were crowded into the room. There was not a seat to be had, except the one Connor had kept for me, right in front of the television. Shyly, I thanked them and took my seat.

The show started, with the distinctive theme music 'Hit or Miss', by the John Barry Orchestra, and David Jacobs introduced the Fab Four, as the Beatles had become known. Then the first record was played - not mine. Then the next. As each one was imminent, my nerves became more stretched, made worse by the boys' blunt comments about some of the tracks, and their irreverent banter.

Then, suddenly, I heard the compère say my name and the room erupted with a huge cheer, followed by silence as the record was played. I was disappointed to note that they only played about half of it, but then became absorbed as my fate was sealed by the number one pop icons of the age. I need not have worried, not only were they very enthusiastic about Bill's song, but they were also generous about my singing, and unanimously voted it a 'Hit.'

There was wild applause from the room, and Connor gave me another big hug. We didn't hear the end of the programme as everyone wanted to congratulate me, but over all the noise I heard a voice in my head say *'Well done, Bell.'*

'Thanks Joey,' I smiled.

~15~
January 1964
Hit The Road

A new television programme called "Top of the Pops" began broadcasting on the first of January. It was the BBC's response to the growing demand for more music and the success of "Ready Steady Go", which had started the year before on the other channel, ITV (in those days, we had only two channels on British television).

It had an exciting format - singers and bands performed their latest hits live in a studio full of young people, introduced by respected presenters such as Pete Murray and Jimmy Saville. In the first edition, the Beatles were at number one, and closed the show with 'I Want To Hold Your Hand'. In the same chart, 'Paddington Nights' arrived at number thirty-two - we weren't invited on the show. I was simultaneously excited and disappointed - excited to see my name on the list, but disappointed that it was at such a low place.

Our first night on the Fortinelli tour was three days later, in the Opera House at the Winter Gardens, in Blackpool. We travelled up on the day, leaving London at six o'clock in the morning in a special coach, which Oberon had extensively modified for the purpose. All the original seats had been stripped out and the interior replaced to make a temporary home for travelling minstrels. The centre section had been fitted with racks and bays to store all the equipment, accessible by removable panels on the outside of the coach, and in the rear was a dormitory, with four tiny bedrooms, a shower and a lavatory. In the area at the front, between the driver's compartment and the hold, was a lounge, with comfortable seating and a galley kitchen.

The streets of London, busy even at that early hour, floated past our misted windows in snapshots, as the sleepy glow from street lamps fell upon small patches of street and was reflected, twinkling, in puddles. The steady rain that had washed away the remaining snow and slush continued to fall. Dawn did not arrive until we were speeding along the new M1 motorway, heading north, and then barely perceptibly in shades of grey.

At first we dozed, but as the day emerged, we did what we always did, what we loved to do, we made music. Andy pulled out his twelve-string acoustic guitar and we jammed the journey away.

We pulled up at the side doors of the Opera House, eight hours later, and our driver honked the horn. Within moments, the doors were flung open and a gang of sturdy men materialised, who began unloading the amplifiers, drums and other gear from the coach. Moments later, a short, rotund man in an ill-fitting suit arrived, puffing and sweating, and introduced himself, in a squeaky voice with a strong American accent, as Mort Winkler, assistant manager of the Opera House.

"Where have you been?" he demanded. "I was expecting you this morning."

Benny opened his mouth and made a sound that was intended to be the start of one of his wisecracks, but he was pulled aside by Andy, and an uncomfortable silence ensued. I broke it by introducing myself. "Hello Mr

Winkler, I'm Belinda," I said, ignoring his silly question, looking straight into his eyes and holding out my hand.

His onslaught parried, he absently accepted my handshake. "I'm a very busy man, you know," he grumbled.

"Of course you are," I replied sweetly. "So if you wouldn't mind just showing us our dressing rooms, and we'll let you get on without any further interruption."

"Dressing rooms?" he snorted. "You have one room, that's all."

"One room? For five men and a girl?" I said carefully. The man's manner and voice were irritating, and I saw Andy step forward, his face angry. But this was not the time for male ego to be asserted. "Very well, Mr Winkler," I said evenly, shaking my head quickly to beg Andy not to speak. "Would you please be so kind as to show us where our dressing room is?"

He led us through corridors to a room about the size of my bedroom at the Jolly Butchers. It was ridiculously small - when the six of us stepped through the door, there was hardly room to move - but it would have to do; we would have to make it work. "Thank you, Mr Winkler," I said, turning to face him. "Goodbye for now," and shut the door quickly to prevent any more exchanges.

-♪-

A moment later, there was a knock on the door. Andy was on it like a tiger, wrenching it open, ready to bite off Winkler's head, but it was one of the stage hands. "Miss Bellini's costumes," he announced, pointing to a trunk on the corridor floor beside him. Andy thanked him and dragged it into the room. It provided the needed final seating for the six of us - two on the only chairs provided, two back-to-back on the trunk, me perched on the shelf that passed as a dressing table, and 'Legs' on the loo in the corner. We sat there in silence, our mood soured.

Believe it or not, Belinda, we've seen worse than this," said Andy.

"Hell yeah," added Marco. "What about that place in Southport?"

They all groaned, then laughed, and in seconds the room was filled with the noise of their reminiscences. So loudly were they all talking that we weren't aware that there was someone at the door until it opened and Tony Fortinelli walked in. I recognised him from his television appearances and album sleeves, in which he looked perpetually young, but close up, in the flesh, was another matter. His lined face was heavily caked with makeup, his hair clearly a wig. As soon as he entered the room, his eyes fixed on me, looking me up and down, assessing me.

"Hey guys, welcome aboard," he gushed, his whiter-than-white, better-than-real, teeth practically illuminating the room.

"Hi Tony," we all chimed, and Andy rose to greet him with a handshake.

"Yeah, hi," Fortinelli said, taking the hand absently, looking over Andy's shoulder at me. "Hey little lady, I hear you have a hit record."

He had only been in the room for one minute, and in that short time had stripped me with his eyes and insulted one of my friends. I decided I did not like him.

"It's a start," I replied, coldly.

He seemed not to notice, or perhaps didn't care. "Yeah, well, I just came to meet and greet, as they say; haha. Bye for now." He flashed another gleaming smile, as sincere as a politician, and was gone. It was as though we had been visited unexpectedly by a member of royalty from a small and unknown principality.

The door closed and I looked around at the boys, who were studying my face with amusement.

"Congratulations, you just met the star of our show," said Andy in a caricatured American accent.

"Is he real?" I asked, still stunned at the man's arrogance. I knew a little about Tony Fortinelli, from the newspapers. He rose to minor fame in the nineteen forties and fifties by miSteveing such real stars as Tony Bennett and Frank Sinatra, but without their talent or charisma. He chose the medium of jazz to disguise his lack of singing ability and, against all odds, he even had a hit record.

"Oh yes," said Marco, wryly, he's a real arsehole."

"The thing is," Andy added, "he has endless belief in himself, and doesn't realise that he's crap. Have you looked at the support acts on the posters?"

"Yeah, but I hardly know any of the names. I assumed they are American acts who just hadn't been promoted over here."

Andy shrugged. "They aren't even big over there. I mean, whoever heard of The Majesterials? Or Buster Damone? The fact is that Tony can't stand competition, so he surrounds himself with minor acts, so he can act Mister Big."

At that moment, there was another knock on the door and a voice called out "Sound check in ten minutes, folks!"

-♪-

Considering what I had been through, it's amazing how naive I still was in some ways. Oh, I had learnt to put on a tough front, that was my defence against the world, but the shell was thin.

The night after the first gig, I was asleep on the bus, but was wakened after only an hour or so by the sound of voices and music. The noise became louder, preventing me from returning to the sleep I had been enjoying, and eventually I got up to investigate. As I pushed through the curtain into the lounge area, the sight that met my eyes hit me like a physical punch, and my mind was jolted into memories of the most unpleasant kind.

The air was thick with the smoke of cannabis, and the floor was a tangled mass of naked bodies. It was just like so many nights had been at The Bricklayers Arms, when that rat Burroughs had held his orgies. The throbbing music, the overpowering smell of drugs, perfume and sweaty bodies, grabbed at my insides, and I was suddenly, uncontrollably, violently sick, able only to quickly turn my head and direct the flow into the sink of the kitchenette.

As I wiped my face with a towel, I heard a young voice laugh, and saw a girl, no older than fourteen, peel her skinny torso from the mass on the floor. "I'ss B'linder! You 'ad too much to drink, sweetie?" she giggled. She waved a splif in my direction. "'ere, 'ave a drag of this."

Angrily I knocked her hand aside, my eyes scanning the squirming sea of flesh on the floor and the couches. "What the hell is going on?" I demanded of everyone and no-one in particular.

There was a splutter of amusement from the crowd, and Ray's head appeared with a pair of slim arms wrapped around his neck. "Just an 'after-show' party, Belinda sweetheart; we're entertaining a few fans. Come and join in, if you want."

For a moment, I couldn't speak, my mind was in turmoil. I wanted to scream at them: *You have no idea what this is doing to me!* But, of course, that was the point, they didn't know. And much as I disapproved of what they were doing, I couldn't blame them for what had happened to me in the past.

When I was finally able to put together a sentence, all I could say was: "I thought you were part of the answer, but you're not! You're part of the problem," before flouncing off back to my bunk. I was disgusted with them. They were married men. For all I knew, they could have daughters the same age as those girls they were having sex with.

-♪-

All that night, whenever I finally drifted back into sleep, images reformed in my mind. Cloudy images, from the Bricklayers Arms. Of distorted faces close to mine - men, grunting, laughing, one after another, sex without feelings. Of music, loud, thumping, piercing. Voices, a babble. Bodies, mine, others, tangled. Then I would wake again, sweating and shaking, crying as the dreams slowly dissipated like wisps of smoke sucked into the extractor fan.

When I was woken by the swaying of the bus as it set off at dawn, I dragged myself from my bunk and into the wash room, unsteady from the movement of the vehicle and lack of sleep, bumping from one wall to another. Inside, I locked the door and stripped off my pyjamas, stepped into the shower, and ran the water lukewarm, to stimulate my skin and tired brain. When I emerged, there was still no sign of any of the guys. I dressed and made my way, one handhold at a time, to the front. I noticed, as I passed through the lounge, that it had all been cleaned up; there was no indication of what had taken place there a few hours earlier.

Adrian, the driver, greeted me with a smile as I settled into the passenger seat. I managed to return the smile, though my mind was in turmoil.

"Who cleared up the mess back there?" I asked after a while, inclining my head towards the lounge, trying to shatter the persistent thoughts that were still teeming through my mind.

He shrugged. "Me. The stink was awful, I couldn't face the drive with that in my nostrils. There are some stains I can't shift. I will have to report it." He turned his head from the road for a moment to fix me with a meaningful glare.

"Don't look at me," I said, defensively. "I spent the night in my bed. But you shouldn't have to deal with stuff like that, it must have been disgusting. I will talk to the boys when they finally surface."

"Ok," he grinned. "Thanks."

Ahead, the road rushed towards us around the next bend, then swished under our wheels like a conveyor belt. The sun was just clearing the horizon off to our right, peering at us through layers of grey cloud. We were already out of Blackpool and heading west, towards Stoke-on-Trent and our next performance.

-♪-

Nick was the first to emerge from the back of the bus. Weaving, hand-over-hand, to stand, blinking in the watery daylight, in the gangway between the front seats.

"Morning," he mumbled.

"Morning," Adrian and I replied in unison, without enthusiasm.

When no further conversation seemed imminent, Nick shambled back to the lounge and collapsed into a couch.

A little later, first Marco, then Benny, arrived, and eventually the others. The lounge began to fill with a hum of subdued voices. Taking a deep breath, and with a little glance at Adrian, I went back to join them.

I glared at each of them in turn, and they fell into silence.

"Hung over?" I asked, acidly. They all nodded.

Having reached that point, I wasn't sure I could go on. It was going to be one of the hardest things I had ever done, and I baulked at the first word. With an effort, I began:

"I'm going to tell you guys something that I have never, ever, admitted to anyone. Not because you deserve it, because, quite honestly, I am disappointed and disgusted in you all."

Their heads came up in synchronisation, ready to protest, but I carried on, quickly. "But I have to put it into words or it will eat at me until I go mad."

This had the desired effect, and they waited for me to continue. I told them about Burroughs, about the drugs and the sex. Forming the words, opening up the memories, was like inserting a knife into my own heart. They sat in respectful silence as I described, as fully as I could, and with tears streaming down my face, the abuse I had suffered. When I stopped, a silence fell over us, with nothing but the hum of the wheels and the swishing of passing vehicles to prove that I had not become deaf. Slowly, as if under the control of a single brain, which had compelled them all to hold their breath, they each exhaled in a long sigh.

Ray rose, came over to my couch and sat beside me. When I looked into his eyes, they were filled with remorse. "I'm so sorry, Belinda." It was all he could say. He took my hands in his and squeezed them, then stood and walked, head down, towards the back of the bus.

One by one, the others did the same, until I was left sitting alone.

-♪-

Traditionally, minor performers open the show and the star appears last. It keeps the fans in a state of expectation and builds the tension. As the unproven act, we were on first, and I discovered that support acts often perform to half-empty theatres. Unoccupied seats, especially in the front rows, awaited the arrival of fans of the star turn;

they were not interested in the unknowns preceding him. But we found, as the tour developed, that many in the audiences had heard our record, and we enjoyed enthusiastic welcomes wherever we performed, to such an extent that word seemed to go before us, and there became fewer and fewer empty seats.

Those performances merge together in my mind. The memories are there, clear and sharp, but the sequence is confused. From my diary I can trace from venue to venue, one theatre after another, but what happened at one show sometimes seems to be cross-referenced to another. From Blackpool we went to Stoke-on-Trent, then Wolverhampton, Birmingham and Sunderland. The layout of one place differed a little from the others, the stage may have been longer or deeper, or the auditorium may have been closer, but it made little difference to us. We travelled, performed, slept, travelled and performed, until it became hard to know where we were, and it is important to know what town you are in. Part of the rapport with an audience comes from identifying with them - they love to hear the name of their town, and if you can comment on some landmark or local celebrity you become their friend, someone to be trusted, adored.

While we were in Hull, a new top twenty was released, and 'Paddington Nights' rose to number eleven. On the strength of that, Jenny got us on Ready Steady Go, which entailed a dash to London to mime to the record in the ITV studios, then immediately back on the bus to get to Brighton for that night's gig. We were so tired from late nights and constant travel that we slept on the coach all the way to Brighton.

As a result of our growing success and popularity with the audiences, we were moved up one place, from opening the show to second on. The Majesterials were clearly put out at being moved down, and I saw much arm waving and angry pacing as they remonstrated with the manager, but with no success. As they stamped past me on their way back to the dressing room, they glared at me as though I had said something to cast doubt on their parentage.

After Brighton, we hit Plymouth, then Manchester, Liverpool and Sheffield. Mostly single shows, but occasionally with a second night.

On the day we travelled southwards to Southend-on-Sea, another new chart put the Dave Clark Five into the number one spot with 'Glad All Over', and 'Paddington Nights' reached number six. Joy for us, but misery for Buster Damone, whose place we took at last-but-one in the running, immediately before Fortinelli came on.

-♪-

London: full circle for us, as we returned to our home base for the last three nights of the tour - ironically, the circle was to close on us.

The first show was at the Dominion, where we were greeted enthusiastically when the compère announced us. As we left the stage, however, Tony Fortinelli was waiting in the wings to be called, and he told me to stay, proclaiming that he wanted me to sing a duet with him.

My heart sank. I had listened to his previous performances with amazement from the wings; he was frequently drunk on stage, his timing was terrible, and he often forgot the words. As he spoke to me then, waves of alcohol fumes were propelled from his mouth into my face, making me gasp for air.

I heard the compère shout his name, and saw him switch on the fake, toothy smile, just before emerging from the wings to the adulation of his fans.

"Thank you, thank you lovely people," he said into his hand mike. "It's really won'erful to be back in your lovely city of Lon-don."

He waited, smiling and waving, for the cheers and clapping to die down.

"Now, you just saw our young rising star, Belinda Bellini - isn't she great?"

The crowd applauded spontaneously with yells and whistles, but I could see him encouraging them with his hands, as though they wouldn't be doing it without his prompting.

He cut in on their cheering, unwilling to let it go on too long. "Let's bring her back, shall we?" As the audience went wild, he turned to the wings where I was waiting, and gestured for me to join him.

"Now I have to tell you good people," he announced, as I walked out to stand beside him, "that our Belinda's first ever record has climbed to number six in the chart this very day. How about that?" Again, he was flapping his hands, pretending to whip them up. They didn't need it, they were going wild without any help from him.

He put his arm around my shoulder, and his body odour nearly knocked me out. In a voice that implied he was offering me riches beyond measure, he asked if I would like to join him in singing 'Forever tomorrow', his well-known hit single. Of course I smiled and agreed. I could hardly decline, in front of his fan club, could I?

-♪-

From the start, it was as bad as I feared it would be. His band played the short instrumental introduction, but he missed his cue and started late. However, they were professionals, experienced at covering for his inadequacies, so they quickly compensated, and the moment passed almost unnoticed. Worse for me was that, throughout the song, his voice constantly wandered off-key; it was as though he had no idea of the correct notes to go with the words. I couldn't tell what note he would be hitting (or missing) next, and it was quite impossible for me to take his lead in order to harmonise with him. All I could do was to pitch myself with the band and sing the right note, hoping he would home in on my voice. Though it only lasted about three minutes, it felt like an eternity as I battled on, trying to look as though I was enjoying myself.

When, gratefully, the song finally ended, and we bowed to the cheering audience, smiling and waving, I thought my ordeal was over, but he had another surprise for me. Off mike, he leaned over and said "You were flat!"

Shocked, I looked at his face. The smile for the crowd never left his lips - it was fixed, like the painted mouth of a clown - but the tone of his voice had been mean.

After a moment of stunned amazement, I angrily retorted: "It wasn't me that was flat, you old fraud, it was you."

We finished bowing and waving, and he roughly took my arm to lead me off the stage, the smile for the audience still unwavering, but his fingers dug into the soft flesh of my upper arm.

"Just take a look at the posters as you leave, little girl, and see who is the star here," he grunted. "You may have a top ten record, but it takes years of experience to get where I am. If I say you were flat, then you were flat."

As we reached the wings, I shook my arm free to wave once more to the cheering fans, then raised my microphone to my mouth and switched it on. "You may have been around a long time, Mister Fortinelli," I snapped for everyone to hear, "and you may once have been able to sing - I wouldn't know, I wasn't even born then - but you can't now." I turned my back on him and marched off to my dressing room.

That was the end of my tour. As I sat fuming, wiping off my stage paint alone in the dressing room - the guys had already cleared up and returned to the bus - Fortinelli's manager barged in and informed me that I was no longer part of the show.

"His loss, not mine," I shouted to the closing door.

~16~
March 1964
All The Time

The next morning, after a short but deep sleep in the first comfortable bed I had spent the night in for five weeks, I had to present myself at the Oberon offices to explain to Dan and Jenny why I had been thrown off the tour. Timidly I entered the lavish boardroom where they were waiting for me, expecting them to be angry, but they seemed to be in high spirits.

"Don't worry about it," Jenny chipped in as I started to tell them what had happened. "The guy is a first-class prick."

"But he's one of your stars," I cried.

Dan cut in: "Maybe, but not for much longer. He has outstayed his welcome, and my solicitor is looking at his contract right now to find the easiest, cleanest way of ending it."

"And anyway, we have better things planned for you," Jenny added.

"Yes," said Dan, pushing a sheet of paper towards me, "we have nearly finished putting together a headline tour for you."

I looked at the page before me. It was a list of about twenty venues, some of which I recognised from the Fortinelli tour.

"I just have to tie up the dates and fees for five or six more, and we will have you back on the road again, this time with your name on the bus."

"Bill has some new songs he's written especially for you," Jenny continued. "You need to go through them with him - you have about six weeks to put down twelve tracks for an album, AND I want to get another single out in good time for the tour."

"And you are on Top of the Pops this Thursday," Dan added.

"Sheesh! Don't I get any rest?"

"Not in this business, matey," laughed Dan. "Success isn't waiting for you to saunter by, you have to chase it and grab it with both hands."

-♪-

On my way to the studios, I noticed that there were more homeless people than ever in the alleyways and doorways on my route. Ever since my own life had improved, I kept thinking about my time on the streets of Great Yarmouth with Joey, and had been trying to think of some way to improve the lives of those with no way out, no hope.

I was in subdued mood when I arrived, but Bill was already at work in one of the rehearsal rooms, and he soon lifted my spirits. "Belinda!" he chimed, putting down his guitar and giving me a big hug. "It's good to see you."

"It's good to be back," I said. "I could have wished for a better ending to the tour, but to be honest, I'd had enough of Fortinelli's ego trip."

"Aye, I heard from the boys. What an arsehole that guy is."

"I was more worried that I had let everyone down, but

no-one seems to mind. Anyway, we had a top ten single, thanks to you."

"Not me, pet. I just gave you the clay, you turned it into a work of art. Speaking of which, I've got some new songs I wrote just for you, shall we go through them?"

He handed me the lyric sheets, eight of them, and we sat down while he sang each one through for me. They were all good, but one shone out as likely for the new single. It was a rhythmic rock song called 'All The Time' - very different from the haunting sound of 'Paddington Nights' - with an unusual broken tempo and meaningful lyrics that spoke to the heart. I ran through it a few times, experimenting with different tones and pitches, playing with ideas. We agreed it was a strong contender for the next A-side.

During a coffee break, my mind wandered back to the plight of the young homeless people I seemed to be seeing increasingly in London. I asked Bill about life for him on the streets, and told him about my nine months with Joey in Great Yarmouth, and about my wish to do something.

He was thoughtful for a minute. "The thing is, if you give cash to anyone, they will most likely use it to buy alcohol or drugs. That's how most of them ended up where they are in the first place. I don't think there's much anyone can do for the older folks, apart from giving them a hot meal or a blanket. I mean, I was lucky, I wasn't addicted to anything, and I always had a way to earn a quid or two, but most of those poor sods don't even have the will to live. What you need to do is find a way to catch the youngsters when they arrive in the city, before the dealers and pimps get to them. Most of those kids are running away from something, and very often that's a violent parent. It makes them vulnerable to the first person who offers them independence and a new life."

I nodded, thinking about Joey's parents and how he ended up living rough. "It's not something I can set up on my own, is it?"

"Heavens no, girl. It will take a sizeable organisation, just to stand any chance of meeting the kids as they arrive at Liverpool Street or Victoria or any of the dozens of other places."

We sat in silence for a while, my mind whirling with the immensity of the problem. Eventually, by mutual, unspoken consent, we returned to the songs.

-♪-

With scarcely time to catch our breath, the boys and I were back on the road, touring the UK and Europe. But I found several big differences from my previous tour. For one thing, the performers with whom I shared the bill were friendly - their route to fame had been more like mine, most could have been the boy next door. As a result, we all had a great time.

Also, Jenny and Dan had put together a smooth operation that gave us all the support we needed. They had engaged a Road Manager, Stan 'The Man' Bancroft. He checked out the theatres, made sure we had dressing rooms, booked us into Bed-and-Breakfast accommodation, if possible (so we didn't have to use the bus every night for sleeping). At the venues, he supervised the set-up of our equipment, dealt with autograph requests from fans, and controlled a constant stream of dressing room visitors, from the daughter of the theatre manager to the niece/wife/mistress of some local dignitary.

There was no way of guessing who would drop in next. We might be sitting in our dressing room and Roy Orbisson could pop his head around the door, or Tab Hunter, or Chuck Berry. One day, Judy Garland called in while we were doing our sound check, and another time we bumped into the Rolling Stones. Of course, I realised that these great artists weren't there to see me, but it was wonderful to feel part of the living entity that was the world of entertainment.

The realities of touring remained the same; town after town, theatre after theatre - we arrive, we perform, we leave. That's life on the road. But this was the sixties, there was a fever in the air. Every venue was filled with girls screaming - not for me, of course (well, mostly not for me), but for the boy bands. It was sometimes quite scary, they were so hysterical, working themselves up into a sexual frenzy that often resulted in them passing out. And when the boys were on stage, they could not hear themselves performing for the noise of the fans.

The Belinda Bellini Phenomenon

I'm sitting in the lounge of the luxurious *Imperial* Hotel, in London's fashionable Russell Square, with Belinda Bellini, the girl everyone is talking about. Her second single is at number three in our chart, she has just returned from a sell-out European tour, and is about to head off again around the UK.

P.W. "So, Belinda, a whirlwind success."
B.B. (laughs) "You could say that."
P.W. "What are you working on at the moment?"
B.B. "Well, as you said, I'm getting ready for my next tour. That starts in Birmingham on the eighteenth. I love performing live, so I'm really looking forward to it. Currently, the boys and I are in the studio, recording an album, which we hope to have in the shops by October, and there's a new single, which is due for release next week."
P.W. "What's it called?"
B.B. "It's called 'Back Again', another brilliant song from Bill Argent."
P.W. "He wrote your first two hits, didn't he?"
B.B. "Yes, that's right, 'Paddington Nights' and the current one, 'All The Time.' And he is working with me on the album. We are writing songs together, now, which is a fantastic experience for me."
P.W. "Tell me a bit about Belinda Bellini; when did you start singing?"

B.B. "The day I was born. My Gran said I never cried as a baby, I just looked at everyone and said 'la la la'."
She giggles, and I am reminded that she is only eighteen.

P.W. "You were brought up by your grandmother?"

B.B. "Yes, my mum died giving birth to me."

P.W. "Any brothers and sisters?"

B.B. "No. But I had a special friend, who was like a brother. His name was Joey. He died, too."
She is suddenly sad, preoccupied.

P.W. "What happened?"

B.B. "We were very young; he got TB." After a short silence, she says: "Talk about something else."

P.W. "Ok. How did you break into the Big Time?"

B.B. "Ah, that was thanks to my friend Dolly. I was staying with her and Steve, her husband, at their pub in Norwich, *The Lion In Winter*. I used to sing with her sometimes, and had also started to get work around Norwich, performing in jazz and folk clubs. She contacted the agency, they came to see me in action, and the rest, as they say, is history."

P.W. "What do you enjoy most, performing live or recording?"

B.B. Laughs. "It depends what I'm doing when you ask me. If I've been on the road for a couple of weeks, I'll probably be dying to get back in the studio, working with Bill and the boys on new material. Don't get me wrong, I love being close to the audience, there's nothing to beat the thrill when you hear your name announced and you step onto the stage with the crowd cheering and clapping. But studio work has its own buzz, when a brand new song is filling out and taking on its own life; I love it. Then, a few weeks or months on and I will find myself longing for the immediacy of a live audience joining in with the songs they know. I am so lucky to be able to spend my time doing something I enjoy."

I'm just about to ask another question when Belinda looks at her watch. "I'm sorry, Penny, I have to go. A car is picking me up in ten minutes, and I have to get ready."
We shake hands, and she winds her way through the tables and chairs towards the lobby, looking for all the world like little schoolgirl; a tiny figure for one with so much talent.

Penny Wardle
(New Musical Express, May 1964)

~17~
August 1964
Paolo

"e a me mi piange il core, e per sempre piangerà."
(Italian traditional song)

In the staff room of La Scuola di Musica di Settignano, a man lowers his tired body into a leather armchair. He is tall, but the stoop he has acquired over the years makes him look shorter, older, an effect emphasised by his prematurely greying, thinning hair. He wears an old, patched jacket over an off-white shirt, which is pulled in at the neck by a badly-knotted, yellow-spotted, blue tie. His trousers are clean but un-ironed. All these are indications that he lives alone, that there is no woman in his life, to check his appearance when he leaves for work each morning.

He takes a pack of cigarettes from his jacket pocket and transfers one methodically to his lips, lighting it with a match which he discards in the ashtray on the small table beside him. Inhaling deeply, he settles back into the chair, and , as the cloud of smoke envelopes him, he closes his eyes wearily. Life is tiresome for Paolo Bellini. He teaches ... *tries* to teach ... pianoforte to talentless students with delusions that they might, one day, be concert pianists. This day has been the same as yesterday, and the day before that, and the future holds an endless chain of similar days, fading numbingly into the distance. There is no purpose to Paolo's life.

How different it all is from the dreams he and Caterina had when they married in 1936, when Josepe was born, and a year later, when his little sister Helena arrived. He had a promising career himself, then. From glittering beginnings here at La Scuola as a star pupil, he won a place in L'Accademia Nazionale di Santa Cecilia. If not for the war, who knows what might have happened. His mind drifts off into memories, ending, as they inevitably must, with replays of the fights and recriminations when he returned from England after the war, and the image, playing in his head again and again, of his wife and children in the car that took them away from him forever.

Shaking his head, he stubs out the cigarette in the ashtray and raises himself from the chair. He shuffles to the door, along the echoing corridor with its polished wooden floor, down the stairs and through the double, oak, front doors into the afternoon sunshine. It has been another dry summer, and dust rises at his feet as he walks purposefully down the driveway, unaware, these days, of the beautiful view of the elegant city of Florence laid out below like a bowl of fruit.

At the Piazza Niccolò Tommaseo, he takes a table outside the Café Rudolfo. He looks, unseeing, across the square towards the fountain of Meo del Caprina while he waits for the waitress, Margo, to bring his usual bottle of wine. There is a newspaper on the table, La Nazione, and when she arrives, Margo picks it up to make room for his drink. Laughing, she points to his name in print at the top of the page. It is an article about a young English singing sensation, Belinda Bellini, touring Europe.

His hand freezes in the act of picking up his wine, because there, in the newspaper, is a photograph, and the face he sees is that of Rita looking accusingly out at him.

-♪-

From that day, Paolo's acquaintances began to notice major changes in him.

He ordered a daily newspaper - not La Nazione, but an English newspaper - and read it avidly. He could be seen, sitting in the sun outside Cafe Rudolfo with a cup of coffee, the newspaper spread out over the table, his finger following the lines of print, his lips moving as he formed unfamiliar words. Often, he referred to an Italian-English dictionary that had taken up residence on the table beside him, becoming fat and brown with constant use. Sometimes he carefully cut out an article or photograph, adding it to a growing collection of clippings; all, of course, about the new English pop star, Belinda Bellini.

He took a trip into Florence on the bus, and returned laden with carrier bags. The next day, he arrived at work wearing new clothes - jeans, even, and trendy shirts.

With his friends, he became brighter, more talkative, laughed more easily. Those who had known him longest said he was like the old Paolo, the man they knew before the war.

His colleagues discovered a new, sharper, guest in the staff room. Accustomed for so long to his surly silences, they were astounded when he began to take an interest in the cut and slash of intellectual discussion (as of, for instance, whether the local football team should dispose of its manager) and proved easily able to parry their lazy verbal lunges with unexpected wit.

Perhaps, though, it was his students who suffered most at the hands of this new master, when he realised that he was letting them down. He had been brooding too long, ignoring the pricking of his conscience that he could do much more for them.

-♪-

"De Luca!"

The boy jumps. "Si, Signore."

Paolo rises from his chair, loping round his desk with that long stride of his, to stand, hands behind his back, facing the class of fourteen-year-olds, leaning towards De Luca.

"Your homework - where is it?" He smiles, benignly.

The youth is laughing, looking around at his friends. "I forgot it, Signore."

"Ah," shrugs the teacher, raising his head to look around. "You forgot to bring it; what a shame. But you did it?"

"Oh yes, Signore."

Paolo, the smile still on his lips, fixes him with an inscrutable stare. "When?"

"Perdone, Signore?"

"When did you do it, De Luca. The homework; when did you do it? Last night?"

"Er ... oh yes, last night, Signore."

"And how long did it take you to do this homework?"

"Umm, about an hour, Signore."

"Ah, very good." Walking back to his desk, Paolo

perches his behind onto one corner of his desk, then beams at the class. "Most commendable, De Luca; I am gratified.

The boy looks relieved.

"So, it's at home, now, is it? On the kitchen table, perhaps?" Paolo resumes.

De Luca starts. His torment is not over yet. "Si, Signore." Then, realising that he needs to placate the Old Man, he makes an offer: "I'll bring it in tomorrow, Signore."

"Oh, we can do better than that, can't we, De Luca? If you were to jump on your bicycle at lunch time, and pedal really hard, I bet you could get home, grab your homework from the kitchen table, and return before the hour is up. You could do that, couldn't you?"

De Luca is unable to answer. Titters can be heard around the classroom.

"Lambardi!" Paolo has fixed another student with his eyes. Lambardi jumps, and stops sniggering.

"What's your excuse, Lambardi? Why have I not received your homework, either? Come to that, I haven't had any homework from you for last week, have I? Nor, as I recall, for the week before that."

Paolo stands again, and takes the half-dozen steps to bring him to Lambardi's desk. The youth is confused. Old Man Bellini is usually a pushover.

"Sorry, Signore," he mumbles, looking up at the teacher, who now seems much taller than he had been.

But instead of pursuing the interrogation, Paolo paces slowly across the front of the class, glaring at each boy and girl as he passes.

"Perhaps I am making it too hard for you all, is that it?" *Or perhaps I have been too preoccupied to care*, he thought, realising that, for nearly twenty years, he has been back-pedalling.

"*Notazione Musicale*," he says; then pauses for effect. "Musical Notation. Is it difficult, class?"

He stops pacing and scans the room. There is a mumble of assent. He shakes his head.

"No, it's not all that difficult at all, if ...."

He raises both arms, outstretched on each side, and looks hopefully around him.

"If ... what?" he asks, his eyes darting from one blank face to another, receiving a wave of incomprehension in return.

He gives a frustrated groan. "*If - we - work - at - it*," he says, carefully enunciating every syllable. "You know, *work*; what people used to have to do to survive."

Still the sea of faces radiates confusion.

He shakes his head. "Very well, here is what we are going to do. I am going to help you to become the best musicians that you can be." His face grew larger with a big smile, then became sad. "Oh, if only that meant I could make all of you into stars of the stage and recording studio. But I'm afraid that is impossible. Some of you, and your parents, will have to reconsider your choice of career." He turns again to the hapless De Luca. "Am I making myself clear, De Luca?" The youth is sitting with his mouth agape. He shuts it at the mention of his name, but is unable to answer.

"Don't believe what some people will tell you: nothing worth having will be yours unless you make an effort - a lot more effort than you have been making so far. Oh, but don't worry, here is the good news: I am going to help you with that, too." He beamed around the room. They had never seen him so self-assured, so ... excited to be teaching them.

"This is how I will help you. From tomorrow, I will be reporting on your progress directly with your parents." Suddenly, their lethargy was replaced with panic; he could see it in their faces. "If you fail to do your homework," he continued, remorselessly, "I will ring them. If I think you are not trying hard enough, I will tell them. Every day, after school, I will sit at the telephone until every parent knows how you are wasting the money they have paid to give you a start in life.

"But," he blessed them with a genuine smile, "if you apply yourselves, if you work hard, and really do your best, I will tell them that too. That is fair, is it not?"

A mumble of voices failed to convince him that they agreed.

He returned to his chair and sat down. Then, to their amazement, he tipped back his chair and put, first one foot, then the other, on his desk and crossed them at the ankles, smiling beneficently around him.

"Now, that's fair, isn't it?"

~18~
September 1964
Shift to Dark

"Is Connor ok?" I asked Garth, one of the young waiters in the hotel restaurant, when he came to take my breakfast order instead of Connor.

"Dunno, love," he shrugged. "He didn't turn up this mornin'. Rest'rant man'ger arsed me to cover his tables. Good job we're quiet, init?" Then he switched into his 'waiter' voice. "What would you like to eat?"

"Nothing, thanks. Where's the manager now?"

He tipped his head towards the restaurant doors. "He went upstairs to reception."

I thanked him and headed for the exit. Before I reached it, though, I saw the manager return and head for the kitchens. I ran to catch him up.

"Charles!" I called as I reached him.

He turned, surprised, then smiled. "Good morning, Miss," he said, warmly.

"Charles, I'm worried about Connor; have you heard anything?"

"No, Miss. I'm quite put out, to be honest. He could have phoned in, if he's sick, but it's thoughtless of him to just not report for work."

"Has he done it before?"

"Well, no; he hasn't missed a day since he started."

"And you didn't think it odd that it's happened now?"

"I suppose so." He looked rather sheepish.

I found I was becoming angry that no-one seemed to be

worried about Connor, only that his absence was inconveniencing them. It didn't occur them to wonder why he would uncharacteristically fail to show up for work.

"He shares a flat with two of the other waiters, doesn't he? Are either of them on duty now?" I realised that I was quizzing him like a headmaster - an odd situation, considering that he was about three times my age.

"Yes ... Katie ... she's over there." He indicated the girl in question.

I crossed quickly to where Katie was clearing a table, and asked about Connor.

"He didn't come home last night. Neil and me figured he had a hot date; know what I mean?" She continued working as she spoke, folding the corners of the white cloth into the centre, then gathering it up under her arm and replacing it with a clean one.

"Do you know where he spent the evening?" I had to check myself; I could hear a harsh note entering my voice - partly rising panic, partly frustration at everyone's apparent lack of concern.

She seemed not to notice my tone, as she carried on setting out cutlery ready for the next diner. "He went to *The Emerald* at about eight. That's all I know."

"Ok. Look, if you get any news, will you leave a message for me at the front desk?"

"Yeah, sure." I was sure she wouldn't, but I was in too much of a hurry to argue. I ran up the stairs, across the entrance hall, and was about to push through the big doors when Connor emerged from them. He was almost unrecognisable; his face was bruised and cut, his clothes torn and dirty, one of his arms was in a sling, and he hobbled like an old man, every step drawing a grunt of pain from his lips. I felt my breath catch as I saw him.

-♪-

Taking his free hand, I held it to my face as I looked him up and down. "Connor, my love, what happened?" I asked, hoarsely.

"A bunch of lads beat me up on my way home last night," he croaked through swollen lips, then smiled ruefully, a twisted grimace. "I guess they were feeling brave. There were four of them and they'd a skinful."

"But why?"

He shrugged, then winced. "Who knows. Because I'm gay? Because I'm Irish? Because they'd had a good night and felt like kicking some innocent sod? Who can tell what goes on in the minds of people like that."

"Have they been arrested?"

A splutter that may have been a laugh. "No hope of that! They ran off when a taxi driver stopped and shouted at them. I think he saved my life. He called the ambulance and I spent the night is hospital."

"But the police ...?"

"Not interested without some kind of identification, and I'd no idea who they were. Never seen them before."

"Hmph! They could at least try. Maybe the taxi driver could identify someone."

"The cops who came at the same time as the ambulance talked to him, but he didn't see any of their faces." Connor reached out his good hand and gently grasped my shoulder. "Don't worry, my lovely friend, I'll heal. Be right as ninepence in no time."

"It just seems wrong to me that they can get away with it."

"Ah, they'll answer for it. God sees everything."

I looked into his eyes; he was perfectly serious. He had never mentioned religion before, and I realised there were still things about him I didn't know. Unsure what to say, I changed the subject. "Well, you're not going back to your flat alone. You can stay with me while I nurse you." I saw that he was about to argue, but I stopped him. "You are in no condition to fight me, Mr O'Connor, so just do as I say. Ok?"

With another rueful grin, he capitulated. "How can I disagree with logic like that. Lead on, kindly light."

-♪-

The next day, I left Connor in my room while I went to the studio to work on the album with the guys. When we finished, at about six o'clock, I met Connor for a drink in The Emerald.

He still looked a sight, but was insistent that he would return to his digs, so when we finished our drinks, we walked the short distance to the shabby house where he shared a floor with Katie and Neil. I had never been there with him before, and was stunned to see the shocking state of the place. The walls were damp, with the paper peeling off and patches of black mould everywhere. The three of them shared a tiny kitchen and a filthy bathroom. I needed a pee, but could not bring myself to use the toilet there.

So we chatted briefly, then I hurried back to the hotel. The cold air made my need even more urgent, and I half regretted not going when I could have. Still, I would soon be in my suite.

The last thing I wanted was to stop to speak to anyone. But as I passed the hotel reception desk on my way to the lift, my bathroom, a wee, and then sleep, the night clerk called to me. Wearily, I crossed to the mahogany and marble desk.

"Sorry to bother you, Miss Bellini, but there's a letter for you, delivered by hand." He held out an envelope.

I took it and studied it - it was grubby and crumpled, with nothing written on it. I turned it over - nothing on the back, either. "Who brought it?" I asked.

"I don't know, Miss, it arrived before I came on duty. But Cheryl told me it was a scruffy man with a limp."

"Ok, thanks Nick. Goodnight."

"Goodnight Miss."

While the lift bore me to the fourth floor, I tore open the envelope and saw that it contained a folded sheet of paper, but my floor arrived before I could open it, and I was in a desperate hurry to get to the loo. Why is it that, the closer you get, the more urgent your need becomes?

I unlocked the door to my suite, and threw my handbag on an armchair as I ran to the loo. Seconds later, sitting there, in blessed relief, I realised I still had the letter in my hand. As I unfolded it, a piece of paper fell out onto the bathroom floor. It was a cutting from a newspaper, and I saw my photograph on it.

My curiosity aroused, I finished unfolding the ruled page, which had been roughly torn from an exercise-book. I was completely unprepared for what I read:

"Doing well for youself arnt you bitch? You owe me and you gonner pay. I know were you are and I'm gonner get you."

-♪-

Shocked, I sat stunned for a while, my knickers around my ankles, my skirt clutched to my chest, as I contemplated the message, made more sinister by its terrible grammar and spelling mistakes. Who was it from? Some madman? My heart was thumping so hard I could almost hear it. Eventually I put the letter down while I dried and dressed myself and washed my shaking hands, then I picked it up again, with the cutting, and took them into my lounge, where I dropped onto the sofa.

The cutting was a page from the New Musical Express, the interview I did with Penny Wardle. As I read it, I realised that, between us, we had revealed rather too much about me.

I looked at the clock - eight fifty, Jenny would still be at work. I rang her.

"Jenny Macarthur," said her tinny voice.

"Jenny, something weird has happened."

"Why, what is it?"

My whole body shivering by then, I told her about the letter and read it out out to her. A face kept flashing before me, I pushed it aside.

"Stars often get this kind of unwanted attention," she said, reassuringly. "Do you have any idea who it could be?"

The more I thought about it, the more likely it began to seem. Gary Buroughs. He had been limping when I last saw him.

"There is someone, but it's complicated," I said, feeling my chest tighten as I remembered the things that man had done. Fear and anger gripped my heart.

"Well, tell me about it tomorrow. Right now I am getting a security firm to put a bodyguard on you, twenty-four hours a day, starting from the time we end this call. Belinda, take this threat seriously, but try not to be frightened. This security outfit is the best, we use them all the time, you have nothing to fear. Ok?"

"Ok."

"Now let me hang up so I can phone Hamblin Security."

Within half an hour, there was a gentle knock on my door. Standing there in the hallway was a well-dressed mountain of a man with blonde hair.

"Hello Miss Bellini," he said softly, with a noticeable Germanic accent. "I am Hans, your bodyguard for tonight. I just want you to know that I shall be in the corridor, right outside your door, all night. You have nothing to fear."

I thanked him, and as I closed my door, he turned and sat on a chair that he had placed in the hallway opposite. So fame has it's price, and it's measured in lost freedoms. From that moment, I could never be alone again.

-♪-

At breakfast, next morning, I quickly showed Connor the

letter, and introduced him to Hans. I couldn't take up much of his time because he was on duty, but I needed the two men to meet, for Connor to know who the stranger was, following me everywhere, and Hans to know that Connor was a friend.

Jenny and John arrived mid morning. By then, I was sitting at a table in the bar, staring into my cup of cold coffee. Hans occupied a table nearby, watching all activity around me from behind a newspaper.

"We have to make some changes," John began, setting his pint on the table. "Jenny told me about the letter. May I read it?" I took it out of my bag and silently handed it to him. As he read it, his eyes narrowed. "I would say that's a fairly clear message of intent," he grunted, passing it back. "Jenny says you have an idea who it might be?"

I knew I would have to tell them something, but how much? And what would they think of me, afterwards. Under Burroughs' control, I had been nothing better than a prostitute, and he was my pimp. I shuddered as the memories flooded back. Would I never be allowed to escape his evil clutches?

John was leaning toward me, a look of concern suddenly on his face. "I'm sorry, Belinda, I can see it's painful for you. You don't have to tell me anything."

His thoughtfulness touched me, and I gave him a smile. "Thank you, John. Let's just say that he is an evil man from my past. His name is Gary Burroughs." Another shiver ran through me as I said that name, but it was done. Just enough of the past was revealed to satisfy the present.

Jenny took over. "John and Dan and I had an

emergency meeting this morning," she said. "We want you to move out of the hotel and into somewhere more secure. There are just too many people wandering about here."

As if to emphasis her point, a hand appeared suddenly from beside me, but it was only Connor, removing my cold coffee and, unbidden, replacing it with a fresh one. I smiled my thanks.

"I understand. What do you suggest?"

John resumed: "I propose that you rent yourself a town house or apartment in a quiet area, where Hamblin Security can control all access."

"But the cost ...?"

He grinned. "You may be surprised to know that you are already financially self-sufficient. Sales of your records and the money from touring have already cleared everything Oberon laid out for you, and you have a comfortable bank balance."

I was, indeed, surprised to be solvent so soon. I nodded. "Ok, but I know nothing about property."

"That's not a problem," smiled Jenny. "We have already contacted a few agencies, and found a couple of places that would be suitable. Do you have any plans for today?"

"Even if I did, this is more important. I feel safe with Hans around, but I would like to get away from here to somewhere Burroughs can't find me."

"Right then. Paul is waiting outside with the Roller, shall we go?" The three of us, with Hans close behind, headed out to the car.

After a short drive, not more that a couple of blocks, Paul cruised to a halt in a quiet, residential street, and we all stepped out into the cool afternoon air. I looked around, thinking that the houses in this street looked far to large for me, but Jenny and John led the way to a narrow opening between two houses, with a cobbled path leading into a closed courtyard. We crossed to a flight of ornate iron steps on the far side, which took us up to the first floor of what appeared to have once been a stable. Jenny produced a key and let us in.

As we processed round the spacious, two-bedroom flat, I fell in love with it; it reminded me a little, for some reason, of my rooms at the top of *The Lion In Winter,* though, of course, far more upmarket. Hans pointed out to me that, from the security point of view, it was ideal, having only one entrance door, and with windows on only the courtyard side. It was a good start to our property search.

As we drove to the next address, Jenny suggested that I should not walk about London as much as I had been, as it would be too easy for someone to hide in waiting.

"But I would go mad if I was shut indoors all day!" The idea was impossible.

"No, silly. I mean you should buy a car," she chuckled.

"Yes," I enthused, falsely, "Great idea! There's one small problem - I can't drive."

"You don't need to, just hire a driver like Paul," she grinned.

At that moment, we arrived at the second destination, another first-floor flat, but, after a quick inspection, ruled it out. It just didn't touch me. It was the courtyard flat for me; I had already made up my mind, and I had plans.

-♪-

"Stop, stop, stop!" I yelled.

We were on our way from signing the contracts for my new apartment, heading back to the hotel to gather up my things.

"What's up?" Jenny asked, a worried look on her face, as Paul pulled over and brought the Roller to a halt at the kerb.

"Back there," I said, excitedly, "I saw the car I want."

She turned to Paul. "Can you park here for a while?"

"Better than that, I'll go round the block and drop you off at the showroom," he grinned. "And I'll give you the benefit of my extensive knowledge of cars. There's more to being a chauffeur than just driving, you know."

He eased the Roller back into the traffic, and, a few minutes later, we were stepping onto the pavement outside an open yard, with rows of used cars laid out like gravestones in a cemetery. Jenny looked up at the flashing neon sign, and her eyes swept the lot before turning to me. "Are you sure about this?" she asked.

"I have no idea," I said. "I never bought a car in my life."

The five of us traipsed into the show yard, Paul beside me, the rest trailing behind. A man in a check suit appeared beside us like a genie popping out of a lantern.

"Good afternoon, folks. How can I help?" he said, wringing his hands.

Before I could say anything, Paul stepped forward. "My friend," he waved a hand in my direction, "wants to buy a reliable little car. I've come along to make sure she doesn't get ripped off." It sounded really strange to hear Paul speaking so assertively - until then he had always seemed quiet and reserved.

"Ah," smiled the man, slightly taken back by Paul's directness, "I'm sure I can help. How much has the young lady to spend?"

"We'll come to that in good time," said Paul, apparently enjoying himself. I began to wonder what his life had been like before he became chauffeur for Oberon. "Let's just see if you have anything she likes, first, shall we?" He turned to me. "Which car was it that caught your eye?"

"That one," I said, beaming, pointing to the pink Cadillac.

-♪-

When Connor finished his breakfast shift I was waiting for him.

"Got any plans for the next hour?" I asked, barely hiding my excitement.

"Nothing more than drinking a cup of coffee and putting me feet up, me darlin'. What you got in mind?"

"It's a surprise. Come with me." I grabbed his hand and headed for the doors. Two blocks down, with Hans strolling behind, we crossed the road and I led the way through the little cobbled alley into the courtyard and up the iron steps to my pad. I had already decided that it qualified as a 'pad', not a 'flat'; this was the sixties, after all.

"Welcome to my new home," I gushed.

He looked around. "Nice. Very nice. So we won't be seeing you at the hotel any more." There was a hint of disappointment in his voice.

"No, I had to move out for security. Because of that letter I showed you."

He nodded, seriously.

"Come with me, I want you to see it all."

I took him to the kitchen, the living room, the bathroom, chattering on about my plans; then my bedroom and finally the second bedroom. There I lingered, suddenly uncertain, lost for words.

"Yes, very nice, all of it," he said, turning to leave. Then saw the expression on my face. "What's up, angel?"

"I .... erm .... I mean .... would you ..... Connor, would you like to have this room - share the flat with me?"

His head tilted to one side, as it does when he's taking in something unexpected, not uncommon when he was around me. I rushed on: "It would help me out. I don't want the place empty when I'm off touring, and we can be company for each other when I'm home. It's much nicer than that bedsit you're in at the moment, and I really would like you to ... be ..." My voice trailed off; I was feeling emotional and lost for words.

"I know, darlin', but I don't think I can afford half the rent on a place like this."

"You don't have to pay half, the rent is already budgeted for, paid by Belinda Bellini limited." He was shaking his head, so I rushed on: "Of course you can pay something, if you want to. Maybe what you are paying already for your room in Cardigan Street? Please say yes, Connor. You're my best friend, my only real friend, actually, and I'm feeling lonely and scared at the moment."

He put his arms around me, like a big brother, which was how I had come to think of him, and hugged me. "You know what?" he sighed. "I <u>would</u> like to live here, and I could help you by cooking and cleaning."

"You don't have to ... " I began, but he cut me off with a look that bore no argument.

I giggled and kissed him. "Ok, you de boss man. Now I have something else to show you." I jumped up and headed for the door.

"What?" he exclaimed. "More?"

"Oh yes. I've bought a car."

A laugh like a question mark escaped his lips. "You <u>are</u> kidding me, right? Belinda darlin', the roads won't be safe if you take up driving. People will lock their doors and stay inside for fear of their lives."

I opened the front door and we began to descend the iron steps, Hans bringing up the rear, as usual. "Bloody cheek! I bet I would make a good driver."

"You would make a good driver cry! Angel, you can't even walk safely, you crash into people because you're so busy looking into shop windows." he laughed again, and I had to smile wryly and agree with him.

"Anyway, I'm not planning to drive myself. I'm going to hire a chauffeur, with a uniform, and a cap he can touch and say 'where to madam?' as he opens the door for me."

We walked the short distance to the car lot, coming to a halt beside my acquisition.

"What do you think?" I grinned.

"This is yours?" he finally managed to ask; I nodded.

"Do you have a driver yet?"

"Nope. Jenny and John are scouring the agencies as we speak."

"Then will you allow me to introduce you to a friend of mine? I think he may be perfect for you ... and for this car."

~19~
October 1964
On The Road Again

I was packing my suitcase, ready for the trip. Most of my stuff - my costumes, day clothes, wigs and personal things - were already on the bus, heading for Birmingham. All I had to carry were some clean knickers, bras, some light clothes and toiletries.

On the coffee table was an envelope, addressed to The Reverend Potter, containing the ten-pound note to pay for Joey's grave. It was a kind of superstition that had grown without me noticing. I could have sent a cheque, which would have been safer and more sensible, but putting cash into an envelope had become a routine that gave me a sense of ... rightness.

My car would be picking me up in an hour - no more sharing with the guys. For security, I had to travel alone, but for my bodyguard, and stay in hotels. It felt as though a fortress was being built up around me - like Norwich Castle, perched up on its mound, remote, intimidating - and all I could do was watch from the walls as the world passed by below me. This was my big tour - sixty-six gigs over ninety-one days - why did I not feel excited?

The Rolling Stones had just finished singing 'Route 66' on my record-player, when there was a knock at the front door. I heard Hans open it, then a few moments later, he came into my lounge. "My boss is here to take over now, Miss."

There was someone else in the hallway, partly hidden by the door frame and Hans' huge shoulders.

"Thanks Hans, see you again soon, I expect."

"Oh yes Miss."

He moved away and the other man approached. "Hello Belinda."

For a moment I was confused. The face was familiar, but out of context. It took several seconds before I realised. "Oliver?"

He grinned, and that clinched it. The smile was still the same. I ran and threw my arms around his neck. "What are you doing here?"

"As Hans said, I'm his boss. That means I get to choose who takes care of you, and from now on it's going to be me."

"You mean, Hamblin Security is yours?"

"Yep. When I finished my National Service, I was well trained and had some money saved up, so I started my own business. Done quite well, too, I'm glad to say."

"Well, so am I."

Emotions swamped me, first elation at seeing him, then confusion and ... and what? ... the beginnings of a stirring inside?

"Come in while I finish getting ready."

He followed me across my room and sat on the big sofa while I stuffed the last few things into my case. I couldn't concentrate, and found myself checking every few seconds that he really was there with me. Each time I did, he was watching me, and we both smiled, then looked away, embarrassed at being caught looking.

-♪-

Neither of us spoke for a few minutes, while I busied myself throwing undies and things into my little case, but, as I closed the lid and snapped the catches, I had to say what was on my mind:

"Oliver, I spent the last two years thinking you were dead; Burroughs told me his thugs had killed you."

"They nearly did. I was lucky that a woman saw what was happening through her window and called the police. Two of the cowards ran off when the woman came out and started screeching at them, but I managed to sit on the third one until the boys in blue arrived."

"Were you badly hurt?" I moved over to the settee and sat beside him.

"They made a mess of my face." He rubbed a scar on his cheek. "I won't win any more beauty contests," he grinned.

I touched the scar. It was long and jagged, and I could see that his cheekbone under it was misshaped. I gently pressed my fingers on the flesh, feeling strange ridges. "How did they do this?"

He shrugged. "Knuckle dusters, boots, I lost track of what they were doing. But, luckily, they didn't connect with my skull. So, although I spent a week in hospital, there's no brain damage."

"You know I've had a threatening letter from Burroughs?"

"I guessed it was him when Jenny told me about it." He gripped my shoulders gently with his big hands, and stared intensely into my eyes. "He'll have to get past me, and this time I'm ready for him," he growled.

His presence was having a strange effect on me. He had certainly developed into a fine example of manhood - tall, physically toned, with broad shoulders and thick arms that stretched the material of his suit. And his voice, with that warm, comfortable Yorkshire accent, was seductive. I leaned over and kissed his damaged cheek. "I'm so happy to see you again," I whispered, rather more huskily than I had intended.

-♪-

As we emerged from the courtyard, Oliver stopped in his tracks and set my case down. "Please tell me that's not your car," he said, staring at the pink Cadillac, with my chauffeur standing beside it. "You are supposed to be keeping a low profile."

"A girl has to show a bit of style," I pouted.

"That's not style, that's ..... showbiz!" he spluttered.

I laughed. "Look, buster, if Elvis can have one, so can I. Come on, meet Leroy."

He picked up my case and passed it to my driver as I introduced them.

"I'm sure Leroy is not his real name, but it suits him, don't you think? Connor found him for me." Leroy rewarded me with a huge smile, revealing ranks of beautiful creamy-white teeth, as he and Oliver shook hands.

"Did you choose this uniform?" Oliver frowned at me. He was beginning to realise that my taste was definitely not conservative. Leroy was dressed in a very well tailored jacket and trousers in a shade of purple, with crimson piping and a cap to match.

"Of course," I replied as I slid into the rear seat.

With a non-commital grunt, he took his place beside me, and Leroy closed the door.

"Leroy, darlin', would you stop off and get some champagne, please?" I called to him on the intercom as he took his seat behind the wheel.

"Sure thing, boss," he replied in an awful fake Bronx accent.

-♪-

I saw nothing of the journey that took us to Birmingham. Oliver and I had missed so much of each other's lives and, though I had pushed it always to the back of my mind, I had missed him, dreadfully. We drank champagne and talked, both of us with a million questions to be answered.

He told me about the week he spent in hospital after the beating he received from Gary Burroughs' boys, and I told him about my imprisonment in the cellar and subsequent escape.

He informed me that Burroughs and his gang were held by the police for a day, following his assault - and that was why I was left alone for long enough to get away.

I recounted how I found Dolly in Norwich, and she helped me with my career, as well as being a wonderful friend.

Then I listened entranced as he recalled his time in the army. He was conscripted into National Service for eighteen months, and he loved it. He was equal with every other newcomer, enjoyed good food and a warm bed at night, and thrived on the hard work. Within weeks of completing his basic training, he was promoted to corporal, then made up to sergeant before a year had passed. He even considered signing up for a career in the new, professional army, but not for long; he had a mission, and that was to find me.

Not one for hitting the town on his evenings off, he had saved his wages, so that when he completed his term, he had a comfortable bank balance. But then he read about my success, and his nerve failed him; he dithered, afraid I would think he was only interested because of my fame. The phone call from Jenny, assigning Hamblin Security to the task of protecting me, was an unexpected stroke of luck.

With every moment in his company, I found myself falling deeper in love with him. At last I could admit it to myself, now that he was there with me. Maybe it was the wine, but the sound of his voice was soothing, and his presence, so close after our prolonged separation, made me feel dreamy. I could see that he was deeply affected, too - his eyes were constantly on my face, his hands gripped mine as though afraid we would be parted again, and before long we were locked together in a passionate kiss that could only lead to one thing.

-♪-

"What about Leroy, can't he see us?" Oliver asked, anxiously, dragging his lips from mine and looking towards the glass screen between the front and back of the car.

"Nope, this is all one-way glass," I waved my hand around at the windows and partition. "We can see out, but no-one can see in. And he can't hear us either, it's soundproofed."

I raised my voice. "You can't hear us, can you, Leroy dear?"

There was a moment's silence, and I was about to resume our embrace, when Leroy's voice said, hesitantly: "Er, shall I turn off the intercom now, miss?"

I gasped and stared wide-eyed at Oliver, my hand over my mouth. He was shaking with barely suppressed laughter. Summoning all my self-control, I managed to answer: "Yes please, dear."

As soon as we heard the 'pop' of the speakers being turned off, we collapsed in hysterical, alcohol enhanced, tearful giggling, rolling on the seat, hugging each other.

With bodies, arms and legs entangled like that, however, it wasn't long before we began kissing again. And, though we may have been drunk, we both knew what we were doing, what we were telling each other. My heart was thundering in my chest. We snatched what breaths we could without breaking the kiss. At that moment, I knew that I wanted nothing in the world more than to feel him inside me.

-♪-

By an effort of will, I eased my lips from his, staring into his eyes, stroking his face with my fingers, feeling myself being drawn into him, longing to be possessed by him. Then I pulled away and knelt on the thickly carpeted floor of the car, facing him, my eyes still locked with his.

Reaching behind me, I ran the zip of my dress down to my waist. He watched, hypnotized, as I shrugged it from my shoulders and let it fall to the floor around my legs. My little bra was next; I unhooked it and slipped it off, sliding it down my arms to join my dress on the floor. Wantonly, I raised my hands to my head and posed, turning a little left and right. He tilted his head, a smile pulling at his lips, and his eyes narrowed in appreciation as he gazed up and down my body.

In the confined space of the back of a Cadillac, I realised that some gymnastics were needed to remove the rest of my clothes. I had to half stand, bent at the hips, leaning across the width of the car, steadying myself with my hands on the window frame, so I could step from the heap of blue material that had been my dress.

From that position, nearly naked, with my arse in the air, I unexpectedly found myself face to face with crowds of people waiting to cross the road only a foot away from me. I gasped, before remembering that they could not see me, and was then shocked to find that their closeness actually seemed to feed my passion; I felt as though I wanted them to watch us making love.

Oliver moved from his seat to crouch in the little space that remained on the floor behind me. I felt his hands sliding up and down my legs, stroking first the outside of one, then the inside of the other, his breath hot on my bottom. With a fluid movement, he suddenly slipped his fingers into each side of my knickers, and eased them down to my thighs. I wriggled a little to help him, and heard his breath catch at the sight of my naked bum jiggling before his eyes. Then, grasping my hips with both hands, he pulled me closer and pushed his face between my legs, so that his mouth was pressed hard against my vulva. I cried out at the exquisite sensations that flooded through me as he moved his face and lips against me, nibbling at my labia, pressing his tongue into the wet cleft between.

-♪-

He released me, and I looked back to see that he was unhooking his belt.

Quickly, I turned and, kneeling again, helped him to remove it, then began undoing the buttons below, acutely aware of the tightness of the fabric beneath my fingers. His trousers fell away, and I felt a violent force take control of me when I saw the bulge of his erection forcing against the thin material of his underpants.

Unable to hold back, I stretched and pulled down his pants and grabbed his manhood as it sprang forth, holding it lovingly between my hands, stroking it with my fingertips, feeling it twitch in my hands. I kissed it, licked the shiny head, then opened my mouth and engulfed it. I heard him gasp, then sigh, as I slid my tongue over it, savouring the musky saltiness of it, pushing my face into his groin as I took the full length of it into the back of my throat. I held it as long as I could, then slid it almost out again, wrapping the fullness of the head with my lips while I breathed again through my nose.

He took my face between his hands and raised it to his own, kissing my lips and nose. Then, easing away from me for a moment, he twisted his body so that he was lying on the carpet, then drew me to him, wrapping his arms about my shoulders like the wings of an angel. I rested my head on his chest, feeling it rise and fall as he breathed heavily, hearing his heart beating a frantic rhythm.

His voice, when he spoke, boomed in my ear: "I have to know, my love. Are you sure?"

I raised my head to gaze up at his face, so earnest, so concerned. "Yes, my darling, I have never been so certain of anything in my life. I love you with all my heart, I want us to be one."

To leave him in no doubt, I arched my body and slid over his until I was lying on top of him, my breasts brushing the coarse hair on his chest, my feet on either side of his legs. I kissed him hard, then wriggled my hips to capture his cock on the entrance to my vagina. Holding it like that for a moment, I felt it swell rock hard, pressing against my opening. I swayed my body a little, each movement easing him a little further inside. My whole body was screaming with desire, I needed to feel every inch of him tightly inside me.

I placed my hands on his chest and sat up, all my weight pushing his beautiful prick into me as far as it would go. His pubic bone pressed against my clitoris and I shuddered with delight, raising myself a little to press down again, and then again, gasping with the intensity of the sensations that flooded every part of me. I wriggled, each movement filling me with fire.

Oliver drew me down to kiss my face. As he did so, and while we were still joined together, he grabbed my buttocks, pulling my hips tight against his, then rolled us both over, so that he was on top of me. He grinned, impishly, then straightened both his arms, so that his torso was raised above me, and began to slide his cock in and out, each time plunging deeply, then holding still before withdrawing and repeating the action. Each movement was like a wave bursting over me, I found I was climbing to a climax. "Oh yes!" I cried. "Oh, my love, yes, yes, yes." And suddenly, we were grinding at each other, thrashing on the carpet, sweating and gasping and crying out together. As I reached my orgasm, he thrust into me, and I felt each pulse as he released his fluids deep inside.

~20~
January 1965
Warning

Touring creates a false world, filled with the oddest feelings. There's the nerves before going on stage. Even though you are used to it all, you still can't quite believe it can keep going so well, it can so easily fall down around your ears. Many people become obsessively superstitious, and accumulate all kinds of talismans and routines, afraid to stop in case they unleash all their worst nightmares.

And then there's the emotional high while you perform to a thousand, or ten thousand, adoring fans; there is nothing like it. You have them, they love you, want you. Your heart pounds with a kind of ecstasy. Then, after the encores, you sit in the silence of your dressing room, with echoes of your performance still resounding in your head, until the exhaustion catches up with you and you start to shake.

Every show, on and on, day after day, highs and lows, up and down, and up again, and down again.

That's when I can understand the artists who take drugs ... to relax, to prevent throwing up from nerves, to get a feeling of creativity when your mind is numb, or just for an escape. I had always known that the boys in the band smoked hash, I had smelt it in the bus the first time we travelled together, and had also seen them buying packets of gear from shady looking characters in expensive cars. And there had been the night on the bus when I was sickened to find them high on other substances, and having sex with young girls.

If not for my experiences when Burroughs was pumping me full of stuff, maybe I would have followed that same road, just as so many other performers have done. In a way, what happened then had prepared me for this part of my life, though I could never bring myself to feel thankful. I'm also convinced that, if he had not fed me such a mixture of drugs, if he had just got me hooked on heroin, for instance, I may never have recovered. Once drugs have their evil hold on your mind and body, they never let go. There can be only one outcome.

Without Oliver, I would have hated that tour. I was already disillusioned by the falseness of the life and the pressures imposed by the people who wanted a piece of me. I had made up my mind at the end of the last one that I would take a long holiday once my current obligations were fulfilled.

But this tour was suddenly different; I had my Ollie with me. He was there in the wings when I performed, in the dressing room with me, in the car with me, and in my bed. It created a weird dichotomy: two worlds running parallel - the insane, unreal existence of the pop star, offset by the security of a lover's arms. For a little while, I was happy.

-♪-

Manchester.

I came off the stage, waving to the audience, skipping past the band, who were still playing the closing bars of the last encore.

Oliver, waiting in the wings as always, took me in his

arms and hugged me. Together we waited while the crowd clapped and cheered. This is where, after two encores, we need to let them show their appreciation, but start to wind down towards the moment when I would return to the stage for the last time, and rejoin the boys for our curtain call. The fans understand, they know the drill as well as we do. It is part of the love affair they have with me. So I wait, and they clap until their hands are sore, and shout until they are hoarse.

A stage hand called across from around a partition: "Telephone call for you, Miss Bellini!"

"I'll be right there," I shouted. "I have to finish."

I turned and ran back on stage, to a surging wave of cheers and applause. Whoever was ringing would have to wait - the show always comes first.

The band ended the number with chords and a drum-roll, and we left together as the curtain came down and the compère ran on.

Panting, after two hours energetic performance, I took the phone from the stage-hand.

"Hello, Belinda Bellini," I smiled.

"Yeah," growled a distorted but familiar voice. "I know who you are. You gonna die, you fuf-fucking cow, and there ain't nothing you or your sus-sus-smart-arse boyfriend can do about it. In fact, I'm - I'm - fuff-fuckin' gonna kill him too."

There was a click, and the call was cut off. I stood, unable to move, shivering, hearing the purring sound of the dead line in my ear. Oliver had been in conversation with the stage manager, but ran over when he saw my face.

"It's Burroughs," I said.

A shocked expression crossed his face. He snatched the phone from me and put it to his ear.

"He hung up," I added, needlessly.

"What did he say?"

"He said he's going to kill both of us."

With a grim expression on his face, he returned the handset to its cradle on the wall-phone, and led me back to my dressing room.

~21~
June 1965
Too Close For Comfort

Leroy eased us out of Leeds city limits and onto the M1 motorway, heading for home.

I was exhausted. Apart from the phone call at Manchester, two days earlier, it had been a good tour - the fans had been wonderful, the guys in the band and I had bonded, and my Olly had been with me - but it was physically hard work, and the constant worry about Burroughs had placed a heavy burden on us. At last we could relax a little, and I settled back into the cushions piled on the back seat and closed my eyes.

Maybe I dozed for a few miles, or perhaps I was just letting my mind wander, but I heard Oliver's voice say softly: "Sheffield. That's where I was born."

I looked out of the window to the right and saw the huge cooling towers of the steel works, plumes of steam rising and dispersing in the grey skies.

"Shall we visit?" I mused.

He thought for a moment. "I was only seven when we left, and the place had been bombed to bits. There won't be anything there that means anything to me. No, my love. Thanks, but it wouldn't be a good idea."

We snuggled down into the cushions and fell asleep.

-♪-

Travelling in a car always has the same effect on me; the swaying motion, the droning of the tyres and and the repetitive swishing of other vehicles, all conspire to make me sleep, like a baby in a pram. Oliver and I lay wrapped in each others arms, blissfully unaware of the passing miles. Occasionally, I opened my eyes, looked at the face beside me, smiled contentedly, and floated away again.

But our poor driver had to concentrate, hour after hour. We had an agreement that he could stop at any time, if he wanted or needed to, and in no circumstances would he drive for more than three hours continuously. So it was that I became aware of a change in the motion of the car. I heard the ticking sound of the indicators, and looked out of the window. A sign for Nottingham drifted past, then we slipped off the motorway into a service area.

We all made use of the facilities, first the toilets, then the coffee shop. In our time together, I had grown to love Leroy. He hid a clever mind and a wonderful, subtle sense of humour behind a quiet façade. He had become an essential part of the background to our lives, and I respected him enormously.

As we waited in the queue for our coffees, I picked up a leaflet of local attractions and began to thumb through. "Why do they think everyone wants an exciting time," I said, pushing the leaflet back in its display box.

"Are you thinking of stopping off?" Leroy asked.

"Well I would, but I just want peace and quiet. I need to unwind."

Our coffees arrived, and we moved to a table.

"It would be nice to have a day or two away from everything," added Oliver.

Leroy gave us one of his beautiful smiles. I never saw a face light up like his did; it wasn't just his perfect teeth, shining out of a dark face, his eyes seemed to crinkle in a way that made me want to smile back. "Shall I take you somewhere special?" he said, with an impish dimple in his cheeks.

"Where?" I demanded.

"Oh, that would spoil the surprise," he grinned.

I looked at Oliver, who shrugged. "I'm game," he said.

"Ok, Leroy my dear," I nodded. "We are in your hands."

-♪-

Two hours later, after miles of country roads that would have had me lost, we pulled into a pretty little town on the north Norfolk coast. Neatly painted rows of old fishermen's cottages led down to a wide beach, where colourful boats sat at unnatural angles on the sand, waiting to put out to sea again. Heads turned at the sight of our pink Cadillac with the striking chauffeur as we drove slowly through. I couldn't resist, I waved to everyone, pretending to be someone important.

Leroy parked the car opposite a cluster of small hotels, and we piled out, stretching our stiff backs. "Which one?" I asked, absently, looking up and down at a dozen or so similar hotels. All had 'Vacancies' signs outside; I knew from experience that it was a quiet time of year. The other two shrugged.

"Ok, first one with a name that begins with a .... N," I announced, thinking about Gran's little B & B, *The Nest*.

So it was that we booked into *Namaste House*, a thirties-style, bay-fronted house overlooking the sea. Once checked in, we walked into the centre of town, bought fish and chips, and sat on the promenade eating them, with the gulls screeching and swooping overhead. It was a mild spring evening, so after eating we wandered among the amusement arcades. I savoured the feeling of detachment, watching others enjoying themselves with a sense of voyeurism; for once, I didn't have to do anything at all.

-♪-

But the weather changed overnight, and the next morning, as we sat in the dining room of Namaste House, eating our bacon and eggs, we looked out of the window upon a wild scene. Strong winds had the trees leaning and swaying, hail and rain bounced against the pavements, and huge waves crashed upon the deserted beach.

I was looking glumly upon the storm-lashed promenade, when Leroy leaned across the table. "Fancy a walk?" he beamed. I thought he must be joking, but something about his expression suggested otherwise.

"You're serious, aren't you?" I said. He nodded.

I thought for a moment. It wasn't cold, we would be alright if we covered up well against the rain. It could be fun. I remembered 'my' beach at Great Yarmouth, and all its moods.

"Yeah!" I grinned, before I could change my mind.

Oliver laughed out loud. "You two are completely mad," he declared. "Now I will have to go too. I can't let you out on your own, who knows what trouble you could get into."

The landlord of the hotel lent us all some boots and raincoats, tutting good-naturedly as he did so, and we set out into the raging gale.

Once we reached the beach, we were slightly sheltered from the wind by the cliff face, and we made our way slowly along the base of it. It was one of the most amazing experiences of my life. Off to our right, the waves curled and broke onto the sand in great plumes of stinging, salty spray as we walked, leaning into the wind, along the avenue between the cliff and the tides edge. We passed a wreck, a statuesque steel monument that was once a steam trawler, smashed onto the shore, perhaps, on a day like this.

I felt free, for the first time since those innocent days of my childhood. I smiled at Oliver, remembering how we had met, and he returned the smile; perhaps he was recalling that time, too.

We reached a flight of stone steps, rising up a less steep part of the cliff in a long zigzag. By silent agreement, we started to climb. I found myself counting the steps - sixty-four to the top. Then, hand in hand, we allowed ourselves to be carried back to the hotel like sailing ships before the wind. I felt elated.

When we were once more in the warmth and shelter of the hotel, I hugged both of them.

"Thank you, this was just what I needed."

-♪-

At my request, we stayed a second night. The closeness of the sea, and the lack of pressure on me to do something, be somewhere, deal with someone, were washing from me the tensions of the past weeks. We resumed our journey southwards early the next day, arriving in London just after noon.

Chattering away, we pulled up at the entrance to the yard. While the boys started to get our bags from the boot, I headed for the alley.

"I'll go ahead to open the pad," I shouted. Their heads lifted in acknowledgement, then disappeared again into the trunk.

I didn't get far. They found me standing at the end of the cobbled passageway, where it opens out into the open space, staring at the ruin that stood where my home used to be.

"Sweet Jesus!" muttered Leroy as they came up behind me.

The top half of the building was a blackened shell. Most of the roof was gone; just a few beams remained, charred and smoking, silhouetted against the sky like the skeleton of some great, dead beast. Ghostly grey shapes shimmered behind the gaping holes that had once been windows, but were now blind eyes in a wall of soot.

A faint sound, like a handful of stones thrown into a pool, announced that something had collapsed inside the building, and a puff of dirty smoke, speckled with glowing sparks, rose through the gaping roof timbers and drifted away into the bleak afternoon.

I heard Oliver and Leroy put the luggage down, and they brushed past me, running across the yard to the foot of the iron stairs, crunching over broken glass and charred debris.

"Be careful!" I shouted.

Oliver tested the stairway with several hard pulls at the railings, before taking each step gingerly to the top. I watched, anxiously.

Now that I had absorbed the initial shock, I realised that I could smell the aftermath of the fire, a combination of stale smoke, acid charcoal and steam - the stench of my home destroyed. And there was another smell ... petrol! Water lay in puddles all over the yard, glistening with an oily sheen.

At the top of the steps, Oliver peered in through the gaping doorway. "There's no way anyone is going in there," he called down. "I can see daylight through the ceiling, and half the floors are missing."

"Come down, please," I begged, and followed every step as he carefully climbed down. At about the moment he reached the ground, a dreadful thought occurred to me. "Connor!" I exclaimed. "Oh my god! Where is Connor?"

-♪-

Oliver reached my side. "You run down to the hotel," he said, urgently. "See if you can find out if he's ok. Leroy and I will put the bags in the car and drive round."

"No," interrupted Leroy. "You go with Belinda; I can manage here. I'll get there as quickly as I can."

Oliver nodded, and we sprinted out of the yard, heading west for the two blocks to the *Imperial*.

The streets were crowded, as they always seem to be in London, regardless of the time of year. I was shouting "Get out of my way!" and receiving reproachful looks from people. I didn't care. If they blocked my headlong charge, I shoved them aside.

A man came out of a shop doorway right in front of me; I couldn't miss him, and hurtled into his unresisting bulk. He was tall and wide, *built like a brick shed,* as Joey would have said, and it was, indeed, just as though I had run into a solid building. I bounced off him, crashing against the shop window and falling to the ground. He scarcely seemed to notice, or care; he looked down at me disinterestedly, then continued on his way. Oliver helped me to my feet and we ran on; I didn't notice the scrapes to my arms and legs, or the dirty wet stains on my clothes.

Oliver made it to the doors a few seconds before me, and held them open for me to run through to the reception desk.

"Connor O'Connor," I blurted to the astonished receptionist. "Is he here?"

She stared at me uncomprehendingly, and I realised I must look a sight: chest heaving, scratched and dirty from my fall, my eyes wide with near hysteria.

"Don't bother," I said, "I'll go down." I turned and ran for the stairs, Oliver easily maintaining station beside me.

We burst into the restaurant, empty of diners at that time, and no staff in sight.

"The kitchens," I said, pointing.

Hotel kitchens are rarely quiet, never deserted. The huge cave echoed to the clattering of pots and raised voices. Chefs and staff were bustling around, preparing the evening meals, and there was Charles, the restaurant manager, talking to the head chef.

"Charles," I cried, running over to him.

"Miss Bellini," he smiled, holding up his hands to steady me. "Don't worry. I know why you are here, and I can assure you he is perfectly safe."

The relief I felt at his words was intense; I felt it flood through me, replacing the panic that had been driving me, occupying every corner of my consciousness. I tried to speak, but the words echoed in my head. I turned to Oliver, saw his his mouth moving, heard his voice, watched as the camera zoomed out until the world vanished in a pin point..

-♪-

"She's coming round," I heard Oliver say, close by my face. I opened my eyes. An ornate, vaulted ceiling was swinging wildly above me, replaced almost immediately by a small, plain panel, with glaring lights inset.

Leroy's voice behind me said: "I'll bring up the cases," and Oliver acknowledged with a grunt. A humming sound followed, then I experienced a heavy feeling.

Seeing my puzzled expression, Oliver smiled. "We're in the lift, my love. I'm taking you up to your suite. The hotel reserved it for you when Connor told them about the fire."

"What happened? Why are you carrying me?" My voice sounded blurred, the words ill-formed, as though my lips belonged to a stranger.

"You fainted, in the kitchen, when Charles told you that Connor is ok. Do you remember?"

"Yes. Yes, I remember, now. Where is he? I must see

him." I tried to turn, but, of course, I was in Oliver's arms, being carried like a baby.

"Relax, my love," he said quickly. "Charles has gone to tell him you are here."

A momentary sense of weightlessness announced our arrival at the fourth floor. Oliver carried me through doors into my bedroom, and laid me on the bed.

"You're shivering," he said, carefully covering my body with a sheet and a thin blanket. "It's the shock of all that has happened.

I held out my arms to him, and he leant over to embrace me. I was still clinging to him when I heard the soft sounds of someone approaching. Oliver looked up, then stepped back.

"Connor?" he asked.

"That's me," replied the familiar voice with its sweet Irish lilt.

The two men shook hands, then Oliver moved away to allow Connor to reach me. Again, I held out my arms, afraid to speak in case my emotions took over again, and we hugged each other tightly. When he released me, I kissed his cheek, feeling better.

-♪-

"Connor, my darlin' boy," I said, mimicking his accent, as I often did - not mocking, but an intimacy we could share - "this is Oliver, my long lost love." I smiled proudly at the two men I loved most, equally but quite differently.

They smiled at each other. After a shy moment, Connor opened his arms, and they hugged. I felt so happy that the tears began to flow again. Quickly, I wiped them away with the sheet.

"What do you know about the fire?" I croaked, trying to become businesslike.

Connor told us how he had arrived home late, two nights ago, after an evening shift and a drink at *The Emerald* with friends. As he entered the passageway, a man pushed past him, running out onto the street.

"He was hunched forwards, holding his coat up to cover his face, so I couldn't identify him. He would have been about my height, with dark hair, and ran with a limp," he explained.

When he continued on into the yard, Connor saw flames shooting from the front door of the flat, and more through the windows, as the fire spread from room to room. He realised he had to alert the occupants of the adjoining flat or they would be engulfed in the inferno. He ran up their stairs and hammered on their door until they emerged, blinking, from their bed.

"After warning them, I ran back to the pub to call the fire brigade, then returned to the yard, by which time the flats were completely ablaze. I stood with the couple from next door, watching helplessly as our homes disappeared. The Fire Brigade arrived quickly, but it was too late to save anything."

"Where are you staying?" I asked, acutely aware that he was now as homeless as me. *Homeless*, I never expected to be <u>that</u> again.

"Oh, I'm ok. I stayed here the first couple of nights, but a friend is going to let me stay with him from now on." Something in the way he said it made me examine his face, and he realised I had caught something. He smiled. "Ok, you were going to find out soon enough. Leroy and I, we seem to be getting along rather well."

I was so pleased for him that I forgot for a moment about everything that had happened, and I jumped into his arms and gave him a huge hug and a kiss, then stood back, grinning like an idiot, shaking my head in amazement. What a day this had been.

"Oh," he said, suddenly, "I have to give you this." He pulled a piece of paper from his pocket and passed it to me. It had the name 'Inspector Chennery' handwritten on it, and a phone number.

"He wants you to ring him. He says it was definitely arson - there was a petrol can on the landing at the top of the stairs."

-♪-

Detective Inspector Chennery proved to be a tall man in his fifties, dressed in a smart, but well-worn, dark grey suit, a new, pale blue tie, and polished black shoes. I decided that there must be a Mrs Chennery. His face was large, with a jutting chin, a white moustache - stained yellow with cigarette smoke - and thick, white eyebrows. It was topped with a pale, shiny bald patch, wrapped in white hair, looking for all the world like a coral island in the pacific.

"We know it was arson, Miss Bellini," he told me. "The fire was started by pouring petrol through the letterbox, then igniting it with a petrol-soaked rag. We know this from the can that was abandoned by the front door. But it is more than that. Whoever did it knew they were cutting off the only exit, and that makes it attempted murder. Mr O'Connor said he saw a man leaving the scene; do you have any idea who that could have been?"

I nodded. "I know a man with a limp, and he has threatened my life."

"Threatened? In what way?"

"By letter, and a phone call." I remembered the menace in Burroughs' voice.

"Can I see the letter?"

"No, it was in the flat. I showed it to several people; I could quote it word for word, if you wish."

He shrugged. "I was hoping forensics could have a look at it, analyse it for fingerprints, that kind of thing. I wish you had reported it at the time."

He stared accusingly at me for a moment, and I flushed. "Sorry," I answered.

"Never mind. Yes, would you write it out for me? It may not be admissible in a courtroom, but I'd like it on the file. What is the man's name?"

"Gary Burroughs. I was in a relationship with him a few years ago." How much to say? Should I tell him all the details? I decided to wait.

"Why would he want to kill you?"

"He was a drug dealer. When I ran away from him, I ...." *stole his money?* That would be a great admission! "I destroyed all his drug stock; flushed it down the toilet. Probably a thousand pounds worth."

His eyebrows shot up, and he studied my face intently.

"I can see how that might upset him. What was your relationship with him?"

My stomach churned. Would I never be allowed to push the memories into obscurity? "If I had to choose a word, it would be *slave*. He controlled me - by filling me up with drugs - then, when I had no self-control, he sold me for sex to his friends. He is an evil man, Inspector."

Oliver, who had been sitting silently beside me for the whole interview, put his arm round my shoulders. I leaned in and rested my head against him.

The Inspector rose to leave. "We will set about finding this Gary Burroughs. From what you've told me, I'm definitely treating this as an attempt on your life. Miss Bellini, please let us know if you receive any more threats, or any kind of contact from him." The last line was delivered with another meaningful glare.

I nodded. "Thank you, inspector."

Oliver escorted the officer to the door, then returned to my side.

"You ok?" he asked.

I realised that I was trembling. I couldn't answer. I shook my head as the tears began to fill my eyes. He took me in his arms and held me tightly until the storm passed.

~22~
July 1965
So This Is Death

With my pad destroyed, we needed somewhere to stay for a while; not a hotel, somewhere I could think of as home. I also needed a break. I had been performing and recording for nearly two years, and felt jaded, resentful even. I told Oberon to give me a month off, and we went to stay with my dear friends Dolly and Steve at *The Lion In Winter*. Walking through the door of my old room at the top of the pub was like stepping into a cool shower on a scorching summer's day; I felt all the tension slip away ... I was home.

I spent the first day relaxing, walking the streets of Norwich, showing Oliver the sights, meeting some of my old friends. But the need to sing is never far from me, and that evening, as soon as the music started, I was joining in from the floor - I wanted to get up on the little stage and duet with Dolly again. And when I did, it was as though I had never been away.

It was not like working, it was my way of letting my hair down. All the tiredness of the past two years left me, and when Oliver and I slipped into bed at the end of the evening, I was still buzzing.

The next night was a repeat of the first, and the next, and as word spread that I was home, more people arrived. Each night, I sang with Dolly, or George, or on my own. Tensions of the past year just slipped from my shoulders as my old friends greeted me and joined in the songs we all used to sing together. I even spotted Luke Fisher in the crowd - the Luke who's sister Daisy had opened my mind so unexpectedly. He didn't acknowledge me, though, and he disappeared soon after I saw him.

The evening progressed. Sometimes I would take a break and sit with Oliver for a while, before the crowd demanded my presence back on the stage. At some stage, all the free drinks caught up with me, and I jumped down from the platform and went over to Oliver, who was sitting where he could see both me and the room - the instinct to protect me never leaving him. "Just going for a wee," I told him. "I'll only be a minute."

"I'll come with you, anyway." He looked tense. The confined space with so many people and so much noise was making him jittery. His eyes were never still, flicking around the room, checking anyone who passed close by me.

As we reached the door that led out of the bar into the corridor beyond, we found Luke leaning against the wall. He pushed himself away from the wall as we approached, and I was strangely reminded of the day I met Burroughs for the first time. He had also been holding up a wall until I arrived.

"Hello, Belinda," he said, standing in the doorway, preventing us passing through. He had a smile on his face, but there was no warmth in it; his eye were cold and calculating.

"Hello Luke," I responded cautiously. "How are you?"

"Oh, fine ... fine," he mumbled.

"Good. Look, I can't stop, I have to get to the loo." He made no move.

Oliver stepped around me and stood over the young man. "Step aside, please," he said in a voice that, though polite, allowed no argument. Luke moved out of the way, and I darted through, gratefully. As I turned into the door to the ladies, I saw the outer door at the end of the hallway begin to open, but thought nothing of it.

-♪-

As with most pubs, the men's urinal at *The Lion In Winter* was in a hut outside, at the back, where the smell could escape into the night air. But, for the ladies, Dolly and Steve had created a nice loo indoors, with two booths and a washbasin. I burst in and headed for the doors.

The nearest cubicle was occupied - someone smoking a joint, by the smell of it - so I headed for the second, grateful to see it open. But as I was about to enter, the first door opened behind me, and I heard the rustle of clothing as the occupant stepped out in a cloud of sweet-smelling smoke. Then, with a shock, I felt their hand grab my hair, yanking me to a halt. I turned my head, as far as I could, to see who it was, and found myself inches from the twisted face of Gary Burroughs.

"At last," he hissed, glaring down at me.

I gasped, and went to speak, but he punched me, the blow glancing off my side as I tried to turn. He punched again, this time hitting me in the stomach, a vile torrent of obscenities gushing from his mouth. With the air knocked from my lungs, I began to double over, but he dragged me upright again by my hair and punched me again. As his foul breath and spittle bombarded my face, I heard a noise like a door slamming in the hallway. I tried to call for help, but had no breath.

Then, over his shoulder, I saw the door open, and heard that noise again, loud and very close. Simultaneously, the left side of Burroughs' head seemed to change shape, bursting open in an explosion of flesh, bone and blood, which spattered against my cheek. His grip on me loosened, and he folded up, slowly, falling like a leaf to the floor.

Then the walls around me began to swirl, my legs gave way and I collapsed on top of him. As I felt consciousness slipping away from me, the last thing I saw was Oliver running towards me, shouting into a walkie-talkie held up to his ear with one hand, and pushing a smoking gun into a holster under his jacket with the other.

-♪-

Oliver ran over to my body, tearing at the front of his shirt, ripping off a handful. He knelt beside me and pressed the white cloth against my belly, where a huge red patch was oozing. *Blood?* I thought. Then I saw the knife laying on the floor next to Burroughs' right hand. The bastard had stabbed me!

"*Yeah, made a mess, hasn't he?*" Joey's voice popped into my head.

It was then that I realised that I was not in my body, but floating in the air above it, near the ceiling, looking down on the carnage laid out on the floor of the wash-room. Under my inert form, down there, was the equally still shape of Burroughs, a pool of blood spreading across the floor around his smashed head. Beside me, hovering like a gull on the breeze was a face I loved.

"Joey! What's going on?"

"Burroughs wanted to get even." The voice was just as I remembered it, his face unchanged. *"You remember when you escaped from the cellar at the Bricklayer's Arms? You took his cash, and flushed his drugs stash down the toilet? It was like a death sentence to him. He had no money to pay his suppliers, and no goods to sell to earn any, so they punished him. You don't want to get on the wrong side of people like that. They smashed his knees with a hammer."*

"Oh no! That's awful. I didn't realise anything like that would happen."

"Of course not, you're a good person, you wouldn't have done it if you'd known. But remember, he chose to mix with those criminals, and he was selling hard drugs to anyone he could get his claws into. He ruined hundreds of lives, including kids. He screwed up yours just as badly. The only difference is that you rose above it."

"He did, didn't he? He deliberately got me hooked on drugs so he could control me, make money out of me. If Oliver hadn't rescued me, helped me get clean, I would never have got away."

Below us, I saw two ambulance-men arrive. After working quickly to stem the flow of blood from my abdomen, they carefully transferred me, my body, to a stretcher and carried it out.

The conscious part of me, that hovered in the air, observing, seemed to be attached to my body by an invisible cord, and felt myself being pulled along, passing effortlessly through walls to stay with it. Joey floated beside me.

In the hallway, someone was sitting on the floor, one hand raised to cover a bloodstained shoulder. When he looked up to glare at the passing figure of Oliver, I saw that it was Graham, Maggie's boyfriend - the man I had seen from the bus, walking with Burroughs. So he had helped Burroughs to find me and set up this ambush.

Two police officers arrived in the corridor. A few words passed between them and Oliver, then one began to question Graham, while the other entered the toilets. I heard him gasp as he saw the horrific scene inside.

Joey and I hovered near the ambulance as the stretcher was quickly loaded and the driver ran to the front and started the engine, then we swooped down and sat together beside my still body.

-♪-

With sirens blaring in discordant two-tone, I was carried through the streets of Norwich towards the hospital. I could feel that my life, the spirit of all I had been, was unravelling from the cage that had held it. My chest barely moved as each tiny breath kept my heart beating.

"*I haven't died yet,*" I noted.

"*No, that's the cord keeping you close.*"

"*Are you with me all the time?*" I suddenly asked him.

"*Only when you need me, and that's much less often than you think. Most times you do pretty damn good by yourself. In fact, for the last couple of years, all I have done is stand by and enjoy the show.*" That cheeky grin split his face.

"*Am I going to die? Is that why you're here now, to take me away?*"

"*I don't know. The future is not like the script of a film, it can go in any direction. But it doesn't look good for you right now, I must say.*"

The ambulance arrived at the Norfolk and Norwich hospital and the back doors were thrown open. Men and women in uniforms of pale blue and white fussed over me as I was trundled along corridors to an operating theatre.

In a sudden flash, as my body was transferred to a steel table, I was reminded of the scene of my birth - the blood, the green gowns, the gleaming metal tools. How like my mother I looked as I lay still and white on the table.

"*Is my mother with you?*" I asked Joey.

"*No, she moved on long ago,*" he grinned.

"*To what?*"

"*She was with you until your Gran came over, then she went to look after a little boy in Africa and your Gran took over with you.*"

"*So that's how it works,*" I pondered. "*I always felt a strength from somewhere when I needed it.*"

Sudden activity below brought our exchange to an end. Doctors and technicians were hastily hooking up a machine and attaching it to my body. At the same time, I felt the tenuous cord between the two parts of me loosening.

"I'm dying!" I cried.

~23~
October 1965
From The Brink

Blackness. Wisps of a dream floating away, already forgotten; taunting words of a song as yet unwritten, its rhythm measured by the click-hiss of the weight on my chest.

A voice emerges from afar, reciting poetry. It passes me slowly, like a monk gliding across a courtyard. A light blossoms above me, piercing, hurting my eyes. I shut it out, returning to the comforting darkness.

Time slips past like a river, swirling, eddying, grey and cold.

My eyes open again. There is a room, but now it is dark, soothing. I hear gentle breathing as someone sleeps in a chair beside me. I smile; it is Oliver. Comforted, I drift off, back to my dreams.

Activity around me. It is day, and people are busy. Someone exclaims. "She's awake!" A face looms, a stranger, he speaks, but his voice is distorted. Already I am floating again.

Now a familiar voice. "Belinda my love, can you hear me?"
Oliver! I open my eyes and see his worried face. I try to

speak, but the words formed in my head are lost.

His expression changes; he smiles. "Hello," he says, hoarsely. "Welcome back, beautiful one."

I think I smile back, but my mouth feels odd. He leans toward me and removes a mask that covers my face, then gently kisses my lips.

-♪-

Later, a day later, when I could speak, I asked Oliver how long I had been there.

"Three months," he said through tight lips. "We thought we had lost you."

Three months? "What happened to me?" I asked, confused.

"Don't you recall anything?"

Try as I may, I could not think why I would be unconscious for three months. Slowly I shook my head.

"It's just as well," he murmured grimly. "I hope you never remember."

"But what happened? Was I hit by a bus?"

Again, his lips tightened. "No, my love, you were attacked."

I tried to ask him more, but he stopped me with a finger on my lips. "Don't think about it now." He stood. "I have a visitor for you. Well, several, really, but only one at a time, we mustn't tire you.

He returned a moment later with Connor. "You came all this way to see me?" I said as he carefully leaned over me and rested his cheek against mine, leaving a tender kiss as he withdrew.

"I took a sabbatical from the *Imperial*, with their blessing I'm glad to say, and found a job in Norwich until you're better. Everyone back in London wants a regular report on your progress; I have to phone them every day."

"But how did you know?"

"Leroy drove back to tell me, then brought me here when the hotel allowed me to leave; they were really good, releasing me at short notice."

I looked from Connor to Oliver and back again, feeling a great sense of peace. Here were the two men I loved most in this world. I grabbed Connor's hand, squeezing it tightly and holding it to my breast; then I waved Oliver over, and the three of us clung together like drowning sailors to a lifeboat. Tears of happiness were running down my face.

-♪-

Days passed, and I grew stronger. One by one the drips and ventilators and drains were removed, as my body took over from the machines that had kept me alive for the past three months.

As the doctors worked, I became aware of the scars - three of them; a long jagged mark on my right side, just below my ribs, and two smaller ones on my belly. The wounds had healed while I was in a coma, now all that could be seen were jagged brown blemishes on my pale skin. With the sight of them came a recollection of pain, or was I just imagining?

Again I asked Oliver what had happened to me. At first he shook his head, but I persisted. Eventually, he relented.

"Do you remember going to stay with Dolly, after the tour?" he asked.

Did I? Could I trust my mind not to use old memories? I shook my head. "I'm not sure; perhaps."

"All right, let's go back a step further. What can you tell me about your flat in London?" He was deliberately avoiding giving me any leads.

I remembered my pad. I recalled viewing it the first time, with Jenny. "It's in a yard, a cobbled yard. Up a flight of cast iron steps ....." I stopped, a vision intruding my reverie, a black-and-white photograph of charred bricks, a smell of smoke, Oliver climbing those steps.

He squeezed my hand, but didn't speak, just gazed into my eyes, a concerned, seeking expression on his face.

"There was a fire, I remember. It's gone, isn't it?"

He nodded.

"But what happened to me? These scars, how did I get them?"

"I'm not going to tell you, my love. I will protect you from that memory, even though I failed to protect you from what happened." His face became a mask, hiding whatever feelings were behind it, but his voice betrayed angry self-recrimination.

-♪-

A procession of doctors came to my room, checking my readings, asking questions, poking, listening with stethoscopes. Nurses bathed me, changed my urine bag, dispensed my pills. Oliver was away in London for a few days, dealing with business matters, worried about leaving me, but happy that I was making good progress.

I plagued the doctors to allow allow me out of bed, and eventually they relented. With a nurse on each side to steady me, I swung my legs over the side; it felt good. But I had hardly put my weight on my feet when the room began to swirl around me and I felt enormous pressure behind my eyes; I resisted it, but consciousness was escaping and my legs gave way. The nurses supported me and eased me back into bed. I laid my head on my pillow, cursing as I fought the nausea that swept through me. *I will beat this*, I vowed.

An hour later I called the nurses back and asked to try again. It had become a mission, a way to prove that I was strong enough to go home. I made it to the chair, and sat for an hour before they escorted me back to bed. Three paces each way, but it felt like a victory.

The next day, they removed the catheter; I could go to the toilet - what a treat! The day after that I was sitting in an armchair in the patients' lounge, reading a magazine, yet not really reading. You know how it is, when you're mind is elsewhere, and you turn the pages without seeing what is written? It was nearly four weeks since I had regained consciousness, and all I was allowed to do was to walk from my private bed to the lounge.

Outside, drops of autumn rain slithered down the glass, distorting the view of the car park beyond.

I was licking an envelope containing ten pounds for Joey's grave, when, out of the corner of my eye I saw the door slowly open a little, and the top of Connor's head, as far as the bridge of his nose, peered around it. It disappeared again, quickly, and I heard him say "She's in here." The three of them, Oliver, Connor and Leroy, came in, bustling and grinning like schoolboys.

I folded my arms across my chest, trying to look stern. "Right! What are you up to?" I demanded. "I'm pretty sure you two are not supposed to be here for a couple of days."

"Nothing miss, honest, miss," Connor giggled. He and Leroy sat on the sofa, beaming like a couple of Buddhas, Oliver sat on the arm of my chair, bent down and kissed me, then announced:

"The doctors have agreed to let us take you home, tomorrow."

"That's fantastic!" I said.

"Yes, but," he added seriously, "they say you must have someone with you at all times, and you aren't allowed to do anything strenuous. I have got to bully you on that point, no lifting, pushing, pulling, twisting, jumping, running or dancing. Got it, madame?"

"Yes, boss. I can live with that; being waited on hand, foot and mouth. Will you book us in at the *Imperial*?"

"Ok, consider it done. But, remembering how much you liked Hunstanton, we wondered if you may like to go there for a week first."

I nodded, smiling in recollection of the two delightful days we had spent beside the sea. "But not now," I said. "It would be lovely for a break, but I already miss the bustle and anonymity of London. Besides, I want to start searching for somewhere permanent to live."

-♪-

It was a grey October day when we arrived back in The Smoke. A steady drizzle smeared the windows of the

Caddy, and dripped from a sea of umbrellas onto the pavements beyond, as Leroy drove slowly through the streets of London. But I was smiling, happy to be out of hospital, pleased to be alive and part of the bustle of the best city in the world.

We arrived at the *Imperial*, and Leroy lifted my wheelchair from the trunk of the Caddy, unfolding it on the pavement beside my door. It was one of the conditions of my release that I should not try to walk until my abdominal muscles had healed enough to allow me to balance. I slid carefully to the edge of my seat in the back of the limo, and swung my legs out onto the damp pavement. Oliver's hands steadied me as he eased me into the wheelchair. So far, so good.

But the steps up to the hotel entrance presented an immediate obstacle. Oliver overcame it easily by tilting the wheelchair backwards, with me in it, then lifting it effortlessly from the side and carrying it up the steps, with Leroy trotting alongside, holding an umbrella over us. At the top, Oliver deposited me before the big doors, and bowed, with a flourish.

The boys wheeled me through the foyer, waving one hand regally as I passed the staff on the desk, and into the elevator.

Connor was waiting in my suite; so were Jenny and the guys from the band. They had decorated the lounge with streamers and a banner saying 'Welcome Home Belinda.' It was a wonderful and emotional homecoming.

However, I was still weak, and soon tired. So, after a while, they made their excuses and left, and Oliver carried me to bed, where I immediately fell asleep.

-♪-

After a couple of hours, I awoke at the sound of a tap on the outer door, and heard quiet voices in the lounge, fading as someone carefully closed my bedroom door. I floated off again.

Drifting in and out of sleep, thoughts came and went; most were lost, but an idea for the words of a song was forming. I tried them in my head, looking for a structure to bind them together.

Out of the corner of my eye I saw the door open slowly and silently, and Connor's head peered around it. "Ah, you're awake," he said gently. "You have a visitor, if you're up to it. Someone you haven't met before."

"A fan?" I ask, apprehensively. "Oh no, not a reporter!"

He pulled a face, and put his hands on his hips in a deliberately camp gesture. "Do you really think I would let a reporter see you?"

I laughed and shook my head.

"Do you want to see him in here?"

"Yes, please."

Connor disappeared for a moment.

When he returned, he was with Oliver and a man I did not recognise. He was about forty, greying, tanned and dressed in a smart, new jacket and jeans. Connor indicated the chair beside my bed, and the man sat in it.

"Hello, Belinda," he said in a thick accent. "My name is Paolo Bellini."

-♪-

Of course, I remembered the name Paolo - Gran had told me it was my father's name - and I had lived with his surname for all my eighteen years.

I glared at him. "Are you my father?"

"I think so, yes," he answered shyly.

A surge of anger and bitterness rose up inside me. "Why did you leave me? Why did you leave my mother?"

He pursed his lips and looked at the floor. "I was very stupid. I listened to the bad things people were telling me. They said the baby was not mine, that Rita had many men. When the papers for my repatriation arrived, I ran away."

"Did you know she died giving birth to me?" I fixed him with my fiercest look, probably not as fierce as I wanted because I was lying in bed, and still weak, but he was gracious enough to acknowledge my feelings.

He hung his head in silence. When he spoke, it was in a hoarse whisper. "I swear to you, cara mia, I did not know about it until I met your man, Oliver, a few days ago, when I arrived in England."

"Why have you come here?"

"I read about you in the newspaper, some months before. You have my name, and you are Belinda - the name your mother and I chose for you if you were born a girl. There was a photograph - it amazed me to see how much like your mother you are. I knew that you must be her daughter, and that I must be your father. I have not been a good father; perhaps I can make up a little for that."

I found myself shaking with anger. "You have not been any kind of father," I snapped. "Why wait until I am famous before wanting to make it up to me? Do you want a share of my wealth?"

Oliver, sitting in the other chair, on the opposite side of my bed, laid his hand gently on my forehead. "Try not to get upset, my love. I have already given Paolo the third degree."

"If it is distressing for you," Paolo added, "I will leave, and only return if you want me to."

"Yes, I think it will be best. I need time to get used to the idea."

Wearily, he pushed himself up from the chair. He seemed worn out, too old for his years. "I understand," he said sadly. "I will wait until I hear from you. Oliver has the address where I am staying." As he turned to leave, he gently brushed my arm with his fingers before opening the door. The expression on his face was of dejection, of a life wasted. Despite my anger and confusion, I felt a tinge of sympathy for him.

"Paolo," I called.

He looked back.

"Come tomorrow," I said.

A wan smile illuminated his face, and he nodded before departing.

-♪-

I heard a few quiet words pass between Paolo and Connor in the hallway, then the sound of the front door being gently closed. A long silence settled over the flat.

"Wop!" A chorus of children's voices suddenly chanted, in my head; "Wop, wop, wop!"

The twisted face of Uncle Ernie reared up before me; "Damned foreigner's spawn!" he spat.

"My mother is dead!" my own voice shouted, echoing like a cracked record, trapped in an endless loop.

Did I say that out loud? A moan pushed itself from my heart, vibrating in my chest.

A movement beside me brought my attention back from the past, and I realised that I had been staring at the bedroom door, biting my bottom lip, trying to stop the tears that were running down my face. Oliver's hand cupped my head, his fingers combed in my hair, his thumb caressing my cheek, while his eyes probed mine, tenderly.

"All this time I have survived without a father," I croaked. "I thought I didn't need one. But I did! When I was growing up, when things went wrong. Gran did her best for me, but a father would have made it different. He should have been there! If he hadn't left, perhaps my mummy wouldn't have died." The last words shot out in a flood of tears as more memories exploded over me.

Oliver wordlessly slipped onto the bed and laid beside me, his arms wrapped reassuringly around me, so that my head was buried in his chest. For five minutes we lay like that as I sobbed into his shirt, until I drifted off again into restless sleep.

-♪-

In my head, a list of questions jostled to be asked, but

Oliver and I talked into the night, and I knew that I wanted to give my father a chance. Now that he had entered my life, I didn't intend to lose him again; at least, not by my own actions.

We sent Leroy to pick him up, and I sat in my chair fretting until he arrived. If I had been allowed to walk, I would have paced the room; instead, my eyes swept the walls, the pictures, the window, as I rehearsed what to say.

He arrived, nervously entering the room like a deer venturing into a clearing, expecting to hear a shot from a hunter's gun. To show he was welcome, I stood and opened my arms. An expression of relief swept his face of its concerns, and a big smile filled it with teeth as he quickly crossed the short distance between us and embraced me. When he stepped back to study me, his hands lightly gripping my upper arms, the smile was still there, but tears were flowing unrestrained down his cheeks.

"You are so like your mother," he said, emotionally.

"My Gran showed me some pictures of her," I replied, returning to my place on the sofa, and patting the space beside me, inviting him to join me. "I could never see the similarity."

Before sitting, Paolo - I could not yet think of him as father - looked first to Oliver for approval. Only after it was granted by a small nod did he take the offered seat.

Oliver came around behind me and kissed me lightly on the forehead from above. "I have some work to do in the kitchen," he announced, leaving Paolo and me to talk freely.

"Ah yes, your Gran was signora Gladys?" Paolo nodded. "A fine woman. Formidable, but a woman of much love."

"She brought me up; took my mother's place," I said, simply, then fixed him with an enquiring gaze; "And my father's."

His eyes broke from mine, and he looked down at his hands for a minute. After some thought, he raised his head again. "You deserve a full telling ... explaining?"

"Explanation," I offered.

"Yes, a full ex-plan-a-tion." He smiled, shyly. "I am sorry that my speaking English is bad. It has been many years. When I first was captured, I could not one word."

With some help from me, and a few misunderstandings, he went on to tell me how he met my mother, and fell in love with her.

"But there was something I did not tell signora Gladys, or my Rita. They never knew. I am ashamed to say I was already married, in Italy, with two children." His voice trailed away, and his eyes dropped to his lap again.

I took a deep breath. I felt angry for Gran and my mother, but it was too late for recriminations, not the time for letting out anger. "That was rather a big thing to keep secret from them," I said, tightly.

He nodded. "I know. When I realised how I had fallen in love with Rita, I wanted to tell her. But then she became with child ...?"

"Pregnant."

"Yes, she became preg-nant, and signora Gladys said we must be married. It was too late to tell, and somehow, Italy seemed so far away, another world." Again his voice trailed off as he relived those days, and the dilemma in which he had landed himself.

My anger drifted away. I could not help feeling sorry for him. I sensed a man with values, who had fallen short of his own standards, and deeply regretted what he had done.

Despite everything, I could see that he and I were going to get along.

-♪-

Over the next few days we became a family. I came to understand and love the man who had given me life, then abandoned me. He told me about the constant ribbing he had received from his colleagues at work and drinking companions, over Rita's reputation. He was emphatic in his defence of her, but also honest in acknowledging the stories told to him, including some by people who claimed to have slept with her. I was shocked to hear such things about my mother, yet, somehow, not completely surprised. After all, there had been the mocking I received from kids at school, and the names they had called her.

He explained that, when his repatriation papers arrived, he had a hasty decision to make. He would not be allowed to remain in England unless he was able to show that he had a good reason to stay. Torn between two homes, with nagging doubts about Rita, and missing his children, he accepted the free passage back to the land of his birth.

But, when he arrived, nothing was the same. Italy's

economy had been damaged by its involvement in the war; not just because of the cost of maintaining its armed forces, but also in terms of lost trade with the countries allied to England. Jobs were few, with thousands of ex-servicemen looking for work. He was unemployed for two years following his return.

And his relationship with his family had changed, too. His wife, Caterina, had learned to be independent, raising two children on her own for the five years he had been absent, and the bambinos themselves did not know their father. He found that he had become unneeded, unwanted, unwelcome.

In deep financial difficulties, trying to survive on only Caterina's wages, they argued constantly, and, when their home was repossessed, she left, taking the children. He never saw any of them again.

-♪-

To celebrate our 'reunion' (is it possible to be reunited with someone who is a complete stranger, an essential part of your life, but with whom you were never, actually, united?) we booked a table at a busy Italian restaurant, a short trundle in a wheelchair from the hotel. Once inside, we left the wheelchair in a corner and I walked to our table, where we found Paolo already waiting.

Before sitting, I decided that a visit to the ladies would be wise.

"Just going for a wee," I told them. "I'll only be a minute."

For some reason, the words started an echo in my head:

"Going for a wee - going for a wee - a wee - a wee - only be a minute - minute - minute." A picture of the packed bar of The Lion In Winter flashed across my mind. I clutched at the back of a chair, suddenly feeling dizzy. Oliver, a concerned expression on his face, was at my side in an instant, lowering me into the seat.

"No!" I cried, clutching at his arm. "I can't sit down."

"Why?" he asked, confused.

"Because ..... because I just wet myself!" I bleated, feeling the warm liquid running down my legs, filling my shoes. Heads turned at some nearby tables, faces with disgusted expressions stared at me.

Paolo jumped to his feet and ran to grab a waiter, returning a moment later with a large towel. He folded it into a thick cushion and, after he had placed it on my chair, Oliver lowered me gently onto it.

He crouched beside me, staring into my eyes. "What's happened?" he whispered.

"I remember," I gasped, my heart pounding so hard I was sure it would burst from my chest. "I remember Burroughs stabbing me!"

~24~
December 1965
A Song For Joey

At the close of 1965, we began the process of rebuilding. Not my old flat, that was beyond repair - the whole block was condemned and had to be demolished. And, anyway, this time my home would not be rented; I wanted a sense of permanence, somewhere for Oliver and me to settle down. So, we scouted around and, after a few disappointments, acquired a new home.

"*Situated in quiet Caterham Square, with access to private gardens*," said the blurb from the Estate Agents, "*this extensive complex consists of two luxury, self-contained apartments; ideal for owner-occupation or for letting.*"

We signed the contracts in December, and moved in on the first of January. It seemed to be symbolic of a new start. We brought in builders to divide one of the apartments into two. They erected partition walls and installed another kitchen and bathroom. For a while, the place was filled with noise and dust, which was inconvenient, and sweaty, half-naked, muscular bodies, which I didn't mind at all.

While they were busy preparing the building, we went shopping for furnishings. My three men patiently wheeled me from furniture store to auction room, junk shop to haberdashery.

The two smaller apartments were for Connor and Paolo, and they had free hand in the layout and decoration. But this was my dream. My family, together for the first time.

-♪-

Bill called to see me, with some new songs he had composed. I handed him my notebook, open at the page in which I been writing. It was the latest of twenty or more attempts at some words I was struggling to put together. Already I had scribbled out some lines and replaced them with others.

"It's an idea that started in hospital. I want to write a song for Joey, but you know me, I get too emotional. I've got some the words buzzing around, but when I try to write them down they get confused in my mind. Will you read it for me?"

He studied the jumble of words.

<u>A Song For Joey</u>
I was beaten by the world,
and in my darkest night,
You picked me up, and led me
out of fear into the morning light,
From the wreckage of my life, you rescued me
Set my feet down on the road again,
and step by step you guided me
But I looked away and you were gone,
The world still turns and life goes on,
Though now I face the world alone
I love you still, much more than words can say
And I will miss you, Joey, from now until my dying day ....

"Is it too heavy?" I asked, rereading the lines yet again.

"The last two lines are naff, pet," he said, candidly - I expected nothing less from him on a professional level. - "But the rest is mostly ok. Do you have a tune in mind?"

"No, and the words change every day, to be honest."

"A melody will probably help. It gives you a framework around which you can arrange the song, and sometimes words will come to you naturally. I'll bring my guitar tomorrow and we can see how it goes."

-♪-

With Bill's help, the song came to life, and I contacted Hughie White to book some studio time. At first, I worked with Daylight Robbery, and we produced a track that was good, but not what I was trying to achieve.

It was then that I discovered something amazing about my father. Paolo revealed to me that he had been an established concert pianist, before the madness of war engulfed his country. He helped me with an arrangement of the song that would incorporate a full orchestra.

We took the idea to Hughie, who fixed up a recording session with The Amadeus Studio Orchestra. I found myself singing with sixty top class musicians, drawn from some of the best orchestras in the land. It was a little bit like my time with Barry Spence, but on a bigger scale. I found it daunting and challenging, but it was ultimately an incredibly rewarding experience.

-♪-

The song was only part of my plan. When the record

was released, I announced to my family what I wanted to do next. Generally, they were receptive, and understood my motives, but it was still an ambitious idea and they wondered if it wasn't just too big.

Oliver leant forward and rested his elbows on the table. "How do you think the church will react?"

"I really don't know; that's why I have to go up there and find someone to talk to. If it comes off, St John's Church won't be big enough, that's for sure. I just have to hope there's a church in Yarmouth that can hold ... well, I reckon it could be two- or three-hundred people."

Their eyebrows all raised in unison, as though operated by the same puppeteer; I had to smile. Leroy let out a whistle, and Oliver's hands flipped open, as though in supplication. He opened his mouth to speak, but closed it again, shaking his head.

"Don't look at me like that!" I said to all of them. "I know it's not going to be easy to organise. But it's worth it; I made a promise to Joey, and I intend to keep it."

From that day, I began contacting everyone I had met since leaving Great Yarmouth: publicans, groups, singers, agents, anyone I counted as more than a casual acquaintance. Each one I asked the same question: "If I can arrange a date when everyone is available, will you do it for me?"

The response, of course, was mixed. Some people who I had thought of as friends were dismissive, while others surprised me with their warmth and enthusiasm. With the help of Jenny and Hugh White, I also contacted performers who I had never met. By the end of two months, I had spoken, or written, to nearly six hundred people - of whom four hundred had agreed to sign up - and I had an idea of several possible dates when most of them would be available.

-♪-

My heart was fluttering like a caged bird when Leroy and I arrived on the outskirts of Great Yarmouth. It was the first time I had returned since the day I escaped from Burroughs. Oliver had to stay in London, supervising a big operation in which his company was providing the security for a top American star's visit to the UK, and, for once, I didn't mind making this pilgrimage alone.

As we drove across the bridge, with the red-brick Town Hall on our right and the grey river rushing below us, I was swamped with memories. They leapt at me from the doors of every building, taunted me with every sound, overwhelmed me with every smell. I tried not to look out, but my eyes were dragged back to the windows to stare at the past as it floated by.

We booked into a large hotel overlooking the river, then took the short walk to the town centre. It had changed enormously, though not completely. New shops had sprung up around the market, but the shape and feel of the place was much the same. At the far end of the square, however, one new landmark stood out and grabbed my attention. The steeple of a church rose where none existed in my memory.

Drawn, as though by a Pied Piper's mesmerising melody, I led Leroy to the great iron gates at the entrance, and stood gazing in amazement at the huge, beautiful building. It looked as though it had always been there, yet I knew I had never seen it before. I walked, wide-eyed, down the path to the big oak doors, turned the wrought-iron handle and pushed - the door glided open - I entered.

-♪-

Stiletto heels clicking, embarrassingly, on the stone floor, bringing back echoes from the distant walls like the crackling of twigs underfoot, I entered the nave. Stone and oak pillars climbed each wall, between pointed windows of coloured glass, to meet far overhead, like God's fingertips arching in contemplation.

Seeing no-one, and in awe of the place I had entered unbidden, I sat in a pew and opened my mind. Never before had I prayed, but, as I sat under that roof, between those walls, I felt part of something I didn't understand. I closed my eyes and silently asked the question that had always nagged me: "*Are you real?*"

In the silence that followed, I tried to tune my mind in to the cosmic frequency, reaching out, searching for a response, but all I heard was the hiss of my own static.

"I expect you're on holiday somewhere warm," I said out loud, smirking at my wit.

There was a soft sound, like a dove stretching its wings, and a voice beside me answered: "One can always dream."

I sprang to my feet, a cold shiver passing across my shoulders, and clutched the back of the chair in front of me, breathing hard. Looking up again towards the ceiling, I stammered: "You answered me. Who are you?"

The quiet voice, with a hint of humour to it, replied: "I'm the verger here at St Nicholas. Sorry if I startled you."

I turned, my mouth hanging open, to find a man sitting on the pew next to me, dressed in a black robe. He smiled. "You should close that before something flies into it."

"So you're not ....? No, of course not! That would be ... impossible, wouldn't it?" I remembered to close my mouth, but I knew I was babbling.

"God?" He gave a little laugh. "No, just one of His servants." His voice was gentle and warm; hearing it was like floating in a relaxing bath, a totally inappropriate image forming at once in my mind, and I felt my face turn red at the thought.

Quickly clearing the picture from my mind, I said: "Last time I was in Great Yarmouth, there was nothing here but a pile of rubble. This is beautiful."

"Thank you," he replied. "It took years of fund raising, and then painstaking work to restore him to his former glory. Are you from around here?"

I told him my story. Somehow, although he was a stranger, he was easy to talk to. I explained about Joey and my mission, and asked if I would be able to have the service at St Nicholas.

"I would have to check with the trustees," he said, thoughtfully, "and consult the Bishop, but as long as it's an orderly service, in keeping with our tradition, I expect we could help you."

-♪-

The cemetery was not as I remembered it. There had been trees in those days, and an open grave, Reverend Potter and a hearse. All so clear in my memory, so different now.

Far off to the east, through the serried iron railings, I could see the pink of my Caddy, where Leroy was waiting. Piercing the skyline in the opposite direction rose the restored spire of St Nicholas church. In between, stretching away from me on all sides, rows of gravestones that seemed to go on forever. Finding Joey's plot, with no stone to read, looked impossible.

Thank goodness the snow had held off. I looked up at the towering banks of heavy, grey cloud marching in from the north, feeling a chill wind against my cheek; it would not be long arriving. I was glad I had my winter coat and gloves, but it was not a day for loitering.

Casting my eyes around at ground level again, I searched for a clue, something familiar. I remembered that there had been a grave beside Joey's, belonging to "Samuel Raines, 1897-1941." I studied the stones near me, but Samuel's was not one of them.

The first stinging spots of sleet began to hit my face. It would be madness to prolong this fruitless search; I would have to return another day. I was not despondent; Joey had taught me to *'keep trying until you succeed.'* So I turned back to the path.

Something touched my hand, as softly as though it had brushed against a flower. I looked down. There was nothing to be seen but my glove; yet the touch remained, like a hand taking mine and tugging me back to where I had been standing. I allowed him to lead me until we stopped at a bare, overgrown patch, then his hand withdrew. I could sense him waiting, expectantly.

I poked about with my foot at the nettles and long grass covering the plot, pushing them aside, unsure what I was hoping to find. I guessed that the little wooden cross would not have survived, and without that, there was no way of telling for sure that this was Joey's.

Which end was the head? I tried to remember the landmarks as they had been, five years earlier. I scanned the rooftops on the skyline, which were now swiftly disappearing in the swirling deluge of sleet. There! A large white house stood out among the red-brick and concrete; I remembered it. As I had stood beside the grave, with the head of Joey's coffin to my right, that house had been directly in front of me. Taking my lead from that, I knelt on the wet ground where the cross would have been, and began to pull at the weeds with my gloved hands.

At soil level, my fingers felt a rough stump, and I scraped away the dirt until it was revealed. I was sure it was the broken base of the wooden cross I had placed there, and with a surge of excitement, I began tearing at the coarse foliage around it. A few seconds later, there on the ground, lay the cross. I knew it at once, could still see the words etched on it "Joey - 14th November 1960." I snatched it up and held it to my heart, looking up into the curtain of snow, which by then was filling the sky, and shouted: "Thank you darlin'."

~25~
May 1966
A Kiss From An Angel

May is an unpredictable month - I've known it to be as cold as January, as wet as September, or as hot as July; I can even remember snow, one year - so as I arrived at the church on the day of the funeral, I looked up anxiously at the busy sky. Small, fluffy, white clouds - bright against the deep blue background - were rushing through on a flighty breeze, not pausing to share the time of day, while a bank of tall, menacing thunder heads rose like a range of mountains on the horizon to the east.

To say I was tense would be like saying the North Sea is a bit cold and wet; understating the obvious. I was there early - two hours early, such was my state of agitation. I checked out Joey's plot. The stone was in position, covered with a tarpaulin, and an enormous area around it had been protected against being trampled by my army of guests by a vast area of raised wooden decking. A piano, an upright, borrowed from the small hall, stood to one side, a man at work making sure it was in perfect pitch.

As I strolled slowly back to the church, I saw the Caddy arrive and deposit Oliver and Paolo at the main doors. I entered by the side door, and walked up the aisle to meet them.

The first guests had also started to arrive, and I welcomed them at the door. As the numbers increased, Oliver and Paolo shared the load. More famous people were gathered for Joey that day than I had met in my whole life before. Whether it was the tension inside me, the lack of food, the stars who were shaking my hand, or the atmosphere created within that awesome building, I don't know, but I began to feel as though I was watching a movie.

Brian Poole was there, Mick Jagger and Keith Richards, Cilla Black, Russ Conway, all passed before me. But I swear that I also saw Buddy Holly and Eddie Cochran, both of whom had died many years before. They were there, in the crowd, then I lost sight of them. Brenda Lee arrived, taking time from her UK tour, Lonnie Donegan, Marty Wilde, the best and greatest entertainers in the world were congregating in Great Yarmouth to honour my beloved Joey. My heart was filled with pride.

-♪-

Who said show-business is a cynical industry? As I took my place at the lectern at the end of the service, and looked around the huge church, packed as it was from front to back with some of the most famous people in the world, I felt a surge of gratitude.

"Oh, Joey would have loved you!" I said, departing from my prepared notes before I even started to read them. I smiled at them, and there was a soft flutter of laughter. "How can this be a sad occasion when I have so many wonderful friends?

"I didn't know what to expect when I started planning this, but in my wildest dreams I could not have dared to hope that so many of you would come. I know many of you have flown in from all around the world, and all of you have gone to a great deal of trouble to make a space in your busy schedules, just to be here. Thank you, from me and from Joey.

"You never knew Joey, but you know me, and I am what I am because of him. Joey was a little man I met when my world had fallen apart. He taught me how to be strong, brave, determined, self-confident, and yet to never lose sight of the things that matter. To Joey, the things that matter stretch from helping others to helping yourself.

"We were homeless together for six months before he died from ......" my voice caught, and I stared up at the roof, blinking away the tears that had leapt into my eyes. Oliver, who had been standing just out of my sight behind me, put an arm around my waist and thrust a glass of water into my hand. I looked at it blankly for a moment, then took a sip. The action, and the cold water, helped to steady me. After a deep breath, I was able to resume.

"He had a tough life: abused as a small child and homeless for eight years. In the end, it killed him. When he died, I made a promise, and today is the fulfilment of that promise. I couldn't even afford to give him a gravestone, but I swore I would come back and put that right. You have all helped to make that dream come true. God bless you."

-♪-

Outside, when all the shuffling and creaking of boards had settled, I stood beside the piano and nodded to the two men who were waiting to remove the tarpaulin from the grave. As it slid back, the marble stone was revealed. It lay flat, the size of the grave, with a granite border, highlighted at each corner with a little square block containing flowers. During the service in the church, the wreaths and floral displays brought by the guests had been laid out around the grave, stretching right out to the edge of the decking.

Cut into the marble slab, picked out in gold, were the words we had chosen, picked from the song Bill and I had written ...

> Joseph Bellini
> Died 14th November 1960
> aged about 13
>
> --
>
> "I looked away and you were gone"
>
> --
>
> All my love, Belinda
> 23rd May 1966

The lilting sound of a piano melody drifted across the graveyard, as Paolo played the introduction we had prepared for the day. I had serious fears that my voice would fail me as, surrounded by my guests, I began to sing my song to Joey, but somehow I held it together for the first verse.

But the chorus stole my equanimity. Despite weeks of preparation, days of rehearsal and my most steely determination, I stood before my peers and dried up; my mouth was open, but no words would form in my lips. Blinking away the tears that cascaded down my cheeks, I looked from one face to another, begging them to forgive me for being so unprofessional.

Then, a miracle occurred. From the congregation of battle-hardened pop stars came, first one or two, then two hundred, then three hundred, four hundred voices singing the words of my song in sweet harmony. They carried me right through to the end, then stood and applauded me - me! It was they who had saved the day, I didn't deserve anything. I applauded them right back, thanking them with my tearful smile.

Oliver stood beside me on my right, his arm about my shoulder, Paolo on my left and Connor beside him. I gazed adoringly up at each of them, but still could not speak. Paolo took the microphone and spoke for me.

"Ladies and gen'men. My little girl has lost her voice."

He smiled at the concerned faces around us, and there was a gentle rumble of polite laughter. "She has come so far on her own - I am very proud of her - but today she needed her friends to share this moment. Thank you for coming. Prego che Dio vi benedica tutti."

The guests began to file away, most pausing to speak to me as they passed. We stayed until the last had left. Wistfully, I watched them dwindle along the path back to the church and the car park, small groups, chattering together, arms gesticulating.

The sky had cleared, the dark clouds had vanished, and a warm May sun beamed down.

"Ready to go home, my love?" I heard Oliver ask.

"Can I have a few minutes alone with Joey first?"

"Of course. I'll get onto the contractors to come and remove the decking." He put his arms round me, holding me to his big chest, then, releasing me, looked down, seeking out my eyes. "Are you ok?"

Was I? It had been a long day, and I was exhausted, yet it wasn't tiredness that filled my senses, but relief. After all the years since his death, I had carried the weight of my promise to Joey. At last, I had kept my word. Yes, I was ok. I felt good.

"Yes, I am, thanks my darling. It has been a wonderful day." I smiled up at his worried face and stretched up to kiss him. "I'll catch you up."

They picked their way to the path, where they turned to wave before walking slowly away. I sat on the edge of the boards, swinging my legs, my feet brushing the flower tributes below, and studied the rectangle of polished marble that symbolised what this day had been about. How incongruous that we use cold stone to represent the warmth of love. I stared into the patterns set by the forces of nature into the rock from which this piece came - greys and greens, a hint of pink, a streak of purple, whirls of gold.

As I gazed, the hard outline shimmered.

It may have been the tears in my eyes, of course - and the whispering in my ears could have been the wind as it ruffled the grass - but the warmth that washed over me was not caused by the sun.

"*Thanks, Bell,*" I heard in my head.

"*It was a pleasure, Joey.*" I replied, smiling, wiping a lingering tear from my cheek. "*Goodbye - I love you.*"

A peaceful feeling wrapped itself around me, a kiss from an angel, then he was gone.

Printed in Great Britain
by Amazon.co.uk, Ltd.,
Marston Gate.